# Stones and Secrets
## Book Five of The Shattered Moon
## Jon Sparks

Copyright ©2025 by Jon Sparks (including text, cover design, and original photographs).

No part of this publication may be reproduced, distributed, or transmitted in any form or by any means, including photocopying, recording, or other electronic or mechanical methods, nor used for the training of AI systems, without the prior written permission of the author, except as permitted by UK and international copyright law. For permission requests, contact jon@jonsparksauthor.com.

The story, all names, characters, and incidents portrayed in this production are fictitious. No identification with actual persons (living or deceased), places, buildings, and products is intended or should be inferred.

No generative AI was used in the creation of text or images for any part of this book.

For Claire and Bridget

# Contents

Part One

    1. Sumyra     2

    2. Embrel     9

    3. Embrel     12

    4. Sumyra     18

    5. Sumyra     24

    6. Embrel     33

    7. Sumyra     41

    8. Sumyra     47

Part Two

    9. Embrel     54

    10. Sumyra     58

    11. Sumyra     63

    12. Sumyra     67

    13. Sumyra     76

    14. Embrel     82

    15. Sumyra     90

    16. Embrel     102

| | | |
|---|---|---:|
| 17. | Sumyra | 110 |
| 18. | Sumyra | 119 |
| 19. | Embrel | 127 |
| 20. | Sumyra | 133 |
| 21. | Embrel | 141 |
| 22. | Embrel | 145 |
| 23. | Sumyra | 148 |
| 24. | Embrel | 154 |
| 25. | Sumyra | 158 |
| 26. | Embrel | 163 |
| 27. | Embrel | 170 |
| 28. | Embrel | 175 |
| 29. | Sumyra | 185 |

Part Three

| | | |
|---|---|---:|
| 30. | Sumyra | 198 |
| 31. | Sumyra | 207 |
| 32. | Sumyra | 211 |
| 33. | Embrel | 218 |
| 34. | Sumyra | 224 |
| 35. | Embrel | 230 |
| 36. | Sumyra | 235 |
| 37. | Sumyra | 240 |

Part Four

| | | |
|---|---|---:|
| 38. | Embrel | 246 |

| | | |
|---|---|---|
| 39. | Sumyra | 251 |
| 40. | Embrel | 256 |
| 41. | Sumyra | 262 |
| 42. | Sumyra | 267 |
| 43. | Embrel | 274 |
| 44. | Sumyra | 279 |
| 45. | Embrel | 284 |
| 46. | Sumyra | 288 |
| 47. | Sumyra | 295 |
| 48. | Sumyra | 300 |
| 49. | Embrel | 311 |
| 50. | Sumyra | 316 |
| 51. | Sumyra | 320 |
| 52. | Sumyra | 324 |
| 53. | Embrel | 333 |
| 54. | Embrel | 341 |
| 55. | Sumyra | 345 |
| 56. | Embrel | 352 |
| About the author | | 361 |
| Acknowledgements | | 363 |

# Part One
## Secrets

# Chapter 1

# Sumyra

"The swallows always return before the Dawnsingers arrive," Papa had said a few years back, and it had always been true. Usually the swallows would appear before the end of Floreander, with the Dawnsingers a few weeks later, rarely before the middle of Meadander.

It made sense, thought Sumyra, because both depended on the weather. The Dawnsingers couldn't make the Crossing until the deep snow was gone from the passes, and the swallows—presumably—also needed warmth for their journeys from… wherever it was they went for more than half the year. Though how, she wondered, did they know what the weather would be like when they got here?

There were always more questions.

Anyway, this year had followed the pattern, with the swallows back and settled into their nests before the Dawnsingers came down from the hills. She'd been pleased, but not greatly surprised, to see Master Analind at the head of the party.

What was a surprise was the arrival of Jerya just one day later. She greeted Analind with warmth, and her companions with perfect friendliness, but Sumyra had the clear impression it was Mamma she'd really come to see.

❉

At first, their conversation seemed perfectly innocuous, and Sumyra saw no reason to announce her presence until she had finished in the instrument store. But then Mamma said something too low for her to hear, and Jerya's reply had an edge of what sounded like weariness. "It's a promise I made him years ago. Ten... no, eleven years now. And I don't know when I'll get a better chance."

"And you're happy leaving Torvyn for weeks on end?"

She imagined Jerya shrugging. "Happy isn't exactly the word. Riding away yesterday, I was pretty much broken for a long while. I've hardly worn a veil lately, but I was glad of it then... But Tor's six now. Hedric's going to enjoy being the sole parent, Elleret dotes on her, and there'll be a whole load of Dawnsingers and summer-school girls to fuss over her too... I reckon she'll be just fine."

Mamma sighed audibly. "I'm not going to be able to talk you out of this, am I?"

"It's not just my promise to Embrel. I want to see my mother again. She must be over seventy, and... well, you know. And Yanil, and Jossena, and Evisyn. But if I went without taking him... I'm not sure he'd ever forgive me."

"I understand that. But you could take him to Carwerid without..."

"Without seeing Rodal? Do you really think that would work?"

"I suppose not. But that doesn't mean he has to know."

"If we get to that point, no one's going to need to tell him."

This was all very mysterious, and more than ever Sumyra knew she should not be listening. But as long as she was in the instrument store there was no getting away from it, and there was no other exit. She glanced up at the skylight and thought that in theory she could climb out, but she surely couldn't do it quietly enough to escape detection.

Deliberately she rattled the lid of the sterilising vessel. Jerya, who'd just been saying, "...never quite understood why you're so dead set against..." broke off and called out, "Someone there?"

Sumyra could feel her cheeks warm as she emerged. "I'm sorry." Mamma just looked at her, in the way that was almost worse than a scolding. "I didn't mean to eavesdrop."

"Well, I'm glad you came clean when you did," said Jerya. Mamma looked less forgiving. Sumyra decided she would wait for another moment.

※

"Countess..."

"Ah, Sumyra. We've hardly had a moment to talk, have we, just the two of us? All these Dawnsingers cluttering up the place..."

"Oh, I like Dawnsingers. But that's why I..."

Jerya saw her hesitation and smiled. "Let's see if I can guess what you're wanting to say. You heard that I'm planning a trip to the Sung Lands, and taking Embrel with me... And you wondered if there might be room for one more?"

"You read my mind."

"Hardly needed to," said Jerya, smiling. "Simple deduction. I've known you a few years now, I know you're fascinated by Dawnsingers and their knowledge; you've been to every summer-school so far. I can hardly imagine you'd pass up an opportunity to see Carwerid, the College, maybe the Observatory."

"Then do you think it's possible?"

"Let me put it this way. For myself, I have no objection. No, that came out wrong. I'd be very happy to have your company. But I'm not the only one who'd have to agree. I made the promise to Embrel, not to you."

"I can't see any reason why he'd object." They'd always been good friends, and the possibility of something more had never quite gone away.

"I'm glad to hear it. But you still need your parents' agreement."

"Do I, though? I'm eighteen."

"All right, legally you don't need their permission. Legally, you could set out and tackle the Crossing all on your own. But if they objected, would you really want to go against them?"

"No, but why would they?"

"Well, there's one sure way to find out. And by the way, you don't need to call me Countess."

"I can't quite call you Preceptor any more, can I? Now I've finished school."

"Perhaps not. But friends call me by my name."

❅

"The route's really very safe these days," said Jerya. "I've been talking with Analind. I'd think twice—and more than twice—about taking them over the Northern Crossing, but taking two sensible young people—" Mamma made a small sound.

"I'm eighteen, Mamma. I'm not a child any more. Or don't you think I'm sensible?"

"Of course I do, sweetheart. It's not that."

"And I'm not suddenly going to decide I want to stay in Carwerid and be a Dawnsinger. I promise you that."

Jerya chuckled. "They wouldn't have you anyway. The Guild was never in the habit of taking any Postulants after the usual age, and I reckon I put them off completely."

That was an interesting thought. "You weren't much older than me, were you?"

"Nineteen."

"You did the Northern Crossing, hardly older than I am now, when it was completely unknown. Just the two of you."

Neither Mamma nor Jerya said anything to this. They were looking at each other; Jerya's expression seemed particularly challenging. Mamma was pale, or as pale as she could be under her coppery skin. There were things going on between them, undercurrents, that Sumyra was at a loss to understand. And for the first time since she'd known them—a full six years for Mamma, and only a few months less for Jerya—they seemed to be at odds.

Mamma pulled her gaze away, turned to Sumyra, took a deep breath. "Sumyra, my darling, do you trust me?"

"Of course I do, Mamma."

"Then will you trust me when I say that there is a reason I don't want you to do this? A reason that has nothing to do with you or my opinion of you. Nothing to do with thinking you aren't sensible or capable. Quite the opposite, I have the highest opinion… Sumyra, maybe I haven't told you often enough how very proud I am of you."

For a moment they gazed at each other. There was much love in Mamma's gaze, but sometimes love wasn't quite enough. "Thank you, Mamma. And I am proud of you too. But if you think so highly of me, can't you trust me enough to tell me the reason?"

Mamma frowned. "It's something in my past; I can tell you that much. I'd tell you all if I was the only one involved, but it bears on other people too. People close to me, people I also care about. People you care about."

Sumyra shot a glance at her father, but his eyes were fixed on Mamma. Mamma, however, saw. "This was long before I knew your father."

"Does he know? Do you, Papa?"

"If Mamma is referring to what I think she is, she told me before we were married."

"But I can't be trusted to know?"

"If trust were the only issue, I would say we should tell you in a heartbeat. But Mamma… in my judgement, your Mamma has absolutely no call to feel the slightest sense of shame. As I have told her many times."

"Sometimes," said Jerya, "You can hear an answer and then wish you'd never asked the question. But then it's too late. You can't un-hear it."

Mamma's head was bowed, her posture rigid. Sumyra loved her Mamma too much to ignore her distress; but something in her still drove her on. "And you're saying that if I go to Carwerid I will hear the answer?"

When Mamma said nothing, Jerya supplied the answer. "Almost certainly, I'd say."

"It's something to do with when you were Dawnsingers, then. It must be. But I already know that you broke your Vows."

Mamma's head snapped up. "How do you know that?"

"I know Countess Jerya did. Last year, at summer-school, she talked about it. She didn't mention you, Mamma, but when I learned what the Vows said, it was obvious you must have broken yours too. And I know that would—that you would feel ashamed."

"I suppose I did, at first," said Mamma. "And I should have talked with you about it... why didn't you say anything when you came back from last year's summer-school? Ask me about it?"

"Because I supposed it would be painful for you. I thought if you wanted to talk about it you'd have told me..." Thoughts whirled in her head like moths around a lantern. "But there's something else, isn't there? The reason you don't want me to... it's not just about breaking your Vows."

"No." That was all Mamma said.

"Rai, my dear," said Jerya. "You know we haven't always seen eye to eye on this. But you know I've never revealed the truth to anyone, save Hedric, and then only with your permission."

Sumyra wondered if she should feel resentful that Mamma apparently trusted Jerya's husband with the secret, but not her own daughter. Step-daughter, she thought, but even at this hard moment she knew that was unworthy. Railu was the only mother she had ever known, and she did not see how a true mother could have loved her more.

Jerya was still speaking. "And I won't break your confidence now... but I urge you to consider that the truth may well escape now anyway. How would you prefer Sumyra find out?"

Mamma said nothing, but Sumyra could see that this last question troubled her deeply. She rose, took three strides, crouched by her mamma's chair, her skirts pooling on the floor. She grasped Mamma's hands in both her own. "I'm sorry, Mamma—mother. I've pushed too hard."

Tears stood in Mamma's eyes. "No, my darling. I can't blame you. Without knowing this secret, you can't understand why I... why I feel the way I do."

Sumyra brushed the tears away, then ran a hand over Mamma's ever-smooth scalp. "No, but I do know, now, how much you feel. I won't push you any more."

"Thank you. Would you... I need to think. Think about the last thing Jerya said. I need to talk to your father."

"Come on," said Jerya, holding out a hand to help Sumyra rise—not that she needed aid, of course. "Let's go find Analind. There's someone she wants you to meet."

## Chapter 2

# Embrel

It was no great surprise, stepping down from the Drumlenn diligence, to see Jerya waiting at the end of the Duncal lane. The Countess of Skilthorn, alone, in a well-worn blue riding-habit, her hair braided over one shoulder.

"Well met, aunt," he said, stepping forward to embrace her. In his schooldays he'd been stiff about expressing his affection for her, especially when they might be observed, but now he saw that for the adolescent foolishness it was.

"Draff!" she said, an expression no one else used. "Are you ever going to stop growing?" She was tall for a woman, but there was no longer any question: he was taller now, and broader too.

"I should hope so, or my tailor's bills will get completely out of hand." He lifted his holdall, which the coachman had dropped carelessly half on the grass and half on the dusty strip at the edge of the road. *At least it's not muddy.*

Jerya took his arm as they started up the lane. Her horse followed a few paces behind, not needing a lead-rein.

"I'm surprised," he said. "Surprised that I'm not more surprised to see you here."

She laughed, exactly as he'd intended. "Ah, but can you guess exactly why I'm here? Not just here in Drumlenn, I mean; can you guess, or should I say deduce, why I wanted to meet you at this exact spot?"

He thought about it for some moments. "I'm sorry, aunt, I cannot fathom it, not immediately."

"Very well, cast your mind back ten years."

*When I was ten...* "My word, aunt, are you thinking of the time I tried to run away?"

"With twenty pence in your pocket, and nothing else but the clothes you stood up in."

"I'd practically forgotten... d'you think the coachman would even have let me on? That fellow today didn't seem to be too particular."

She shrugged. "I'm just glad I got to you first. But the real point is... Embrel, do you remember what I said to you that day? The promise I made?"

He stopped walking. They faced each other. "I believe I recall your exact words. *One day, when you're older, we'll go on a journey together.*"

"Near enough, I reckon." She held his gaze. "Had you made any plans for this vacation?"

"I'd sort of promised to visit one of the fellows later on. There's good fishing in their river, or so he claims. But nothing I can't make an excuse for." They swung into motion again. "So where are we going, aunt?"

She smiled, that testing, teasing smile he'd known ever since she was his governess. Since before, probably. "Where would you like to go? Anywhere in the known world: I'm not proposing to leave my child for six months or a year so we can go sailing off over the horizon."

"Well, then," he said, "The answer's clear. The Sung Lands."

"Exactly what I was thinking."

He dropped his bag and swung her into a hug. This time he lifted her clean off the ground.

"Put me down, you gurt lummock!" she laughed.

"Gurt lummock?" he repeated, releasing her.

"You can take the girl out of Delven but you can't take Delven out of the girl."

This he only half-understood, but half would have to do. There were bigger questions. "How soon can we start?" was the first of them, as they walked on.

Jerya smiled. "Well, there's a few things to settle first. For a start, there's someone else who'd love to come with us."

"Who?"

"Sumyra. Would you have a problem with that?"

He hardly needed to think. "No, not at all. We've always been good friends. And of course she'd love to see where Railu came from."

"That's good. But I have to tell you, Railu isn't keen on the idea."

"Why? Does she think Sumyra's still too young?"

"It's more... complicated than that. I really can't tell you; it's Railu's private business. We may need to give them a couple of days to resolve it."

"But we can still go? I mean, I'd be sorry if Sumyra can't come, but it wouldn't mean we couldn't?"

"Well, we need to talk to your parents about that."

## Chapter 3

# Embrel

Because Jerya had her horse with her, they went round by the yard. Rhenya must have been looking from the kitchen window because she came running out. But two paces short she stopped.

"Don't you dare," said Jerya, stepping forward, enveloping Rhenya in her arms. This time it was Rhenya's feet that left the ground. She might be shorter than Jerya, but she surely outweighed her. There was a deceptive strength in Jerya's frame, he thought. He was still wondering about 'Don't you dare', but as Jerya returned Rhenya to the ground she said, "'Countess' is just a title, flimflam. Sometimes it's useful... but here... I hoped I was still one of the family."

"Course yow are," said Rhenya.

*Family*... he thought. For much of his life they had been family; not in the same sense as Mamma and Pap but maybe just as important. Jerya, Railu and Rhenya. Rhenya was the only one still resident; after bearing the Crest as a mark of honour for years, she was now free, but still Cook and housekeeper, so that really it seemed like little had changed.

"I hope you're not going to curtsey to me, either," he said, reaching out. Rhenya had some strength, too, her arms almost crushing the breath out of him. It was a chivalric pretence that ladies were barely capable of picking up their own dropped handkerchief. Real women weren't like that. It was good to remember that, here with two of the women who meant the most to him in all the world.

Rhenya picked up his bag and drew him into the house, leaving Jerya to settle the horse. She rejoined them a few minutes later, having left a decent interval for the first greetings with his parents. As they turned from him to welcome the new arrival, Rhenya stepped closer. "I 'xpect yow'll be wanting to wash up, maybe change yowr clothes," she said privately.

"Oh, it can wait. I've only been sitting in a coach, it's not like I've been riding for hours."

Her tone grew firmer. "I *'xpect* yow'll be wanting to come upstairs." She was a free woman now, he remembered.

As they climbed the stairs, he remembered to complement her on her hair; it was growing out into a fuzzy halo, though you could still easily see it was longer down the centre, where her Crest had been

"Yow reckon?" she asked. "I reckon I look like a dandelion clock."

He could see what she meant, and it was too new for him to be sure. He'd known her all his life, and she'd been fully bald for most of it, only growing a Crest—always tightly braided—in the last few years. He thought that style had particularly suited the shape of her head, but the only decent thing to say was, "I think it looks lovely."

As she hurried off to fetch hot water, he threw his bag on the bed and thought about Rhenya. It had taken long enough for her clearance to come through. The law dictated that no enslaved under the age of thirty could be freed save in exceptional circumstances. Since there was no record of Rhenya's birth (the story of her early life was a closed book to Embrel; he wasn't sure that even Jerya knew the whole of it), it had required a juristic review to certify her age. There'd been plenty of evidence, including the sworn statement of a Countess (*it's flim-flam, but sometimes it's useful*) that Rhenya had been at least fifteen when they first met. That had been before Embrel was born, so even by the most conservative estimate she could not be less than thirty-five now. There was no good explanation except bureaucratic foot-dragging to make an already restrictive law even more so.

Or so it seemed from the perspective of a home that had always stood for a better deal for the enslaved. There were plenty among his classmates—decent fellows, too, on the whole—who took a different view.

His train of thought was halted as Rhenya bustled back in. Yes, he thought, she was a bustler. Always had been, bald or Crested or free.

"Are you going to watch me change?" he asked a moment later.

"I doubt I'd see anythin' I han't seen a thousand times afore," she said, but she turned her back. He knew he could trust her not to look.

"So," he said as he stripped off his shirt, "Seems like there's something you wanted to say to me."

"Aye, there is. It's yowr Mamma."

A sudden wrench of alarm in his bowels. "What's wrong?"

"Maybe nothin'. Only she's been gettin' pains in her guts, cramps. Off her food, e'en when I try to tempt her with her fav'rites. Yow might ha' noticed she's got thinner."

Embrel was ashamed to admit he hadn't.

"Well, I dun't want to 'xaggerate," said Rhenya. "It comes an' goes. But she's had th' doctor out a few times."

"Skelber?"

"Most times it's bin Railu. Mebbe yow should go talk to her."

"I'd want to see her anyway." Now there was another reason.

※

Somehow he had to put that worry aside and talk about the Crossing. Or, as it turned out, let Jerya do most of the talking while he, as discreetly as he could, observed his mother.

The trouble was, she'd always been slender. She knew other ladies envied her, paid compliments that weren't always as well-meaning as they sounded, jested about never needing to wear a corset. She was not one of those who might say 'it wouldn't hurt to lose a few pounds'. She still looked the same, as far as he could tell given her full skirts and the newly fashionable puffed sleeves (newer in Drumlenn than in Denvirran, no doubt). Her face, naturally pale, was no more so than last time he'd seen her and there was no obvious constraint in her movement; but then she'd always been one to whom stillness came naturally. *The opposite of me*, he thought wryly.

Perhaps Rhenya had been exaggerating. She was a worrier, for sure. Still, he wouldn't be entirely easy in his mind until he'd seen Railu.

Meanwhile, the other half of his attention followed Jerya. She began by reminding his parents about the promise she'd made eleven years ago, which they'd known about all along. "I can't see we'll get a better chance than this. Torvyn's old enough to leave now and Hedric's looking forward to spoiling her rotten. And I've finally convinced myself I can leave other people to run the summer-school."

Naturally Father and Mamma had questions about that. Embrel was more or less up to date, which made him chafe at the distraction, but he reminded himself that it was because Jerya wrote to him more often than to them. He suspected that during his University terms they got most of the Skilthorn news second-hand, via Railu.

"Well," said Jerya, seizing a moment when his mother was pouring more tea to grasp the initiative again. "There couldn't be a better chance from my point of view, and doing this before Embrel's final year seems to work well too." She smiled at him. "Who knows where you'll be after that?"

She turned back to his parents, mother in the window-seat, father standing beside her against the curtain.

※

"It's hard to be sure," said Railu. "If only we could see inside the body... but you don't cut someone open just to have a look. So much of what we know comes from autopsies, dissections; never see inside a healthy living body." She sighed. "But if she'd just come in we could do a more thorough examination, a full set of samples."

Embrel dug his nails into his palm. This was his mother they were talking about. He didn't much relish being an adult right now, but he had to play the part. "She's refusing to come in?"

"It's not like a flat-out refusal, just keeps putting it off."

"I could try and have a word with her." That was hardly a conversation he looked forward to. However, Railu's grateful look told him he had to try. "So what *do* you know? What do you think it might be?"

"Well, it's often hard to say exactly where internal pain is centred. It sometimes feels like there's tumefaction in the bowel, but it's intermittent, so it must be inflammation, or a temporary blockage. And she says there's no blood in her stool, but I don't know how closely she's looked."

"I can't imagine Mamma examining her own... movements."

"No one likes it," she said. "That's what we're here for. If she'd just come in..."

"But till then... you must have some suspicions."

"Well, there are several possibilities." She gave a swift explanation. "Possibly gall-stones, for instance. And since the gall-bladder is mostly concerned with the digestion of fat, the symptoms can sometimes be eased with a few adjustments to diet. But it can be acutely painful, and often the best thing to do is take the thing out. Which is a relatively simple surgery."

"But you don't know for sure?"

"Embrel, you're old enough for the truth. At this point I'm not certain of anything. I don't think it's cancer..."

"That's good, then?"

"Yes, but I said I don't think. As far as we can tell there's no sign of a tumour. But not all of the bowel is equally accessible to palpation... Get her in here and maybe we can be more certain."

"I'll do everything I can." He paused, looked at her. To look at, Railu had hardly changed from his earliest memories. Still bald, so there could be no grey, like the few strands he'd noticed in Jerya's hair. No, of all the people he considered as his broader family, Railu had changed the least, in appearance anyway. Her position and her role had changed enormously and there was a confidence about her that hadn't always been so evident. "Railu..."

"Yes?"

"You know Jerya's talking about taking me to the Sung Lands?"

"Of course."

"Only now I'm wondering if I should... If Mamma's sick, should I be disappearing for a month or more? Can you look me in the eye and tell me she'll still be here when I get back?"

"Look, you know anything can happen to any of us at any time. I rode over a bridge last week and the next day half of it collapsed when the cows were crossing. I can't look you in the eye and tell you with utter certainty *I'll* be here in a month or two. But as far as your Mamma is concerned, I'd be surprised if she got seriously worse in that time."

"So you think I should go?"

"No, my dear, I'm not saying that. That's for you to decide, no one else. That's what being an adult means."

"Jerya says you don't want Sumyra to go."

Railu sighed. "No, but not for any reason like that. Both Skelber and I are in excellent health."

"I'm glad to hear it. But then... you'll understand I'm curious as to what other reason there could be. It seems like a wonderful educational opportunity."

Railu only sighed.

# Chapter 4

# Sumyra

Mamma turned to Papa. "Have you nothing to say?"

"I have, but it may not be exactly what you were hoping to hear." He studied her face. "You know, my dearest, I have supported you in all your struggles. But I beg you to consider that you may lack a certain... perspective... in this case."

"Perspective?"

He took a moment. "Let me be clear, I may seek to persuade you to change your view, but I will never betray the secret without your consent. And therefore I must be exceedingly careful what I say now. So please bear with me..." His glance shifted from wife to daughter and back. He drew a long breath. "First, let me say that I see no reason—none whatever—for you to feel shame or embarrassment over this. Not twenty years ago and even less so now."

*Twenty years?* thought Sumyra. *Wasn't Mamma a Dawnsinger twenty years ago? Is that what all this is about?* It was true that the matter came to a head when Jerya invited her to join the trip to Carwerid. But Mamma had already denied that her reluctance had anything to do with the breaking of her Dawnsinger's Vows.

"And if there's no reason for you to feel embarrassed," continued Papa, "There is surely no reason for anyone else to. Let us suppose—hypothetically—that Embrel and Sumyra do learn the truth. Do you think either of them will think less of you?"

Sumyra pressed Mamma's hand. "I'm sure nothing could diminish my love for you. Love *and* admiration." The answering smile was brave but watery. "Oh, Mamma, I don't want anything to make you feel this way."

"Thank you, sweetheart, but I fear it may be too late for that... not your fault," she added hastily. "None of this is your fault. It happened before you were born."

*But what was it that happened?* Sumyra was torn between the hunger to know and the wish to say, 'no more', to spare her Mamma's feelings.

"The crux is this, I think," Papa continued, his voice steady, very much like the voice he used for serious conversations with patients. "It seems almost certain now that Embrel and Jerya are going. And if they go, it's equally close to a certainty that Embrel will learn the truth."

"Which is what Jerya's wanted all along." Mamma's tone startled Sumyra. What was it? She sounded almost... bitter. What could it be that made her feel like that toward her oldest friend?

"She has," agreed Papa. "But for twenty years she has never broken confidence. Never even, to the best of my knowledge, dropped a hint. But Embrel is not a boy any longer and she believes he has the right to know. It's my impression she believes it very strongly. Have you never considered that she may have a point?"

"But think of the consequences if it becomes more widely known."

"I suppose at the moment there are six people who know. Four who knew from the start, plus Hedric and myself. And none of us have ever breathed a word of it."

"Seven," said Mamma. "You're forgetting Rhenya."

Papa smiled. "Seven, then. And you would hardly describe Rhenya as close-mouthed, would you? Yet she too has said nothing. Do you really think our daughter is less to be trusted?"

Mamma looked away. Sumyra knew that in saying 'our daughter'—not 'my daughter' or 'your step-daughter'—Papa was stirring deep feelings in her. Whether he intended this as a tactic or whether it was simply how he thought of her anyway, she could not have said.

"You must know I think nothing of the kind," said Mamma after a moment. She let out a long breath. "Ah, I suppose if Embrel does learn..."

"He will think no less of you than he does now, I am sure," said Papa firmly.

"I must have one more talk with Jerya before I agree to anything. Do you know where she is?"

"Most likely at the inn with the Dawnsingers," said Sumyra.

"I'll go there now." Mamma got to her feet.

"I'll walk with you," said Sumyra, also rising. "Not to linger: I promised to show Singer Corysse the vertical tramway." She gave her father a quick hug, threw her arm around her Mamma's waist as they left the room. They were almost the same height now.

❅

"It's funny," said Sumyra. It had grown warm, down in Lowertown, and she'd been wishing she'd chosen a lighter skirt this morning. But the tea-garden was shaded by trees and there was a cooling breeze off the river.

"What's funny?" asked Corysse, looking at her over the rim of her cup.

"Just thinking, I'm as old as you now."

The corners of Corysse's mouth twitched. "If you're the same age as me now, you must have been the same age ever since you were born."

Sumyra had to laugh. "Sorry, I said that in the most muddled-up way, didn't I? What I meant was I never met a Dawnsinger my own age before."

"Ah... and a year ago you couldn't have. A year ago I was still a Novice."

"That's what I was thinking. I just said it all wrong." She studied Corysse a moment. The young Singer had green eyes and pale skin; pale, at least, where it wasn't swathed in freckles. They were densest over her nose and cheeks, but scattered all over her scalp too. "And I've seen Dawnsingers every year since I was twelve, but never one as young as you before. You must be freshly... you say Ordained, don't you?"

"Last Autumn Equinox, so not yet nine months. But I don't know why Master Analind decided to bring me. She said it would be good experience for me, but it would be for anyone." She stopped, her eyes gazing over Sumyra's shoulder. "Why are those people staring at us?"

Sumyra resisted the temptation to turn and look. "Maybe they've never seen a Dawnsinger before."

"They don't look friendly."

"Maybe they think you're a slave. An enslaved."

"But then why would they stare? There are enslaved everywhere."

"There are... but how many do you see sitting at these tables? Slaves don't do that. In strict households they'd never sit in the presence of free folk."

Corysse looked exactly as if her chamomile tea—which she'd enthused over just a few minutes earlier—had transmuted into something foul.

"I know," said Sumyra. "I know it's wrong. In fact it's a good thing you're here. The way you see it reminds me... My Mamma says, when it's around you every day it's easy to stop seeing it. Or only seeing the very worst abuses."

"She was a slave herself once, wasn't she?"

"Not exactly." She explained how Mamma and Jerya had been taken—miss-taken—for slaves, and had lived as enslaved for some time.

The conversation flowed easily, and they lingered even after a second round of teas had been drunk. The people who'd been staring were lingering too, and when she and Corysse eventually left she made a point of saying in a clear voice, as they passed their table, "So, Dawnsinger, how do you find our Drumlenn hospitality?"

By chance they had the tramway carriage to themselves. No sooner had it grumbled into motion than Corysse was grasping Sumyra's shoulders and then she was kissing her. And it was not a kiss like any she had experienced before.

Sumyra, still slightly breathless, led Corysse out of the terminus. Almost without thinking she turned right, the way that led to the Overlook, rather than straight ahead, the direct route home. Corysse was quiet as they walked. The only thing that stirred her to speech was the three-legged spaniel at the cooperage, which lolloped out of the gate with its usual startling speed, barking in a way that could seem fierce until you saw how its tail was almost wagging it off its one hind leg. Then she was silent again until they were leaning on the railing at the edge of the precipice.

"I think I shocked you," said Corysse.

"Surprised me, most certainly."

The young Dawnsinger smiled and laid a hand lightly over hers on the parapet. It seemed to tingle, like a mild form of the galvanic force she'd seen demonstrated in Denvirran city. "I'm sorry to... pounce on you like that. But I knew the ride only lasts three minutes, and I wanted..." She stopped, lifted her hand away. Sumyra couldn't tell whether she was relieved or sorry.

Corysse looked out over the fall of land, the river and the port, her eyes seeming to seek the summer-hazy distance. "I have to keep reminding myself everything's different here. Back home, in the College, it's all women. Women and girls. And when you're there, as a Novice, it starts to seem like the whole world. I mean, you can go up the bell-tower and look out and see how much more there is, but life, your life, is all contained within the precincts. And in that life... what I mean is, I know it's different here, that women..." Her hesitancy now was at odds with the swift, decisive way she'd kissed her, thought Sumyra. "I mean, if I did that with another Novice—another Singer—they might or might not welcome it, but it wouldn't be such a shock."

"I've never been kissed that way by anyone. Not a boy or a girl. So I don't know... I think it might have been just as much of a shock if a boy had done that. Maybe..."

"Maybe?"

"Maybe almost more so. Boys are more frightening, I think. Or some of them," she added, thinking of Embrel. They had kissed each other a few times, in an experimental sort of way, a few years ago. The experience had been strange, even unsettling, but never frightening. But then again, after that month, they had never repeated it.

Corysse looked at her for what seemed a long time. Her eyes were really very green, almost as intense as the fresh foliage of the treetops below them. "Then would you mind very much if I kissed you again?"

"I don't believe I would."

## Chapter 5

# Sumyra

She'd thought everything was ready in advance, but somehow the morning still turned into a rushed affair. Jerya didn't say anything, but she would glance at her wristpiece whenever she thought no one was looking.

There was no moment when she could say anything to Corysse, and whenever their eyes met she found her own gaze sliding away. She didn't know what she would have said if she had got the chance, anyway.

Then everything finally seemed to be ready, and Jerya was already swinging up into the saddle. Sumyra gave Dortis a quick farewell hug; senior nurse now, someone from whom she'd learned much. Then much longer ones for Mamma and Papa. It was strange, she thought. She'd left them before, and nine weeks at Skilthorn was longer than the planned six weeks in the Sung Lands; but Skilthorn wasn't half as far, and there were letters, and if anything was really urgent there were—weather permitting—birds and the helio-relay. It wasn't impossible to get messages across the mountains, but it took a lot longer. *No, you can pretend this trip isn't bigger, but really it is. Even though I'm older.*

She climbed into the saddle, knowing that she hadn't done it as elegantly as Jerya, even though the Countess was more than twice her age. Well, it was harder when your vision was swimmy.

All the Dawnsingers had come out by now to see them off. This was a great honour, she knew. Perhaps it was mostly for Jerya, but Sumyra was happy to share in it. She brushed her eyes with her sleeve, and found

Corysse. This time her gaze didn't stray. She smiled and mouthed thank you then turned to wave to her parents as the four horses and four riders passed out of the yard and turned down the street that led to the high road.

Jerya looked at her wrist, gave a satisfied chuckle. "Nicely ahead of time."

Sumyra glanced in puzzlement at her own watch. "We're more than twenty minutes behind... aren't we?"

"That's the idea. I learned years ago the only way to get a journey started on time is to tell everyone you absolutely have to be on the move at least half an hour before you really need to."

Embrel, coming alongside, groaned theatrically. "You mean I could have had another half-hour in bed?"

※

Embrel was a few lengths ahead, talking earnestly with Mavrys. Sumyra's mount was happy to match her pace with Jerya's.

"Countess," she began.

"Didn't I say already, you needn't call me that? In fact... I was going to say this to you, probably tonight. You know Embrel never calls me 'Countess' anyway." She smiled at his broad back. "I cured him of that years ago. And now... 'Countess' means nothing in the Sung Lands. Literally nothing; people will just look at you blankly. Over there, I'm just plain Jerya. Jerya of Skilthorn, I suppose, if we're doing formal introductions. And whether we're there or here, I think we know each other well enough... Embrel calls me 'aunt'; why don't you do the same?"

"That's... I... thank you very much. But he's known you all his life, I only..."

"Must be a third of yours." Jerya smiled. "I don't do so much maths any more but I can still divide six into eighteen." It was a jest, Sumyra knew: Jerya might not pursue pure mathematics but she still practised—and taught—astronomy, and there was lots of complicated maths in that.

"I'm very flattered, but I'm not truly your niece."

Jerya shrugged. "Not by blood. But Embrel's not my nephew by blood either. I don't entirely go along with the 'blood's thicker than water' notion anyway. It's important, to be sure..." Her voice tailed off. For a few moments they rode in a silence punctuated by the steady thudding of hooves on sheep-cropped turf.

Then Jerya gave a little shake, almost like a wet dog shaking itself dry. "If blood was all, you wouldn't call Railu 'Mamma', would you? But you do, and it warms my heart. But don't let me browbeat you; you can call me 'Jerya' if you want. I just thought 'aunt' might be easier for you. And you say you're flattered, but, honestly, if you feel you could call me 'aunt' I believe I'd be the more honoured."

"I don't suppose there's any gain in debating which of us is really more flattered..."

"No, that's true."

"...Though I will always believe it's me."

Jerya gave one of her uninhibited laughs, raising a faint echo off the grey crag that loomed over the meadow on their right. Embrel and Mavrys both glanced back curiously.

"Nicely played, niece," she said.

❈

"I keep thinking about secrets," said Sumyra a little later.

Jerya—*Aunt* Jerya—gave her an appraising look. "Well, there's been a fair deal of talk around that subject lately."

"Yes, and of course I think about that. I'm full of curiosity. I can't think why we have to find it out for ourselves somehow, when we reach the Sung Lands; why you can't just tell us."

"As to that, I do think it might be best, but I can't explain my reasons without pretty well revealing the secret. But also it's a promise I made to Railu; it was her condition for finally agreeing you could come with us. And I set great store by promises."

Once, many years ago, before she or Embrel were even born, Jerya had broken her Dawnsinger's Vows. (So had Railu, but Jerya felt responsible for this too.) Sumyra didn't pretend to understand all the background, but she knew Jerya now was fiercely resolved never to make a promise she could not keep.

She had to ask, "What did you promise Mamma?"

"Whatever happens, I'm not to tell you the secret, either of you. I can answer any questions you put to me, but I can't volunteer any information."

"But you think we'll discover the secret when we get to the Sung Lands?"

"When we get to Carwerid, to be precise. At the least, I reckon you'll see enough to start asking questions."

Meadow gave way to forest, a sand-and-stone trail rising through the trees. As the horses slowed to tackle a steep pitch, Jerya treated Sumyra to another of those assessing looks. "You said you keep thinking about secrets. Should I surmise you have more than one secret in mind?"

"You could say that... aunt," she said, as if trying 'aunt' on for size.

A fleeting smile tweaked at Jerya's lips, then she grew serious again. "Some people have secrets they never want to tell anyone, and some are just waiting for the right person to tell it to. And sometimes aunts are the right people."

"I need to think about it."

"Of course. Sometimes people spill the beans and then regret it."

Sumyra nodded. Off to the left she could hear falling water, and then through the trees she glimpsed a white cascade. As they rose above it, the trail became almost level again. "Can I ask you a question?"

"You can ask me anything. I can't promise I'll always have a good answer."

Sumyra thought such occasions would probably be rare. "When you were a Dawnsinger, did you... I mean, in the College, there were only women there; that's right, isn't it?"

"Yes, Dawnsingers and women who worked for them. Who did all sorts of jobs that would be done by men anywhere else."

That was interesting, but it wasn't what she wanted to ask now. "And you never saw any men? You never spoke to any?"

"Well, it's a little more complicated than that. Officially, Novices would only ever leave the precincts to travel to the Observatory at Kendrigg. A carriage ride down to the river and then, if the wind was right, a boat for a few hours. Then another carriage up to the Observatory, though on that road it would probably have been just as quick to walk." She chuckled. "I only did that trip once, but most Novices would do it every year; several times if they were specialising in astronomy. Your Mamma must have done it several times.

"Anyway, you'd see out of the carriage window, and on the boat the crew would be men."

"But you wouldn't speak to them?"

"You weren't supposed to. But when I did it someone sneaked a few words on a dare." Jerya shrugged. "The majority of Singers leave the College after Ordination and most of them will be sent to a village or a town. They have to communicate with the people and they usually do it through the local headman, like my—like the Singer in Delven." She gave herself another of those quick shakes. "Most Dawnsingers can't entirely avoid contact with men. And I think that's right. The Guild is there to serve everyone, after all."

"A minute ago you said, '*Officially, Novices would only ever leave*' for that one reason. I wasn't sure what you meant."

"I was wondering if you'd caught that. There were a couple of discreet ways out of the precincts. I guess we thought only we knew about them, but... well, every senior Singer was a Novice once. And if you put on coloured clothing and covered your head... as far as I know, most people never did more than wander the streets, just looking. Maybe if they were really bold they'd have a drink in a quiet tavern... though I never knew how they got hold of the money for that. Railu'd probably know. She was there eight years." She was silent for a spell, presumably thinking back.

Jerya sighed. "It was a long time ago. More than half my lifetime. Nineteen then, forty now, and I wasn't there much longer than one of your seasons at summer-school... You've done six now, haven't you? Only person to have done every one."

Sumyra agreed, not without pride.

"I hope you'll think this trip's worth missing your seventh... but, already, six seasons makes nearly a year of your life, doesn't it?"

"I hadn't thought of it like that."

"Less than four months," said Jerya. "That was all I had. All the official education I've ever had, in fact. But it's still more than most girls get, either side of the Dividing Range."

Sumyra gestured toward Embrel, still a short distance ahead. "Whereas Embrel can go to school for six years and then three years at college and it's perfectly normal."

"For lads of his class, not for most. But I take your point. Take Mavrys, there. I don't know how much of her story you know...?"

"I know she's the only female Master of Horse I ever heard of."

"Yes, as far as I know too, she's unique. And, when she first took the position, every single hand in those stables was older than she was."

"I didn't know that." Sumyra looked again at the young woman, riding with enviable ease on a leggy brindled gelding. Mavrys was unique in another way too, sporting hair of a brevity you normally only saw on someone recently freed: but she'd looked exactly the same every time Sumyra had seen her, hair shorn close at back and sides, and never above an inch long anywhere.

"She's worth talking to," said Jerya. "But I mentioned her now because... did you know she's a gentleman's daughter?"

"No... she never sounds like it when she's talking to the stable hands."

"No, and she can parl Patter like she was born to it, but she sounds ladylike enough when she chooses. Her father was a noted horse-breeder, but he died when she was still a girl, and then... long story short, the family lost pretty much everything; the stables, the horses, the house. But get Mav to tell you herself. What I really meant to say... she had a governess for a few years, some woman who herself might have had a governess for a few years... I'm not disrespecting governesses, I've been one myself. But mostly no one thinks a girl needs more than that. That's what it's all about; the summer-schools and the main school.."

Sumyra knew this, of course. "And it's a great achievement. But... what happens next? Novices become Dawnsingers..."

"Present company excepted, obviously."

"Yes... And Embrel goes on from school to university, and that's what you have to do before you can enter any of the professions."

"I know. And believe me I wish I could do more. I wish I could change things faster."

"I wish you could too." Sumyra knew she sounded bitter, and she knew that Jerya, of all people, was not to blame. But she had to say it. "Mamma has her licence, she's properly recognised as a doctor, she can practise without any subterfuge... but that's because she trained in the Dawnsingers' College. I can't go there, but there isn't a medical school in the Five Principalities that admits females. If I want to be a doctor..."

"*Is* that what you want?" asked Jerya gently after a moment.

"I don't quite know. But I think maybe that's because I never allowed myself to dream of it, because I couldn't see any way it could ever come to pass."

"I know how that feels. I was nineteen before I realised any sort of life was possible other than what was set out for me in Delven."

"Here's a secret," said Sumyra. It wasn't the one she'd been thinking of when the conversation started, but it was something she'd never told anyone. "When the letter finally came, agreeing that Mamma could be recognised, get her certificate and everything... I hugged her and we did a kind of dance and we celebrated with a special meal and everything... and that night when I went to bed and I was finally alone, I cried for a long time."

"Oh my dear girl..."

"I know that shows I'm horribly selfish..."

"No!" said Jerya. Manoeuvring her horse closer, she leaned across to squeeze Sumyra's knee. "If you were truly selfish, you wouldn't have danced with your Mamma. You wouldn't have shared her joy. Selfish isn't thinking of yourself... it's when you only think of yourself."

"I suppose..."

"Does your Mamma know anything about how you feel?"

"Oh, she knows. It's obvious whenever we talk about what I can do. She just doesn't know about that night... and the other times..."

"And you don't want to tell her because you think it would make her feel bad. Which, again, wouldn't concern you at all if you were truly selfish... but don't you think Mammas are supposed to know when their daughters feel bad? Isn't that part of what they—and fathers too—are *for*?"

"And aunts?"

Jerya gave her knee another squeeze. "Of course. And maybe sometimes it is easier to talk to someone not quite so close. So, yes, remember I'll always have an ear for you."

She looked up as the trail opened out again, winding between scattered boulders that seemed to be cushioned in thickets of bilberry and heather, months away from blooming. "Speaking of aunts, did you know I was raised by aunts? I mean, I called them aunt, but... well, there was a blood tie, on one side, but nothing as close as a true aunt."

She pressed her lips together, thinking, then said. "Sumyra, I've a mind to tell you a secret of my own. I know I can trust you, but you should know that only two people this side of the mountain know it, and one's your Mamma. Four or five in the Sung Lands, I reckon."

"Not Embrel?"

"Not even Embrel. And I could tell him, now he's grown, but so far I haven't. Like I said, I was raised by aunts. What I didn't say was that I didn't know who my mother was. Or my father, for that matter. As far as anyone knew, or at least as far as anyone told, I'd just appeared one day, a newborn baby from nowhere."

"How's that even possible?"

"It's not. As I grew older I realised that. Delven was a tight community. I knew about pregnancy and birth, knew it pretty well before I was ten. I couldn't see how anyone could hide a pregnancy, let alone give birth in secret... That word again. And I realised I didn't quite look like anyone else. My skin was darker than anyone in the village—I know I'm not dark like Rhenya or Analind, but Delvenfolk are proper pale, when they're not tanned. But I knew, from early on, I couldn't just have been left by woodland spirits.

"I got to nineteen and I still had no idea. I was Chosen, sent to Carwerid, spent those months in the College and still I was none the wiser. It wasn't till I was here in the Five Principalities, living at Duncal... it was just after they set me free... you do know that story, don't you? How we were never really slaves but for a while we lived as if we were?"

"Yes, Mamma's talked about it."

"So they 'freed' me and I got a room of my own and for the first time in my life I got to see myself in a really good mirror. And more or less at once I realised. I could see her face..."

She stopped. Sumyra supposed she was affected by the memory. She tried to steer her horse closer, as Jerya had done for her a little earlier, but Musken was not quite so well-schooled as Jerya's Oronsa, or she herself was not such a skilled rider, and before she could get within touching distance Jerya let out a long breath. "I'm sorry, Sumyra, I should have thought. You never knew your mother either, did you? And unlike me you never will have the chance..."

"It's quite all right. Really. I didn't know her, but I've always known who she was; Papa often talked about her. And now I have Mamma."

"I'm glad you see it that way. Well, I finally knew who my mother was, but by then I..." She gave a brief little laugh. "I'd dragged myself and Railu across the mountains and got myself sort of committed to a life this side... and of course my mother was in the Sung Lands. I didn't see her again for ten years."

## Chapter 6
# Embrel

The first night's stop had been little different from any wayside inn, of the simpler, more rustic kind. The second was different, but no less welcome; it had been a long day. Jerya had made it clear they should be riding by seven, fixing him with a look as she added. "And this time I'm not saying that so we'll actually be off at half past. I say seven, I mean seven."

"You're very confusing," he'd protested, but with a grin.

They rode for nearly four hours, the trail getting narrower and less rutted as they went, before stopping in a grassy space beside a small waterfall. This was as far as the horses could go. They transferred things from saddlebags into backpacks, said their farewells to Mavrys, and stood for a few minutes watching as she rode off at the head of the string.

Embrel groaned as he lifted his pack, then felt abashed as he saw Jerya lift hers onto a handy boulder then slide backwards into the straps. She made no comment as she stood up, settling the weight level on her shoulders and adjusting the belt. *She's a woman, and twice my age. If she can do it, I surely can.*

Sumyra had been watching, and now copied Jerya's actions. She, slighter of build, must feel the weight even more, but she too merely appeared intent on getting the pack set just so.

It was clear at once why they'd had to leave the horses, as the path wound up through broken rocks. It wasn't really difficult: a good mule could probably manage it, but no one in their right mind would risk a thoroughbred, or even a decent hack. More passages of similar nature came at intervals throughout the day.

After what was already a decent half-day in the saddle, legs took a while to adjust to walking, all the longer with close to forty pounds on his back. Jerya's only comment had been, "Just be glad we aren't carrying tents and sleeping bags as well."

It was almost six of the evening when they reached their night's rest, which meant they'd been walking for seven hours. If you discounted the time they'd spent resting—only brief stops, apart from half an hour for lunch—actual time in motion must be close on six hours. It felt like plenty for the first day. Following Jerya's example, they rested their packs on a bench outside the refuge before wriggling out of the straps. Sumyra made no complaint, but leaned back against the rough stone wall and closed her eyes. "That should be the longest day," said Jerya quietly.

"Should be?" asked Embrel.

Jerya shrugged. "If the way's clear. There might be snowdrifts higher up. Rockfalls can change the path. That sort of thing."

"Rockfalls?" said Sumyra, not opening her eyes.

"Frost can loosen stones, or a storm. The Dawnsingers didn't report any problems from their crossing, but things change."

"For a moment I imagined rocks falling all around us."

"Not likely," said Jerya firmly. She didn't say impossible, Embrel noted.

Inside, the place was plain and simply furnished. A bare wooden floor, which looked as if you'd risk splinters if you went about unshod, boards cladding the walls, a single long table and benches. Steep stairs, little better than ladders, led up to the sleeping lofts, each three-quarters filled by a single low platform covered with crudely stuffed mattresses. Horsehair, it felt like through the ticking. Shelves in one corner held dozens of coarse blankets. Jerya and Sumyra claimed one loft and Embrel dumped his pack in a corner of the other.

Downstairs again, Jerya drew the paraffin stove from her pack. "I'll make a drink, then we need to decide who takes first turn to cook. Any volunteers?"

He knew that a few of his friends would take the view that a man travelling with two women should not be asked to cook. He also knew that Jerya would give short shrift to any such suggestion. He suspected Sumyra would be equally unimpressed. Beside, he'd grown up in a household where the kitchen was the centre. As a small boy he'd often helped Rhenya—though he doubted, now, how much 'help' he'd truly been. Still, he wasn't a complete stranger to pots and pans. "What do we have for tonight?"

"Use up the fresh produce tonight and in the morning. Can you make an omelette?"

"I can," said Sumyra.

"Why don't you show me?" he said.

"Analind said we could gather some fresh herbs round about," said Jerya, setting a soot-blackened kettle—one of the few utensils the refuge did supply—on the flame. "I'll have a look after we've had this drink."

She returned with not only a bunch of chervil, thyme and chives but a selection of mushrooms. "All safe, I assure you."

They had almost finished their meal when the door was flung open. A burly bearded man entered, followed by two enslaved.

※

The bearded man nodded to Embrel and threw a blanket down at the opposite end of the platform. He rolled himself up and appeared to be settling right down to sleep.

After a few minutes Embrel knew he had to ask. "Pardon me, but what's become of your... companions?"

"Them two?" the other grunted. "They'll bed down outside."

"Outside? Have they a tent? Anything to lie on?"

"Yow want 'em in here wi' us? They've had th'other loft afore, but there's ladies in there now." He rolled over, turning his back.

Embrel thought a little longer, then threw off his own blanket and crossed the landing. He hesitated at the door of the second loft, until he heard low voices within. He knocked.

Sumyra opened the door just a fraction, peering round the edge. The merest glimpse of a bare shoulder explained her caution. He summarised the situation, and heard Jerya's voice. "Give me a moment to throw some clothes back on."

He doubted very much the fellow was genuinely asleep already, but he was doing his best to pretend, ignoring the first attempts to claim his attention. "Listen," said Embrel, growing impatient, "You were particular enough about the delicate feelings of the ladies a few minutes ago. Yet now you insult them by ignoring them."

The man sat up with a grunt. "Pardon me, I'm sure. What c'n I do for yow, ladies?" He sounded neither penitent nor notably concerned for anyone's 'delicate feelings'.

Jerya moved a few steps closer. Embrel wondered briefly if she might make play of her noble status, but she simply said, "My nephew tells me you expect your companions to sleep outside. Was he mistaken?"

"No mistake, m'lady."

"And they have no tent? No mats to sleep on? It looked to me like it'd be hard to find a spot with no stones."

"Yow do know they're slaves, dun't yow, m'lady?" Oh dear, thought Embrel; and then the fellow went and made it worse. "I'm sure yow wun't want 'em sleepin' in here with yowr nephew. And I know yow wun't want 'em in th'other room with yow and yowr... daughter, is it?"

Jerya had not mentioned her title, but she could sound as haughty as any aristocrat in the Principality when it suited her. "I'll thank you not to presume to tell me what I want, or my niece. Surprisingly, we are quite capable of thinking for ourselves."

There was a tiny sound from Sumyra. He dared not meet her eye.

"Well, beggin' yowr pardon, yowr ladyship. P'raps yow'd be so good as to tell me what yow do want?"

"I want those men to spend the night under cover, not lying on stony ground and waking up drenched with dew."

The bearded man vouchsafed another grunt. "I s'pose they could sleep downstairs."

"On the floor?"

"Pile up a few blankets, they'll be comf'table enough."

"And you think that's sufficient?"

"I dun't know what else yow 'xpect me to do, m'lady. I ain't sharing my bed wi' no slaves."

"Your bed? It's twenty feet across if it's an inch. You think you can claim all of it?" Jerya didn't wait for an answer. She turned to Sumyra. "We'll go and find those men. Tell them there's plenty of room in our loft."

Sumyra nodded, but Embrel wondered just how happy she'd be with that arrangement. Enslaved or not, they were two men she didn't know, and he'd have been prepared to lay a bet she'd never shared a room with any man before, save possibly her father. He hoped she'd conclude, as he had, that Jerya's aim was to shame the unpleasant man into conceding.

Jerya and Sumyra's departure left him alone with the fellow. He considered his next utterance carefully before speaking. "You know who she is, don't you?"

"Am I s'posed to?"

"She's well known. There've been engravings in all the papers."

"I don't read papers." *Probably doesn't read at all*, he realised.

"Still, maybe you've heard of the Countess of Skiltthorn?"

"She's that cra—" The man clapped his mouth shut. *You were about to say 'crazy', weren't you? Crazy what? Crazy bitch? Or Crazy Countess?* He knew that label had been bandied about. But the man had been wise to clam up. *If he had said 'crazy bitch'... I couldn't have ignored that.*

*Good thing I didn't need to make that choice.* Jerya would never have approved if he'd got into a scrap. And there was no certainty that he would come out on top. The woodman looked to outweigh him, and he might well be handy with his fists. *We're a long way from any constabulary as well...*

As it turned out, the two enslaved could not have looked more horrified at the notion of sharing quarters with two ladies. They were, however, more than grateful for the opportunity to sleep indoors.

※

The wind was blowing directly in their faces. The slopes on either side were nothing but shadows behind the streaming snow. Any path there might have been was hidden under the slow soft buildup. There was nothing but grey and white, the only dim hints of colour the vague shapes of Jerya and Sumyra in front of him.

After a while, Jerya paused. She turned to face them and he saw how snow had crusted the front of her coat like a breastplate, how it clung to her eyebrows and lashes, white arcs against which her face looked dark as a shadow.

As they watched, she removed her right glove, held up her hand, turned it this way and that. Then she pulled out the map. "We're here," she said, pointing. "Head up to the right about a mile and we'll find the bothy."

He had to ask. "How can you tell?"

"The wind told me. And speaking of wind, let's get on and get out of it as soon as we can."

She'd refolded the map as she spoke, and was now pulling her glove on and turning in the direction she'd indicated.

A few yards on, she pointed to a vague white mound. "That'll be the cairn marking the change of direction."

You had to crawl to enter the bothy, but once inside it was possible to stand up with a foot to spare, at least at one side. There was no light but a couple of flickering candles, and no sign of a fireplace, but simply being out of the wind and snow made it feel almost warm.

"It's like a cave," said Sumyra.

Jerya smiled. "It reminds me of where I grew up."

"You lived in caves, didn't you?" said Embrel.

"I lived mostly outdoors, but I slept in a cave. I loved my own little cell. It was tiny but it was all mine. Now..." She looked around. "Would you put those boards across the entrance? Keep the last of that wind out."

There were slots chipped into the rock walls to accommodate the boards, but he and Sumyra had to figure out which board belonged to which pair of slots. By the time they had it sorted, Jerya had assembled the stove and had a pan of water over the flame.

"What do we do when we need more water?" asked Sumyra.

"There's a spring nearby," said Jerya, "If we can find it under the snow. If not, we melt snow, though that'll use a lot of fuel."

"Aunt," he said when they were all settled on the thin pads that were all that the place provided in terms of seating, or indeed mattresses. "What did you mean, the wind told you?"

"Ah, yes. I'm sorry if I was a bit terse, but we needed to keep moving. Didn't you feel the wind shift direction?"

"I thought it was in our faces the whole time."

"The wind is funnelled by the mountains, so it nearly always blows straight up or down a valley like the one we came up. But we were looking for a side-valley. In Selton's book he said they dismissed it at first, but what seemed to be the main valley soon got steeper and steeper, then ran out in a cirque of crags. And I remembered coming down it, the side-valley, eleven years ago. I thought there was a good chance it would catch the wind from the West, so when I started feeling it more on my right cheek I thought we were in about the right place."

"So why did you remove your glove?" asked Sumyra.

"To get a better feel for the wind."

Embrel sat back a little and regarded his aunt. It was funny how rapidly it had come to feel natural calling her that. It felt almost as if she'd always been 'aunt'. She'd removed her hat, but none of her other garments. Sitting on the ground, bundled up in woollens and oilcloth, still she looked utterly at ease.

She had said this chamber reminded her of home—a home that, with luck, he and Sumyra might get to see in a few weeks. He already knew that Delven lay in, or at least close to, the mountains, the Northward extension of this same range. He knew that she had crossed this very route, albeit in the other direction, when he was much younger. He recalled his own childish outrage that she could leave him for so long; that had led to her promise, of which this very journey was the fulfilment.

She had 'only' been his governess then, but he had loved her fiercely. Calling her 'aunt' only felt like recognition of a long-standing truth.

But then a new thought struck. If she was his aunt, was he now to call Hedric 'uncle'?

He studied her again. The oaf in the first refuge had called her crazy. Embrel knew that she'd been called 'the crazy Countess', and worse. He'd all but come to blows with one of his University friends for repeating the slur.

Looking at her now, and listening to her in the last few minutes, he thought in fact he had never met anyone more sane.

And in the next moment he was wondering exactly what he meant by that.

## Chapter 7

# Sumyra

The final refuge was a solid stone building, placed on a slight rise, far enough (Sumyra surmised) from the crags to be safe from rockfall. At the same time those rearing crags curved round into three-quarters of a bowl, giving shelter from all winds but southerlies. It would be a sunny spot, too, when the clouds broke. There were patches of cultivation alongside the refuge, salad leaves showing russet and emerald alongside what might be onions and carrots.

As they approached, a Singer emerged. A bald woman, anyway: *I should know better than to make assumptions.* Bald, but not in white: she wore rusty-brown trousers and a sturdy knitted pullover in wool the colour of buttermilk, probably undyed. "Welcome," she said, but her tone was guarded and she looked them all over closely.

"Greetings," said Jerya, smiling. "Just the three of us."

"I know," said the other, with a different kind of smile. "We spotted you a couple of hours ago."

"You keep a lookout, then?"

"Aye, that's half our purpose here. There's hospitality for all friendly travellers, but we're also first warning if anyone comes with... malign intent." *And I haven't finally decided which you are*, her tone said.

Sumyra saw truculent creases on Embrel's broad brow. She gave a slight shake of her head, hoping he'd take the hint: *Leave it to Jerya.*

For her part, Jerya just smiled again. "Very prudent. Well, we bear no malice, but there's no reason you have to take my word for it. My name's Jerya, and this is my niece Sumyra and my nephew Embrel."

"Pleased to meet you, Singer...?" said Sumyra.

"My name's Acklyn. You'd better come in."

Very soon they were settled at a long wooden table, mugs of coffee steaming in front of them, and soup promised within minutes.

"I must admit I'm curious," said Jerya. "I have some idea of the terrain below us. It's hardly suitable for pack animals. I wonder how you keep yourselves so well supplied."

Acklyn hesitated. "That information could have value to anyone who does bear ill will."

"Really, Sister?" said another voice; Sumyra looked up to see a second Singer, a dark, lanky, figure, bearing a large tray. "You know who this is, don't you?" She shifted her gaze. "You did say your name is Jerya, didn't you? Jerya of Delven, if I'm not mistaken."

"It's a long time since I named myself by Delven; I'm Jerya of Skilthorn now. But I'm the same person."

The Singer placed the tray and began passing out bowls. "Then you're the reason we're here. Certainly the reason we keep such a careful lookout."

"I can't claim the credit, really," said Jerya. "That belongs to a courageous young woman called Mavrys."

Sumyra and Embrel exchanged glances. They both knew Mavrys was remarkable, but this suggested she'd played some part in a history they didn't know.

The second Singer nodded, taking a seat next to Acklyn. "You're also the one who set up the Skilthorn Congress, and the summer-schools."

"There I do take some credit. Though neither was solely my idea, and neither would have been possible without many other people."

"I think we can be sure you're a friend of the Guild, anyway."

Jerya just nodded to that. This seemed to draw her attention to the soup in front of her. "This smells wonderful. But perhaps we should let it cool another minute or two."

"I know who you are now," said Acklyn. "I wasn't in Carwerid when you... I was out on Visitation. But I heard all about you when I got back for Solstice."

"I'm sure there were some harsh things said," said Jerya, smiling.

"To be sure," said the second Singer. "But we heard a different story when you returned—what was it? Ten years later?"

"From some," said Acklyn.

"From Master Evisyn, for one."

"Master Prime Evisyn," said Acklyn and Jerya almost together. Their eyes met and for the first time Acklyn vouchsafed a real smile.

"I hope I'll find her well when we get to Carwerid," said Jerya. "Now, I wonder if you'll trust us enough to satisfy my curiosity about your supply-lines?"

❋

Acklyn still looked wary, but her companion, who gave her name as Shamiah, was more forthcoming. The refuge was supplied by a cableway, its upper terminus at a point on the clifftop a few hundred yards away, but hidden by an intervening outcrop. Shamiah was happy to lead them to it, and they stood gazing down the catenary sweep of the cable to its base station, which stood on a rise, maybe three hundred feet lower, flanking the long strath. A faint track could be made out winding its way up the slope, and Shamiah confirmed that it was possible for mules.

Sumyra could readily see how much easier it would be transporting loads that way than lugging them on human backs through the Defile, of which she'd heard much already, and up the scrambly steps above. She would see it all for herself tomorrow.

In fact, said Shamiah, the cableway had been the first thing to be completed, allowing building materials for the refuge to be transported. The stone had been found in the vicinity, among the jumbled rocks, not even needing to be quarried, but there was much else to be brought in: mortar, timber, all manner of fixtures and fittings.

She could see it would still be hard, winching loads up the cable, its curve making the final part of the haul the steepest. It all underlined the commitment the Guild of Dawnsingers had made in building the refuge, and sustaining it since (five years, said Shamiah, since a part-completed structure had first been occupied).

"What did you mean about Mavrys?" asked Sumyra as they walked back, Shamiah striding ahead.

"Ah. Almost said too much there." Jerya sighed. "Well, let's just say… it was during the first Congress. Mavrys hadn't been with us long; it was when she was still masquerading; well, she was trying very hard to be a slave. But—" She checked herself again. Sumyra had hardly ever seen her so hesitant. "She overheard a conversation between the Prince of Sessapont and one of his henchmen. Seemed they were at least contemplating some sort of incursion—an armed incursion—into the Sung Lands."

"How would they…? Sessapont doesn't even share a border—"

"—I know. But if he had allies in Denvirran… anyway, Mavrys came and told me, and I told Master Prime Evisyn, and she used her address to make clear the Sung Lands were ready to defend themselves, if forced to it. But the point here—the point about Mavrys—is that there were very few people who could have overheard that conversation. So, if the Prince realised that Master Evisyn wasn't just indulging in speculation… it would put her at significant risk, you see?"

"That's why you called her courageous… but wait." A flash of memory. "Is that when Mavrys was… kidnapped?"

"You heard about that, did you?"

"I thought it was just a rumour."

"Well, Railu and I brought her back in full view of at least a dozen people. I suppose it would have been strange if stories *hadn't* got around... but it's when stories turn into rumour that it gets tricky. I'd be interested to know what they're saying now, in case it's wandered too far from the truth. But later..."

She stopped, facing Sumyra. "One thing to remember is that Mavrys was seventeen at the time. Seventeen and trying hard to live the life of a slave. As if that wasn't enough of a challenge for a well-brought-up daughter of the gentry, she had a couple—at least a couple—of difficult experiences." Jerya gave a short laugh. "And less than six months later, she was Mistress of Horse."

"She's another remarkable woman."

"Another?" They began to walk again.

"Well, you are, obviously. You smile, aunt, but you can't deny it. And so's Mamma, of course."

Jerya shrugged, but how could she gainsay it? "Your Mamma, indeed. And you may think her even more so before this trip's finished." Her voice trailed off for a moment, her eyes went distant, but then she turned back to Sumyra with a brisker tone. "I'll tell you another remarkable woman."

"Who?"

"Vireddi."

The name was unexpected, but Sumyra's surprise was short-lived.

"Yes," said Jerya, "Like I said, Mavrys had two or three difficult experiences in not too many weeks. And the person, above all, who got her through was Vireddi. I'll give Hedric a lot of credit too, for having faith in Mavrys, giving her that chance—well, you must know the circumstances."

"I hadn't realised she was quite so young."

"She's still only twenty-four now. And Vireddi is still her... her rock."

They mounted the steps onto the terrace of the refuge, but Jerya showed no inclination to enter, turning aside to seat herself on the low bounding wall. It did not look like a fortress, thought Sumyra, and then reconsidered. Nature herself had given it all the ramparts it could ever need.

"I don't believe I'd have achieved anything without someone beside me," said Jerya. "When I was a Dawnsinger, and for years after, it was Railu, and now of course it's Hedric. I won't say everyone needs a Railu, a Hedric, a Vireddi, but most of us do, besure."

*And who'll be my rock?* wondered Sumyra, but Jerya hadn't finished. "I wanted to say more about Vireddi. When she first met Mavrys, she was an illiterate enslaved, a housemaid. Just the sort of person we all too easily overlook, even those of us who're committed to making life better for them. But in seven years, she's not only been the mainstay for Mavrys, she's learned to read and now..." A soft chuckle. "Did you know she's one of the most prolific borrowers from the Library?"

"I know she loves to read, and I've seen her in there, but I didn't know that specifically."

"Aye, and... I don't know how many enslaved, young and old, she's taught to read in the last few years. As well as running the kitchen, and pretty much everything else for the stable-hands. As well as going from terrified of horses to being a pretty competent horsewoman. I've even seen her going over jumps. Small ones, true, but you know even that's no slight thing."

Sumyra nodded. "I didn't know all of this, but... I do admire her."

"Aye, and she's worth it." Jerya's gaze roamed over the wild landscape, even the level ground supporting only pale, straggling herbs and scattered clumps of heather. "But you know, Sumyra, I think you might turn out to be quite a remarkable woman too."

"Me?"

"Why not? You have all these good examples in your life already... and you'll meet a few more in these next weeks."

She must have seen Sumyra was still dubious. She smiled and patted her niece on the shoulder. "And I dare say none of them—of us—really think ourselves remarkable. I'm not even sure I'd trust anyone who did. Believe too much in yourself and you get... well, the Prince of Sessapont, for one."

## Chapter 8

# Sumyra

"It's a good deal higher than when I came this way before," said Jerya, looking at the ribbon of dark water. "Nice that they've contrived an alternative for that first pool, but this one's three times longer."

"So how do we do this, aunt?" she asked.

"We take our clothes off."

"What?" cried Embrel, as Sumyra said, "You're jesting, surely?"

"I wish I was. But if you wade through with your clothes on, you then have to walk the rest of the day in wet clothes. We'll be in this defile a while longer, and it's cold enough even now when we're dry. And then a couple more hours to Blawith, out in the wind. If you've never experienced that, you can hardly imagine just how cold you'll get. But if you keep your clothes dry, you have a few minutes of real cold, but put your dry things back on and you'll be warm again five minutes later."

"But..." She made a point of not looking at Embrel.

Jerya understood. "We go through one at a time. The others look away. And we're not going to get any warmer standing here blethering about it. Who's going first?"

They looked at each other a moment, then Sumyra heard herself saying. "I'll go. May as well get it over with."

"Good for you. Now..." Jerya gave a few more detailed instructions: strip off everything, including your socks, then put your boots back on: "You'll need them to keep your footing, and there are sharp rocks under the water. Roll up all your clothes in the oilcloth they gave us at the refuge. Carry your pack however feels most comfortable; rest it on your head, or on one shoulder. You'll probably want one hand free for balance. And then go steady, don't rush, but keep moving."

Jerya gave Sumyra's shoulders an encouraging squeeze before she and Embrel retreated a few paces and turned away.

It was lucky there was no wind in the defile, but still she shivered as she hurriedly packed her clothes and closed her rucksack. She stood a moment, naked except for her boots, summoning her resolve. *It's not going to get any warmer*, she thought, echoing Jerya. *Just get on with it.*

She hefted the pack onto her right shoulder. Having left almost all the remaining food with the Singers at the refuge, it was probably half the weight it had been when they set out, but taking all the weight on one shoulder made it feel heavier as well as much more unwieldy. But there was nothing for it. *Just get on with it.*

She stepped forward. At once chill water filled her boots, but she could feel the roughness underfoot, pebbles strewn over finned ribs of rock. It would be much worse without boots on. A few more steps and the water was up to her knees. It was hard to look down and, though the water was crystal clear, it still distorted everything, so she could not confidently judge the depth of the next step. As Jerya had advised, she trailed her left hand along the rock wall. It was carved and scalloped and darkly glossy; beyond doubt, torrents had filled this defile many times in the past. Maybe they still did, when there was a big storm, or in the height of the thaw. *Don't think about that now.*

She gasped aloud as the water slid up her loins. As if it were somehow ten degrees colder than around her legs.

"Are you all right?" Jerya's voice. Sumyra didn't—couldn't—turn to see if her aunt still had her back turned. The sound was clear, but she supposed the narrow space contained it.

"It's cold, that's all," she called back.

"Getting in's always the worst part."

"Keep going," added Embrel. She trusted he wasn't looking, though if he did look now all he'd see was her upper back. A Sessapontine ball-gown would reveal almost as much, though she'd never worn anything like that.

Another shocking moment, like being slapped with ice, as the water reached her breasts, but it got no deeper. she began to feel... the chill wasn't less, it couldn't be, but it seemed to change its nature. Not the icicle sharpness of those first moments, now more a kind of... pressure. Like iron bands around her chest, her belly, her hips. Iron dragging at her feet as she moved.

"How deep?" called Jerya.

"Not quite up to my clavicle."

A merry laugh echoed off the grey walls. "I can tell your parents are doctors!" Jerya paused, then, "I'm going to turn and look now, if that's all right with you."

*Why not?* she thought, and then repeated it aloud.

"You're doing well," said Jerya. "Almost half way. I seem to remember that's as deep as it gets. Keep going. Steady."

"It seems easier if I lean forward just a bit."

"Aye, lean into it. But not too much, or your own buoyancy can flip you. I remember when I was learning to swim..."

Jerya talked on, a memory of her early years in Delven. At any other time Sumyra would have been fascinated; Jerya had only ever shared a few stories of her girlhood. Now, though, she couldn't spare even half of her attention. Everything was focused on the process of... what would you call it? Walking? Wading? Something in between: walding? But that, too, was distraction. Place the front foot, test the footing, transfer your weight; repeat, repeat, repeat.

And then the water was growing shallower. She assumed they would turn away again, said nothing, all her concentration for one thing: don't stumble now. As the water's support fell away, she felt herself heavier with every step,.

And then her boots were splashing through a couple of yards of shallows. "I'm through," she called back.

"Well done! Now get dried off as fast as you can and get into every stitch of clothing you've got. We won't look until you're dressed."

"There's a rock just ahead that'll hide me well enough. You can start, whoever's coming next."

Strangely, just after she finished dressing was when she felt coldest. She couldn't remember her teeth ever chattering quite so dramatically. But she remembered what Jerya had said: move about. Jump up and down, wave your arms around. Movement was a little hampered, having taken Jerya's advice about *every stitch of clothing*, including her divided skirt over her narrower walking trousers, leaving only her smarter skirt in the pack. Still she could stride briskly up and down a few yards along the gritty bed of the defile, swing her arms. Maybe the added resistance of too many layers of clothing made the muscles work harder. Whatever the reason, warmth did began to spread. Pins-and-needles made her feet clumsy, made her shake her hands vigorously.

By the time she heard Jerya's feet swishing in the shallows, Sumyra felt herself *glowing*.

※

She removed the skirt before they walked on, but left everything else in place. Her sense of warmth still felt somehow... fragile.

The extra layers made her a little clumsy in the places where they had to scramble over boulders or down smooth rock steps, but none of these were too difficult—if never as easy as Jerya made them look. But then Jerya had grown up in a rocky place; all this seemed to come naturally to her.

And then, of a sudden, they were out of the defile, the sky no longer a dazzling sliver far above but a sprawl of pale cloud that seemed almost to hang closer. A thin breeze greeted them and Sumyra pulled her hat lower on her head.

"Well, my dears," said Jerya, "I think I can finally say this: Welcome to the Sung Lands."

"Is it always this cold?" said Embrel.

# Part Two

## The Sung Lands

## Chapter 9

# Embrel

An hour or more into the walk down the broad bare strath, Jerya stopped. "About here, somewhere," she said almost to herself.

"Something happened here?" asked Sumyra, looking around, though there was nothing obvious to distinguish this spot from any other part of the valley.

"Several things, actually, starting with the first meeting between Dawnsingers and men from the Five Principalities."

"That would be Selton's expedition?" said Embrel. Jerya nodded. "I've met his son, you know."

"Young Tavy?"

"Tavistan? Not so very young."

"He'd be about ten years older than you, I suppose. Young enough, to an old woman like me."

"You're not old," he and Sumyra protested in near-perfect unison.

Jerya laughed. "Exactly the reaction I'd hoped for, thank you both... how did you meet him?"

"He gave a talk at school, in my final year, about the exploration of the Outer Isles. I was fascinated. I managed to have a few minutes' converse with him afterward. It was that day, more than anything else, that led me to choose Pre-History and Archaeology at University. If I distinguish myself, I hope one day I too may be able to take part in such investigations."

"I would have loved that myself," said Jerya. There was a hint of yearning in her tone. He saw Sumyra notice it too; something, anyway, that made her turn her gaze on their aunt.

"You have to leave a few discoveries for the rest of us," he said, hoping to cheer her. "And... he may have enthused me about Archaeology, but it's from you I learned to love the idea of travel."

"And look where we are now," said Sumyra. He smiled at her; it was a fine thought. But she was already turning back to Jerya. "You said 'several things'. What else happened here?"

"Well, that's a longer story, and it's not like there's anything left here to show for it. Keep walking and I'll tell you as we go."

They flanked her, and settled back into the rhythm of walking. "The question is where to start," she said. "There's what happened here, but you need to know a little about what preceded it. Maybe you need to know a bit about it anyway. We'll be in Carwerid in a few days, after all.

"Stop me if I repeat too much that you already know—but I'm sure I haven't said much, and who else would you meet who knows it all? Hedric was only around for half of it, Tavy only saw the end... You've met Master Evisyn, of course, and you both know Analind, and they were right in the thick of it, but I doubt they've told you this tale.

"Well, before Evisyn was Master Prime, there was another. The one I said my Novitial Vows to, for all the good that did..." She laughed shortly, not sounding truly amused. "What was her name? I only ever heard it once or twice... Katellen, that's it. She was still in office when I returned to the Sung Lands..."

"After the Second Crossing," said Sumyra. "With Hedric and Lallon."

"You've been paying attention," said Jerya. Sumyra blushed faintly, fetchingly. "Though strictly it was the Third Crossing, but that's another story. And by the Northern route; the Duke and his party did fairly discover this Southern one. Well, between Katellen and Evisyn, there was another Master Prime for a short time, and her name was Perriad..."

A tangled tale unfolded over the next mile or so. There were deceits and betrayals, incarcerations—Jerya had been confined twice, though the notion of 'imprisoning' people in a tent had obvious flaws which had swiftly been exploited by none other than Analind—not yet a Master then. This took place right where they had stopped—if Jerya had identified the spot correctly—as had the dramatic confrontation which followed. It seemed as if the stakes had been nothing less than the future of the Guild of Dawnsingers, maybe even its soul.

And then, in a final twist, a seemingly unbalanced Perriad, holed up in a tent at the mouth of the defile they had descended earlier, made a feeble and ultimately futile attempt to stop Jerya leaving the Sung Lands. Defeated, she had collapsed, revealing herself to be half-starved.

"That was the last I saw of her," said Jerya. "But I hear news every year, and she's still around and still trying to stir up trouble."

※

"You know," said Jerya a little later, "As historian—as a potential archaeologist—you'd love to see the Four Fragments."

"What are they?"

"Actual texts from the Age Before."

"Texts? On paper?"

Jerya frowned, digging in memory. "I think they said it wasn't quite like any paper known today."

"I suppose... I mean how could paper survive when there are no buildings, not even ruins, from Before?"

"I've thought about that too, and I think the answer might be quite simple. Paper is easily portable. Buildings stay in the same place. I suppose that was true even in the Age Before."

He considered that. "Then that suggests that the Known Lands were unpopulated, back then..."

"Or at least sparsely populated... Yes. And we know that the lands to the South, both here and in the Five Principalities, are dangerous to enter, that they seem to be toxic."

There was much to think about here, but he had a particular question. "Where are these Fragments?"

"In the Library of the Guild of Dawnsingers."

"In the College?" Jerya nodded. "Then I suppose I'm not allowed to see them."

"I'm afraid not. As far as I know no man's been allowed into the main Precincts since the foundation."

"That hardly seems fair."

"Perhaps not," she said gently, "But you might like to consider this... How many female students are there in your University?"

"Yes, but that's not fair either. Two injustices don't cancel each other out."

She gave a soft chuckle. "That's an interesting argument, and I have a lot of sympathy with it. But it's also fruitless to pursue it. There's precious little sign of the University authorities in Denvirran making any concessions to the admission of women... and even less that the Guild is about to change its position."

# Chapter 10

# Sumyra

At one end of the table, Blawith's Dawnsinger had spent most of the meal immersed in conversation with Jerya. Her name was Sellet, though the villagers only ever addressed her as 'Dawnsinger'. Being regarded, for some reason, as guests of honour, she and Embrel were seated at the same table, with only each other to talk to.

And Embrel seemed strangely abstracted. He answered remarks that Sumyra put to him, commented on the food, but kept drifting off into silence and not really looking at her. She had never seen him like this before, in six years of knowing each other.

When the villagers were taking their leave, Jerya left her seat to inform them she was going back to Sellet's cottage. "We've still got a lot to talk about. I may be late, so don't wait up if you're tired."

Sumyra and Embrel walked silently back to the guest-house. The One was hidden and the Three were low in the west, not casting enough light to be useful, unless perhaps you waited a long time for your eyes to adapt. There were just enough lanterns scattered around the compact, huddled, cottages for them to pick their way.

The night air was cool, but the house was still warm. Embrel knelt to add another log to the glowing embers. As he stood up, Sumyra found herself yawning. "Jerya said not to wait up...."

Embrel looked dismayed. "Could you hold on a few minutes? There's something I want to say to you."

"You've had all evening and you haven't said one word worth remembering."

His look made her feel cruel, but then he nodded. "Aye, you're right. I'm sorry, but I... I've spent all day trying to work out how to say it."

"All right, then."

She gathered her skirt and took the nearest chair. The stuffing was a little lumpy, but it was softer than anything she'd sat on for a week.

Embrel sank heavily into the facing chair and for a moment just looked at her. He pushed his hands through his hair, black in the low light, unruly as ever.

"How long have we known each other?" he said. "Six years?"

"Six and a half."

"Yes, since the night of your father's wedding. When we danced." He grinned, but it looked uneasy in the shifting light. "But what I don't suppose you know is that Jerya asked me to dance with you. Didn't give me much of a choice, to tell the truth."

"You're saying you didn't want to?"

He shrugged. "I was fourteen. Maybe fourteen's the worst age for boys. I was fourteen and you were twelve, and two years seemed like a big gap—then, I mean. And I imagined if any of my schoolfellows had been there, how they'd have sniggered at me. Impressing your friends is the most important thing at that age."

"That's probably true for girls too," she said, thinking back four years.

"Well, I danced the first dance with you because Jerya asked me—for Railu's sake, I think—but I danced the others because *I* wanted to. And I didn't really think much more about it—" He broke off, ploughing a hand through his hair again. "I didn't mean that how it might sound. I liked you, we were friends, that's all I thought. I never really thought about what anyone else might think. But, you know, you're not a little girl any more, you're a woman. And I dare say you've got friends who're courting, maybe betrothed?"

"Coming on this journey means I'm missing a wedding." She wasn't sure Hadwen would forgive her in a hurry.

"There you are. We're at that age, and people talk. When I was getting ready to come home at the end of term, one of the fellows said, 'I suppose you'll be seeing the lovely Sumyra, then?'"

"You must have talked about me."

Embrel frowned. "I'd've mentioned you a few times. But I'm sure I never said you were lovely." He winced at his own words, tried a hasty codicil. "I don't mean you're not, of course."

Sumyra laughed. "I don't expect you to lie for me."

"What? No, but you—" He collected himself. "I don't believe I ever said anything about your appearance. I'm sure when I mentioned you it was because we were talking about education for females; I probably said how your Mamma's a doctor but you never can be, and how unfair it is.

"But the point is, the thing I'm trying to say... I always thought of you as a friend. A *good* friend. You're as important to me as any of the fellows in Denvirran. And I admire you. Maybe you can't be a doctor, but I'm sure you'll do *something* extraordinary."

Sumyra wished she felt as sure as he sounded; but he was still speaking. "The thing is, that's how other people think. The fellows... Rhenya... maybe our families too. You know how people think; how it would *make sense*."

Then his face took on a look of horror. Sumyra laughed again. "It's all right, Embrel, I didn't take that as a proposal of marriage." She met his gaze. "I think I understand what you're trying to say. We've reached the age, like you said, our friends are courting, getting married. I know exactly what you mean by make sense... though if you think about it, it would make even more sense for you to marry the daughter of one of the neighbouring estates."

"That's true. Especially as... well, the finances have never been the same since Grevel... you know."

Sumyra nodded. She knew the outlines at least, the fraud that Jerya had eventually uncovered just a month or two before her marriage. The Duncals' manager, Grevel, had been skimming here and there for years and, just before being unmasked he had absconded with a hefty sum in cash.

"But there's only Stasha," said Embrel. "And... well, you know her."

Sumyra did. And perhaps all that needed to be said was that Stasha not only had no interest in education for herself, but absolutely failed to comprehend why any woman should wish to know anything beyond what was needed to run a household. "I'm sure she'll make a very good wife and mother."

"But not for me. As soon as I compare her to you... Well, there is no comparison."

"I think I should introduce you to a few of my friends. Then you'd see I'm not really that unusual."

"I doubt that," he said stoutly, and Sumyra was sure he meant it. "But I still don't know if I've said what I meant to say. People look at us, I suppose; young man, young woman, they obviously like each other, and they start thinking about all the other things. But in my head we're still the friends we've always been... and that's important too. I'd hate to do anything that would jeopardise that. Only I don't know if you feel the same..."

*I wish I knew.* That was her first thought. *I kissed Corysse... and I liked it.* But she could hardly say that. "I would hate to jeopardise our friendship too. It's important to me. And... there's one thing I do know. Just because people we know are courting and all the rest of it, doesn't mean we have to be in a tearing hurry. I think Jerya was thirty, or nearly, when she married Hedric. And when Mamma married Papa, she was... she'd just turned thirty-three, I think. And also... there's a real chance that the University in Velyadero might be admitting women in the next year or two. I want to be one of them."

She'd never said it so openly before; perhaps she'd never seen it so clearly for herself. Marriage, or any entanglement, would be a complication. And, really, what was everyone in such a rush about?

For a moment they just sat looking at each other. Then the door opened and Jerya stepped in. Both she and Embrel sprang to their feet. Sumyra didn't know whether to be relieved or dismayed.

"You didn't have to wait up for me" said Jerya. "It's not such a long day tomorrow, not in terms of walking, but the earlier we start the better the chance of picking up a boat or a coach from Varsett."

Sumyra gave Embrel one more look. She couldn't think of a single thing that she could say in front of Jerya, but hoped her eyes would convey the message: we'll talk tomorrow.

First, though, she wanted to talk to Jerya. But that, too, was best left for the morning.

# Chapter 11

# Sumyra

The sun was hot; the difference from yesterday could hardly have been more stark. She and Jerya had soon concluded that they would be cooler in the summer-weight skirts they had brought than in trousers, and had found a screen of juniper scrub so they could change.

Trousers could be a good thing, Sumyra now knew. Other things being equal, trousers would be warmer, skirts cooler because air could circulate more freely. When there was rough ground to negotiate, the kind of scrambling they had faced a dozen times during the Crossing, trousers had to be easier than trying to manage a long skirt. Now the walking was easy, a cart-wide track that almost qualified as a rough road, dipping and winding over rumpled dusty hills. In the startling sunshine, she was immediately happier now she'd changed. She looked across at Embrel and felt sorry for him. But surely he could take his jacket off...?

On a longer rise he seemed to draw ahead naturally, lost in his own thoughts. She feared he might be brooding. It was hardly in his nature, but he had rather unburdened himself last night, and she had conspicuously failed to respond as he must have hoped.

She would have to deal with that, with him, and the sooner the better. But until she had spoken with Jerya she would struggle to know what to say to him.

"Aunt," she said, moving a little closer to Jerya.

"Something on your mind?"

"I've had something on my mind since before we left home."

"I had a feeling... and I'm listening."

"First, can I ask you something?"

"Always. I don't promise you'll always like the answer." She'd said something similar before, thought Sumyra.

"No... well, when you were a Dawnsinger..."

"I barely was, you know. Only for a few months. Your Mamma was there eight years."

"I know... but I don't think I could ask her this."

Jerya just looked at her, one of those looks that seemed to see more than most people ever did.

"It's a little embarrassing to talk about..."

"Maybe that's what aunts are for."

"I hoped you'd think so."

"Go on, then. It takes quite a lot to embarrass me."

"Well, when you were a Dawnsinger..." She could feel her cheeks growing warm. She wished her skin were darker, like her Mamma, or better still like Rhenya. It would make a blush harder to see. But she'd begun this, she had to see it through. "Someone told me that Dawnsingers... swyve other Dawnsingers."

Jerya pushed back a strand of hair that had escaped her braid. "An interesting choice of word. I'm not keen on 'swyve' myself. How about 'make love with'?"

"That sounds better, I suppose."

"Someone told you that Dawnsingers make love with Dawnsingers, and I guess you want to know if it's true."

"Yes."

"Yes, it's true. And maybe your next question is... did I?"

"You were only there a few months."

"Aye," said Jerya, "But long enough. Not everything I learned was maths and science."

"And Mamma...?"

Jerya pursed her lips. "You should probably ask her that, when you get the chance. I'd be pretty sure she won't mind. But maybe just my saying that gives you a clue. Well, two facts: Dawnsingers make love with Dawnsingers, and Railu was there eight years."

"Does it... does it happen outside too?" She checked herself. She knew it did; Corysse hadn't been the first girl to kiss her. But Corysse was more than a girl; she was a woman, and a Dawnsinger.

"You mean do other women do it?" Jerya smiled. "Yes, I can personally confirm it."

"Women in the Five Principalities?"

"Yes. And yes to your next question too."

"How do you know what my next question was?"

"Let's just say I'd be very surprised if you weren't about to ask me if I've made love with women in the Five Principalities." Jerya chuckled. "Well, strictly speaking, I haven't. I've only made love with women in one Principality. Denvirran."

"But you're married now."

"Yes. I'm married, to a man, and I haven't made love with anyone else, man or woman, since I agreed to marry him."

"But..."

"Why's there a but? I've made love with women—more than one, though not many more—and I've made love with a man. Just one of them. To me the important questions aren't what sex they are—except that making love with a man can have consequences that you don't get from making love with a woman. But I'm sure your Mamma has discussed that with you already. Avoiding consequences. But I don't think that's your concern right now...?"

"No, not really. And I know what you mean about consequences."

"What was I saying? Yes, important questions. To me the important questions aren't whether it's a man or a woman but whether you care for each other, whether you respect each other. That's what matters."

"I thought..." She could not finish the thought.

"What did you think?" Jerya's voice was gentle, almost lost on the soft warm breeze that had begun to tease at their hair and their skirts.

"I though maybe if you... made love with women, you wouldn't be able to love a man."

"Hm." Jerya walked on a few paces, thinking. "First thing, making love and loving someone aren't necessarily the same. They can overlap, and that's the best thing, but they don't always. Which maybe suggests the vocabulary's misleading. But on what you said... I promise you, Sumyra, niece, from my own experience, it's absolutely not true. When it comes to love, I don't see any difference at all. And as for making love, yes, there are differences in how you do it, things that can take a little getting used to. But if you have that care and respect—and love, with luck—and maybe a little patience, then it's not a problem."

❈

They caught up with Embrel, and then he asked her something, and it was Sumyra's turn to be lost in her own thoughts. She hadn't walked far before she found herself thinking, *I must have sounded really stupid. 'Do women in the Five Principalities make love with women...'* Perhaps she and Corysse hadn't quite crossed the line from kiss-and-cuddle to 'making love'. Perhaps the same was true of the times she'd been close with girls at school.

But Mavrys and Vireddi called each other 'wife', and lived together exactly like a married couple. They were a married couple, in every sense except the legalistic. Their love and intimacy were obvious to all who knew them. *Am I to suppose they don't... cross the line?*

Jerya must have thought of this, but she hadn't mentioned them. Sumyra was grateful for her aunt's tact, but her cheeks grew hot anyway, and not just because the sun was on them.

## Chapter 12

# Sumyra

A mass of black ringlets swished across the shoulders of a vivid yellow blouse as the woman turned. She seemed around the same age as Jerya or Mamma, with a few fine lines around the eyes and, just like Jerya, a scattering of silver threads amid the black.

"Well," she said, obviously recognising Jerya, "It's been a while."

"Eleven years, near enough. How are you?"

"Three kids, and a tavern to run; I wouldn't have time to be ill." She said it with a shrug, but sounded cheerful enough.

"And Rodal?"

"Down at the brewery, giving his verdict on a new ale they're trying. And he'll be calling on the vegetable merchant about some produce that wasn't fresh." Her eyes flicked past Jerya as if noticing for the first time that she wasn't alone.

"Sorry," said Jerya, "Forgetting my manners. Annyt, this is my niece Sumyra, and..." She stepped aside to reveal Embrel, who'd been behind her. "This is Embrel."

The warm smile Annyt had given Sumyra curdled as she looked at Embrel.

Though there were sounds around them, conversations in the bar, the clatter of clogs on the setts outside, Sumyra suddenly felt as if Annyt and the three of them had been enveloped in a kind of bubble of silence.

Annyt stared at Embrel a moment longer, then turned back to Jerya. "Tell me I'm imagining it."

"I can't."

"Then how—" She broke off, moved to a door behind the bar, and called out, "Sokkie, come and serve." Without waiting for a reply, she gestured to the nearest of the booths along the right-hand wall. "Just you and me," she said to Jerya. "The girl too, if you want. Not him."

Sumyra glanced back at Embrel, whose face registered honest bewilderment. She felt she ought to stand with him, but what could she say? If she joined the other two women, she might learn something. *Maybe I'll be more help to him that way*, she thought, though she had to wonder if that wasn't more of a pretext than a reason. There was a puzzle here, and she'd always found puzzles hard to resist.

She waited for Jerya's nod before joining her on the worn leather seat. She had barely settled before Annyt stabbed a question at Jerya. "Is he yours?"

"Not mine, no... look, are you sure you want to do this before Rodal gets back?"

"I need to know where I stand by then."

"As you wish."

"If he's not yours, whose is he? No, wait... he's got to be Railu's, right?"

*What are they talking about?* Sumyra was asking herself. But in a moment it came to her. She jolted in her seat as if a dozen wasps had stung her all at once.

"You didn't know?" the woman, Annyt, said, looking at her neutrally. "No, you said 'niece'."

"Honorary niece," said Jerya. "As I call Embrel my nephew. But there's no blood tie between any of us. Although... Railu is Sumyra's step-mother."

"This is getting even more tangled."

"I'm still not sure I understand," said Sumyra. "But this... this is the secret, it must be. The reason Mamma didn't want me to come."

"Oh, it's a secret, is it?" said Annyt. "I wondered if everyone in the Five Principalities knew."

"I didn't know until this last minute."

"Does the boy know?"

Sumyra glanced at Embrel. He had taken position on a stool further along the bar, his eyes fixed on the three in the booth. A girl of thirteen or fourteen had appeared behind the bar.

"He doesn't know," said Jerya. "Very few people do. And in general we want to keep it that way."

"And you said, what's your name, Sumyra, Railu didn't want you to come? She's who you mean when you say Mamma?"

"That's right."

"Didn't want her dirty little secret getting out, is it?"

Sumyra bristled reflexively at the insult to her Mamma... but, really, what was she supposed to think?

"Please," said Jerya, "At least hear the full story before you judge her too harshly."

"Do I want to?" asked Annyt.

"You might need to. Remember how young we all were, and Railu was youngest of all. And she'd been in the College of the Dawnsingers for eight years. You know how she was with Rodal at first, could hardly speak to him. But when he came to help us cross the mountains, she began to see him differently."

"It made me look at him differently too. Except I didn't see him for nigh on a year." Abruptly, Annyt leaned out of the booth, called to the girl at the bar. "Sokkie! Half of the Pale for me. What about you?" Jerya and Sumyra ordered the same. When the girl fetched the drinks, Annyt told her, "Get the lad whatever he wants, too.

"Guess it's not his fault," she said when her daughter was back behind the counter.

"Not in the slightest," agreed Jerya.

"Still not sure I want to look at him..."

"Aren't you worried your daughter'll see the likeness too?" asked Sumyra.

"Not likely. I'm seeing Rodal twenty years ago, not now, with the beard and all." She sipped her ale, fixed her gaze on Jerya again. "Finish your tale."

As Jerya's story unfolded, Sumyra tried to imagine the young Railu. Not the near-forty-year-old doctor, wife, and beloved step-mother, but a girl her own age, propelled far outside her previous experience, far beyond anything life had prepared her for. The three—not two—had endured blizzards and made what sounded like a terrifying descent of a huge steep rockface before reaching easier ground. She knew most of it already, but now she could add on a different narrative. When Jerya said that the mood, on finally finding a congenial stop to camp and recover, was 'euphoric', she could readily believe it.

"And it only happened once," said Jerya as she drew her account to a close.

"You expect me to believe that?"

"You know this part. The very next day Railu and I were taken for slaves. Rodal was off in the forest. We never saw him again for best part of a year."

Annyt *hmphed*. "*S'pose* I can believe that... but how come he never told me he had a son?"

"He never knew. He still doesn't."

"You really expect me to believe that?"

"It's true. Next time he saw Railu, Embrel was eight or nine weeks old. And he never came into the house; he never saw him, he had no reason to suspect there was a baby."

"And you never told him."

"I wanted to but Railu had other ideas. And I know that sounds like I'm putting responsibility on her when she isn't here to speak for herself, but Sumyra knows she wasn't keen on Embrel finding out even now."

"That's quite right," agreed Sumyra.

"Why not?" demanded Annyt. "Is she ashamed?"

"It's not that," said Jerya.

"Then why?"

Sumyra, who was wondering the same thing, didn't get to hear Jerya's answer. A shadow fell over the table. And then things seemed to happen in staccato, like a dark scene lit by flashes of lightning. Blink-glimpses of a bearded man; his face changing as—she supposed—he recognised Jerya. Then, before anyone else could move or speak, Annyt was on her feet, grasping the man's arm, hustling him into the back-room.

This left her looking at Embrel, who was staring, evidently more bewildered than ever. Before she could think she was out of her seat, crossing the floor. She drew up another stool and climbed onto it.

He had one question. "*What's going on?* Do you know?"

She shrugged. "Some of it."

"Seems like I'm the last to know," he said sourly.

That wasn't fair, she saw. He was right at the heart of it, and of course entirely innocent.

"This isn't going to be easy. You may not want to believe it."

"Just tell me. I can't stand the suspense any longer."

She took a deep breath. "The Squire and Lady Pichenta are not your real parents."

For a moment he seemed frozen, as if he had not heard her. But then she saw his eyes.

All she could do was finish what she'd started. "They adopted you from birth. I think it was all agreed before you were born."

"Then who..." A whisper, barely audible over the background hum of the bar, folk carrying on normal everyday conversations.

"Your mother is Railu... and that man who was there a moment ago. Rodal. He's your—"

"No." The word sounded flat but his actions weren't. He almost catapulted himself off the stool, darted to the street-door and was gone.

❋

Before Sumyra could think what to do, Jerya was beside her.

"I guess you told him," she said.

"I started to."

Jerya sighed. "I always thought he should have known all along. Maybe this is what I was afraid of... I suppose we should go after him." Her tone was strange, uncertain; she seemed at a loss, in a way Sumyra had never seen before.

After a moment she realised Jerya was looking at her as if looking for advice, or at least to share the decision. "I should go," she said. "I'm the one who messed up telling him."

"I'm not sure you did. I don't think there'd ever be a painless way. But maybe... you weren't any part of the original decision. He can blame me, but he can't blame you."

"I'd better get a move on."

"Listen." Jerya held Sumyra's hand a moment. "He ran away once before. Long time ago, when I was about to set out, first time I came back here. I found him at the road-end waiting for the diligence. But I don't know if he'd had that much of a plan when he started out."

"You think he just followed the road?"

Jerya shrugged. "Maybe just that it was downhill. Easiest way to get away quickly."

That was something, Sumyra supposed, but there was an immediate problem. The tavern was at the bottom of a dip, so that whichever way you turned from the door was uphill.

There was, of course, no sign of Embrel. No handy tracks, as on the snowfield they'd crossed a few days ago. *Think... if I turn to the right, that's the way we came, down from the hilltop.* Jerya hadn't known a direct route from the waterfront to Old Tanpits Lane, had only been able to find her way from the environs of the College. Sumyra remembered Embrel's half-ironic grumbling about going all the way up the hill only to come half-way back down again.

She turned left. A sharp rise, an odd kink, and then the lane turned downward once more. At each succeeding junction, she took the most obvious downward route. She kept an eye out for Embrel, though there was no apparent reason for him to linger at any spot she passed. She could only hope he wasn't in some other tavern, perhaps less salubrious, drinking himself into oblivion. How would he do that? *I'm sure he hasn't any Sung Lands money.* It didn't quite seem the sort of thing he would do anyway.

Mostly, her thoughts kept running over the last hour. She fixed on her one glimpse of the bearded man. The beard, of course, making it harder to see any likeness there might be between them, at least in the jawline or the mouth. The beard was reddish, redder than the sandy hair, shot with grey, especially near the corners of the mouth. Nothing like the deep umber, edging towards black, of Embrel's curls.

She realised that she'd been looking for something that proved Rodal was Embrel's true father; or perhaps she'd really been hoping for contrary evidence.

The plain fact was, there was no such evidence to tie him to his... official parents either. They had both been grey as long as she had known them, and though she knew there was a portrait of Lady Pichenta as a young woman in the hall at Duncal, she could not recall what colour her hair had been. They both had straight hair, though.

Embrel's hair colour was closer to Jerya's, but he was not Jerya's child—if you could believe anything any more. And Railu, Mamma... her mind flinched away from the thought, but she made herself consider it. Mamma was bald, but she must have had hair once, and black or near-black hair could easily go with the copper hue of her skin. And her eyes were a rich deep brown, not unlike Embrel's, though Lady Pichenta's weren't so very different.

She took another turning, down a flight of shallow steps between tall houses. Blank arches overhead buttressed the houses, as if the builders had feared they would topple toward each other.

Her mind went back to the bearded man. There'd been no introductions, but she had no doubt he was Rodal. His hair was swept back from a broad squarish brow. When Embrel pushed the tight curls back off his face, his brow had the same bullish shape.

It wasn't proof; she wasn't sure what would constitute irrefutable proof, if Jerya's word wasn't good enough; but it was suggestive. It made it at least plausible that he was Rodal's son.

She came suddenly from the shadowy stair to the brightness of the waterfront. Half-dazzled, she almost stumbled in front of a cart. The driver ignored her but the mule gave her a disdainful look and a soft snort. She lifted her skirts a few inches to cross the road, its grey setts dotted with a litter of cabbage leaves, scraps of fish-skin, the vivid splat of a crushed carrot. No doubt there were worse ingredients in the mix. She was glad there hadn't been time to remove her walking-boots.

She escaped the roadway onto smoother, cleaner setts. A scattered line of spindly trees demarcated this strip as somewhere reserved for pedestrians. Two more strides took her to the parapet. Despite her urgency to find Embrel, she took a brief moment to take in the scene. She knew from the map how the river drew a great lazy curve, three fourths of a circle, around the city's heart, the hill crowned by the College of the Dawnsingers. As far as she could estimate, she was close to a hundred and eighty degrees from the wharf where they'd disembarked. Here there were no wharfs, no working boats, only what seemed to be pleasure craft.

A scatter of colourful sails made it an agreeable scene, but she forced herself back to the matter at hand. Jerya's suggestion of heading downhill—easiest way to get away quick—had made sense, or at least given her a direction to follow. Now, however, there was no more 'easiest way'. The river still flowed, so there must be some gradient, but there was no sense of it in the stones under her feet. The slow broad slide of the river might draw him to the left, but the trade-river—and the way home, if that was in his mind—were upstream, to the right.

Logic gave no clear answer. She could only fall back on her own knowledge of Embrel, her sense of what he might do. And take a chance. There was no certainty that he'd even reached this point, after all. Probably the chance was a slender one. *And dithering here isn't going to improve the odds.*

She turned left, with the flow of the river. Better to be doing something than nothing.

## Chapter 13

# Sumyra

She found him within ten or fifteen minutes. He was leaning on the parapet, his attention on a little boat that was skimming along maybe thirty yards out, apparently heading straight for the bridge that spanned the river. It didn't look as if the arch was high enough to admit its mast.

Sumyra quietly took her place next to him, but neither said anything until anything until the boat had slipped safely through, clearing the arch by no more than a foot. It must have lined up pretty precisely on the highest point.

Only then did Embrel turn and look at her. "How did you find me?"

"Gravity," she said. "And then mostly instinct—or pure luck. Anyway..." She looked at his hands, resting on the parapet, wondering if she could, or should, take one in hers. For a moment she was distracted by a flaky curve beside his little finger: a fossil? She'd learned about fossils a couple of years ago at summer-school; Earl Hedric had taken the girls fossicking at an old quarry on the scarp of Skilthorn Wold, found a few modest specimens.

Embrel brought her attention snapping back to here, to now, to himself. "Is it really true?"

"Jerya doesn't make things up. I'd think you'd know that better than I do. And that man, Rodal... I can see something." Feeling very daring, she reached out, brushing his hair back. "Here, for instance." She let her hand fall, landing beside his. "Embrel, I know this must be very shocking for you—"

He snorted, a fleeting laugh that had no merriment in it. "You think so? Can you really imagine how I... To suddenly find that everything I thought I knew was a lie?"

*Not everything*, she wanted to protest, but instead she found herself saying, "I'm shocked too. It's like my Mamma isn't quite who I thought she was."

He met her gaze squarely for the first time. "I suppose... at least you still know who your father is. And... what does it make us? You and me? Some sort of brother and sister?"

"Almost, though there's no blood-tie."

"No..." He pulled away, almost as convulsively as he'd flung himself from the bar-stool. "I need to move. Can we walk?"

"Of course. Where?"

"Anywhere. Over the bridge, maybe."

Perhaps it wasn't the best choice. The pavement was narrower than the riverside promenade, and busier. Still, this meant that Embrel, remembering his manners, placed himself on the side nearer the road and offered his arm. Sumyra didn't need his 'protection' but she didn't think this was the time to protest.

They walked in silence for a few moments, then Embrel released a long sigh. "I feel like I don't know who I am any more."

"Seems to me you're exactly the same person you were yesterday."

"Really? Even though my parents aren't my parents after all?"

"But what your parents... the Squire and Lady, I mean... what they gave you was never in your blood. Your blood-inheritance always was from Railu and Rodal. And the home they gave you, the love, the education... none of that's changed either."

He merely grunted, unconvinced.

"Listen, Embrel. We learned something about blood and inheritance in summer-school last year. And Tutor Marjani, who taught us, virtually the first thing she said was, 'Dawnsingers don't have children'."

"And yet here I am."

"Well, but Railu wasn't really a Dawnsinger any more, was she? In general, Dawnsingers don't have children. They also brought Mavrys in for one session. She's remarkable, you know, in so many ways. Did you know she was younger than I am when she first became Mistress of Horse? Younger than every single lad in the stables. I can't imagine... but that's not what she was there to talk about. She knows all about bloodlines. Every single horse in that yard, she knows every sire and dam going back three or four generations. And she knows a lot about other horses in other yards as well. The breeding of horses seems to be a lot more... scientific... than it is for people. But still, she said, '*It doesn't matter if a horse has a dozen champions in its bloodlines from the sire and a dozen more from the dam. It still has to be properly schooled, properly fed, properly exercised... and even then you still don't know how it will race until it's run a few times. And the proof of that is that people can still bet on the races. If the result was a foregone conclusion no one but a fool would take your bet... and bookmakers aren't fools. My father said they were the only men who ever got rich out of racing.*' And someone stuck her hand up and asked, '*If that's true, why do you take so much trouble over bloodlines?*' Mavrys grinned and said, '*Do you think I never asked myself that? But I'm not saying bloodlines count for nothing, only that they're a long way from being everything*'."

They were half-way across the long bridge now, and there was a little wider spot, a triangular space like a balcony, mirroring the angles of the cutwater below. He didn't resist her gentle tug on his arm; perhaps he was glad to step aside out of the bustle, to look down on the waters smoothly parting around the stone prow. Perhaps this river had flowed here in the First Age—the Age Before, as the Dawnsingers called it—though the bridge surely hadn't existed then.

"D'you really believe that, 'Myra?" he asked. It was years since he'd called her that. "That blood counts for so little?"

"I don't think that's what Mavrys was saying, or what Marjani taught us. All Mavrys really said was that bloodlines weren't everything."

"*A long way from being everything*," he quoted.

"Yes, but how far is that? Is it half blood and half upbringing? More one than the other? Marjani said no one can put a number to it. And most people are raised by their natural parents, particularly their mothers, so that makes it even harder to tell what's what. I mean, if someone has red hair, that's in the blood, clear enough. But when you said, 'I don't know who I am any more', you were talking about character, aren't you? And who can say where that comes from? The old Earl of Skilthorn, you know he had two nephews? One seems to have been just as bad as he was, but the other... the other is Hedric."

"Hmmm." He tugged at his ear as he pondered, and she laughed gently. "What?"

"Who else does that when he's thinking?"

"My father—but what do I call him now?"

"Well, that's something you do have to decide. But you always called him Papa when you were younger?"

"Except when we had company."

"Embrel, you know this isn't all going to get sorted out in one day. How long since I first dropped it in your lap? An hour? Probably less.

"Mamma said there are seven people who know this secret. Now there are four more: you, me, Rodal, and Annyt. Maybe... did Jerya say there are three children? We've only seen one, I think she's the oldest. Maybe they'll want to tell them too, or maybe they'll wait till they're older."

"I never even thought," he said, lightly slapping the parapet. "That girl, she's my half-sister." He ploughed his hand through his curls. "Draff, I really can't take it all in."

She lifted his hand from the pale limestone, wrapped both her own around it. "You know hardly anyone in the Five Principalities says 'draff', don't you? You got that from Jerya, or I'm a Dawnsinger."

"Well," he said, "You don't look like one, that's for sure."

Then he reached up his free hand and slid it slowly down the length of one of her braids.

All at once Sumyra felt herself tingling all over. "Embrel..."

He snatched his hand back. "I'm sorry."

"No, please, don't be. That's not... I liked it. I think... look, let me just say something. I'll stumble. I'll probably stumble a lot and go red and... please, hold my hand, stroke my hair again if you like, but just don't say anything until I've finished."

"How will I know when you've finished?" he asked with a grin that made him look five years younger.

"I think you'll know. I hope so... and if not I'll just have to tell you." She stepped a little closer to him, to make their conversation even more private. "A few nights ago, in Blawith, you said... well, quite a few things And I didn't know what to say in return and I'm sorry about that... but I've been thinking about it ever since.

"I was just a child when we first met; well, you said, that was why you didn't want to dance with me at the wedding, because I was just a kid. But Jerya leaned on you and then you... I suppose you found I wasn't so bad after all."

"Not too bad," he said, then remembered his promise and put a finger to his own lips. Half of her wished he'd take hold of her braid again, half of her thought it was hard enough already to concentrate in what she had to say.

"And we've been friends, so even the idea that we might be something more, or different... it's hard to think about isn't it? You said so, and, well, I feel it too. Just now, you said, I don't know who I am any more; but don't we all feel that way sometimes? Growing up, becoming a woman... Sometimes you feel like you're just the same person but no one else treats you the same; sometimes you don't even know yourself.

"And you went away to Denvirran, and I was always at summer-school in your long vacation. And we were growing up as well. We were never going to go on being exactly how we were when I was twelve and you were fourteen. One of the best things about this journey is having the time with you again. Getting to know the man that boy grew into. And it turns out... the man is so different, and yet he's exactly the same in so many ways. I suppose people are always changing and we're always getting used to each other all over again. Like Papa... he's different since he met Mamma, and yet he's still the same man.

"And you're the same too. And..." She shrugged. "Finding out that my Mamma's your natural mother... it's a big thing, of course it is. A big thing to learn about her, but she's still my Mamma. And you're still Embrel. The boy who didn't want to dance with me, and then didn't want to stop."

She ran out of words then, felt as if she'd almost run out of breath too. They just gazed at each other. Finally he said, "*Have* you finished?"

Sumyra gave a little choking laugh. "No. I don't think I'll ever be finished... but yes."

"Then can I say something?"

"Please do."

"I still want to dance with you."

❋

"Draff!" she said a little later.

"What is it?"

"I don't know the way."

"I don't remember either." His laugh rang off the walls of the narrow lane. "Fine couple of travellers we are, eh? First time we try to do anything without an aunt to guide us and we get lost."

He tightened his grip on her hand. It should have been painful but somehow it wasn't. "At least we're lost together."

"Yes, and I am glad... but if we keep heading uphill we're sure to get to the College eventually, and I'm sure I can remember the way from there."

"Oh joy. Climb to the top of the hill and then come halfway down again—for the second time today."

## Chapter 14

# Embrel

"Now, lad," said Rodal, "Here's how I think we go. We've got womenfolk watching on hoping we'll fall into each other's arms and declare undying love..."

"I thought your wife wasn't happy about me."

"Annyt's a practical woman. Sees how it is." Rodal grunted. "You know I left her in Delven, when I followed Jerya and Railu? Didn't see her again for nigh on a year. An' my folks, reckoning we were betrothed—which we weren't—had it solid in their heads she should stay, permanent-like. So what'd she do? Only got the Dawnsinger on her side." He swigged at his dark ale like a thirsty man. "But that's another story. What I'm saying now is... I'm not expecting you to love me or call me Pa. Let's take it slow. There's things you'll want to know about me, an' things I'll want to know about you. Let's just do some o' that an' see where we get to."

Embrel nodded, sipped more sparingly at his own pint. "Sounds fair enough... Question is, where to start? Yesterday I didn't even know you existed. And even now, all I know—apart from, well, you know—is what I can see and what you just said about following Jerya and Railu."

'Happen that's a place to start, if you like." Rodal grinned. "It's not a story I get to tell very often. Annyt's probably sick o' hearing about it. Sokkie too, by now. An' the boys are still too young to understand it properly. Mayhap Tawno, in a year or two, but it'll be a long while for Elbar."

Rodal shrugged. "We all have our secrets."

"Well, I'd like to hear it."

"Grand." Rodal took a more moderate sip, lubricating his vocal cords. "So how it starts is, coupla days after we'd got down out o' the mountains, I come back from hunting to find the girls gone, an' most of our gear with 'em. What they'd left was thrown around an' the ground was all trampled. The tracks were easy to follow, and then I got to a place where I could see horses had been standing a while. Stony track after that, so mostly I tracked 'em by following the shit." Embrel restrained himself from laughing out loud. He could see this wasn't a happy memory for Rodal. "Two days walking, and then it was the third day afore I got any news of 'em. Heard they'd been taken as slaves, an' sold to this house... well, you'll know that part."

"I surely do. Grew up there."

"An' you grew up with Jerya and Railu?"

"Yes; when I was little I thought they'd always been there... But tell me the rest of your story and then I'll tell you mine."

"Aye, keep it tidy. Growing up in Delven, when we had taletell of an evening it was always finish one story afore you start another... though sometimes it aingt so easy to say where one story ends an' the next one starts, is it? Still..."

The tale unfolded. Rodal satisfied himself that 'the girls' were safe. It was odd for Embrel to hear Jerya and Railu referred to as 'girls', but of course they had been younger than he was now. Reasoning that it made no sense to attempt liberating them before he had some resources, and a better knowledge of the Five Principalities, Rodal looked for work and soon found a position on a trading-ship, a river-coaster or wherry. This took him down-river to Troquharran and then through the Island Passage to Sessapont. "I figured myself for the only man in this age who'd seen both Oceans," he said. "Maybe there's others now, but I was the first, far as I ever heard."

Embrel nodded. "Maybe there's one or two others now. But only in the last few years."

"Happen you could join 'em. It's only a couple of hours on the canal to the seacoast." That was a stirring thought.

Rodal's tale wound on. The nine months or so he'd spent on the Levore sounded like a grand adventure, and Embrel sensed there was part of him that had been sorry to take his leave. But he'd made promises, to Annyt as well as to Jerya and Railu, and he kept them. When he returned to Duncal, he found that Jerya had already been freed, though not Railu. (Here, Embrel was able to tell him that she'd been freed more recently, after Jerya's return from her second Crossing. Or so he'd understood it at the time; now he knew that their enslavement had never been valid.)

"You'd'a been about two months old, I s'pose," added Rodal. "But neither o' them said a word about you."

"I think Jerya might have wanted to but Railu set her face against it."

"So you didn't find out till today..." He grinned as he lowered his glass. "You an' me both, eh? D'you know why Railu was so agin it?"

"Not really. I guess you'd have to ask Jerya. I can guess why my parents... I mean..."

"I know what you mean," said Rodal helpfully. "The folks what adopted you, what raised you."

Embrel nodded. "Though Jerya and Railu raised me just as much. And Rhenya... but I'll tell you properly when you've finished."

"Aye, well, there's not too much more to tell. Turned out they reckoned they were as well off staying where they was as anything else. Which surprised me, but I s'posed they knew best. So I came back—"

"You crossed the mountains alone?"

Rodal shrugged. "I was lucky with the weather. It wasn't too hard, really. There's only the crag, an' I was raised in Delven... So I got back here, to Annyt, a few days ahead of time. But it took a while afore she'd consider having me back, an' a while longer afore her parents came round. But we won 'em over—eventually—an' the rest is... well, not so much of an adventure. Or mebbe a different kind of adventure. Raising three kids an' learning to run this place at the same time... But it's time I heard something about you." He signalled to his daughter and a minute later she brought a second round of drinks.

In the brief hiatus, a thought—an unwelcome thought—lodged itself in Embrel's mind. He didn't really want to think about it, but he knew it wouldn't go away. As Sokkie departed with the empty mugs, he took a hefty draught to fortify himself, then set down his glass. "You seem to have started after... after whatever happened between you and Railu."

Rodal lowered his own tankard and sat back. "I was hoping you wouldn't ask that. I at exactly proud of it."

"Why?"

Rodal must have heard something in his tone. His gaze sharpened. "I hope you're not suggesting anything... If you even have to ask that, lad, you don't know me."

"But that that's just it. I don't."

※

"He's Delven-born, same as I am, and if there's one thing that's drummed into you every day, it's telling the truth."

"But mightn't even the best of men be tempted to..." He saw the fallacy before she could say it. "No, the best of men wouldn't be in that situation, would they?"

"I surely hope you wouldn't."

"Can you think that I would?"

Her gaze was hard to bear; he hardly knew why. But he did not look away.

"No," she said after a moment. "I don't believe you would. But I have to tell you, Embrel, I have the seen the impact it can have on a woman. I'll not say who, or who the offender was—that's one secret I've never shared beyond those who already knew, or guessed. And that was one of the cases where the man might say that the girl put herself in that position. It's..."

She trailed off, biting her lip. "I've often wished we could have made a case against the man, but it would have been her word against his. And what good does it do, raking over those coals now? What matters is you and Rodal.

Jerya grasped his upper arm. "I can tell you I never thought for a moment Rodal forced himself on Railu. I can tell you what she told me, that same day; 'we didn't mean it to happen'; take note that she said 'we'. But I don't want you to lean on that. You need to believe that Rodal, your father, isn't the kind of man who'd force himself on any woman. And you need to believe that he's a man you can trust."

She paused, looking like a woman in need of a strong drink. Embrel felt much the same himself.

"Ask him about his time on the *Levore*," she said.

"The *Levore*?"

"The ship he sailed on, for most of his time in the Five Principalities. I met her Skipper. What would it be? Twelve years later. It was on our sweetmoon; Hedric and I sailed on her. The Skipper remembered Rodal well, clearly thought highly of him. He told me he single-handedly saw off a couple of thieves who'd obviously thought the ship was unattended. He said he'd been thinking seriously about taking him into partnership. But Rodal had made a promise, or he he had an understanding—with Annyt, obviously. And he'd made promises, at least in his own mind, to Railu and me, too. He might have been tempted to stay with the *Levore*, but he stood by his promises. That's the kind of man he is."

She didn't say it aloud this time, but he heard it anyway: *your father*.

※

"Right," said Rodal. "If you're satisfied there's no question of anything sordid... Look, I can't blame you for wond'ring, but you can't blame me for not liking it. And can we... I need a little time to think out how I'm to tell you. So I'm guessing there's other things you want to ask me... and besure there's a few things I'd like to ask you."

"Well, why don't we start there?"

"Jerya's told me a few things. She's got a kid of her own? How old did she say, six?"

"That's right." Rodal hadn't mentioned her being a Countess: had Jerya omitted that bit? It was hardly an insignificant detail.

But Rodal didn't linger on the subject of Jerya's current life. "An' she said she'd been your... governess? Is that the word? I'm not right sure I know what that means."

"Well, I didn't go to school till I was twelve. When I was smaller I had tutors but I didn't get on with any of them. I don't know whether I was a difficult pupil or they just weren't any good, but when I was about eight my parents agreed Jerya could teach me instead."

"An' that went better?"

"*Much* better. She already knew me well, of course, so she knew how to get me interested in things. She didn't just sit me down with an arithmetic text, she showed me how numbers worked in the real world, whether it was the estate accounts or measuring the orbits of the moons."

"She tried to explain a bit o' that to me. When we were crossin' the Sunder... When we were crossing the Sunder... How the sun's rising has nowt to do wi' Dawnsong. S'pose I needed to know, an' o'course once I'd spent a bit o'time in the Five Principalities it was obvious. Sun comes up jus' the same, Dawnsong or no Dawnsong. Still, most o' what she said went right over my head. Don't know how she picked up so much when she'd only been in the College a few months." He stopped, gestured, as if to say, *But we're supposed to be hearing from you now.*

"When I was a kid I thought she knew everything," said Embrel. "I guess she did learn a lot when she was here." He gestured in what he hoped was the right direction, up the hill toward the College. "And then she went through my father's library—" He broke off. "Only I shouldn't say 'father', should I?"

"If that's how you think of him, I don't see why not. Surely seems he was a lot more of a father to you than I ever was."

"I suppose... it's all so confusing."

"You an' me both." Rodal grinned, raised his glass in salute. "Here's to confusion."

Embrel could relate to that, used the toast to finally drain his first pint.

He tried to pick up the story again. "And she used his telescope a lot more than he ever did... but that was mostly after she met Hedric."

"Aye, he came here, but they weren't wed then."

"They were married the year after their Crossing, I think."

"Aye... But tell me where Railu fits in. You said they both had a big part in raising you?"

"Yes, Railu was my nursemaid when I was little."

"Funny," mused Rodal. "She must have done a lot o' the things a mother'd do in most families. And yet you never knew. Never even suspected...?"

"No."

"Yet I sit here and look at you... an' I ain't even seen her for more'n twenty years, but I can still see you have her eyes."

Embrel flinched, almost as if he'd been slapped. It was like the moment when Sumyra had first told him, all over again. A shock, as if the very notion of Railu being his true mother hadn't penetrated beyond some superficial layer of his mind. *You have her eyes...* He still couldn't make sense of it. Perhaps he still didn't quite *believe* it.

Rodal's look seemed sympathetic. "Musta been strange for her."

"I hadn't thought of that. She was always... Oh, I don't even know how to say it. I've called Jerya 'aunt' for a few years, but not Railu. But then she—Jerya—invited me to. She was raised by aunts herself, you know?"

"Aye," said Rodal, a crooked smile creasing his beard.

"Oh, of course you would." Embrel's face felt warm.

"They weren't really aunts, mind, not by blood. Same for you'n'her, reckon."

"I suppose... well, what I was trying to say is that they both raised me, they and Rhenya." He broke off to explain briefly who Rhenya was. "When I was young I probably spent more time with them than with..."

"Your parents. Might as well say it that way."

"It's how I've always thought of them... Well, the three of them looked after me and I loved them all. Still do. Maybe... maybe I loved Jerya best, especially when she became my governess." He managed a short laugh. "I'd never liked any of my tutors, she was like a breath of fresh air.

"Now I know Railu's really my... my mother... it feels a bit wrong saying I loved Jerya better. But I think that's true. I loved them all, but Jerya came first."

# Chapter 15

# Sumyra

The portress was evidently not a Dawnsinger; she was dressed in grey, and not bald, though her hair was severely cropped. "I have to tell you, madam, that it is most unusual for persons from Outwith to be admitted to the Precincts. *If* the Master Prime or any other Singer has business with you, it is more likely that they will see you in the Annexe. You can reach—"

"—I know how to find the Annexe, thank you." Jerya's voice was quiet, polite, but firm. Sumyra knew that tone well. "The Master Prime has been a guest in my home, and in my niece's. If you would just see that the message reaches her, and then we'll see what she says."

The woman's sigh was poorly concealed. Sumyra had the clear impression that she was merely humouring the request to shut up her annoying visitor. "Very well. What did you say your name was? "

"I'm Jerya and this is my niece Sumyra. Shall I write it down for you?"

"That won't be necessary." The portress disappeared into a back room. They heard an exchange in low voices. A door opened, closed.

"There will be a wait," said the woman, returning. "I can't say how long. The Master Prime is extremely busy."

"I don't doubt it," said Jerya.

"There are seats through there."

In fact they occupied the hard upright chairs for less than ten minutes. The portress's demeanour had changed. "I have a note for you from the

Master Prime." Jerya unfolded and scanned the single sheet, showed it to Sumyra:

*Glad to hear you're in Carwerid again, but afraid I can't see you right away. Suggest you call on Sharess first. Come back to the lodge around 11th hour for further word. I'm instructing that you and Sumyra have free access to the Precincts.*

"Who's Sharess?" asked Sumyra as they walked through the first cloister.

"The Singer who Chose me, all those years ago."

Jerya walked on in silence. Sumyra supposed she was reflecting on everything that had followed. She'd learned enough about Dawnsingers to know that it was very unusual, probably unheard-of, for a girl to be Chosen at such an advanced age as nineteen. As Jerya herself had said, had she been Chosen at the usual age, around eleven, "I dare say I'd have become a perfectly ordinary Dawnsinger."

Sumyra wasn't sure any Dawnsinger was perfectly ordinary, and it was even harder to imagine Jerya herself being so… but she could not deny that Jerya's life would have been very different. And, a sobering thought, so would many others. If Jerya had never made the First Crossing, neither would Railu.

*And Papa would never have met her…* It was a disconcerting thought. Would he eventually have settled for some lesser bride? Would he ever have suspected what he had missed?

*Would I now call some other woman Mamma?* She couldn't imagine it.

*Well*, she thought, brisking her thoughts along, *one thing for sure, I wouldn't be here now, in the Sung Lands, walking through the College of the Dawnsingers*. She made herself take better note of her surroundings. *This may be the first and last time.*

❋

"I'm sorry I couldn't come to meet you," said Sharess, hobbling toward them, "But... well, you see how it is. And the retired lodgings, pleasant though they be, are about as far as you can get from the front lodge."

"Nothing to worry about," said Jerya, smiling tenderly at the older woman. She took both Sharess's hands in her own, but lightly, careful of the arthritis that twisted the fingers and knotted the joints. "Do you need to sit down?"

"In a minute. I can still walk, and Berrivan always tells me to do as much as I can. So give me your arm and we'll take a turn around the damson orchard. It's too late for the blossom, of course, but it's still fine. But first, aren't you going to introduce us?"

"I'm sorry. So happy to see you again I forgot my manners. Dawnsinger Sharess, this is my niece Sumyra."

Sharess examined her carefully. Nested in wrinkles, the eyes themselves were clear and green. "Niece, you say? But I know you never had a sister. Or a brother." She chuckled, a soft breathy sound. "Reckon I'd know if anyone does."

"Aye," said Jerya, "It's by way of a courtesy title. But Railu and I are close as any sisters, and Sumyra's Railu's step-daughter."

"Ah, yes; I should have placed the name from your letters. And Railu's properly recognised as a doctor at last? Berrivan was well pleased to hear that."

"I must try and see Master Berrivan before we leave," said Jerya. "And Yanil, Jossena... I just hope there's time for everyone."

"You'll be here for a few weeks, I suppose?"

Jerya shrugged. "We haven't fully settled our plans. This trip's for Sumyra as much as for me... and for Embrel, of course, my nephew—also not by blood, but I've known him all his life. They may want to see more of the Sung Lands. Maybe even as far as Delven."

"But you'll not be going back across the mountains from there?"

Jerya gave the old woman's gnarled hand a gentle pat of reassurance. "Not now there are refuges all the way on the Southern route. Beside, I don't know how I'd do on the crag descent these days. I'm out of practice... and I'm not as young as I was."

"You still look young to me," said Sharess.

"Well," said Jerya, "I hadn't thought of going back that way. Though it could save time overall..." For a moment she seemed to consider it, then gave herself a little shake, like a wet dog. "No, it'd be foolishness. We've got six weeks. If Sumyra and Embrel would like to see Delven, it's a couple of weeks out of that."

"I know someone else who'd like to see Delven," said Sumyra.

"Who's that?" asked Jerya.

"Sokkie. She's only seen her grandparents once, when they came to Carwerid, and she was still quite young, doesn't remember them very well."

Jerya grunted. "I wonder what Annyt would think of that? I get the feeling she couldn't wait to get out of Delven last time... but we'll talk about that later. Except... if we were going to Delven, are there any messages you'd like us to take?"

Sharess shook her head. "I write to Marit often enough... well, I dictate, now. Evisyn's seen to it the mail is regular now, and Visitations every couple of years."

Then they had to explain to Sumyra what Visitations meant. One part of the process was the Choosing of young girls as Postulants. Jerya became thoughtfully quiet at this point, and Sumyra guessed she was thinking, as she herself had so recently, how different things might have been if she'd been Chosen at the customary age. After a moment Jerya stirred herself. "Has anyone been Chosen from Delven since my time?"

"Sadly, no," said Sharess. "You know how it is, most of the girls can't even read well enough."

"Still?"

"It's changing slowly. Marit does what she can, and Meladne.... but you remember how it was; even getting most of the women to stand and talk when you approach them is hard enough."

"I was just the same," said Jerya, laughing a little. "Never knew any different."

"Until you did."

"Aye, and then I wished I'd known you long afore... but you mentioned Meladne? I remember her."

"Aye, she'd be a year or two younger than you. Apparently she got friendly with... what was her name, the one who was betrothed to Rodal?"

"Annyt. They're married now."

"Of course they are, and they have three children. My memory's a little slow sometimes, but it still works. Anyway, Meladne came to the city, stayed a few years—lodged with Annyt and Rodal, I believe. I think she was there when their first was born, the girl... now what's her name?"

"Sokkie."

"Sokisel," said Sharess at the same moment, obviously recalling the girl's little-used full name.

"Maybe that's why she wants to visit Delven now," said Sumyra.

"Maybe," said Jerya, "But don't you go saying anything to her about it. I don't know if Annyt would let her go. Draff, I don't know if I'd want the responsibility. You and Embrel are enough of a handful as it is."

Before Sumyra could protest this outrageous slander, there was a knock on the door. A young Singer entered. Or not so very young, Sumyra reconsidered as she got a better look; the Singer might easily be ten years older than herself.

The newcomer stopped as she took in the fact of visitors. Her gaze locked on to Jerya's face. Jerya smiled. "Hello, Elifian."

"You know each other?" said Sharess in surprise.

"We met when I was here before," said Jerya.

"Jerya saved me from myself," said Elifian.

"Saved you from something, maybe," said Jerya. "Or... all I'd say is I helped you reflect on what your choices really meant."

"Anyway, I'm grateful. Though of course I'll never know what my life would have been like if..."

"That's always the way. We make choices, we live with them. There's not much to be gained in second-guessing yourself."

"Do you still feel that way?" asked Sharess. "When it's someone else's choice you've had to live with?"

Jerya leaned across to press the older woman's hand. Sumyra got a sharp glimpse of their profiles, and a sudden jolt made her miss Jerya's initial response. She barely managed to catch on when Jerya addressed her directly. "Have you ever heard me complain?"

She smiled. "I've heard you complain about many things, aunt."

"But not about being Chosen...?"

"No, never that."

Belatedly they completed the introductions and Sumyra learned that Elifian was 'on rotation', spending some time at the College before resuming her primary role as a Peripatetic. This was an innovation of Master Analind, strongly supported by Master Prime Evisyn, intended to keep Peripatetics, the vital link between the centre and Singers at a distance, in touch with developments at the heart of the Guild.

Jerya smiled. "I'm sure it's entirely secondary that you get some time to enjoy comfortable beds and good food and wine after months enduring the rigours of life on the road."

Elifian grinned back, clearly understanding that Jerya had been teasing her. They seemed strangely familiar considering they had not met for ten years.

"I won't say I don't enjoy the break," said Elifian, "But I like the 'rigours' too. Most of the time, anyway. Nearly all, really."

Jerya nodded, and Sumyra thought of how many new experiences she herself had tasted since they left Drumlenn... was it really still only ten days ago?

Talk flowed comfortably for another hour, until Jerya declared it was time for them to report back to the gatehouse. The warmth of the embrace between her and Sharess set Sumyra's mind in motion again.

She waited until they were out of the building, walking down a broad path flanked on the north side by pleached limes, before broaching. "May I ask you a question, aunt?"

"You can ask me anything. And mostly you'll get an answer."

"About Sharess..."

Jerya gave her a sharp look. "What about her?"

"Well..." *If I'm wrong about this*, she thought, *this could be very awkward*. "She looks a lot like you."

"I couldn't deny that even if I wanted to." That wasn't the rebuff she'd feared, but it seemed Jerya wasn't about to help her along either.

"I mean... it almost looks to me as if you must be related somehow."

"Almost?"

"But you said no one in Delven looked like you."

"Well, that's very nearly true, but there was one, only I'd never seen her up close... until the day I was Chosen."

Sumyra knew she was gaping. There was only one solution to this conundrum... but it couldn't be right. Could it?

Jerya smiled. "Follow the trail."

"Sharess is your mother?"

"Before I say yea or nay, Sumyra, you need to know; there are probably even fewer people who know this than know about Embrel's parentage. Sharess herself, and Delven's headman. His mother, if she's still alive. Hedric, of course, and your Mamma, but I don't think she's ever told your father. Rodal knows, but I doubt he's told Annyt. In the College here, only Yanil and possibly Jossena."

"Not the Master Prime?"

"Not as far as I know."

"It would be a scandal, wouldn't it? A Dawnsinger having a child?"

"If it ever became known, yes. And the moons know I'm all for the truth, but who would it benefit to spread this?"

"I won't say a word, I promise."

※

They had passed numerous Dawnsingers, from young girls who must be Novices, or even Postulants, to women probably older than Sharess. Some barely glanced at them; others, especially the younger ones, looked at them curiously; several greeted Jerya by name. For her part, Jerya gave a courteous nod to everyone who met her gaze.

No one they'd seen provoked any notable reaction, until a tall Singer emerged under the archway that linked the second and third courts. With her hand on Jerya's arm, she felt her aunt stiffen. Her stride faltered.

They halted, facing each other a couple of paces apart.

"Master Perriad," said Jerya quietly, and Sumyra got a glimmer of understanding.

"Not Master now, or so they say."

"I understood that it was a courtesy to any former Master."

"Courtesy, is it? Then how should I address you? Novice Jerya?"

"I wouldn't ask that. I think I forfeited the right to be called Novice, or Singer, or anything of the sort."

"Then how are we to address you?"

Jerya sighed. It was so soft Sumyra wondered if Perriad even heard it. "In the Five Principalities I'm called Countess."

"Aye, I'd heard. Of course no one here had ever heard of Countesses and whatnot, but we got the tale from those who'd Crossed." She narrowed her eyes, which had never yet left Jerya's face. "Countess Jerya. Really, is there no end to your self-aggrandisement?"

Jerya's sigh this time was distinctly more audible. "I never expected we'd be best friends, Master Perriad, but I had hoped we could be civil." She waited a moment, but Perriad made no reply. "And I don't know if you've space for facts, but I might as well offer them anyway. It's true that I married a man who was heir to a title, but I didn't know that when I first met him. And when I did find out I couldn't decide if it would be a gift or a burden. " She chuckled ruefully. "Sometimes I still wonder."

Perriad's eyes narrowed again. "Tell me this, *Countess*... how many slaves do you own?"

"Under the laws of Denvirran Principality, as a married woman, I don't own a single thing. Not the clothes I wear, or the chair I sit upon. Everything is by grace of my husband." Her tone aimed for neutrality, but if you knew her well enough, you could hear the rancour underneath. It was true, of course, in strictly legal terms, though if you had a husband like Hedric, or like her own father, you could reasonably call your possessions your own. But it was still by their grace, by proxy, not by right.

Perriad seemed unimpressed. You might even say she was strenuously radiating unimpressed-ness. Though she'd never seen the woman until five minutes ago, Sumyra found her reaction strangely predictable. "Skew the words as much as you want, you cannot deny you benefit."

"Master Perriad," said Jerya, a tightness in her voice betraying her effort to remain 'civil'. "I have never sought to deny it. And I know what slavery is. I should think I know a good deal better than you. At my side most of the time at home is a woman who had to learn to speak all over again after her tongue was cut for speaking out of turn. Yes, we bought her, because it was the only thing we could do to help her. What would you have done?"

Perriad simply ignored the challenge, hit back with one of her own. "You admit that it's monstrous."

"I've said so many times."

"And yet you maintain we—the Guild—should have commerce with the home of such monstrousness."

"With caution, yes. But I don't make those decisions."

Perriad snorted derisively.

"If that's how you respond, Master Perriad, you and I are wasting our time here."

"What's your purpose here this time?" demanded Perriad.

"Are you going to believe me if I tell you?"

"Are you refusing to answer?"

"I'm hardly obliged to answer you, and it never seems to matter what I say... but since you ask, I'm here to see some old friends, and to show my niece, and my nephew, something of where I came from. Nothing more than that. And now, Master Perriad, if you'll excuse us, we're running a little late."

Neither Jerya nor Sumyra said anything until they were crossing the second court. Sumyra broke the silence with, "So that's the famous Perriad."

"Famous, infamous, notorious... So what did you make of her?"

"It was strange; she never looked at me. I was beginning to wonder if I'd become invisible."

"That woman's had an unhealthy obsession with me for a very long time. It seems she took it badly when I broke my Vow, when Railu and I took ourselves off, as if we'd done it all purely as a personal affront to her. Gnawed on it for ten years till I came back. Thought she'd finally got her revenge—and fulfilled her ambition—but it all fell apart for her when it turned out I had been telling the truth... though it seems she hasn't accepted that even now. That reversal pushed her right over the edge; last time I saw her she was in a pretty poor way. Half-starved and ranting. I almost—I did feel sorry for her, at least a little.

"Now... well, you saw, she seems lucid again, but, I don't know, she still seems to have a somewhat disjointed relationship with the truth."

※

"Can't deny she's still a thorn in my side," said Master Prime Evisyn with a sigh. "A few too many people here still pay attention to her... At least, I don't think she has much influence among Singers Outwith. Trouble is, she can spend pretty well all her time bending the ear of anyone who'll listen. We present Masters have better things to do."

"Doesn't she have anything else to occupy her?"

Evisyn shrugged. "What would you suggest? Teaching? Jossena would have my guts for a skipping rope if I put Perriad in charge of impressionable Novices."

"You never thought of sending her Outwith?"

Evisyn laughed cursorily. "Nothing I'd like better... but how would that look? To anyone who even wonders if there's a grain of truth in her ramblings? *The Master Prime's scared of the truth, sending Perriad away to silence her.*"

"I suppose..."

"Well, what we have done is move Singers around rather more. If someone's done ten years in the field, especially in the more remote places where they may not see another Singer from one year's end to the next... then she's offered the chance to rotate back here, or to an Adjunct House... why are you smiling, Jerya?"

"Just... you reminded me of something we were saying a few hours ago, with Sharess. How many things would have been different if she hadn't Chosen me. I'm sure Master Perriad would wish she hadn't... But Sharess had been in Delven longer than ten years, hadn't she? Must have been twenty, at least. I was nineteen when she Chose me, after all."

That, Sumyra reflected, would have made no sense at all but for the morning's revelation about Sharess and Jerya's true relationship. Was Evisyn one of the 'barely a handful' who knew? Certainly the Master Prime nodded as if she understood. But all she said was, "If 'what ifs' were pastry, we'd all be drowning in pies."

Sumyra tried, but she couldn't help herself, bursting out in giggles. "I'm so sorry, Master Prime," she gasped when she could get the words out.

But Evisyn herself was chuckling now. "Don't fret yourself, Sumyra. It was hardly my finest display of elegant phrasing."

Jerya was also smiling, but her question was serious enough. "You don't think she's a major problem?"

The Master Prime spread her hands wide. "She's been a niggling annoyance for ten years. Like a fly buzzing at a high window. But you know as well as I do, Jerya, she's particularly unbalanced when you're mentioned. Seeing you again... If she's ever likely to become a serious nuisance, it's most likely now."

"I'm sorry. I could have been more discreet, I suppose."

"No, we can't all steal around like thieves just because Perriad might be set off. How could you see Sharess without walking through the College? I'm tempted to take you to lunch in Refec just to make the point: you're welcome here."

"Thank you, Master Prime, but I'm not sure that would go down well."

"I said 'I'm tempted', not 'let's go and do it'. But I'll walk you out to the lodge when you leave, friendly as can be. It'll get back to her and I'll not be sorry." She paused, redirected her gaze. "Now, Sumyra, I want to hear about you. You're missing your summer-school this year."

"Yes, Master Prime, but I reckon this is just as much of an education."

# Chapter 16

# Embrel

"So," said Rodal. "I reckon what you still want to know is about me an' Railu."

"To be honest, I'm not sure I exactly *want* to know..."

"But you *need* to?"

"If I don't, I'll always wonder."

"S'pose I ease into it, as you might say. You can always stop me if, you know, it's too much."

"Thanks. But I think I have to be brave about this."

"See how we go. Well, first time I met her, it was right here in this parlour, Jerya brought her, when they were still thinking about her—Railu—being sent to Delven. But she could barely even look at me. Although..." He chuckled softly. There was something oddly familiar about the sound. Do I laugh like that? "Happen that was at least half my fault. I didn't make a good first impression. Came in drunk. I'd been beat at wrestling, which I wasn't used to, I was right out o' sorts. An' o' course, reckon you'll know, she'd been up the hill for seven-eight years. Hardly seen a man all that time, certainly not spoke to one."

He sipped pensively. "I know I'm not wise, nor educated like you are. Still can't hardly figure how Jerya came out o' the same place I did and ended up knowing so much... Anyroad, wise or not, I can't help wondering. Keep girls right away from men for eight years an' then send 'em straight out into villages like Delven. Well, ain't my place to question the ways o' the Guild, but it'd explain a lot about how Railu was with me...

"Then when we were on the road to Delven, the four of us, she was still shy o' me for a long time. In the end when we were on the Scorched Plains Jerya more or less made her walk wi' me an' we finally got to talking a bit. I still don't think she were best pleased when I caught 'em up after she and Jerya left Delven, but in time she saw I had my uses. Me an' Jerya both, o'course. I know you come the South way, so you ain't seen the route we used, but mostly it was a lot like the country we knew, the high moors, the foothills. Bigger an' emptier, but kind of the same too. So we were sort of at home, knew what we were doing. Even simple things like walking on rough ground, how to place your feet, keep looking a few paces ahead. You get tired a lot quicker when you don't know. We hardly had to think about it, she had to learn.

"So I reckon she started to think I couldn't be all bad. An' then... I reckon we were both thinking the same thing sometimes. When we were cold or tired, missing a hot meal, nowhere to sleep but huddled under sheepskins in a hollow on the side of a mountain. It's 'cause o' Jerya we're here."

He took another sip. "Always did know her own mind, Jerya. Right from a little girl. You know, when we were small, we played together, girls and boys. An' Jerya... if she didn't like the game she'd just take herself off somewhere. When we got older... an' it seemed to happen earlier with the girls, being set to learn sewing or whatever... anyroad, it seemed natural to us that girls and boys did different things. So I didn't see so much of her, not close. But it was a small place, you knew what was going on. Because Jerya didn't have a mother, several different women had charge of her, an' she soon learned that if one didn't see her she would prob'ly assume one o' th'others had her."

He stopped abruptly. "An' why am I gabbing on about Jerya? It's Railu you want to hear about."

Embrel smiled, keen to be accommodating. "I'm interested in Jerya too."

"Aye, no doubt. Happen you know her a lot better'n I do, now, calling her aunt an' all that... But maybe it's also that I'm a bit shy about talking about what happened wi' me an' Railu... But that's not fair on you."

He lifted his coffee-cup, sipped. "A bit shy, did I say? More'n a bit, if I'm honest. I've never really talked about this; never knew till yesterday that I'd need to. Well, mayhap if I can get it straight in my head telling you, I can make a better job explaining to Annyt.

"Anyroad, like I say, it wasn't too strange for me an' Jerya, but Railu found it harder. Afore long we were carrying most o' her stuff. Packs got lighter as we went through the food, but still, it was hard for all of us. Coming down the crag by the waterfall towards the end... I mean, Railu did right well, 'cause it was far ayont anything she'd ever done. She was scared, besure, but she kept her head. Still, by the time we got down to the valley, we were all tired, and getting hungry. We were pretty much out o' food. We'd been able to see afore we started down the crags that there was forest below. We had to think that where there was forest there'd be game. 'Cause if there weren't, if we couldn't get food into us, we'd be in a bad way. Getting back across on empty bellies don't bear thinking about.

"An' o' course, soon as we did get down we were finding berries. But it was late, we were tired, we didn't have much but a few oatcakes an' late-season bilberries that night afore we bedded down.

"Next day... we walked a few hours, an' then suddenly... sun came out, it got warm, there were soft banks to sit on, loads o' bilberries. It was like everything had shifted. You know, none of us knew what we'd find beyond the mountains. Oh, Jerya talked like she was sure, but she couldn't have known, not really. But she looked me in the eye as if to say, 'See? What did I tell you?' I hardly knew whether to be mad wi' her or give her a cheer. Anyroad, she took herself off, said she was going to see what else she could see. So then it was just me an' Railu..."

He lifted his cup, but did not drink, only staring into it for some moments, as if he could see something in there; a reflection, a vision, a memory. He set it down again, not hard, but the solid sound still reverberated in the stillness of the parlour, the morning calm of the inn.

The clock ticked.

"So," said Rodal finally, still looking at his cup, "There we were; jus' Railu an' me. An'... I remember feeling how good it all felt. Sunshine, a beautiful spot, the whole feeling of... of ease. An' being there wi' her, wi' Railu, an' just feeling at last like we were friends. I dunno, I'm not such a great one wi' words, it's hard to describe how I was feeling—and I guess she was feeling something the same. It was almost like... you know when you've had a couple o' drinks; not really drunk, but you start feeling a bit of a glow? That day was like that."

"Intoxicating?" suggested Embrel.

"Aye, intoxicating. Even... what's the word? Euphoric? That sound right?"

"Sounds like what you're describing."

"Aye. A good feeling, but mayhap sometimes a dangerous one. 'Cause... well, I hope I don't need to spell out what happened next. It's what men an' women have been doing since the Age Before, an' no doubt the ages afore that." Then he did meet Embrel's gaze, if only for an instant. "An', sure, if we'd stopped an' thought about it, talked about it, it would all probably have been different."

*And I wouldn't be here now...* he thought. *Not anywhere... I just wouldn't be.*

Perhaps Rodal read this thought. Could you do that, when you were someone's natural father, their *biological* father? Or was it just the natural thing to think? Anyway, he gave a short nod. A brief smile flickered through the grey-and-ginger of his beard. "Well," he said, "It wasn't wise, besure. But still, then and there, in that moment, it felt good. It felt right."

He gave Embrel a steadier look. "I hope you can see that. Whatever else, that moment, where you began, it wasn't bad." *And don't ask me to go into any more detail...* his look also seemed to say. Embrel was happy with that. He didn't want anything to solidify the image that was already there, vague and misty, in his mind.

"What happened next?"

"Jerya came back."

"So she saw...?"

"She couldn't have mistook what'd just happened."

"And?"

"She ran off again. Din't see her till evening. An' then... we talked a bit, but not like we really settled anything. But we still had to... you know, we needed each other. Or that's how I saw it then." He took another quick gulp. "Far as we knew there was only the three of us. An'... see, the way I was thinking of it, however rich the land was—an' it did seem good, even there still in the foothills—it was going to be hard. Jerya'd been saying all we needed was to find some caves."

"Because you grew up in caves?" Jerya's stories about her childhood, living in caves, had enthralled him when he was small.

"Aye, we did, but Delven's not like someone just wandered in and found everything jus' right. People have lived there hundreds o' years, and they've made it so you can hardly tell what was natural cave and what's been carved out. There's shafts for ventilation, conduits for water, all sorts. We didn't have the tools to do any o' that work. We had one small axe, but that was for firewood, splitting dead wood. Not a felling axe.

"See, I'd been thinking all along, this idea o' living there all alone, just the two of 'em... how was it ever going to work? Can't blame Railu, she din't know anything about it. But Jerya... she should have known better. An' I could try an' tell her but... when did Jerya ever listen to me? Even now, does she listen to anybody?"

"A few people. Not many."

Rodal smiled. "I'd'a been disappointed if you'd said any different. Jerya's still Jerya, eh...? Well, way I reasoned it, we'd have shelter, we'd have fire, we'd have food. We'd get through the winter. But it wouldn't be easy, it wouldn't be comfortable. Let them see how it was, let them feel the cold... Then come spring maybe we'd all be coming back over the mountains together."

"Only it didn't work out like that."

"It didn't, lad, it certainly didn't." His eyes went unfocused, distant. "Very next day, it all changed; well, I told you the bones o' this part. Went off hunting, I said, but mostly I was aiming to get my mind clear. I don't know, now, if I did, but it din't signify... 'cause when I got back, they were gone. And the rest... well, I don't need to tell you, do I? They can tell you better'n I could. But I scouted it out, and I asked around—careful like, not to give myself away, but soon enough I knew that if they had to be taken as slaves they couldn't have landed much better. That's right, ain't it?"

"I think so. Of course, you might say I'm biased, it being my home, but genuinely I think so."

"An' proof o' the puddin', next time I saw 'em, eleven months later, they chose to stay, not to try crossing back West. O'course, I din't know anythin' about a baby, they never told me."

"If you had known...?"

"Draff, I don't know. I'd made a promise to Annyt, that was always in my head. What could I have done?" Again he levelled his gaze. "I'd'a wanted to do something more, I'm sure. But I don't know what..."

""It's all what-ifs and might-have-beens, though, isn't it? I've often heard Jerya say don't waste time on what-ifs." He grinned. "The Master Prime said something too: Sumyra told me. 'If 'what ifs' were pastry, we'd all be drowning in pies'."

Rodal looked at him. He chuckled, and again Embrel had that eerie sense of familiarity. The chuckle swelled into a full-grown laugh. "By the moons, lad, I needed that," he said presently, wiping his eyes. "The Master Prime said that? Really?"

"That's what Sumyra told me."

"Well, I guess she's right, and Jerya too. You can wish things had been different, but if you get too caught up in it it can drive you crazy. I might wish I'd known you sooner, o'course I do, but I didn't—an' that weren't my choice. An' now you're a man grown, I can hardly start thinking you'll call me Pa... what'd you say in the Five Principalities?"

"Dadda when I was smaller, then Papa, mostly Father now."

Rodal wrinkled his nose. "Jus' sounds odd, don't it? That's not what we are. I reckon best we can hope for is to be friends."

"That sounds good to me."

"Aye. Your father'll always be the man as raised you, not me." He held out his hand and Embrel took it. Rodal's grasp was strong, his hand warm and dry. "Now, if you don't mind, lad, I need to talk to my wife. Spelling it out for you's given me the sense o' how to tell her how it happened. 'Course, it dun't mean she'll take it as well as you did, but I have to try."

"I hope it does go well."

"Well if you'd ask Annyt to step in, I'll be grateful.. And maybe you can give Sokkie a hand, whate'er needs doing."

"I don't know how it all works."

"She'll see you right—and we'll talk again soon."

❈

"I've been thinking," said Rodal the next morning. "About things I didn't know, and what I might have done different if I had... but there's no use in that, is there? What could I have done anyway? They all thought Railu was a slave, and one thing I learned over there, slaves and frees can't marry. But it's pointless; I didn't know. I never had that choice in front o'me.

"But I did have choices. I told you how I spent most o' my time, workin' on the Levore. What I didn't tell you... I loved that life. And it turned out I was pretty handy at it. Skipper even talked about taking me into partnership one day." His eyes were looking beyond the walls of the bar-room. "And there was a girl." He chuckled, mirth masking something deeper. "I can't say, now, if I truly loved her, but she were a good sort, and I could imagine setting her up in a little house in Sessapont or somewhere and coming home to her...

"But that's what I'm trying to tell you. That's a life I might have had, if I'd chosen different, or just if something happened a different way. But I can't ever know for sure how it would have been. In the end you only get one life, and the others are… I don't have the words to say it properly. Jerya could, mebbe… but it seems to me you can imagine this other life and that other life, but they're not real. They're no more real than dreams are."

"I think that says it very well."

"Ah, well, mebbe. But the point is, lad, there's nothing to gain by dwelling on them. You can't live on dreams. You get one life, like I said, and the thing is to make the best job of it you can. We can dream about a life where Railu and I raised you, but it's only a dream. I'm not the man who put a roof over your head and food in your belly. I'm not the man who sat you on his knee when you were little, told you stories. Maybe he taught you to read; maybe he taught you to ride? Anyroad, he taught you all those things, he made your life what it is. Not me. And you're the man you are because…. you have all that in you."

## Chapter 17

# Sumyra

"Somefin' funny 'bout them two," had been Sokkie's observation. She probably hadn't intended anything more than a casual remark, but Sumyra was curious enough to grab a tray and wander round picking up empty glasses. Under this cover she stole a few glances at the two women Sokkie had indicated.

She deposited the tray beside the sink, promising to help as soon as she could, but first she had to find Jerya.

Her aunt was in the kitchen helping Annyt chop vegetables. "Sorry to interrupt," said Sumyra, "But I think we might have a couple of incognito Dawnsingers out front."

The knife in Jerya's hands was suddenly still. "How sure are you?"

"I've seen Dawnsingers in wigs before. I remember you saying a few years ago how hair colour needs to marry up with skin colour."

"And someone's doesn't?"

"Skin as dark as Rhenya but hair like Rodal."

"Well," said Jerya, "There can be other reasons why a woman would wear a wig. But I'd like to take a look..." She cast an enquiring look at Annyt, who rolled her eyes in a long-suffering way. The willingness of all three visitors to pitch in and help whenever they could had done a lot to reconcile her to their presence—and especially to Embrel—but there were still limits to her tolerance.

"I'm supposed to be helping Sokkie..." said Sumyra, anticipating what both older women were likely thinking.

Annyt rolled her eyes again. "Can you at least finish those last two carrots?"

Jerya shrugged. "Don't suppose it's that urgent."

Sumyra was fulfilling her promise to Sokkie before Jerya emerged. There could be no mistaking the way the two women sat up, the way that after a moment they tried to make it look as if they weren't really interested. She almost laughed. If they were trying to be 'discreet' in their observation they were doing a very poor job of it.

Jerya joined her. "I'll help you finish these and then why don't we go and have a friendly word?"

"We?"

"Why not? You may find it interesting."

Two pairs of hands made quick work of the pots and it couldn't have been more than five minutes later as she followed Jerya to the women's table.

"Mind if we join you?" Jerya didn't wait for an answer, dropping into a chair with a cheery complaint about having 'been on my feet for hours'; a slight exaggeration, but not excessive. Sumyra snagged a spare stool from the next table and settled beside her aunt.

"Did Perriad send you?" was Jerya's next question.

"No!" said one, but simultaneously the other was saying, "Who? I don't—" before she caught up. They looked at each other in confusion.

"Relax," said Jerya. "Whatever Master Perriad's told you, I don't bite. In fact... I'd be really interested to know what she has said about me."

Again the women looked at each other. It was obvious they were trying to agree, purely by looks, whether to continue denying they had any connection with Perriad or whether to accept that they had been rumbled. Sumyra thought only a fool would persist in denial, so their next decision would have to be how to react to Jerya's question.

Both were young. The one in the too-obvious wig might have been no more than Embrel's age, the other a few years older. Pale and green-eyed, with a scattering of freckles, this one looked perfectly convincing in auburn tresses. Sharp features and an alert look put Sumyra in mind of a fox. After a few more moments, she drew a slightly shaky breath and said, "I'm sure you know the charges against you."

"If I knew exactly what she's told you, I wouldn't need to ask, would I?" Jerya levelled her gaze on the freckled woman. "Look, I'm a Vow-breaker. I've never denied that, and everyone knows it. But… if it wasn't before you were born, it certainly was when you were far too young to know or care."

"A transgression like that never goes away."

"That's true. I live with it every day. But it doesn't seem like a good enough reason for you to come here, incog, just to get a look at me."

"And you brought men from the East to the Sung Lands."

Jerya sighed. "*That's* your best shot? There's no charge easier to refute than that. But I guess I'm a tainted witness… Why don't you try, Sumyra?"

Sumyra leaned forward. She knew, from school debates, the tone and the look she wanted; gently challenging, but never aggressive. "If Jerya 'brought' the Selton expedition here… why did they spend weeks trying blind alleys before they found the Southern route? When Jerya already knew the Northern route?"

The two Singers looked at each other but said nothing. "Besides," continued Sumyra, "Selton describes it all in his book. The first meeting." She recalled that bleak strath; an unpromising place for a momentous encounter. "How he was surprised—astonished—to be addressed by name… because as far as he knew no one had ever made the Crossing before."

"And no one had," said Jerya. "Not by that route."

"Anyone can write anything in a book," said the fox-faced one.

"But there were eyewitnesses." She turned to Jerya. "Master Evisyn was there, wasn't she? Master Analind too."

"We can hardly go demanding answers from the Master Prime. And Master Analind is conveniently absent for the summer."

"They weren't the only ones," said Jerya. "Do you know a Singer called Elifian?"

Again that shared look, that silent communication. Sumyra found herself wondering if they were lovers. And then she wondered if, since Corysse, she was simply reading too much into innocent glances, into every instance of female closeness.

The result, it seemed, was a new line of attack. The darker woman leaned forward, her gaze accusing. "You keep slaves."

When Jerya didn't answer at once, Sumyra spoke up again. "Have you been to the Five Principalities?"

"No!" As if she'd offered a serious insult.

"It's a fair question. Dozens of Dawnsingers have. But what I'm really asking is, if you haven't visited, can you really understand how things work? I've heard plenty about the Sung Lands, but even after just a few days, I understand better now I'm actually here."

"I don't need to see it to know that slavery is evil."

"And many people in the Five Principalities would agree with you. Including me… and including Jerya." She glanced sideways, but Jerya only smiled, as if to say, carry on, you're doing fine. "Slavery is terrible, but what would happen if the people who feel that way gave up their enslaved? D'you imagine all those people would suddenly become free?" She was repeating something Railu had once said to her, she realised, when she was fourteen or fifteen. "The law doesn't allow it. There are strict limits on how many enslaved an owner can free in any one year. The only way an owner can divest himself of more enslaved is to sell them."

She studied the two faces, wondering if she was making any impression. "Yes, there are thousands of enslaved on the Skilthorn estates. And before Hed—before Jerya's husband inherited, they belonged to the old Earl, his uncle. He didn't care much for their welfare. I know one woman in particular who grew up as a slave under him." She thought of Dortis, how different her life was now, and felt new confidence in her argument.

"When he died, Jerya and her husband could have repudiated the title. The enslaved of Skilthorn wouldn't have been set free; they'd just have got another master." Hedric's cousin Ferrowby, whose name occasionally cropped up in the newspapers, and never for a worthy reason. "They'd have been no better off than under the previous Earl. Instead, Hedric and Jerya have rebuilt and extended the living accommodation, improved working conditions, given the enslaved more free time."

"Sumyra's right," said Jerya. "We've done what we can to improve life for the enslaved we're responsible for. Is it enough? That's a question we ask ourselves regularly—and we ask the enslaved too." She shrugged. "Come to Skilthorn and you can ask them yourselves." She watched as the two once again communed in wordless fashion, then she smiled. "You know, we've been sat here a while, and I still don't know your names."

"I'm Sesmy," said the darker one. Fox-face looked briefly startled, as if she thought giving their names a rash move, then shrugged slightly and said, "Chamion."

"Pleased to meet you," said Jerya, sounding as if she meant it. Her chair creaked again as she shifted forward. "Thing is, if you're going to talk about slavery, it's like anything else, you need to be sure you know your ground. Sumyra and I, we live with it every day. And I know it from the other side too…

"Did Master Perriad ever tell you *this*? Railu and I, for a time, we *were* enslaved. We were bald; that was all the reason they needed to take us for runaway slaves. They put metal collars on us, they dragged us for hours behind horses. It's a wonder I ever wanted to look at a horse again. After that… well, you don't need all the sordid details. It wasn't pretty, I'll just say that. But none of it scars your soul quite like being paraded on a platform to be *sold*." She took a hasty gulp from her tankard, brushed the back of her hand over her top lip. "You know, we were lucky, Railu and I. Lucky that we were kept together, that we were bought by decent people. But still, they were owners, and though they never abused it, they could, in law, do pretty much whatever they liked with us. So you don't need to tell me slavery is evil. Monstrous, as Master Perriad said to me yesterday."

Railu had long avoided revisiting that dark time, but had finally opened up a couple of years ago; and once she started she'd evidently found it hard to stop. Sumyra had heard more of the tale than she'd bargained for; but she had encouraged her to continue. *I think I need to know*, Mamma, she'd said; but she'd thought, *And I think you need to tell it.*

None of it was news to Sumyra now, but Jerya's brief account had left Sesmy and Chamion looking shaken. Sumyra turned, caught Sokkie's eye, gestured for more drinks.

"I'm guessing Master Perriad didn't tell you all of that?" said Jerya. The women neither agreed nor denied it. "Yes, with Perriad, what you get is her side. Maybe that's true with most people, but some have a way of only seeing things from their particular perspective. Well, judge for yourselves."

She paused as Sokkie delivered new glasses and removed the empty ones. "On my account," Jerya told her, before turning back to the Dawnsingers. "Well, you probably know, I wasn't Chosen in the regular way, nothing like it. Don't need to go into why... but I was nineteen when I arrived in the College. And the first time I met Perriad—Senior Tutor Perriad, she was then—I thought she was going to send me right back again." Jerya chuckled. "I reckon there've been a few times since she's wished she'd done just that. But she didn't, she sent me round the other Tutors, and some of them thought they saw something in me.

"Now I've never known exactly what Perriad had in mind for me. She had some notion that because I'd lived Outwith for longer, somehow I'd have a better idea how the wider world worked." She shook her head. "But the only place I knew was Delven, which is about as remote as you can get. I'd bet any seasoned Peripatetic could have told her far more than I could."

Jerya sipped her ale. "I didn't expect to be here for long, just trained up enough to serve in Delven, then sent home. When Perriad decided she had a different plan, it meant someone else would have to be sent instead. And she wanted to send... someone who wasn't suited for that at all. Someone who'd be wasted there, and miserable."

"It's not for newly-Ordained Singers to decide where they serve," said Chamion severely.

"Perhaps not to decide, but is it reasonable to ignore their inclinations, their aptitudes? A village Singer, especially in a place like Delven... it can be a lonely life. And in this case a complete waste of talents that could have given much to the Guild if she'd stayed in Carwerid."

She was talking about Railu, Sumyra knew. She wondered if Chamion and Sesmy did too. Well, Railu had found rich scope for her talents in the Five Principalities. *And if she'd stayed here, she'd never have met Papa and she wouldn't be my Mamma now.* Some things really did work out for the best.

"Well," said Jerya, "Perriad was keen to have my experience of life Outwith... but my experience told me her plan was wrong. And when I found out the truth about the Dawnsong, that seemed wrong to me too."

"I suppose that's when you started to hate the Guild," said Chamion. Sesmy frowned; Sumyra wondered if she was starting to waver.

"Hate the Guild? Nothing of the sort Oh, I know: *she's a Vow-breaker, why should we believe a word she says*? Well, the fact is, I learned a lot in the months I was here, and I'll always be grateful for that; and there are people here I now count as lifelong friends. I never hated the Guild, I only knew I couldn't be part of it." She watched their faces, perhaps waiting to see if they would respond. "When we left, I thought I'd never return, but when I heard about the Selton expedition, I came back. It was a risk, it turned my life upside down, but I thought the Guild's leaders should know about it, be prepared, decide what they wanted to do.

"And your precious Master Perriad tried everything she could to obstruct me and my message. To discredit the physical evidence I'd brought. Draff, even when the actual expedition turned up, she was trying to make out I'd fabricated that too. You look doubtful, but there were plenty of witnesses to that, including your current Master Prime.

"Well, Perriad managed to get me locked up at one point—twice, if you count being shut in a tent." Jerya laughed softly. "Not a very effective means of incarceration. She even physically attacked me... that happened twice, too, come to think of it."

She lifted her tankard, drank briefly. "Way it looks to me, when I left—yes, when I broke my Vow—she didn't just see it as an affront to the Guild. She took it personally. And by the next time I saw her, ten, eleven years later, she'd been gnawing on her grievance ever since. The way it looked to me, and to others in the Guild, it had turned into an obsession. She wasn't quite rational any longer, not when I came into the picture."

"How dare—" began Chamion, then stopped. Sumyra had seen a slight movement from Sesmy, imagined a restraining hand settling on a thigh, out of sight below table-top level.

"Locked up twice," said Jerya quietly. "Assaulted twice. And on the second occasion, when she clearly wasn't well, I took time to make sure she'd be cared for. That's how I dare."

Chamion glowered, but Sesmy leaned closer. "Were there witnesses to either of these assaults? Alleged assaults."

"To the first, several, including Master Prime Evisyn. As for the second, the only Dawnsinger present was Master Analind. She could tell you a good deal about Perriad's conduct around that time, when she gets back from the Five Principalities."

"But for now she's conveniently absent," said Chamion.

"If I'm looking for corroboration, it's not so convenient at all."

"What *is* your business here this time?" asked Sesmy.

"Personal. Family matters, essentially. I promised my nephew I'd take him travelling when he was old enough, and then my niece wanted to come too." She rested a hand on Sumyra's shoulder for a moment. "Old friends right here in this tavern... And I wanted to visit my mother." She didn't specify who or where her mother was, Sumyra observed, and of course she said nothing about Embrel's parentage.

"But you visited the Master Prime."

"Who is also an old friend. There are others I want to see before we leave, too."

"So you and the Master Prime never discussed anything relating to the future of the Guild or relations with the Five Principalities."

"I'd say I forfeited any right to pronounce on the future of the Guild twenty-one years ago. But if I can offer the Master Prime any insight into how things stand in the Five Principalities, is there any good reason why I shouldn't do that?"

※

"When we were with Sharess..." said Sumyra as she and Jerya prepared for bed.

"Is this about our secret?"

"No. At least I don't think so... No. You said something about seeing more of the Sung Lands. *Maybe even as far as Delven*, you said."

"I did."

"Are you still thinking of it?"

Jerya turned in her chair, hairbrush stilled in her hand. "Sumyra, this trip has always been... well, you know it began with the promise I'd made to Embrel. And now you too. It's for you, at least as much as it is for me."

"Well, I know I'd love it."

"Seeing more in general, or Delven in particular?"

"All—any—of it; anywhere new. But, yes, Delven sounds fascinating. The whole thing of living in caves... And it's where you came from, of course. But would you want to go back?"

"Why not? There are people there I wouldn't mind seeing. And the place itself... but what d'you think Embrel would say to it?"

"I'm not sure. When we started out, he was full of talk about wanting to see as much as possible. But now he's got a father, a half-sister, brothers..."

"He also has grandparents in Delven."

"He does, doesn't he?"

"And perhaps it wouldn't hurt to put some distance between us and Perriad..."

## Chapter 18

# Sumyra

About half an hour beyond the bridges, where houses were mostly scattered here and there among market gardens and orchards, they heard hoofbeats coming up fast behind them. Jerya and Embrel moved to the left to allow the faster rider to pass, but she reined in as she came level with them. A Dawnsinger, Sumyra saw. After a moment she realised that she'd seen the freckled face before, but then it had been framed by an auburn wig.

"Singer Sesmy," said Jerya, with a subtle note of enquiry.

Sesmy took a moment to calm her breathing. Sumyra wondered how much practice she'd had in riding that fast. "I thought you should know… Master Perriad and Chamion and some others are planning to waylay you on the road."

"Waylay us and do what?"

"I don't know exactly. They saw I wasn't sure, and they clammed up. Didn't say another word till I left the room."

"Do you know where?"

"The heathlands beyond Aynsome. 'It's a lonely road,' Taini said. She used to be a Peripatetic, so I guess she knows it. 'Course, they might have changed their plans, seeing I'd heard that part."

"That's a chance we'll have to take," said Jerya, although she glanced at Sokkie and Sumyra knew she was having second thoughts about taking the youngster on a trip that was suddenly looking a sight more hazardous. "If they're looking for 'lonely', there's nowhere else until they get right past

Stainscomb and into the Scorched Plains." She laughed suddenly. "And if that's their plan now, maybe they won't think it so cunning after they've been waiting there a few nights."

"You're thinking we'll take a different route?" asked Embrel.

"Exactly," said Jerya, examining the map which she'd extricated from her battered leather satchel. "And it seems to me the best way to do that would be to take a detour along the coast after Hunsley. Here, take a look."

Embrel and Sumyra brought their horses close on either side of her, but Sokkie was not so used to precise manoeuvring. When Embrel had taken a look, Sumyra backed her mount so she could show Sokkie the map. "It's a longer way," said Jerya, "Which is why I didn't pick it in the first place, though I was tempted, having done the high road three times before. If Kerrsands Bay is as beautiful as I've heard, maybe we'll end up thinking Master Perriad's done us a favour."

She retrieved the map and stowed it away carefully, then turned to Sesmy. "And we most certainly owe you our gratitude. But I have to ask... it seems you've changed your mind about Master Perriad."

Sesmy looked down, biting her lip. "I still think some of the things she says make sense. How treating with the Five Principalities could be dangerous."

"Only a fool would think otherwise," said Jerya. "If Perriad could actually listen to me for once in her life... and recognise that I know a great deal more about the Five Principalities than she ever will... we might be able to have a reasonable conversation about it."

Sesmy nodded. "I see that. And some of the things you said, that night in the tavern, seemed to make sense. But Chamion wasn't having any of it. So I... I'm a Healer, you see, and the other day I asked Master Berrivan what she thought of Master Perriad."

Jerya laughed. "I'd like to have been a fly on the wall for that one."

"You know Master Berrivan?"

"I helped out in the Infirmary a few times. I wouldn't say I knew her well, but my friend Railu certainly did."

"Yes, that was one of the first things she said. 'Perriad lost me one of the best Healers I ever saw.' And something about it not being much consolation that Railu's a doctor in the Five Principalities now... Is that right?"

"It certainly is," said Jerya. Sumyra felt a thrill of pride. That's my Mamma...

"And Master Berrivan also said... well, it was much like what you said. That she had... 'a bee in her bonnet', she said, about you, and then she laughed and said, 'A bee! More like a hive full of them!'"

Jerya laughed too. "That sounds like Berrivan."

"Then she said that Master Perriad seems to lose the power of thinking rationally when there's any mention of you. And that's what you said too." The young Singer shrugged uncomfortably, shoulders constricted. "I don't know you, never seen you before that night, and most of what I'd heard was from Master Perriad and others who follow her. But you weren't quite what I'd expected, and Master Berrivan told a different story, and then I went and asked a couple of others. People I knew had known you. Like Tutor Brinbeth..."

"Ah..." said Jerya, as if not expecting good news.

"Well," said Sesmy, "She said you'd been unruly. Asked questions out of turn, that sort of thing. But she said, 'For all the vexation she caused me, I can't say I share Master Perriad's view. It may be Jerya's done more good for the Guild outwith it than she ever would have if she'd stayed in.'"

Jerya looked surprised, even moved. She sat her horse in silence for a few moments, then gathered herself. "Well, once again, Sesmy, you have my thanks."

"All our thanks," added Sumyra, and Embrel quickly echoed her.

Jerya smiled. "I'm sure it wasn't easy. I applaud your courage. And if you'll take one word of advice from me... Take it easier going back. Let the horse settle to his own pace. He could probably do with a drink, too, soon as you see somewhere."

"We crossed a brook about a half-mile back," said Sokkie unexpectedly.

"We did, didn't we?" said Jerya. "There you are, then. Let him walk back to the brook, give him a good drink and a rest, then take the rest of the journey as it comes."

"I will," said Sesmy.

"And I hope to see you again before too long."

❄

They all watched Sesmy ride slowly away until she disappeared over a brow. *That'll be the slope down to the brook*, thought Sumyra.

"Now," said Jerya, "We need to think. And we may as well give the horses a rest."

They dismounted and led the beasts to a patch of lush grass under ash trees. A fallen tree made a handy seat.

"I don't know what Master Perriad's latest scheme is, but would she really be planning to waylay us on the loneliest road between here and Stainscomb just to have a friendly chat?" Jerya snickered sardonically. "I don't see it myself. Sumyra... you've at least seen her."

"Yes. Only for a few minutes, but I got a feeling... a very strange woman." She glanced at Embrel, at Sokkie beyond him leaning forward to see. "She never even looked at me. And I could quite see why you said she has... what was the word? A *disjointed* relationship with the truth."

"And," said Jerya quietly, "She has attempted actual violence against me twice before. So I think we dare not take this news lightly."

"But you said we could go around," said Embrel.

"Aye, and if she's waiting where Sesmy heard them say, that works. But we have a return journey to make as well, and if she figures out what we've done she might decide to try another spot. In the Scorched Plains, maybe. There's no such obvious way to avoid that road. Pretty tangled country north and south."

"What are you thinking?" asked Sumyra.

"Well, we could change our plans entirely. Go to Kerrsands Bay and on round the coast a bit. But we set our minds on Delven. I know I'd like to see the place again. You know, it might be the last time.... And it sticks in my craw to be put off by someone like Perriad. But..."

Sighing, she looked at them: Sumyra on her left, Embrel and Sokkie to her right. "I'm responsible. I'm responsible because I'm the one who gets Perriad all riled up. But also I'm responsible because I'm the aunt here—and for simplicity I'm calling myself your aunt too, Sokkie, if you don't mind." The girl murmured something Sumyra could not make out, but Jerya evidently took it as assent. "Thank you. I'm supposedly the seasoned traveller—"

"—Supposedly?" said Embrel. "Who made the First Crossing? And the Second?"

"I was much younger and more foolish when we made the First Crossing. The Second was Rodal—on his own." She glanced at Sokkie. "Hedric and Lallon and I made the Third... but anyway, that's different. This is about knowing there's someone out there, somewhere on the road, who almost certainly wants to do us harm."

"Surely she has no reason to wish harm to any of the rest of us?" said Sumyra. "I don't suppose she even knows who we are."

"If she were rational, I'm sure you'd be right. But if she were truly rational, we wouldn't be having this discussion in the first place. Sumyra, Embrel, you're old enough to decide for yourselves, but Sokkie... if anything happened to you, your mother would kill me."

Sokkie sprang to her feet and faced Jerya, hands on hips, face hot with indignation. "I'm not a child."

"I didn't say you were."

"Then what did you mean? You said Sumyra an' Embrel are old enough. That's as good as sayin' I'm not."

"You're thirteen."

"I'm very nearly fourteen. You know that; we said I might be havin' my birthday in Delven. I'm old enough to tend bar. Old enough to mind my brothers, to walk 'em to school. Ma an' Pa can't think I'm still a child."

Jerya smiled. "I like your spirit, I really do. But—"

"—I'm not scared o' bullies. More'n'once some scruff's tried to grab one o'th'lads lunch-sacks. I saw 'em off right and proper."

"May I say something?" asked Embrel quietly.

"Please," said Jerya.

He fixed his gaze on the girl. "Sokkie, I understand what Jerya's saying. I only just found out I have a sister."

"Half-sister."

"Let's not quibble. Sister, half-sister, I only just found out. But already I know I'd hate for anything to happen to you."

"Don't s'pose I'd want anythin' to happen to you either. But you're not talkin' 'bout goin' back, are you?"

"Thank you. Can't say I want anything to happen to me either. But I've only said half of what I wanted." Sokkie lowered her gaze and Embrel turned to Jerya. "Aunt, you say this Perriad and whoever she has with her may mean to do us harm. My question is... how?"

"What do you mean?"

"Well, to start, do they have weapons?"

Jerya blinked several times. "I never thought about that."

"Do Dawnsingers usually carry weapons?"

"Not that I ever heard of. I think... they sent Rodal as my escort when I was first Chosen, but there was probably no need. I've never heard of Dawnsingers being attacked or anything... But what are you thinking, Embrel?"

"My friend Trevmy—he's been to Duncal but you wouldn't have met him—his father's Supervisor of Constabulary in Kenskell. Trev's thinking about joining when he finishes college, maybe... anyway, he knows something about all this. His father showed him some tricks for looking after himself and he showed us.

"Well, what he said was, really hurting someone without a weapon isn't easy. Unless you're a lot stronger, or you have some skill, and most people don't."

"Or the element of surprise," said Jerya. "Perriad did catch me on the hop once. Slapped me hard enough to make my head ring."

"I doubt she'd be stronger than you," said Sumyra, recalling the woman she'd seen: tall, but bony, angular. In fact, thinking about it, there'd been something fragile about Perriad.

Embrel nodded. "Aye, surprise. Still, if you really wanted to hurt someone, you wouldn't just rely on your fists. Trev's father said a lot of murders are done with whatever was to hand. You know, kitchen knives, a kindling-axe… But would this Perriad and her companions think of it? It's one thing to lay hands on a knife in a city, not so easy in the middle of nowhere."

Jerya considered. "That would imply some level of forethought. Would she actually think of it? She only used her hands before."

"Well, in any case, someone with an axe or a knife is dangerous, but only if you let them get close to you. And even then, most people have no skill, no experience."

"I doubt Perriad's ever hefted an axe in her life. Likely she's never used a knife beyond a table-knife either, or not since…" Jerya laughed suddenly. "I never thought of Perriad being a girl before. You know every Dawnsinger had a life before she was Chosen, but mostly they don't talk about it, not much. And someone like her… of course, when I first met her, she must have been at least the age I am now. Just seemed like she'd always been a Singer."

"So she must be over sixty now?" said Sumyra.

"I should think so. Yes, surely. Of course her companions might be younger… Draff, we should have asked Sesmy who they were!"

"She did say, '*Master Perriad and Chamion and one or two others*'," said Sumyra. "And we've seen Chamion. She's young… but she's smaller than me."

"But after that we don't even know if we might be facing three or four of them. Well, we can ask along the road." Jerya turned back to Embrel. "Was there more?"

"Aye, a couple of things. Like I said, Trev showed us a few things. Like what you can do if someone comes at you with a knife. It's actually not that hard to disarm them, especially if they don't know what they're doing. I can show you."

"I already know," said Sokkie, startling everyone. She put her hands on her hips again. "Told you, I'm not some helpless kid. Look, you've seen. There's times when I'm in the taproom on my own; Ma in the kitchen, Pa swapping over casks or somethin'. An' it's not the kind o' place where you get a lot o' fights. They're mostly down by the waterfront, on the trade river; especially Over." She meant across the bridges, Sumyra knew, further from the heart of the city. "But every now an' then you get someone. So Pa said afore he'd ever leave me on my own I had to know what to do. An' we keep a kerry-knob behind the bar. Nine time out o' ten, he reckons, you jus' need to bang that down loud somewhere, on the bar or a table or the floor. An' he'll hear and come runnin'."

"If we did get into a fight," said Sumyra, "It sounds like you'd be more use than I would."

Embrel started to protest. Sumyra smiled inwardly; being good in a fight was hardly a ladylike virtue. But Jerya raised a hand. "My plan is not to get into any fight in the first place. We'll go by Kerrsands Bay, nothing to lose by that but a couple of days. And while we're on the common road we'll enquire wherever we stop. A group of Dawnsingers riding north... people are going to notice."

"Does that mean I'm still comin' with you?" asked Sokkie.

"For now," said Jerya. "And if we find out Perriad's got more than two or three cohorts, we might change our plans entirely. But, for now, if everyone's happy, we carry on."

## Chapter 19

# Embrel

Arvelyn, who greeted them at the gates of the Kerrsands Bay Adjunct House, was the sort of person some might call 'motherly'. Which was odd, when you considered it, because Dawnsingers weren't mothers. She ands Jerya were obviously old friends. Embrel let them talk, taken by his own thoughts. Of course, his mother wasn't his mother at all, that was the fact of it. It was hard to stomach but he couldn't keep denying it. But how, in the end, did nine months that she hadn't carried him weigh in the balance against twenty years when in his mind she *had* been his mother? And how was he going to feel when he saw her again?

And then... how was he going to feel when next he saw *Railu*?

It was strange, in all this, how little thought he'd given to his true mother. Yes, there'd been all the business of trying to get to know Rodal, and his half-siblings. A mouthful, but there it was. He still didn't feel he knew the boys, but he was starting to like Sokkie very much. There was something about her you'd almost call fierce... and that, he'd wager, came from her mother, not from the father they shared.

But Railu... Railu, like Jerya, had always been there, part of the landscape of his childhood. Both of them, and Rhenya, were family, in every sense except the dogmatically legal. And the strictly biological, in the word Jerya favoured—or so he'd thought. But Railu was his biological mother.

Funny, though, of the three of them, the first you'd label 'motherly' was surely Rhenya; the only one who had no child of her own. You'd probably attach the tag to Railu before Jerya. There was the way she'd settled into the role of Sumyra's Mamma; but she'd always had that warmth, that nurturing way about her. Jerya was many things, including, now, a devoted mother to her own child, but... she was a wonderful aunt, he knew that, but being an aunt was somehow quite different.

*Ah, it's all beyond me.* He made himself attend to the talk that had been flowing on around him.

"...welcome, and more than welcome," Singer Arvelyn was saying now. To Sokkie, he realised. What was this? "We hardly ever have the company of young people your age. We get girls passing through on their way from being Chosen, Postulants, but they're much younger, of course."

Arvelyn had to be flattering Sokkie. Girls were Chosen at ten or eleven, he knew; three years younger. at most. Still, flattery is often hard to resist and Sokkie didn't appear to be trying. She beamed at their hostess and said, "If you're happy to have me, Dawnsinger, I'd be honoured to be your guest." *A very graceful little speech*, he thought, impressed.

"I'm delighted," said Arvelyn, "And I'm certain my sisters will be too."

*Sisters?* he wondered. She couldn't mean real sisters, not even in the way Sokkie was his; it had to be what Dawnsingers called each other. But now Arvelyn was turning to him. "However, I'm afraid we can't offer you the same hospitality."

"Of course, I understand."

"But we can recommend a guest-house in the town. They've often put up Postulants when we're full. Mention my name and they'll give you a good rate on the room."

That was all fair and reasonable. What he hadn't quite grasped—though it was very welcome—was how Sumyra came to be walking down the street with him, boots rasping on grainy granite setts. He must have missed something when he was brooding on other matters.

When he raised the question Sumyra only laughed. "Jerya seemed to manage everything with a look or two. I guess she thought you'd be lonely on your own."

"Well, I'm glad." She took his arm and they carried on down the narrow corkscrew way.

※

Arvelyn's name did indeed seem to carry a kind of power. The proprietress of the guest-house, a small, brown, wiry woman named Rinian, smiled broadly and ushered them into a small parlour discreetly separated from the busier main room.

"*Two* rooms?" she said. She looked at them in turn. "Are you sure about that?" And then she actually winked. She was facing Embrel but he was pretty sure Sumyra would see it too.

"Thank you, yes, if that's possible."

"Well, I'll tell you what I can do. There are two rooms on the top floor with a sitting-room between them. We lock the connecting doors when the rooms are let separately, but it makes a kind of suite. And the view over the bay... I sometimes go up and sit there myself just to enjoy it, on the rare occasions I get two quiet moments to myself. You can order dinner now, if you like, and we'll bring it up later. And I'll just charge for two singles."

She was right about the view. The Bay was a vast expanse, the far shore at least ten miles distant, and stretching even further from left to right. Glittering channels laced the tracts of what must be sand and mud; darker patches might be banks of shingle. Beyond, high hills mounted into a long roughhewn skyline, all purple shadow now as the evening advanced.

"I guess the tide is low," said Sumyra, settling into the second chair before the window. He was suddenly very aware of her presence, as if Rinian's winking insinuation had fired up something in him.

He fumbled for a response. "I don't know much about tides."

"Well, we live a long way inland, don't we? But it's all about the pull of the moons, isn't it?"

"I think so."

"Must have been simpler when there was only one moon. I wonder what that was like... I suppose predicting the tides is another thing Dawnsingers hold to themselves here."

Any other time, he would have been interested in this. Now, he had to clear the air. Clear his own head. "Sumyra, that woman..."

"She was charming, wasn't she?"

"In a way, but... I suppose things are different here. At home the way she spoke would have seemed highly impertinent. Yet I think I might have reason to be grateful to her."

"Grateful?"

"Aye. All that smiling and winking and *are you sure you need two rooms*... it's almost the same way other people look at us. I mean, people at home. Papa, Mamma; your Mamma too, a little; and Rhenya. Rhenya's the worst; well, she's always been a matchmaker, putting people together. And people have been putting us together ever since we danced at your Papa and Mamma's wedding."

Sumyra smiled. "We did dance four straight dances together—or was it five?"

Embrel shrugged. "I think I lost count. Only stopped when I got too hungry to continue. D'you know, I hadn't really wanted to dance with you? Thought you were too young, I guess."

"While you were such a grown-up," she said, smiling, not at all affronted.

"Well, that's obvious now... but that's the whole thing about it, d'you see? We were kids. And once I got over my stupid stubbornness, I liked dancing with you. That's all there was to it; but people wanted to see more in it, and they've been reading more into our friendship ever since. Until it's hard to just be friends. And even harder to know if I really want us to be something more... or not."

Sumyra turned away from the window to look squarely at him. The late-afternoon light gave a ruddy glow to her sepia skin. He half-hoped she would say something, help him along, but she only appeared to be waiting for whatever came next. *So am I...* he thought with grim amusement.

He drew breath. "It's hard to think straight, sometimes. And among the fellows in Hall, at a tavern... well, there's a lot of talk, you know. I don't know... I mean, I'm sure girls talk too, but I don't know if they brag and boast like boys do."

"You might be surprised."

"Anyway, there's a lot of talk about girls—about young ladies, I mean, and... I don't mean that it's unsavoury, or not often, but it does all seem to be thinking about young ladies in a particular way. Who'll marry whom, or what you want in a wife." And that's only what I can mention... "Which is why being away with you and Jerya has been good, there's been none of that... but still it's taken me till now to see things straight."

She said nothing. "I just hope you're not going to hate me for saying this, Sumyra, because you are, you'll always be, very important to me. You mean more to me than any of those silly fellows... just not in that way. In fact... when I thought about..." he tried to swallow, his throat strangely dry. "Marrying you... I realised it would feel more like marrying a sister."

"Well," she said, "I almost am, aren't I?"

"What do you mean?"

"Your mother... your real mother... no, I shouldn't say that. What did Jerya say? Your biological mother is my Mamma."

"So what does that make us?"

"I'm your step-half-sister."

He laughed. Mostly it was relief that she didn't seem to be upset by his blundering declaration... but still... "Step-half-sister? Is that even real?"

"If I say it is, why not?"

"It's as real as calling Jerya 'aunt', I suppose."

"More so. Railu really is your mother, and she really is my Mamma."

"Well," he said, "It's as you like. But I hope you won't mind if I shorten it to just 'sister'."

She reached across, over the low table, and took his hand. For a while they just sat, looking out again as the sun declined and the skyline faded into darkness. Then she said, "What would you call them? Mountains? Or just hills?"

"I don't know. They're rugged enough, but nowhere near as big as some of the mountains we saw on the Crossing. Small mountains, maybe?"

"Ah yes, small mountains. Tiny-wee mountains. Knee-high mountains. No, not even that; look, I can cover them with my hand."

Then they were both laughing helplessly—laughing at more than just her flight of absurdity—laughing until they were too breathless to continue. And then they just sat again, content in quiet sibling togetherness, watching as the fat red sun rolled slowly down to meet the slate-blue mountains.

## Chapter 20

# Sumyra

The sands stretched away for miles in both directions. As soon as they'd passed the strandline, Jerya pulled off her shoes and stockings and kept on walking. When she reached the water, she lifted her skirt and continued until she stood about knee-deep.

Something about this had given both Embrel and Sumyra the feeling that this was a private moment for their aunt, and they stayed a little way back from the waves, looking at shells and shards of wood worn smooth by long tumbling in the sea.

After maybe ten minutes, Jerya began to make her way back to them. "Not as cold as the pool in the Defile," she said. "If we could find a more secluded spot I'd take a swim. But at least now I've dipped my feet in the Eastern Ocean and the Western, and I don't suppose there are many who can say that."

She looked at Embrel. "Did you know... the first person at least to see both oceans—in this age of the world—can you guess who that is?'

He shrugged. "Rodal reckons it might be him... but didn't you...?"

"No, when I left the Guild I'd only ever seen the ocean as a glimmer on the horizon, from the grounds of the College. And it was years after I came to the Five Principalities before I saw the Eastern Ocean. First time I properly stood at its edge was on my sweetmoon, and the first time I sailed on it was a couple of days later. No, as far as anyone can be sure, it was Rodal.

"He'd been to the Western shore; it's an easy day-trip from Carwerid. And then he spent months working on a trading vessel, up and down the rivers and along the coast. Troquharran, Sessapont, the Archipelago... And then, at the end of his year, he came back across the mountains, entirely alone." Her gaze rested on Embrel now. "When we talk about people doing remarkable things, we have to include him."

※

"I know you're missing the summer-school for the first time," said Jerya as the road curled around another cove. "I am too. I'm surprised just how much I miss it, in fact. But maybe that's not altogether a bad thing."

"I'm not sure what you mean."

"I mean... it reminds me that I really do care about education. Which helps when I'm battling the doubts that I'm doing the right thing fighting to get women admitted to a University... when they are so many who think even setting up a full-time school was a step too far."

"I find it hard to believe you have doubts."

Jerya laughed ruefully. "Oh, draff, is that how I come across, even to you? Always sure of myself?"

Sumyra chose her words with care. "Sometimes, perhaps, but I think probably you have to. It's hard enough for a woman to be heard, to be heeded; if you look like you're not sure, it's even easier to disregard you. What I meant, though, was doubts about the rightness of establishing the school. Surely... I mean, it seems to me it was absolutely the right thing to do. If my opinion helps..."

Jerya gave her a warm smile. "Your opinion counts for a lot, Sumyra. Because you're my niece, because you're a bright young woman... and because you're a lot closer than I am to the girls we're fighting for in Velyadero."

"I don't know if it's the girls you'll have to persuade; it's the parents who'll decide. And in the end, I suppose, it's the fathers."

"That's very true," Jerya agreed with a sigh. "However much some people talk about wives ruling their husbands... it's always struck me that's a story both wives and husbands tell themselves to relieve their feelings about the injustice. Anyway, you're right, and that's why I'm full of doubt. Not that it's the right thing to do, I'm quite certain about that; but can we make it work? What if we get agreement from Velyadero and then there aren't any students?"

"I'm sure most of the girls girls who graduated with me would be keen."

"I'm glad you think so, but, like you said, it's the parents we have to convince." She gave a wry chuckle. "When we were trying to set up the school, the biggest problem was... where would we get the teachers? We couldn't very well ask Dawnsingers to base themselves in the Five Principalities year-round. It's no small matter that we've had five or six of them for six or eight weeks every summer. I'm pretty sure not everyone in the Guild approves."

"Like that Master Perriad?"

"Let's not talk about her, not while we're as sure as we can be she's nowhere near. No, let's talk about teachers. Because, after all, where are the educated women? That's why we set up the school... but until you've educated some women, where do you find women who can teach?"

Sumyra thought about that. In many ways it was self-evident. She naturally thought at once of the two highly educated women she knew well: Jerya herself, and her Mamma. Hardly typical females of the Five Principalities. After that... "You obviously managed somehow."

"Aye, but only by stretching the definition of 'educated'." She chuckled again. "Now you've graduated, Sumyra, I'll tell you this: the first year or two, we all lived, pretty constantly, on the edge of panic. None of us had been teachers before; most of us had never even been in a classroom. I was the exception there, thanks to four months at the College of the Dawnsingers. So when I tried to advise the others how to teach, the only models I had were Dawnsingers, Tutors like Yanil and Jossena."

"Earl Hedric must have had a full schooling?"

"Aye, he did, and he was a great help. But it soon became clear that the way things were done in boys' schools in the Five Principalities, and the way they're done in the College, were very different. I couldn't quite believe how... *punitive* the system was. How *adversarial*. I don't know how I knew, but I knew that wasn't how we'd do things at Skilthorn."

"Do you think it's to do with the differences between male and female?"

"I'm sure it is, but in what way? I mean, does the difference in pedagogical styles arise from differences between the sexes... or does it explain them, or at least some of them?"

Sumyra was pondering that, but Jerya's mind was already onto a new tack. "Another thing I was sure about from the start: education isn't only measured by the time you spend sitting in a classroom. I didn't arrive in the College knowing nothing. My mind wasn't a blank; Sharess wouldn't have sent me there if it was. I'd read every book Delven had, and I'd spent a lot of time looking at the world and trying to understand everything I could; even devised a few experiments. And when I got to Duncal, there was a decent library there, a telescope... I'd learned a good deal before I met Hedric, and I learned a lot more afterward."

"I was just thinking about him. And thinking how much I learned from my father; and from Mamma, too, of course. I wondered... I know it's all about educating girls, but does that mean all the teachers need to be women?"

"Well, we've always had Hedric, and Docent Ishe followed his wife to us after the first year... I think he'd been waiting to see if we'd even make it to a second."

She chuckled. "A few parents needed reassurance about having their daughters taught by men. But that's not why I want as many female teachers as possible. It's showing that we can do it for ourselves. But we still have subjects we aren't covering as well as I'd like. Which is why I've been wondering..." She settled her gaze on Sumyra, trusting the horse to hold its course. "How would you like to be one of our teachers?"

Sumyra startled violently enough that her horse made a slight hitch in its stride. The animal glanced back as her as if in reproof. Another time, she would have laughed, but she could think of nothing but what Jerya had just said. "*Me?*"

"Absolutely."

"But I... I'm not qualified."

"Isn't that what I've been saying for the last half mile? None of us are, except Docent Ishe. I'm not."

"But you were a Dawnsinger—"

"—For four months."

"You've done original scientific work. You've published papers. Aunt Jerya, if you're not qualified, I'm not sure who is."

"That's rather the point I'm making." Jerya glanced ahead briefly, just while she manoeuvred her mount a little closer. "If we'd insisted on qualified teachers, then the school would probably never have opened. It's a vicious cycle. If we were ever going to break it, we had to start somewhere. Not with people who hold some sort of certificate, but people I thought would do a good job. People I liked and trusted and respected. And you're all of those, Sumyra."

For a moment Sumyra didn't trust herself to answer. She loved her Mamma, above all other women; that was clear. But if she was asked who she admired the most, Railu or Jerya, she wouldn't be able to answer without thinking. Perhaps the answer was that she admired both of them beyond measure. To have Jerya look her in the eye and use a word like 'respect' meant more than she could say.

Finally she found her voice, and if the question was mundane, Jerya didn't seem to mind. "What do you think I could teach?"

"What subjects?" Jerya smiled. "At the start, almost anything. No, I'm serious. Let me tell you something Analind said to me. She was never a Tutor, you know. She had to teach her Peripatetics lots of things, but practical stuff, in the field. I'm not sure she'd ever stood in front of twenty girls in a classroom. And it is daunting, believe me. So before the first summer-school she said to someone, might have been Yanil, how nervous she was, and... d'you know what Yanil said? *If you understand today's chapter in the textbook, you can teach it. If you understand a couple of chapters ahead, you can teach it well."*

"I don't think I ever even saw Yanil look at the book."

Jerya chuckled. "She didn't need to; she *wrote* the book. And she's been teaching mathematics for... oh, at least thirty years, I should think."

"I don't think I could teach mathematics even with the book in front of me."

"You won't have to; I can do that myself. Maths, astronomy, a bit of physics. But what about biology, anatomy, physiology? I know you've picked up plenty of that."

It was true, she supposed. Ever since Papa and Mamma had taken over the clinic in Drumlenn, she'd helped out in whatever way she could, from sterilising instruments to making fair copies of scribbled (and occasionally bloodstained) notes. She'd asked a million questions, too. She'd often wondered exactly what she could do with the knowledge she'd gained. It was something of a sore point that the exemption which allowed Railu to practise would never apply to her. Teaching would never be a replacement for actually practising medicine... but it would be *something*.

"Would we use the Dawnsingers' textbooks?" she asked finally.

"We already do, as much as we can. Apart from anything else, it gives the girls hard evidence that women can do these things. Of course, we still need Five Principalities books for some things, local history and so on... but there's another one for you. What about geography?"

"Geography? I don't know anything about geography."

Jerya held her gaze for a moment, then said. "Look around you, Sumyra. Where are we?"

Obediently, Sumyra looked. One one side, low mounded hills clad in a medley of fields and woods. On the other, the narrowing bay, merging into the estuary of the Caburn; beyond that, more low hills, gradually mounting in crumpled steps toward the skyline peaks. "At the head of Kerrsands Bay," she said.

"And where is Kerrsands Bay?"

She puzzled a moment, unsure what precise kind of answer Jerya wanted. The Sung Lands didn't have simple divisions like the Five Principalities—or if it did, no one had told her. "The West coast, three or four, days' ride from Carwerid."

"The West coast of what?"

"The Sung Lands."

Jerya smiled. Evidently, that was the answer she'd been looking for. "How many women from the Five Principalities have visited the Sung Lands?"

"You and Mamma."

"Yes, if you even count us, since we were both born here... though we have now lived longer in the Five Principalities than we did here... Who else?"

"Well, me, now."

"Quite so. And I'm not saying straight out you're the first, but I honestly haven't heard of any others. Disappointing, but hardly surprising... You're a rarity, besure, if not unique. You've seen—you are seeing—the Sung Lands with the eyes of a woman raised in the Five Principalities.

"I'll make a prediction, Sumyra, You won't need a textbook. We'll get you good maps and then you just need to tell them where you went and what you saw. What you ate, what you drank, what you wore... If they're not avid to know as much as you can tell them, if they don't bombard you with questions, well, they aren't the kind of girls we want in our school."

Sumyra looked again to her left, over the strip of coarse grass splashed with wildflowers, over the low broken fringe of rocks, the rippled sand. At the water's edge a heron stalked, step by fastidious step. Then she turned back to her aunt. "Can I ask you one thing?"

"Of course."

"Did you think of all this before you invited me on this trip?"

Jerya chuckled. "I seem to remember you came pretty close to inviting yourself."

"Maybe I did... but the question stands. Did you think of it before?"

"My dear, you give me way too much credit for forethought. I thought of asking you to teach biology a few days ago. I thought of asking you to teach geography about five seconds before I said it."

## Chapter 21

# Embrel

Sokkie had a kind of dazed look, maybe even dazzled. It wasn't hard to figure out why, but he asked anyway.

"Sittin' at dinner wi' Dawnsingers…" she said. "An' again at breakfast… Mostly they wanted to talk wi' Jerya so they got one to talk wi' me. One o' the youngest."

He thought about that. "I think when they're newly… Ordained, they call it, they're about Sumyra's age."

"That'll be right enough. An' she seemed like she were really interested in me. In my life."

"That's hardly surprising. They're Chosen when they're about ten or eleven and then they spend seven or eight years in the College. They hardly ever go out, far as I know. So maybe your life's as much of a mystery to her as hers is to you."

She shot him a curious look. "How come you know so much about Dawnsingers?"

"I've met a few, too. Our house is one of the first places they stop when they come to the Five Principalities. Ours or Sumyra's. And… well, Jerya was a Dawnsinger. Railu too."

"Jerya don't look like a Dawnsinger now," she said with a hint of doubt.

"She wasn't one for very long. But Railu was, she was there the full eight years."

"Railu's Sumyra's Ma, right?"

He sighed. "It's confusing, I know. I'm still making sense of it myself. Remember, I only found out after we arrived in Carwerid. Railu's my natural mother, though I never knew it. She's Sumyra's step-mother."

"Step-mother?"

"Her mother died when she was a baby. Her father married Railu about six years ago. Sumyra calls her Mamma."

"So she's kind of your sister too?"

"Step-half-sister," he said, chuckling. "And when we were smaller I thought of her like a sister." *I still do, it seems.* "But we're not related by blood at all. Not like you and me."

"It's funny. Suddenly findin' out I got a brother I knew nothin' about. Half-brother, whatever it is."

"Half-brother's technically correct, but I'd be happy if you just called me brother."

"You ain't like my other brothers…"

"Oh no," he said, filling his tone with gloom. "I'm so very sorry."

She laughed, a bright sound in the dull morning. "I don't want you to be like them!"

"I know, they drive you crazy. I was probably the same when I was that age. But I must be twice Tawno's age now, and probably three times Elbar's. People change, grow up."

Sokkie grunted, unimpressed. "Tawno growin' up? I'll b'lieve that when I see it."

"That's how it generally goes, I reckon."

She gave him another considering look, reverted to the earlier subject. "So you know lots o' Dawnsingers?"

"I wouldn't say I know them. I've met quite a few." He looked ahead. "Sumyra knows them better than I do." He explained about Skilthorn, the summer-school. "And of course Jerya was one, for a while."

"I thought there must be somethin'. Way she was with Dawnsinger Arvelyn… They must've known each other afore."

Yes, it had been a warm welcome, and there had been a familiarity between Jerya and the superintendent of the Adjunct House. But they never forgot that not all Dawnsingers felt so warmly toward her.

※

"I wouldn't mind if we had to go on," said Sokkie later. "Cross into the Five Principalities. I want to see more of the world."

"Maybe you can," said Jerya. "Next year, the year after."

"Following in your father's footsteps?" asked Sumyra.

"Good steps to follow," said Jerya. "First to make a double Crossing, after all."

"But now he never goes anywhere," said Sokkie. Her tone was quiet, matter-of-fact, but there was something behind it that made Jerya look at her closely.

"Let me tell you about your father," she said after a moment. "I'm not saying Railu and I wouldn't have made it across without him, but it would have been harder for sure. And, if we had ended up having to fend for ourselves like we expected, we'd have been a lot less ready. But, of course, we were taken for slaves. He must have taken some risks to find where we were, what our situation was, but he realised there was no point in trying to get us out straight away, with no money and nowhere to go. So he set out to earn some money and at the same time to learn as much as he could about the Five Principalities.

"I don't know how much he's told you about all this..."

"It was like bedtime stories," said Sokkie. "I think I was too young to understand."

"I'm sure you could ask to hear them again. So I won't say too much, don't want to steal his thunder, but I'll say this. In the time he was there, before he came back to Duncal to find us again, he learned a completely new trade, and he sailed the Eastern Sea. So, as I was saying to Embrel and Sumyra yesterday, he's the first person in this age to have seen both seas. And after that, he was the first to cross the Sundering Wall in both directions. Those are pretty big achievements."

"So why does hardly anyone know about them? And why does he never go further than Canalfoot now?"

"Because he kept—keeps—his promises." Jerya's words were quiet but emphatic. "All of them. He made a promise to Railu and me, and he kept it. He made a promise to your mother, and he kept that too. And I guess he made promises to you and your brothers as well, before you were born as well as after, and he's honouring those also. Whereas I… I made one big promise when I was a Dawnsinger, and within weeks I'd torn it to shreds."

"That's why Perriad calls you a Vow-breaker," said Sumyra, half a question.

"Yes, and she's absolutely right about that. She's wrong about plenty of other things, but not that."

Sokkie wasn't finished with her preoccupation. "I can't see how he can go on a great adventure like that and then just come back to opening the Tavern every day."

Jerya smiled. "Taverns are important too."

## Chapter 22

# Embrel

As they splashed through a shallow rill, Jerya was in the lead. A moment later she held up a hand, reined in, and dismounted. Embrel and the girls found her peering at a sandy patch of ground.

"Someone's been this way recently," she said. "Four horses, wouldn't you say?"

They all swung down to join her, and after examining the tracks agreed that there had probably been four horses.

"Singer Sesmy said Perriad had three companions," said Jerya, still studying the tracks. "And we know there are no Peripatetics due to be heading this way just now. The only places this road leads to are Thrushgill and Delven. I don't know quite so much about Thrushgill, but I can't recall a single time in all my years in Delven when we had four outside visitors at once."

She straightened. "Can't be a hundred per cent certain, but I'd say it's highly likely it's Perriad and her friends. Did they know we were making for Kerrsands Bay and just guess we'd come round to Delven this way? Wonder how far ahead they are... Draff! Why didn't I ask when we passed through Stainscomb?"

"No one said anything to us," said Sumyra.

"No, but if a Dawnsinger told them not to..." She pulled the map from inside her shirt. "And there's an obvious place to catch us with no one else around." Her finger fell on a spot that must lie a few miles ahead.

"The thing about obvious places is they're obvious to us too... Sollom; I never knew its name before. It was just a cluster of dots on the map Rodal and I had. There's no real hills around there—they do call it the Scorched Plains, after all—but the land does roll a bit. If we do a wide loop around and stay off the highest ground, we won't be visible even if anyone's looking in the right direction at the right time."

She grinned fiercely. "If I was trying to do what Perriad's trying to do, I'd have my people riding wide loops around the place, or posted on the highest points. But she's a city person, I'm sure. She won't think about straying off the road."

"Can you be sure all her companions are city-bred too?" asked Embrel.

"No... but Perriad's a teller, not a listener. Besides, they've all been Dawnsingers since they were ten or eleven, lived in the College at least eight years. I don't think any of them are Peripatetics. They don't have the experience."

※

The detour around Sollom must have cost them well over an hour, but they saw no one, nor even the wild horses Jerya recalled from her first time crossing the Plains. "The first time," she said, "I ever saw a horse."

On an overcast day like today, reflected Embrel, 'Scorched' was a poor descriptor. Instead, the land looked... bleached. Pale, dusty soil showed through a threadbare covering of straggling grasses and stunted herbs. He'd heard that some of the land to the South of Velyadero and Buscanya looked like this, and wondered how similar it really was. And of course he wondered why those places, and this, looked the way they did. Jerya only shrugged when he mentioned it. "No one knows that I ever heard of. But it looks more like there's something toxic in the ground doesn't it?"

They didn't stop, and they didn't let the horses drink from any of the occasional streams, until they came to greener terrain. By then humans as well as horses were overdue for a good rest and a long drink. After a few minutes Jerya set off to climb a nearby knoll, and Embrel followed her.

As he joined her at the crest, she was already studying the map. "I think we should meet the track again just beyond those trees. Then not more than an hour to Thrushgill. We'll see what they say but I think we're best leaving the horses there. We'd be leading them much of the way on the path up to Delven and even then they'd probably balk at the last bit."

"You think we'll reach Delven tonight, aunt?"

"It's three or four hours' walking, if we push on steadily. So yes."

## Chapter 23

# Sumyra

Jerya's tactic of detouring around the deserted village, Sollom, must have worked. No one in Thrushgill had seen any Dawnsingers, or any other travellers, for some time; as far as they could judge the answers were honest. As Jerya had suggested, they left the horses there. Hiking on up, Sumyra's pack felt heavy after letting the horse do all the work for a week, but she told herself it was little more than half the weight of what she'd carried at the start of the Crossing.

She thought of Master Perriad and her confederates, their fruitless wait at Sollom. From Jerya's description, it did not sound like a place to linger. Sumyra wondered how long they would sit it out there before giving up, and what they would do then.

※

Someone must have spotted them well before they reached Delven, because the village was out in force to greet them. Sumyra had already gathered that visitors of any kind were rare, so every arrival would be an event, but had they realised who was in this party?

Her questions were soon answered as a tall, lean, man stepped forward, several paces in front of the rest. This had to be Holdren, the headman. She knew from Jerya's account that he must be in his late sixties at least. His hair was sparse and mostly white, his face lined, but he looked more…

weathered than aged. His eyes were clear and his voice as he greeted them was strong.

And he was Jerya's father...

Naturally, she looked for signs of resemblance, but it was hard to see anything in that seamed face. Something in the jawline, perhaps, though loose skin beneath the chin made it unclear.

There was no great display of affection between them. Sumyra recalled what Jerya had said about the secret of her parentage being known to even fewer people than Embrel's. No, there would be no acknowledgement in public. In his first greeting, he'd addressed Jerya as 'daughter of Delven', and if there was anything more than usual stress in the word 'daughter', she could not detect it.

It was different when he gathered who Jerya's companions were. At once he called a couple forward, both perhaps ten years younger than himself, presenting them first to Sokkie. "I don't know if you rightly remember your gran'parents."

"A little," said Sokkie. She looked for a moment uncharacteristically shy, but there was no such restraint from her grandmother, who seized her in a fervent embrace.

Jerya was left to explain who her other two companions were. Holdren nodded comprehension as she named Sumyra as 'Railu's step-daughter'; of course, Railu too had passed through Delven on the eve of the First Crossing, had even been intended for service as the village's Dawnsinger.

When it came to Embrel, Jerya hesitated, just long enough for Embrel himself to take the initiative, naming himself before saying. "Railu is also my mother—my natural mother. And Rodal is my father."

That could not have been easy, she knew, but she was glad to hear him acknowledge it.

"How's that possible?" asked Rodal's father, Sardain. "And how's it we never knew?"

"Rodal didn't know until two weeks ago. No one did, not this side of the mountains."

Soon, Embrel, Sokkie, and the two grandparents had drawn aside, deep in talk, though Sumyra noted that Embrel did not receive the same embrace his sister had.

She had no time to notice more. A stir in the gathering, and then a spreading silence, was quickly explained. All eyes had turned toward the tor that rose a short distance from the stonecourt. A figure in white, a bald woman, was descending the rough steps that slanted down two sides.

"Dawnsinger Marit," said Jerya as the Singer approached.

"Welcome, Jerya," replied Marit. "We meet again. A pleasure I never dared hope for."

"You're too kind, Dawnsinger. Might I present my niece, Sumyra?"

"Niece, is it? Yet I had heard you were an only child..." Sumyra found it hard to hold the Singer's gaze. Hazel eyes, skin of a warm hue; like Mamma's only a shade or two lighter. A tall woman, taller than Jerya.

Jerya had said something she hadn't heard, and now Marit replied, "We have a few things to discuss, I think. Will you be my guest for a third time? And you too, Sumyra, if you like."

"I'm honoured, Dawnsinger," she managed to say.

※

The chamber atop the tor was roughly hexagonal, about seven paces across. The walls were more than half covered with ornate and colourful hangings; what remained exposed was a mix of natural rock and masonry. Marit indicated a chair for Jerya, apologising that there was only a simple stool for Sumyra, "But set it closer to the wall if you want to rest your back." The only natural light came from the door, left ajar, and from an opening in the ceiling where a ladder led up to what must be the songstead.

Marit was offering coffee and Jerya responded with, "That reminds me." She produced a paper-wrapped packet from her satchel.

"Guild Blend?" asked Marit with a smile.

"I know you have your own supply," said Jerya, "But I couldn't think of anything else more fitting."

"Yes, most appropriate, thank you. You won't feel slighted, though, if I brew from the one already open?"

As Marit prepared the drinks in an alcove revealed behind one of the hangings, Sumyra saw that Jerya was looking around with particular intensity. When she realised she'd been observed, she smiled. "This is where it all began."

"Where you were Chosen," said Marit over one shoulder. "How many years ago?"

Jerya replied without hesitation, "Twenty-one years and a couple of months... I do believe she sat me in this very chair to shave me."

"It's a big moment for every girl Chosen," said Marit, bearing two mugs to her guests. "I told you, didn't I, I was proud... proud beyond measure."

"And I was terrified."

Marit smiled. She fetched her own mug and settled into a second chair before continuing. "And maybe you had more the right of it than I did. Or maybe the only truly rational response is to feel both." She lifted the mug, inhaled, but did not drink. "I know I lost the pride for a while. I was near my lowest ebb that first time." She must mean the first time they'd met, thought Sumyra. "I can't have done much for your state of terror."

Jerya, perhaps diplomatically, did not answer that, only sipping her coffee and complimenting Marit on the brew.

Sumyra, remembering the old Singer they had met, said, "This was Sharess's chamber then, wasn't it?"

"It was," said Jerya.

"And not six months after it was mine too," added Marit. "In fact we were both here that winter."

"Seems like it'd get crowded," said Sumyra.

"Not so bad as you might think. There's a bed-chamber through there..." Marit indicated another of the hanging tapestries. "Sharess gave that to me, she slept in the nook."

"I supposed there might be another room," said Jerya, "But I never knew."

"Is it usual to have two Dawnsingers in such a small place?" asked Sumyra. She'd thought it an innocent question, but both Jerya and Marit stiffened and looked at each other.

"I was supposed to replace Sharess, but when the troika brought me here they didn't think she was well enough to be moved. You can't bring horses all the way—well, you'll know that—and you couldn't get a carriage any nearer than Thrushgill." Marit sighed. "The truth is, though, the first month or two, I needed her more than she needed me."

Sumyra wondered at that, but Marit did not elaborate. She was silent for a moment, as if looking into memory, then gave her head a small shake. "And Meladne—you remember Meladne?"

"Aye," said Jerya. "She'd be a couple of years younger than me."

"Well, she'd made herself the one who knew all about herbs, and where they grew. After Pentrunne couldn't get about so well. I think they said it was Annyt—that's Rodal's wife, aye?—had started her on bringing borage and things to Sharess, massaging her hands. And after Annyt had gone, Meladne carried on, the massage too. I think that's how she and Holdren…"

"Meladne and Holdren?" asked Jerya.

"They've been married nine years now. Got a boy and a girl."

Sumyra thought of the man who'd greeted them, and that Jerya had said Meladne was younger than herself. There had to be thirty years between them. Well, that wasn't unheard of in the Five Principalities either… And then there were the stories about what owners did with young female enslaved. There'd been talk at Skilthorn about the former Earl, Hedric's uncle; if even half of it were true, he'd been a monster. Though she cautioned herself about the way gossip and rumour could feed on itself in a close community like a school.

Jerya was shaking her head at the latest news. "Draff, I'd never have thought… but I suppose that's what I get for only coming back every ten, eleven, years."

"I'm sure I'm not the only one who'd be happy to see you more often," said Marit.

## Chapter 24

# Embrel

"I'm sorry Ash's a bit..."

"Stand-offish?" he suggested.

"Aye. Stiff, like. She's a good woman, and there's none got a kinder heart, but she's got a way of thinkin' there's nobbut one right way to do things."

"There are people like that everywhere," said Embrel. If what Jerya had said about ex-Master Perriad was true, she was another one.

"I dare say," said Sardain. "Anyroad, give her time. It's a lot for her to take in. Findin' out our Rodal had been... had lain wi' another woman—and her a Dawnsinger and all."

"It's been a lot for me to take in too....."

"I dare say..." The path swung to the right, winding up the rocky slope in broken steps, more stone than dirt. "How long since you found out?"

"A couple of weeks. I couldn't even take it in at first."

"Well, then, mayhap you can see how it is for Ash. But she'll see soon enough. Whate'er fault may lie with Rodal or Railu, it's none o' yours. You're the result, not the cause."

They climbed more gradually, keeping to the west side of the swell. Then the ground levelled, and in the space of a few strides, the East opened before him; the East, and the mountains.

The mountains he knew, around Drumlenn, gathered themselves gradually, in modest foothills. As Jerya had once told him, you could even think of the knowe, just a few minutes' walk from home, as a first tentative rise.

There was nothing tentative about the mountains he saw now, springing up who-knew-how-many thousands of feet with all the swagger of a prizefighter.

At this time of the morning they were still mostly in shadow, sun only catching the peaks and the higher ridges, but it was enough. He could see how there was one great rank of them, apparently unbroken, walling off the horizon, stretching away to the North as far as the eye could see. In front of it, a second line, perhaps lower but still high enough to obscure most of the ridge behind; but this line came to an abrupt end, its final peak falling away in a snow-streaked chaos of rock and scree, almost opposite the point where they stood. Behind it, between it and the greater ridge, a hint of what might be a long valley that would run away to the South-East.

"That must be where they went," he said.

"Aye," said Sardain. "And who knew what lay ayont?"

"No one had explored it before?"

"Well, that's summat you need to understand. To us it was always… you didn't go ayont reach o' Dawnsong. Not further'n you could get back afore night. No one ever quite said what might happen if you did wander too far, but no one wanted to find out."

"But they did…"

"Aye, and that were quite a puzzle. Some folk said, Jerya and Railu were Dawnsingers, so they'd take the Song wi' em. And it seemed the Dawnsinger—our Dawnsinger—had bid Rodal go wi' em. So that way it seemed it oughter be all right, but same again it was all irregular. If it were right and above board, you'd have thought they'd'a said summat aforetimes, 'stead o' sneakin' off while it were still dark." Sardain's shrug seemed to say as much as his words. "And then we heard nothin' for nigh on a year…"

"And then Rodal came back."

"Aye, all by hisself. And he had a tale or two. Draff, if he hadn't been my own son, if we hadn't raised him honest like any good Delven man, I'd'a thought he were makin' up half of it." His gaze sharpened. "But he never said owt about you."

"He never knew. He found out the same time I did."

"That must ha' been a moment, then, for both o' you."

Embrel laughed, though there was nothing funny about it. At once he was glad that the wide sweep of the moor swallowed the sound, that the mountains were too far off to return any echo.

His mind reached for another topic. "It's strange to think... it's really not that far. If you were an eagle, you could fly it in a day." How fast did eagles fly? "Maybe just a few hours."

"To where you live?"

"Yes. But of course it's a hard journey on foot. Hardly anyone uses this Crossing, do they?

"Aye. Only one lot from t'other side since Jerya came back. What was it, ten years ago?"

"Eleven. I was nine. Made a big fuss; I didn't want her to go."

They talked about Jerya then, and what she was to Embrel, and what it meant that she was a Countess now. But as long as the mountains were in his sight, at the back of his mind remained the thought that Rodal had crossed them twice.

He thought more about it as they descended. Of course, Jerya had also returned this way; but she had had Hedric with her, and... what was the fellow's name? Lallon. Rodal had made the journey entirely alone.

From an early age, and especially after Jerya's return in '92, Embrel had taken an interest in the tales of Crossings. He had always remembered Jerya's promise.

*"One day, when you're a bit older, we will go on a journey together."*

*"A real journey?"*

*"A real journey."*

Jerya had never been more specific, but 'a real journey', in his mind, had always meant a Crossing. Now he had done that, and seen a good part of the Sung Lands too. Jerya had fulfilled her promise; no doubt about that; but he was beginning to wonder how long he would be satisfied with that. He could hardly expect her, with all the other demands on her time, to arrange another journey for his benefit. Next time, it might be up to himself. And the number of Crossings by the Northern route... it sounded like it could still be counted on one hand.

He caught a glimpse of the Dawnsinger's tor, still some way below, and his thoughts came back to Rodal; he must have descended this very path many times.

Not only had Rodal made the first return Crossing; he had made what, in all his reading about the subject, all the tales he had heard, was to this day the only solo Crossing—by either route—Embrel knew of. And he had done more. He had spent almost a whole year in the Five Principalities. Starting out penniless, unacquainted with the lands and their customs, he had made his way with remarkable success. He had become an accomplished seaman; had he mentioned that himself, or did it come from Jerya? No matter.

It must have been quite a year.

Embrel smiled as he recalled what Sokkie had said, just a few days ago. *"I can't see how he can go on a great adventure like that and then just come back to opening the Tavern every day."*

Her remembered, too, what Jerya had said in reply. *"Taverns are important too."*

*Pesk!* he thought. *I could do with a drink.*

# Chapter 25

# Sumyra

Sumyra had only seen Master Perriad for five minutes, but she recognised her even from twenty yards away. She hurried closer, in time to hear Perriad's peremptory demand of Sardain. "Are you the headman?"

"Begging your pardon, Dawnsinger, but th'headman's off huntin' wi' some o'th'others."

"Well, you'll do, I dare say." She pointed at Jerya. "Place this woman in confinement."

Sardain looked honestly bewildered. "Confinement, Dawnsinger?"

Perriad's lip curled. "Lock her up."

"I don't rightly know as we've got any doors wi' locks."

"By the moons, what kind of place is this?"

"One where people trust each other," said Jerya quietly.

Perriad scowled furiously at her but swiftly returned to the unfortunate Sardain. "Put her in a room. You do have rooms, don't you? My people will—"

"Just one moment," another voice broke in. Everyone turned, with a swift unison that would have been amusing in less fraught circumstances. Delven's Singer was descending the rough steps at the base of the tor. "Ex-Master Perriad," she said.

"Singer... Marith, is it?"

"Marit."

"I beg your pardon."

Singer Marit paused on the lowest step, which left her a head above anyone else. She gave Perriad a long cool look. "I must say I'm wondering if my ears deceived me. I *was* still halfway up the steps. Did you really ask—or should I say *order?*—that Jerya be locked up?"

"That's exactly what I ordered."

Marit sighed. "I am Dawnsinger in Delven, not you. This village is my responsibility."

"I am a Master of the Guild."

"Ex-Master, I believe—or have you been reinstated? Too recently for the news to have reached me?" Perriad did not answer. "I thought not. In any case, I answer to the Conclave of the Guild, not to an individual Master. Besides which, in this village, I do not order people to do things. I offer counsel and advice. I don't believe I've issued a direct command in the twelve years I've been here."

"Singer Marit, this woman—"

"—I know very well who this woman is. And let's pay her the courtesy of using her name. I've met Jerya before, on two occasions... and to the best of my knowledge she is in good standing with the Conclave and on occasion has the ear of the Master Prime."

"That is exactly the problem."

"In your opinion. But I know Jerya personally. I only know you by reputation. And if I had nothing else to guide me but my experience of Jerya and what I know of you, I would—"

"—Singers," one of Perriad's companions broke in anxiously. "Surely this... conversation would be better in private? It's hardly good protocol to air our disagreements in public."

"If you're such a stickler for protocol," said Marit, "You might have advised ex-Master Perriad that it is a gross impertinence to march into a village and start issuing orders before you've even paid your respects to the resident Dawnsinger."

Sumyra had to turn away to hide her smile, but she could still hear Marit as she continued, "Speaking of paying your respects, Master Perriad, your companion has a proper notion. Perhaps you would care to ascend, and we can discuss your visit in a civilised fashion?" She gestured at the steps. "I just need a word with this good man here."

As Perriad started up the steps, Marit turned to Sardain. "I'm sorry she accosted you like that. And now it appears we have four more unexpected guests to accommodate... do you know if Meladne's within?"

"I couldn't say for sure, Dawnsinger, but on a day like this she's more likely up at the hives, or away somewhere foragin'. But my Ash'll look at findin' beds for 'em. Not as it'll be easy, mind."

Marit sighed. "I think I shall have to offer Master Perriad a place with me... at least that means you only have to find room for three, not four."

Sardain nodded, bowing slightly, and moved off. Marit turned back to Jerya and Sumyra. "That woman doesn't look like she'd appreciate the nook, either. I'm afraid I'll have to offer her my own bed."

"I'm sorry," said Jerya.

"For what?"

"She's only here because I am."

"Perhaps. But, Jerya, Master Perriad's reputation precedes her. We may not get many visitors here, not in the usual run of things, but we do see a Visitation every two years... Come to think of it, don't I have you to thank for that?'

This baffled Sumyra, but Jerya only shrugged. "Or to blame for you being transferred up here."

"Nonsense. It was the best thing that could have happened to me. Well, Sharess was the best thing that could have happened..." She sighed again. "Sharing with Perriad... By the Seven, I may need to start drinking again."

Jerya's turn to heave a sigh. "I wouldn't want to put you through that. And anyway, it's awkward for everyone. People are already displaced because we're here. I think we'd better not prolong our stay overmuch."

"I understand why you say that, but if you leave too soon I think everyone here will know who's really to blame. Besides, won't they pursue you wherever you go? Is there no way to resolve matters?"

"If there is, I don't think it'll happen here. But you're right, they'll follow us..." For a moment a strange light kindled in Jerya's eyes. "Of course, there are two routes out of here."

For a moment Sumyra was puzzled, and she saw Marit was too. Then it dawned. "You mean the Northern Crossing?"

"Aye," said Jerya. "But... draff, I'm twice the age I was then, and I've hardly touched a rock since Hedric and I came this way. I don't know if I could manage it now... and what would your Mamma say?"

"She did it," said Sumyra. In truth, the thought of the Northern Crossing—so much harder than the Southern, by all accounts—sparked something close to terror; but it had a perilous allure, too. "She did it when she was just about my age, didn't she? And she didn't grow up here, among the rocks."

"Well, if we could get everything we need... draff, even then, Perriad's probably crazed enough to follow." Jerya shook her head. "Besides, we all have unfinished business in Carwerid. Embrel especially, I reckon. No, it's a last resort, and a desperate one. We'll have to think of a better plan."

She turned. "And with respect, Dawnsinger Marit, aren't you keeping your guests waiting?"

Marit smiled. "Did you think I'd forgotten them? No, if I'm putting off the moment, it's quite intentional... but I suppose I had better get to it." She started up the steps, a great deal more nimbly than Perriad had done a minute or two before.

❃

"Aunt," said Sumyra when they were alone. "I don't suppose Perriad's interested in me or Embrel..."

Jerya gave her a sideways glance. "Not likely; it's me she's obsessed with. But what are you thinking?"

"It doesn't need all three of us to go by the Northern Crossing. And you said yourself, it's mostly Embrel who needs to go back via Carwerid."

"Perhaps. But I want to spend more time with my mother. Besides, I wasn't joking when I said I don't know if I could manage the Crossing now... let alone on my own. You know Rodal's still the only one to do that?" She grasped Sumyra's shoulders. "I appreciate the offer, besure, but there surely has to be a better way. And in any case, we won't be going anywhere tonight, and if we were going to do anything desperate we'd need time to prepare. Whatever we decide, the earliest we can leave is the day after tomorrow."

## Chapter 26

# Embrel

"What have you done with our horses?" demanded the Dawnsinger. One of Perriad's companions, of course; she was tall, dark-skinned, a little darker than Railu. (That little jolt in the gut that still occurred every time he thought of Railu.) And young, probably much about his own age.

"I beg your pardon?" he said, as politely as he could. She looked worried, he thought, and she was breathless, as if she'd been running.

"Our horses. Where are they?"

"I don't know. Where did you leave them?"

She waved an arm down the path. "In the meadow, down there, below the steep part."

That did make a kind of sense, though even to get that far they'd surely have been leading the horses for at least the last hour. It was far enough from the village to be inconvenient for checking on the horses, but there was shelter, plenty of grazing, and water.

The Dawnsinger was looking hard at him. "You really didn't know?"

"I never thought about your horses; if I had I'd have supposed you'd left them down at Thrushgill, like we did."

"Then who?"

"Look," he said, trying for a soothing tone. "Let's just go down and take a look."

❋

The meadow was much as he recalled from walking through it two days ago. Lush grass golden in the hazy sunshine, a vivid stippling of wildflowers. A few he recognised, like cornflowers, vetch, others he could not name.

What he could not see, at least at first, was any horses. "They were here?" he asked, though the fact hardly needed confirmation.

"Just over there, tethered to that tree." She indicated a spindly sycamore that stood in from the general line of the forest edge. They walked over to it. There were signs of trampling, piles of manure... and an end of rope still tied around the tree.

"Bitten through," he said, inspecting it. "And I think I know why."
"Why?"

"I guess none of you know too much about horses?" She did the silent look; he was beginning to recognise it as her standard response when the answer was 'yes' but she didn't want to admit it. "What can you hear?"

She cocked her head, the way people often did when asked to listen. It didn't help anyone hear any better but he supposed it showed that you were doing as requested.

It didn't take her long. "Bees."

"Mm. Line of hives not ten yards away. Maybe they weren't keen on the horses being so close, maybe the horses got stung a few times. Or just didn't like the buzzing. Anyway, they decided to move."

"Then where are they?"

He turned and looked down the length of the meadow, into the light, sensing the Singer doing the same. There were certainly no horses anywhere to be seen, but the meadow wasn't a simple clear space, a rectangle like you might find in a more formal landscape. It curved to the right, and there were little bays cutting into the enclosing forest. Partway down, a large tree—an oak, he guessed from the silhouette, wider than its height—further impeded their view.

They found the horses about five minutes walk away, not far beyond the sprawling oak. Two of them were still linked by a length of rope, the other two free. "You left the saddles on too?" he asked, slowing his pace so as not to alarm the animals.

"What else we were supposed to do?"

"Stash them somewhere, carry them with you. Leaving them saddled overnight's no kindness...." He stopped walking. All four horses had stooped grazing, lifted their heads from the herbage, were watching them; alert, curious, but not necessarily alarmed. "Which one's the boss?"

"Boss?"

*You really don't know much about horses, do you?* he thought. *But be polite*, he also thought. "Horses are like people. Get a group, you usually end up with a leader. In this group... you've got two geldings and two mares, right?"

"I think so." It was hard not to scoff then: *you don't even know that*? One thing about it, all this seemed to confirm Jerya's earlier hunch that none of them were Peripatetics. He'd met a few, notably Analind; they knew horses. Not the way Mavrys did, maybe but well enough. Knew them, and cared about them.

"Nine times out of ten the boss'll be the senior mare. Which is the dapple grey." Silently he dared her to ask him how he knew, but she didn't oblige. Sighing inwardly, he went on. "If she's happy, the others aren't likely to run off. Not unless something seriously spooks one of them."

At this point it would have been nice to have something to offer the grey mare, an apple or a carrot. Since there were no apple trees or vegetable patches to hand, he contented himself with twisting a tangle of grass, ripping it up.

The mare wasn't overly impressed with his offering, but she wasn't spooked either, tolerated his approach, accepted a scratch behind one ear. Once she was settled, he had no difficulty approaching the others.

"They all seem happy enough," he said after a few minutes.

"So what do we do now?" He restrained the urge to smile. Asking my advice now? "How do we tether them again?"

"We don't."

"But..."

"Look. One, they've made a mess of the rope. You'd have a job making good enough to give them room to graze. Two, where are they going to go anyway?"

"What do you mean?"

"This meadow's got forest all around. Horses aren't forest creatures, and the undergrowth looks pretty dense. It's practically as good as a fence. The only way they'd take, without being driven to it, is the path. And... well, I have to say this, it's not a good..." A sudden, concerning, thought. "Please tell me you didn't try and ride them up. Not all the way."

"No, we led them the last hour to here."

"Well, you got that right, at least. I don't see them heading back down that way on their own... and going up towards Delven, the first bit's even steeper."

"That's why we left them here."

"I have to say you'd have done better leaving them at Thrushgill. Put them in a fallow field like we did. Someone to keep an eye on them, bring them water... That's a thought. I think I remember a stream just a little lower down."

There was, and it got lazy where it crossed the meadow, spreading into little pools in a couple of places. "They've got water, and they've got good grazing. It doesn't look like rain but there's decent shelter under the oak tree. No reason on earth why they'd shift from here."

He got the Singer to help unsaddle the horses. They secured the saddles on low branches of the tree, which seemed the safest place. Worst case, they might get a bit nibbled by rats or squirrels, and by his reckoning Perriad and her crew deserved that at least.

"Thank you for your help," said the Singer as they finally started back up the path. "And I suppose I must apologise for accusing you before."

"It's all right," he said, feeling awkward. "Ah... may I know your name?"

She walked a few strides before answering; it appeared the matter needed some consideration. "My name is Elidir."

"Embrel," he said, thinking that they at least shared an initial. "Pleased to meet you." She glanced across and for a moment met his gaze.

※

*You have beautiful eyes.*

For one vertiginous moment he thought he'd said it aloud, but surely the Dawnsinger would have reacted, instead of merely turning away and continuing toward the village. She would have reacted, and not well. He might have done some good by helping her with the horses: saying anything of such a personal nature would surely have undone it, and probably made things worse.

But they *were* beautiful. A warm brown lighter than her skin, that he couldn't help thinking betokened a warm personality.

Following a few paces behind, he noticed first the grace of her walk, but then found himself captured by the smooth curves of her scalp, the way dappled light and leaf-shadows slipped across the skin. A special loveliness to the little hollow at the base, where the skull met the nape. Was there a special name for that place? Was that what they meant by the occiput? A ponderous word for something so delicate.

There was something Dawnsingers did which meant their hair would never grow back. Their scalps never showed even a hint of stubble, of shadow, as enslaved did.

Somehow Jerya had escaped permanent baldness, but not Railu. She had been a Dawnsinger far longer, he recalled, again feeling that dislocation as he thought of Railu. The sense of how awkward it would be when next he saw her. Strange, when he'd known her, and loved her, all his life; but there it was.

For now, though, his thoughts insisted on returning to the Dawnsinger, Elidir, plying her steady pace ahead of him as the track made the last climb to the threshold of the village.

※

Sleep was proving elusive. It wasn't the hard bed, though with only an inch or so of felt and goats' wool between him and the rock it was hard. He had slept well enough the first night. He didn't think it was the darkness either, absolute though it was. His room at home looked out toward the wilderness and woodland beyond; on cloudy nights, especially when the moons were down, it could be black enough outside the window, but he hadn't needed a nightlight since the first winter he'd come home from school.

Perhaps it was the silence. At home—he stopped, noting that he still thought of Duncal as home. His notions of who he himself was might have been upended, but home was still home.

At home, there was nearly always something. Sheep or cattle in the fields; sheep had a way of coughing that sounded very human. Horses in the stable just round the corner of the house. The shrill whip-crack bark of a fox; the call-and-response of a pair of tawny owls; the harsher cry of a barn-owl.

In the city he'd had to grow used to a different range of sounds. Human voices, amiable or angry or fearful; the rumble of cart-wheels, be it the night-soil collector or deliveries of bread or milk; the discordant serenade of an amorous cat or the furious snarls of squabbling felines. He'd grown accustomed to them all.

Silence, though; the dense silence of rock all around; the mind tried to fill it. And what his mind was mostly filled with right now was…

Was Elidir.

Embrel was not a fool; at least he did not believe so. He knew perfectly well that she was a Dawnsinger, and he knew, more or less, what that meant.

He had heard mention of the Principle of Detachment; Dawnsingers were not supposed to get too close to anyone.

Clearly this Principle was not always scrupulously followed. That there was variation in its interpretation, he had already seen, marking the difference between the free and easy relations between Singer and people in Blawith, and the more constrained. formal, interaction he'd observed here.

And self-evidently the Principle sometimes slipped further; on occasion considerably further. Jerya was evidence of that.

But that was a great secret. He had the impression Jerya had only shared it with him out of a sense of... fairness, after Sumyra had learned the truth.

His birth, and Rodal's part in it, was clearly scandalous; he had seen that in Ashlem's—*his grandmother's*—first reaction. But by that time, Railu had already broken her Dawnsinger's Vows, and that seemed to be an even greater scandal. And in that light, what Jerya's mother, Dawnsinger Sharess, had done would be a still greater scandal.

So, the Principle of Detachment was occasionally violated, but he could hardly ask, or expect, a Dawnsinger to do so. It was probably unreasonable to hope for anything more than the slightly distant politeness which Elidir had shown him already. In fact, given her association with Master Perriad, he probably should see even that was a concession.

He could hardly have said what he *did* want, but surely it was more than that.

But that was another question; what *did* he want?

He rolled onto his left side, seeking a comfort that he knew was not there.

## Chapter 27

# Embrel

He was halfway through his lunch: oatcakes with sharp goats' cheese and moorland honey, an unexpectedly exquisite combination, when he spotted Elidir heading down the path again. Going to check on the horses, no doubt, and good for her.

He finished the food, trying not to look as if he was hurrying. Not that anyone appeared to be watching. Jerya and Sumyra were with the Dawnsinger, Marit; at least he thought so. Not in the tor, somewhere outside the village. Sokkie was sitting with her grandparents. Where Perriad and her other two cohorts might be, he had no idea.

As far as he could tell, no one took any particular notice as he dusted the crumbs from his breeches and started on the downhill path. Only his own conscience, telling him this was not a good idea. Every step of the way he thought he should turn back, and every step was followed by another descending step.

He found her, of course, in the meadow. Her back was toward him and again he found himself marvelling at the elegance of her figure. *Elegant* was usually reserved for genteel young ladies in elaborate frocks, with corseted waists and exaggerated hips. He thought he would never again look at such extravagant caricatures of femininity without an urge to laugh. Elidir in the meadow, in a plain divided skirt and chemise, the sun gilding the arc of her skull, made all that a mockery, a travesty.

He moved closer, and the first of the horses, the boss mare, looked up and whickered softly.

Elidir—*Dawnsinger* Elidir, never forget that—turned. "Everything all right?" asked Embrel.

"Seems to be," she said. "Do they look well to you?"

It warmed him unreasonably that she should ask his opinion. He could tell himself it meant nothing more than recognition that he knew horses better than she, but his heart had its own ideas.

He went round all the animals, checking diligently, and he talked as he went, a mix of greeting and reassurance for the animals and whatever he could think of that might engage Elidir's interest. "A lot of what I know about horses I learned from a woman called Mavrys. She's Mistress of Horse at Skilthorn—Jerya's place, you know. Far as we know, she's the only woman in charge of a significant stable anywhere in the Five Principalities. She was very young when they first gave her the position, too. Might even have been younger than me, in fact."

*I'm talking too much*, he thought. *Babbling, probably*. But he didn't seem to be able to stop. He told how Mavrys had once been a slave, or at least lived as one; how she routinely wore breeches and kept her hair cropped short; how she lived with Vireddi, how they called each other 'wife'... "And that's not legal two ways, because they're both women and because Vireddi's enslaved, but they still had a ceremony, with all the stable-hands, and half the household, *and* the Earl and Countess—Jerya and Hedric. Her husband, you know," he added, thinking Elidir might very well *not* know. He stepped back, eyed the brindle gelding, watched him swishing his tail as he cropped contentedly. "They all look fine to me."

"Thank you for that. I should be heading back."

"Do you mind if I walk with you?"

"Would it make a difference if I didn't want you to?"

"Of course!" he protested. "I'd never impose myself on a lady." Though he wondered if he'd done just that, blathering on about Mavrys. "There isn't another path, far as I know, but I could give you five minutes..."

"No," she said with a shrug, "I don't suppose it does any harm..."

It was hardly a ringing endorsement, let alone a declaration of friendship, but it was something.

He gave the gelding a farewell pat, and they started across the meadow. He managed to hold his tongue, and it was Elidir who broke the silence, as they were passing the sprawling oak. "Why do you follow her?"

"Jerya?" *Dumb question. Who else would she be meaning?*

"The Vow-breaker. Jerya. Call her what you will."

"I call her 'aunt', mostly. I can't remember a time I didn't know her. She helped raise me. She was my governess for several years; but really, she was part of the family." *Though 'family's' got a whole lot more confusing since we came to the Sung Lands...* "But I wouldn't say I *follow* her. We're travelling together, that's all."

"So you take no part in her plans?"

"What plans?" He was genuinely confused, and perhaps it showed, for she stopped abruptly; so much so that he had gone another couple of strides before he caught up and turned back. "What plans?" he repeated, as if he didn't know full well that she'd heard him the first time.

"Well, we don't know exactly, but Master Perriad is sure she means to do the Guild harm."

"Is that why you followed us here?"

"Someone has to take it seriously."

"Do you really believe that? Anyway, if she meant to hurt the Guild, why come here, of all places? A little village, as remote as it gets... what harm could she do here even if she wanted to?."

"You don't think there's anything suspicious about our welcome here? Or lack of it, I should say."

She started walking again, and he scurried to catch up. "I don't know what you mean."

"Don't you? We haven't even got *beds*; I'm sleeping on a kind of stone shelf, with about two centimetres of padding beneath me."

"But *everyone* here sleeps like that," he said. He supposed that, like before, his bewilderment was clear in his tone; she didn't stop, this time, but she looked at him—really looked, he thought, in a way she never had before. "Look at... well, I don't suppose you can come to my room, but... you're on the Maidens' Level, I suppose?"

"That's what they call it, yes."

"Ask Sumyra or Sokkie, then. See where they're sleeping. And... you know that none of these rooms were reserved for guests? How often do you think they even have guests here? And when every chamber has to be chipped out of the rock, would you have several that you keep empty against that one time every few years?

"For each of you some girl's had to double up with someone else, or go back to her parents. Did you—you didn't know that, did you?"

She had the grace to admit it, and to look appropriately abashed.

"Why's Jerya here?" he asked then. "Because she was born here. Grew up here till she was nineteen."

"Nineteen? That can't be right."

"Why not?"

"Dawnsingers are Chosen at ten or eleven, not nineteen."

"Usually, yes, I know. There was something unusual about Jerya's Choosing; I don't know all the details, but why don't you ask her?" Seeing doubt clear in Elidir's face, in those lovely eyes, he added, "She doesn't bite, you know. I can promise you that."

❅

"As long as we're here," said Jerya, "There's nothing they can do. They've got nowhere with Singer Marit, which means Holdren won't take orders from them. And I think the others have finally convinced Perriad that keeping on badgering him, or anyone else, really doesn't show the Guild in its best light.

"But... As soon as we leave, and especially once we get beyond Thrushgill, they'll have a chance to try and ambush us again."

"Can't we just go round, like we did before?" asked Sokkie. Embrel smiled at her; he'd been having the same thought himself.

"They'll surely be wise to that trick this time. Keep a lookout from the hills on the edge of the plains."

"Could we go another way?"

"Well, maybe we could try, but... remember, we can't do anything this side of Thrushgill, because our horses are there."

"We could take theirs..."

Jerya laughed. "Sokkie, I love your spirit, but stealing horses from the Guild would be a great way to sour my relations with them. Maybe there'd be a lot more remembering that I was a Vow-breaker...

"No, that's definitely out. And as for a detour... I'll ask a few people. Holdren, Sardain... maybe Meladne, she's wandered a lot further than most of the women. But I was a wanderer too, when I lived here. And if the day was a bit clearer we'd see pretty well from up here. North of the main trail it's nearly all forest, slow going, and as you go further West there are more and more swamps. If there is a reasonable way through, it'll be Thrushgill folk who can tell us, but we can't bank on that.

"And going South... There's a river, runs down to Aldgrave. If we had boats, it might be a good idea... but you need a sizeable boat to carry four horses, and even if we had one I don't think any of us knows anything about managing one...? No. And either side of the river the terrain gets swampy again.

"We can ask in Thrushgill, but that only means we need even more time in hand. We've got to get a good head-start, because we're walking all the way there, and they'll be able to ride, at least the last few miles. And the only way I can think of to do that is by leaving *really* early. Well before Dawnsong."

Embrel groaned. He caught Sokkie's eye again and saw she felt much the same.

Chapter 28

# Embrel

"So he climbed down," said Jerya. "Back on one wall, feet on the other."

Sokkie, gazing down into the depths of the well, where an almost-circle of mirror-sky gleamed out from blackness, had an unusually thoughtful expression. She was seeing a new facet of her father, he supposed. *My father too*, he reminded himself. Though his picture of Rodal had begun with Jerya's first, condensed, account of their adventures—*First to make a double Crossing, and first to make a solo Crossing*—It had been hard to square that with the cheerful family-man they'd met in Carwerid, apparently quite content with the life of a publican.

"Fortunately for us, someone's replaced the rope," continued Jerya. "Peripatetics of the Guild, is my guess. They're using this track more often these days. Thrushgill, Delven, the other villages out this way, only used to be visited at long intervals. I don't remember ever seeing any Dawnsinger other than Sharess until I left home."

Embrel was checking the rope, which had been coiled in a chest under the nearest tree, when something whizzed past his ear. Something heavy... something thrown.

He spun around, and in that second, everything was confusion. He saw white-clad figures grappling with his companions. Before he could even fully grasp what was happening, a body slammed into him, shoulder driving low and hard into his belly, and all the breath fled his body.

If she'd known how to press home that initial advantage, his assailant might have ended the fight there and then. Fortunately for him, perhaps for all of them, she hesitated. It might only have been half a second, but it gave him the chance he needed, to force himself upright and, even before trying to re-fill his lungs, to push her away with both hands and all the strength he could muster. She staggered back a pace, almost fell over her own feet. Embrel had a sudden vision of her striking her head on the parapet of the well just behind. A fractured skull... what would happen in this land to someone who killed a Dawnsinger? Would the courts even entertain a plea of self-defence? If there were courts...

Besides which, he wanted to stop her, not kill her.

It was only then, in that fragment of stillness, that he realised that his assailant was Elidir. He almost groaned aloud. Not that he wanted to hurt any Dawnsinger—any woman, come to that—but how could he handle this? She was as tall as he was, near enough, but that elegant slenderness he'd admired had to mean she was least a stone lighter, probably nearer two. He had to have an edge there.

Then she darted forward again and he had no more time to think. She might be slender, but there was a surprising strength in those lean arms, and she fought fiercely. If she had matched strength with skill, he quickly saw, he might have been in real trouble. He had another momentary vision, Trevmy's face, a mocking smile, a Denvirran drawl: *let yourself be bested by a girl, Em?*

But that was the trouble: she was a girl, or young woman, and he did feel inhibition. To hit a lady... it simply wasn't done. To hit this particular lady... he wasn't sure what pitch of desperation could ever force him to it. If he could throw one good punch—Trev had taught him that much, at least (*you have the strength, Em, but strength's naught without timing*)—he was sure he'd lay her out. But his instinct, his entire upbringing, rebelled against it. *Has to be another way... but what?*

Then she went for his throat, and his mind went icy clear. They'd covered just this, in one of the few 'noble art' sessions he had attended. A swift thrust upwards with both hands together, to force the other's hands apart, off his neck. Follow through with a hard shove, as he had before, but this time back it up with a heel hooked behind her knee, taking the leg from under her.

She fell again, a safe yard from the well's rim now, and he dropped after her, flipping her onto her front before she knew what he was about. A knee in the small of the back.

"Just stop struggling," he said, bending low so his voice would be clear through all the racket of the other struggles. "If I put my full weight on your spine... well, I don't know what might happen. And I don't want it on my conscience."

She subsided, though he didn't dare let himself relax. And he was suddenly, shockingly, aware of the body beneath him, alive and warm and breathing rapidly. *But I knew that all along...* He had, but now he seemed to know it in a whole new way. He felt... he stopped himself, tore his thoughts away, looked up to see what was happening with the other battles.

Jerya, he saw first, was locked with Perriad, a strangely static struggle. Another, whose name he didn't know, was battling with Sokkie. It should have been an unequal struggle, the Singer half a foot taller, surely two stone heavier, but... he'd thought Elidir had fought furiously, but now he revised his opinion. Sokkie was like a wildcat.

It was Sumyra who seemed to be in difficulty. Her opponent, the heaviest-built of the four Dawnsingers, had forced her to her knees; and Embrel saw, with horror, that there was blood streaking the side of Sumyra's face.

Desperately, he cast about for a way to subdue the woman beneath him so he could go to Sumyra's aid. There was a whole rope, yards and yards of it, just a few steps away, but it might as well have been on one of the moons. Then he thought, if he could somehow free his belt, he could lash the Singer's wrists behind her back. That would give him the time he needed.

But then:

"Stop!" Jerya's cry rang out above all the clamour. "Just *stop*!" When it seemed to have no effect. she turned toward himself and Elidir. "Embrel, release her," he heard her say. "Elidir, come here. Sokkie, stop fighting." She had to repeat the instruction before it got through, but finally the girl settled, and she and the Singer with her fell into panting, glaring, stillness.

Cautiously, he began to lift his weight from Elidir's back. "Let's just keep calm now, shall we?" After a moment Elidir nodded. He scrambled to his feet and thought of offering a hand to help her up, but before he could decide if that was a good idea she was up and in motion. He followed to where Jerya was kneeling, half-supporting an inert form. Sumyra was beside her, holding Perriad's wrist. Then another of the Singers, the one who'd been grappling with Sokkie, pushed in. There was some conversation he couldn't hear, but its intensity was obvious.

As he and Elidir came up to them, he heard Jerya say, "Is there anything we can do, here and now?" Sumyra's reply was softer, but he caught something about 'a Healer'.

"Where is the nearest one, do you know?"

"The Adjunct House in Aldgrave," said the third of Perriad's company.

"That's a long way. I suppose it's possible in a day, but... she obviously can't ride at the moment, not on her own."

Sumyra shrugged. "I don't know about this. She needs food, though. Something sweet, I suppose, but not too heavy. And she probably needs to drink, too."

They had water, and Jerya produced one of her jars of honey—cherished souvenirs of Delven—but it was clear they were struggling to get the barely-conscious Perriad to swallow.

"I don't reckon she's going to be taking the reins any time soon," said Jerya, "And we need to move if we're to have any chance of reaching Aldgrave tonight."

There was an obvious problem: how to transport the stricken Dawnsinger. No one had conveniently left a cart—better still, something fast, like a phaeton—in the abandoned village. Someone suggested wrenching a door off one of the more intact houses to make a stretcher, but no one could see a secure way to carry such a thing between two horses, and they would surely have had to proceed at a sedate walk anyway.

Jerya was growing impatient. "There's nothing else for it. She'll have to double up with someone."

"Let me take her," said Elidir, meeting Jerya's gaze.

They renewed the discussion about whether Perriad could even sit on a horse, finally agreeing that she could not safely do so on her own. Therefore someone must double up. Again Elidir urged, "Let me take her."

"Have you ever ridden double with someone? Someone semiconscious at best? It's not easy, let me tell you. And she's frail enough already... can you imagine what damage she might do if she fell?"

Elidir looked troubled, but he could see she was reluctant to commit Perriad to Jerya's care.

"I know you don't trust me," said Jerya. "And you know I have no reason to love Master Perriad... But I'd be very surprised if I'm not the most experienced horsewoman here. And... Embrel's a good rider, and he might be stronger than me, but I'm quite sure she wouldn't want to double with a man."

Elidir and the other Dawnsingers still looked uneasy, but Jerya was resolute. Embrel knew it was little use arguing with her when her mind was made up. "Look, I'm not going to run off with her. Even if I wanted to, I wouldn't be able to outpace you when we're carrying two."

Embrel, who was probably the strongest, and certainly—apart from Perriad herself—the tallest person present, thought it made sense for him to be one of those to lift Perriad onto the horse with Jerya, but the Dawnsingers balked at that, insisted on doing it themselves.

While they struggled, Embrel and Sokkie stood alone. He strode across to her. "Remind me not to get into fights with you, he said, grinning.

"Were you planning to?" she sparked back.

"No, of course not... look, what I'm trying to say is, you did well. I'm proud of you, little sister."

"Not so little," said Sokkie, trying to make her voice an indignant growl; but then, perhaps surprising herself as much as she did him, she threw her arms around his chest and hugged him hard. He hugged her back.

※

"Singer Elidir. I hope you are not injured?"

She gave him a long cool look before replying. He could understand why she might be wary. "I have bruises in various places. Muscles strained... I am sure I shall be stiff tomorrow."

"I could say the same. You gave as good as—" He stopped himself. It all sounded too flippant. "I'm sorry. What I really wanted to say..."

What I really wanted to say is... *You have beautiful eyes. The way you walk is beyond any words of mine. I could look at the back of your head for an hour...*

"What I really wanted to say is that I regret very much the circumstances which placed us in conflict." Too stiff, too formal, but stiffness and formality might be exactly what he needed if he was to engage her in conversation at all. *What do they call it? The Principle of Detachment...* "From the first time we spoke, in the meadow, looking for the horses, I wanted nothing but... amity between us."

*Amity? Where did I dredge that up from?* He wanted a great deal more than 'amity'. The memory of those moments when she had been on the ground beneath him was so fresh it was almost painful. He thought of a pan on the hob, boiling so violently its lid threatened to fly off. He needed half his mind to keep the lid on, but that left only half to try and hold up a conversation that trod the narrow path between ugly formality and the undue intimacy that would surely outrage and repel her.

He did not know how this could ever go anywhere, but he could not stop himself trying to keep it going anyway.

He sighed. "I really don't understand. What were you hoping to achieve by ambushing... by waylaying us there?"

"You can't be unaware that Jerya is a Vow-breaker. *The* Vow-breaker, some of us call her."

"I'm well aware of that. You mentioned it the other day, but anyway, she told me herself, some years ago."

"But perhaps you are not aware that, on her previous return, the Conclave of Masters committed her to a year in confinement for the offence. Of which she served just five days."

"But... she's been in the College. No one did anything against her."

It didn't seem to impress the Dawnsinger. "That does not alter the fact that three hundred and sixty days of her sentence remain to be served."

He thought about that for a minute. Hooves thudded grittily on the vague trail. His horse flicked its ears at a fly.

Then he thought about another thing. "Even if you were meaning to... confine her again, did you really think... I mean, *here*? Back there, I should say, the abandoned village."

He had the dubious satisfaction of seeing Elidir look uncomfortable. His heart wanted only to say what would please her, but his head saw things differently.

"I'm sure it would only be temporary," she said after a moment.

"And what were you planning on doing with the rest of us? Me and my sisters?" It was the first time, he realised, that he'd said 'my sisters'. It gave him a warm feeling. Again he watched Elidir's face, the pleasure of doing so vitiated by the duty to pursue the argument. "Sokkie's only thirteen." It wasn't until that moment that he recalled: *no, she's fourteen today. Strange sort of birthday...*

"I have another question," said a new voice, startling him; Sumyra, on Elidir's far side. He had no idea how long she'd been there, having been so fixated on the Dawnsinger. "Who gave you a mandate to come after Jerya anyway?"

"The Conclave," said Elidir. Turning away to speak to Sumyra gave him the view of the back of her heard, a delicately-sculpted ear. It reminded him sharply of those moments when she'd been beneath him on the ground.

Some of the thoughts that had arisen then stirred again now, and he missed the beginning of Sumyra's reply; but he caught the end. "—Was ten years ago. Surely it's been repealed?"

"Only the Conclave can rescind its own rulings, and it has not done so."

"But by implication..." He well knew Sumyra's doggedness in debate. "We were received in the College. I was with her."

Elidir said nothing but a tilt of her head seemed to indicate doubt; clearly it seemed so to Sumyra. "I know non-Dawnsingers aren't often admitted, but Master Prime Evisyn invited me. I've met her before, you know." Railu's wedding; Embrel remembered it well. "Why, Master Perriad herself saw us. Confronted Jerya. She didn't say anything about locking her up then, and neither did anyone else. We had an audience with the Master Prime, we saw other people; we were there for several hours."

Again Elidir said nothing, only looking down and ahead, perhaps gazing past her horse's ears to the trail before them. "Well," said Sumyra in an innocuous tone Embrel knew could be deceptive. "Think about it. Meanwhile... can I tell you about my aunt Jerya? And Embrel... well, he's known her all his life."

She still looked dubious, and on impulse he said, "You're wrong about her."

Elidir slowed her pace, half-turned to stare at him. "How are we wrong? She broke her Vow. Walked away from the Guild, from a life of service."

"I guess that's true. But it was a long time ago. Before I was even born. And you can't be much older than me, you can't have been more than a babe, can't have known anything about it."

"No, but I've heard all about it since."

"A lot can happen in twenty years. My whole life, for example. And Sumyra's right, I've known Jerya all that time. She helped raise me. So don't you think, maybe, it's possible I know pretty well who she is? And, whatever happened before I was born, as long as I've known anything about it, she's been a friend to your Guild."

"Then why did she bring men from the Five Principalities into the Sung Lands?"

"What? When?"

"Ten years ago. The... Duke of something."

"Selton? Jerya didn't *bring* him."

"Didn't your friend tell you? Chamion?" said Sumyra, nodding to one of the two Singers riding just ahead. "We told them—her—when she came to the tavern. Told her the truth. And told her there were witnesses. Including the Master Prime.."

"Master Analind, too," said Embrel, who had met her not long after.

Still silence. "Look," said Sumyra, "Every summer since the Southern Crossing was established Jerya's helped the Dawnsingers who've come to the Five Principalities. Since she became Countess of Skilthorn she's been able to do more. Hosted meetings, that sort of thing."

"Sharing our secrets."

"Well, I don't know so much about that. But if anyone's sharing secrets, I don't think it's her. She was only a Dawnsinger—a Novice—for a few months, wasn't she? How many secrets would she even know?"

Once more the Singer had nothing to say. "Look," said Embrel, "I've not been at these congresses and things. But lots of people from your own Guild have. Master Analind's been every second or third year. Summer-schools, too; Sumyra can tell you all about those. But what I do know, I'm sure, is that it's not about giving away secrets; it's about sharing knowledge. In some areas the Five Principalities are ahead and you can learn from them." He saw her look and couldn't refrain from adding, "Believe it or not. But in other areas the Sung Lands lead. Medical matters, stuff like that." *Railu knows all about that*, he thought, and the follow-on came unbidden: *my mother*. It still sat strangely in his mind, but he wrestled his thoughts back to the present, and to Elidir. "Look, I know Jerya. I've known her all my life, like I said. And she's a good person. I don't know anyone... I mean, there's no one I admire more."

Then he wondered if he'd said the wrong thing. Saying you admired someone more than anyone else; was that too close to being a 'follower'?

## Chapter 29

# Sumyra

Having been nominated as the next best thing to a Healer in the party, Sumyra kept a close eye on Jerya and her inert passenger. As she did so, she kept revisiting the scene in her mind, wondering if there was more she could have done.

"I'm really not a doctor," she said.

"You're the closest thing we have," said Jerya.

Sumyra crouched beside the slumped figure. Responsibility settled on her, heavy as her backpack at the start of the Crossing. Did Mamma and Papa feel this way every time?

Suddenly Sumyra wasn't so sure she would want to be a doctor even if the possibility did arise.

But she bent close to listen to Perriad's breathing, aware of Jerya gesturing to the onlookers to be silent; and then she took Perriad's wrist. She was struck immediately by how bony it was. But she was more than half glad; it was usually easier to find a pulse on a thin person. And Perriad was thin; she could see sharp lines of shoulders through her shirt, an ankle where her divided skirt had ridden up.

A few moments later she looked up and saw faces change, reflecting something they'd seen in her own. "Her pulse is really irregular. Sort of... jittery. I'm sure Mamma or Papa could tell much more from it. I just know I don't like it."

"Here, let me," said one of the Dawnsingers, shouldering between Jerya and Sokkie. She grasped Perriad's wrist but after a moment she said, "I can't feel anything."

"Like this," said Sumyra, demonstrating on her own wrist. "Tips of the first two fingers. Just about there..."

The Singer tried again, and then said. "Oh. Yes it does feel... irregular." *Did you think I was making it up?* thought Sumyra, deflecting a surge of irritation.

"Is there anything we can do?" said Jerya. "Here and now, I mean?"

More than ever, Sumyra longed for her parents. To see Mamma or Papa come riding down the gritty track now... But there was no chance of that. She tried, instead, to use the thought of Mamma to summon that sense of calm she always emanated. Mamma herself, when Sumyra had said something like this, had laughed, likened herself to a swan, appearing to drift serenely while its legs paddled frantically under the surface.

"We could wait for a while, make her as comfortable as we can, and hope she improves. But it's only a hope. Really, I'd like to get her to a doc—to a Healer as soon as possible. They'll be able to tell much better what this arrhythmia means, what to do about it."

Jerya had sighed. "It's all too much like what happened ten years ago. I don't remember the arrhythmia, but then I never took her pulse. But the rest, the collapse, the sense that she was too thin; that's eerily similar."

"And what did you do then?" asked the Singer.

"We left her with some men from Blawith and asked them to take her to their Dawnsinger. Maybe we could have done more, but we were anxious to get through the Defile and up the steeps beyond before dark. This time I want to be sure she's seen by a Healer."

※

As the first trees began to show through the haze of early afternoon, Sumyra heard Jerya's urgent voice. "Sit still. Don't be a fool. I'm not going to let you fall. No doubt you'd blame it on me anyway."

If Perriad replied, Sumyra did not hear it, but when she heard no further admonition from Jerya she assumed Perriad had settled.

"I suppose I am now your prisoner," said Perriad after a moment.

"Not at all," said Jerya. "Look around you. All your companions are here. We're taking you to the Adjunct House at Aldgrave, to get some proper care."

There was another pause. Hooves thudded, the sound blurred on the sandy trail. The sky arched pale and empty. Sumyra couldn't recall seeing another living creature since early morning. Perriad seemed to have relapsed into passivity.

"It's not the first time I've had to make arrangements for her care," said Jerya. You said so already, thought Sumyra, but the remark was aimed at Elidir, on Jerya's far side

"What do you mean?"

"Ten years ago, after she attacked me—for the second—"

"—*Attacked* you?" Elidir's tone was full of disbelief.

"Both times before witnesses. The first time in front of the present Master Prime and at least one other current Master…"

"You must have provoked her."

"I've no doubt she'd say I did. But the point I'm really getting at, Elidir, is… the same thing happened, ten years ago, the second time. She'd pitched a tent, all on her own, near the mouth of the Defile—you know, at the start of the Southern Crossing?" Elidir murmured recognition. "And if she'd had any food with her she'd eaten it all, but I didn't even see a plate or a knife. Anyway, she collapsed, just like earlier today—and just like today she seemed frail, and very thin. Worryingly thin."

Her head was turned away: Sumyra imagined her giving the young Dawnsinger a searching look. "Tell me, have you taken note of what she's been eating? You've been travelling together for nearly two weeks..."

※

At Stainscomb, Jerya and Elidir went into a discussion with the Dawnsinger and the headman, while Sumyra and the other Singers tried to persuade Perriad to share some of their hurried lunch of hard flat bread and tangy white cheese. Despite their entreaties, Perriad took only a cup of water sweetened with honey. Nonetheless, she seemed to revive for a while, climbing into the saddle with assistance rather than being inertly manhandled—*woman*handled—into it.

Jerya explained the plan as soon as the rest were mounted. She and Perriad were on a fresh horse, loaned by the village; her previous mount, which had already done two hours with a double load, would rest at Stainscomb and someone would bring her to Aldgrave in the morning

The trail made a gentle climb through a network of small fields and thick stone walls. Sumyra supposed that the walls were made of stones cleared from the fields; cleared, rather, to make the fields. As they emerged onto a plateau of open pasture, Sumyra heard Jerya ask, "If you *had* managed to lay hands on me... what exactly were you going to do next, Master Perriad?"

"The Conclave sentenced you to a year's incarceration. That sentence has never been rescinded. By my reckoning you still have three hundred and sixty-one days to serve. As 364 was a leap year."

Jerya was shaking her head. Seeing Sumyra's wondering look, she gave a crooked smile. "There's actually a twisted kind of logic to it. They did pass that sentence and I suppose with everything else that happened around then, they never did annul it."

"And therefore," said Perriad, "In seeking to place you under incarceration, I do no more than enact the express will of the Conclave."

Jerya shook her head, but she was smiling slightly too. Sumyra supposed this to express a kind of admiration at the depth of Perriad's delusion.

Elidir, meanwhile, was frowning. "And yet," she said, "What you told me about your recent visit to the College, about being received by the Master Prime herself... does that not suggest that the present will of the Conclave is clear, at least by implication?" She paused, chewing her underlip. "But if that *is* the case, wouldn't it be better, for all concerned, to have it clearly stated?"

"Now *that* makes sense," said Jerya. "If I want to come back another time, I'd rather not have to deal with all this again. But it would have to be done quickly. Once we've brought Master Perriad safely to the Aldgrave House, I mean to make good time back to Carwerid, and I don't intend lingering there much more than another week. I have things to do back in the Five Principalities."

"How very convenient for you," said Perriad.

"Convenient? How?"

"I'm sure it's obvious to everyone. You hope for a hastily arranged Conclave, while I am detained in Aldgrave, so that you may exercise your blandishments unopposed."

Jerya puffed her cheeks, blew out a breath in frustration. "Yes, the Healers in Aldgrave will likely want to keep you there some time... but perhaps you can exercise your blandishments on them; perhaps they'll agree you can travel by carriage.

"Anyway, there's another question. Do you really imagine there'd be no one else able and willing to argue your case in your absence? That would suggest... either there are vanishingly few people who share your view, or that you don't think any of them are competent."

Perriad scowled but said nothing.

"Master Perriad," said Elidir. "I see that even riding like this, with support, is trying for you. I would not wish to see you subjected to the rigours of a longer journey until you are well recovered. But we three have ridden with you this last ten days. We are all familiar with your case against Jerya."

There was an undertone to 'familiar'. Sumyra saw Jerya smiling and had to suppress a grin of her own. Evidently, Elidir had heard Perriad's grievances more than once. But she had more to say. "Let one of us go. I will, if you wish, and I will present your case to the best of my ability."

Perriad frowned. "And what happens during your journey? Three days for this woman to turn her wiles on you."

*First blandishments, now wiles...* Sumyra had to subdue another smile.

"If I leave early tomorrow," said Elidir, "And if I use relay horses, I can do it in two days."

Jerya knitted her brows but said nothing; perhaps she was doubting Elidir's fitness for such a ride.

"Tonight," said Elidir, "In the Adjunct House, if there's anything else you think I should know, you can fill me in."

※

"Seems to me you've done well enough," said Margail, the senior Healer of Aldgrave, as Sumyra finished her tale. "It's not ideal, o'course, putting her through a journey like that." Seeing Sumyra's face, she gave her arm a reassuring squeeze. "I don't mean that; anything else you could have done would likely have been worse. Getting her here as fast as you could was the best of a bad choice. We'll get her properly settled now, properly assessed, but I don't reckon she'll be travelling any further for some while."

In the latter hours of the ride, Perriad had again lapsed into somnolence, had been lifted as a dead-weight from the horse when they finally reached Aldgrave. Sumyra watched now as she was settled on a stretcher and carried into the building. Margail gave her another squeeze and a smile and moved off to supervise.

As white-clad Healers and other Singers swirled around, some following the stretcher within, others attending to the horses, Sumyra found herself standing beside Elidir. "Did you hear what she said?"

"About Master Perriad, or about what you did?"

"Both, I guess."

"Enough. And I appreciate it, at least."

Jerya appeared before them. "I'm sure you want to see her settled, Singer Elidir, but would you give me five minutes? If you're set on leaving early, this may be my only chance."

"I *am* set."

"You've taken a lot on yourself. Riding to the city in two days… and then standing up before the Conclave."

Elidir shrugged. "If you agree that the issue should be properly resolved, then it should be done while you're still still in the Sung Lands. And if it's to be done properly, then both sides need to be heard."

"Would it surprise you to know that I do agree? The case should be argued fairly. And I will be there, but a day or two behind you.

"But while you're preparing your case, a little context…

"My problem with Perriad, or her problem with me… It's simple enough at root. I'm a Vow-breaker; we all know that. I left the Guild, left the Sung Lands altogether… and I took Railu with me. Of course Railu made her own choice, she's no one's puppet, but it's true enough she'd never have left if I hadn't been there. Anyway, we made our choice. I've talked before about the reasons behind it.

"Still, reasons or not, I know that's a terrible thing. Whatever else you think of me, don't ever imagine I did it lightly, or that I don't still think about it. I understand that you're outraged by it. But Perriad… Perriad took it personally. It wasn't just an affront to the Guild, it was an affront to her. That's the only way I can explain her attitude to me. Her obsession, really. She took it personally and I guess she brooded on it.

"Now, let's jump forward ten years. For ten years I'd been getting on with my life over there in the Five Principalities—and then I found out that the Duke of Selton was preparing an expedition, making a serious effort to find a Crossing. And at once I thought, *the Guild needs to know about this*. And, since I already knew a route, I came back.

"I presented myself at the College gates; I delivered my message. And immediately Master Perriad declared the whole thing was a fabrication. As if I'd spent ten years forging documents and coins, even clothes, solely for the purpose of... well, you'd have to ask her what she supposed I was trying to achieve. Mischief. Disruption. I don't know. The one thing she seemed unwilling or unable to conceive was that I might simply be telling the truth."

She levelled her gaze on Elidir. "But I was. We all know that now. You know it. In fact there was proof a few weeks after; even Perriad could hardly deny it. So she switched. In almost no time at all she went from saying I was making it all up to saying I'd brought them across. But that makes no sense either. "

Elidir nodded. "Sumyra told me about that."

Jerya nodded appreciation at Sumyra. "There you are then. If I'd 'brought' them to the Sung Lands, why wouldn't I just show them the route I already knew?"

"That's a fair question, I suppose," said Elidir. "But I'm not sure it proves anything."

"Harder to prove a negative, I know," said Jerya. She smiled. "That's something I learned in the College. Who taught me that? Tutor Brinbeth? One of my fellow Novices? By the way, remind me; what was Perriad's subject, when she was a Tutor?"

"History; specifically, history of the Guild."

"I'm not surprised. If she'd been a scientist she might have different notions of proof... I remember some interesting discussions about that." She smiled again. "Got hauled over the coals once; Brinbeth dragged me in front of Perriad for questioning why something was stated as fact when there was no definite evidence.

"Well, let's not get bogged down in my memories. Just to say: in a very small way I am a scientist. I do know something about proof, about evidence. So I don't want to claim anything I can't prove, or refer you to people who can. But..." Her gaze settled more firmly on Elidir. "If that's what you expect of me—and you should—you have to apply the same test to Perriad. And she's made all manner of claims, allegations, against me. Mostly without a shred of evidence that I can see."

Elidir looked thoughtful, but made no comment. Jerya also pondered briefly, leaned forward a little. "You might think I've got some nerve talking about Vows, but bear with me one moment. If I remember rightly, the Novitial Vow says *I shall defer at all times to duly instituted authority*... is that correct? And Final Vows are the same?" Each time, Elidir nodded. "And the duly instituted authority of the Guild is the Conclave and the Master Prime, isn't it?" Again Elidir nodded, but a wary look had crept into her eyes.

"Then I have to ask you. Do you think what Perriad's been doing—pursuing me half the length of the Sung Lands, planning an ambush in the Scorched Plains, ordering the villagers here to lock me up—is any of that compatible with *deference to duly instituted authority*?"

"The Conclave never explicitly forbade us..."

"Explicitly," repeated Jerya, with a small but unmistakable emphasis on the first syllable. She let the word hang in the air for a moment or two before going on. "But you know I've been received in the College. Sumyra and I had a meeting with the Master Prime herself." She glanced at Sumyra for conformation.

Sumyra remembered how she'd burst out laughing at one of the Master Prime's remarks, and then been mortified; but Master Evisyn had quickly set her at ease again. "She was very welcoming."

"Master Perriad would say you have too much influence on the Master Prime," said Elidir with what Sumyra thought was faltering defiance.

"That was the first time I'd seen her in almost six years," said Jerya. "How much influence can I exert from all the way across the Sundering Wall?"

The young Singer had no answer. Jerya seemed to read her troubled expression, and went on in a gentler tone. "I know not everyone agrees with the direction the Guild has taken. I know people are concerned that contact with the Five Principalities could be dangerous. Would it surprise you to know that I think they're right?" Elidir's face answered the question beyond doubt. "It is dangerous. Of course, it's said nothing worthwhile is without risk. And I've lived in the Five Principalities... in fact, I've lived there now longer than I lived in the Sung Lands. So maybe I know better than most... maybe, without sounding arrogant, better than anyone, except perhaps Railu... just what the risks are. And that's a big part, probably the biggest part, of any advice that I can offer to Master Evisyn, Master Analind, to the Conclave or the Guild as a whole.

She gave Elidir another keen look. "That's why I came back ten years ago... and your precious Master Perriad tried to undermine me at every step. To be brutally honest, I can't believe she had the Guild's best interests at heart. Not entirely, anyway. To me—and you'll find plenty of others who see it the same way—her judgement was warped by her obsession with me. And, yes, I was a Vow-breaker. I set my conscience over my Vow, ahead of deference to duly instituted authority. But ask yourself, Elidir, how different is what Perriad's doing? Isn't she setting her conscience ahead of deference in exactly the same way? And if that's true, what does that make her?"

Elidir sprang to her feet. "Are you calling Master Perriad a Vow-breaker?"

"I'm asking a question."

"It's clear what you're implying."

"If I'm wrong, tell me what the difference is."

But Elidir was already leaving. If there had been a door, thought Sumyra, she would have slammed it behind her.

Jerya sighed. "I guess I overplayed my hand there. Shame, I thought I was getting through to her."

"I think you were," said Sumyra consolingly. "Maybe when she thinks about it some more..."

"Maybe... or maybe I just pushed her back into Perriad's corner."

"And she'll be back in Carwerid before us..."

"Aye. But I suppose the Dawnsingers here have access to more rapid means of communication. And even if the Conclave does agree to meet—if

Elidir, and whoever else Perriad counts as allies, make a good enough case—natural justice demands they hear both sides."

Jerya considered a moment longer. "I'll ask the Adjunct House to send a simple message, just say that we'll be back in four days. And I'll be happy to appear before Conclave on the fifth."

# Part Three
## The Conclave

# Chapter 30

# Sumyra

"Master Brinbeth, I believe you have prior knowledge of Dawnsinger Jerya."

"I have prior knowledge of Jerya," said Brinbeth. "I understand she goes by another title now."

"Well," said Elidir, "Can you tell us about your previous interactions?"

"As is well known, Jerya was only here for about four months, and in that time she was not a regular member of any of my classes."

Brinbeth took a sip of water, and before she could resume Elidir jumped in with, "But I believe you had occasion to bring a disciplinary complaint against her?"

"I did." Brinbeth, Sumyra saw, was resolved to do no more than strictly answer the question; and Elidir was finding it unsettling.

"Would you tell us why you took that action?"

"I should say that, owing to her unusual situation, Jerya had licence to sit in on any class when not otherwise committed. On the morning in question she was sitting in with my third-year Novices. And she asked a question which some of the girls found... disconcerting."

"May I ask what that question was?"

"She asked, 'how do we know that the Journal-keeper was female?'"

There was a significant stir at this. Sumyra saw heads shaking, Singers whispering to one another. She didn't grasp the import herself. *Have to ask Jerya later.*

"Of course," said Brinbeth, "Simply asking a question, however outrageous, is not in itself a disciplinary matter. Jerya's offence lay in not desisting when I asked her to. She was rather persistent about it."

"In defiance of duly-constituted authority."

"Indeed. Specifically, in defiance of my authority as a Tutor—I was not a Master then."

"Would you say that her *persistent* defiance presaged the greater defiance she would later enact?"

Brinbeth's tone was tart. "That's too glib a conclusion for my liking. Jerya was overly persistent—unruly, I might say—but at the time I failed to reflect that, though she was of an age with the senior Novices, she had in fact been with us less than a month. Had I so reflected, I might have had second thoughts about instituting a formal process. I think I would have been wiser to speak to her privately, counselled her as to the standards of decorum appropriate to a Novice."

Again, Elidir looked disconcerted, but she rallied quickly. "Even so, Master, is it not possible that her, in your word, unruly conduct suggested a deeper deficiency in respect and due deference?"

Brinbeth gave her a look which Sumyra could easily imagine had quelled many an 'unruly' Novice during what must be a long career. She might do worse than practise such a look herself if she was to be a teacher. "Possible?" the Master said at last. "Yes, I suppose it's possible, but this is altogether too speculative for my liking. Speculation about someone's innermost thoughts and feelings is not evidence, as I regularly counsel my students."

Elidir seemed to have concluded that she would get no further with Master Brinbeth; she thanked her, and turned to Yanil, but Jerya's advocate merely waved a hand. "No questions." A hint of a smile suggested she was better pleased with the outcome of this phase of questioning than Elidir was.

"Thank you, Master Brinbeth," said the Master Prime, "You may stand down."

Brinbeth, however, did not move. "Master Prime, would the Conclave kindly indulge me by permitting me to say a few words?" Evisyn nodded. "As I say, subsequent reflection led me to consider that I was unduly severe on Jerya that day. I have sometimes wondered if, in my intransigence, I myself may unwittingly have provided some of the impetus driving her away from the Guild, though that, too, is speculation, not evidence.

"What I most particularly wish to say, while I have the opportunity, is this. I might not always see eye to eye with Jerya. I might not, indeed, always see eye to eye with you, Master Prime. As you well know, I have often counselled a little more caution in the pace of change, as it is currently enveloping the Guild.

"Nevertheless..." She paused, let the word hang a moment. "It is clear to me that Jerya did the Guild a service, ten years ago, in bringing us forewarning of the imminent arrival of men from the East; warnings which were dismissed by some but which, as we all now know, proved to be nothing more or less than truth.

"I also understand that in doing this, Jerya subjected herself to significant hardship, and placed herself at significant risk. Bearing this in mind, it is my belief that the sentence originally laid down was unduly harsh, and suggestive of rank ingratitude by the Conclave of the day. To seek to enforce it now serves no good purpose; indeed, it seems to me it will deprive the Guild of its most significant aid in the Five Principalities, and may substantially prejudice sentiment there against us. It is my opinion that to do so would be unnecessary, vindictive, and in all probability detrimental to the interest of the Guild."

Another round of whispered talk accompanied Brinbeth's slow progress back to her seat. Looking at Jerya, Sumyra saw that she was watching the limping Master with a fixed gaze, and that her eyes were suspiciously bright.

"Thank you, Master Brinbeth," said the Master Prime. "Singer Elidir, have you any further witnesses to call?"

"Master Prime, the witness I would most like to call is Master Perriad, but she is detained in Aldgrave. I wonder if we could adjourn, or reserve her testimony until later?"

"In ideal circumstances, no doubt the Conclave should hear from Master Perriad, but she holds no position of special privilege. I do not feel adjournment is appropriate, nor will I countenance undue prolongation of these proceedings. If you have no other witnesses, Singer Elidir, I propose to hand the floor to Tutor Yanil. At the conclusion of her witnesses' testimony, my fellow Masters and I will reassess the position."

Elidir had little option but to acquiesce.

"Call your first witness, Tutor Yanil."

"With your permission, Master Prime, my first witness is yourself,."

With a nod, Evisyn yielded the chair to Master Vakosh and took her stance where Elidir's witnesses had stood.

"Master Prime," said Yanil, "If you cast your mind back to the summer of GR 364, what was your position at the time?"

"My position changed more than once during that summer," said Evisyn with a smile. "You will need to be more specific."

"When Jerya first arrived, then?"

"I was Master of Peripatetics."

"And you took an active part in the discussions sparked by Jerya and the news that she brought?"

Evisyn smiled again. "You could say that."

"In fact, was there not an occasion when you castigated the Conclave for the course it was following?"

"There were several, but I think you may be referring to the time I told the Conclave that its course was folly."

"Why did you say that?"

"The simple answer is because it was—as I think subsequent events have amply confirmed. The Conclave was spending more time debating sanctions against one former Dawnsinger than addressing what might pose a threat to our very existence. And may I say, if there is anything on which Master Perriad and I agree, it is that we hold this Guild very dear.

"As we have heard from Master Brinbeth, Jerya did the Guild a service in bringing us forewarning of our impending visitors, but the Conclave was threatening to squander that gift by demanding impossible proofs before contemplating any action."

"This, I take it, was why you took matters into your own hands?

"It is. And I would do the same again."

"And what action did the Conclave take in response to your unilateral action?"

The smile was back. "First they dismissed me, then they made me Master Prime."

Looking around, Sumyra thought very few were surprised by this particular twist in the tale.

"Master Prime," said Yanil, "What was the first step you took at this time?"

"I released Jerya from her confinement and took her to the stables so we could ride to Blawith, where we had reason to believe our Five Principalities visitors would appear."

"And were there any witnesses to this?"

"There were two that I know of."

"Would you name them?"

"The then Master Prime, Master Kurslan, and Singer, now Master, Analind."

"And what action did they take? Did they help you, or try to hinder you?"

"Master Prime Kurslan helped us saddle the horses. Singer Analind rode with us."

"Is it correct that Master Prime Kurslan subsequently resigned, and the Conclave then dismissed you and installed Master Perriad as Master Prime?"

"Quite correct."

"But neither of those actions stood for very long, did they?"

"No, within ten days the Conclave first restored me to Mastership and then elected me Master Prime."

"On the face of it, this seems an extraordinary reversal. To what do you ascribe it?"

"I conclude that once they had received confirmation of the arrivals from the East—and indeed had seen those men for themselves—the Conclave was finally fully convinced that Jerya had been telling the truth all along. The doubts certain people had tried to instil could no longer be sustained. Further, having had a chance to confer with our guests, the Conclave recognised Jerya's important role as a mediator." Evisyn glanced at Jerya, just for a moment, with another hint of a smile. "I might even say she acted as a translator at times. We might be using the same words, more or less, but sometimes they seemed to carry very different meanings."

"Do you draw any further inference from the decisions of the Conclave at the Kendrigg meeting?"

"In restoring me, and then elevating me, it seems undeniable that the Conclave felt that my release of Jerya was a justified step. This, and the fact that at no time did any of the Masters suggest returning her to captivity, says very clearly that the Conclave was quite content to let the sentence lapse."

"Although it was never formally rescinded?"

"No, and of course that was a regrettable oversight. In our defence I can only say that it was a most unusual meeting, and we had much else to consider. But when Jerya left, to return to the Five Principalities, she left with the thanks and good wishes of the Conclave; and Master Analind went with her."

"Thank you, Master Prime. Have you anything further to add?"

"One observation, if I may. Having been a Peripatetic for almost thirty years, and having myself made the Crossing of the Southern route, I think I may claim a better than average understanding of the physical undertaking to which Jerya committed herself. But I must remind the Conclave, and all present, that Jerya had come by the Northern route. By all accounts, this route is more arduous than the Southern, attains higher altitudes, and is more exposed to bad weather. There is also one place, on the Five Principalities side, where it is necessary to tackle a very steep and difficult crag.

"I think the relative difficulty and danger of the two routes is underlined by this fact: in the twenty years since the first Crossing of the Northern route, led by Jerya herself, there have been only five or six more."

Sumyra mentally enumerated the tally of Northern Crossings:

*First: Jerya, Rodal—and her own Mamma;*

*Second, the following year: Rodal, return; still the only known solo Crossing by either route;*

*Third, nine years later: Jerya, Hedric, and Lallon (Jerya returned by the Southern route);*

*Fourth, same year: Hedric and Lallon, return;*

*Fifth, three or four years later: Tavy Selton and three companions (returned by the Southern route).*

There had been two or three more after that, but she couldn't recall the names.

"Bear in mind," added Evisyn, "That Jerya envisaged no benefit to herself in this. She took on the hardships and the physical risks because she believed we needed to hear the news. And what was her reward? Doubt, censure, and finally confinement. How did Master Brinbeth put it? Unnecessary, vindictive, and detrimental to the interests of the Guild."

"Thank you, Master Prime," said Yanil. "I think that is all I wished to ask you."

"Singer Elidir," said Vakosh, "Have you any questions for the Master Prime?"

"Thank you, Master; just a few brief questions. Master Prime, were you present at the Conclave when Jerya was sentenced to a year's confinement?"

"I was. I opposed it, of course."

"But how did the Conclave vote?"

"By... I think it was eleven to seven for confinement."

"And how long did she serve?"

"Approximately four days."

Elidir took a shaky breath. Clearly confronting the Master Prime, the head of her Guild, was hard for her; but she stuck to her mission. "And we have already heard you testify that you released her." Her voice went husky, and she hastily sipped water. "Let's move forward to the Conclave at Kendrigg, when you were reinstated and then elected to the Primacy. Did that Conclave also rescind Jerya's sentence?"

"As I've already said, in the heat of the moment, we overlooked that."

"I think the question required only a simple yes or no," said Elidir. Evisyn reacted with a slight smile. One might get the impression, thought Sumyra, that she was enjoying herself; and that she rather approved of Dawnsinger Elidir. "Master Prime, did any subsequent Conclave at which you were present rectify that... oversight?"

Evisyn smiled again. "No." *The question required only a simple yes or no...*

"And on the occasions when the Conclave convened in your absence, was there any vote on the question?"

"To the best of my knowledge, no."

"Thank you, Master Prime; I have no further questions."

"If Conclave will allow," said Master Vakosh, "I can speak to Singer Elidir's last question, since I was in the chair on those occasions—seven in number, I think, over the eleven years Master Evisyn has held the Primacy. At no time did we consider the question of rescinding Jerya's sentence." She looked at Evisyn; they seemed to commune a moment without words. "And now, as the time is well past half-past twelve, I propose that we adjourn. Unless you wish to retake the chair first, Master Prime?"

"No, I think it's a good time to adjourn. And perhaps, Master Vakosh, it would be as well if you remained in the chair this afternoon? It could be argued that I have too close an interest in this question."

"I think," said Vakosh, "That those who really wish to argue that might think I also was closely involved in the events of eleven years ago. I was, after all, in the chair at Kendrigg. Perhaps before adjournment the Conclave could decide this: should I continue in the chair, or should another be found?"

The vote was taken, and was sixteen for Vakosh, none against, and three abstentions—including, for reasons Sumyra took a few moments to understand, the Master Prime.

# CHAPTER 31

# SUMYRA

As soon as Master Berrivan grasped the nature of Sumyra's relationship with Railu, she welcomed her warmly, even giving the brow-to-brow 'kiss' which was the customary greeting between Dawnsingers after long parting. Her broad dark face was deeply lined; on first sight it had put Sumyra in mind of the close-packed contour lines on the maps Jerya had carried for the Crossing.

"You must tell me all about Railu's doings now, about her practice."

"Gladly, Master, and if I may beg a favour in exchange, I hope you can tell me a little about her when she was my age."

The Master's eyes twinkled. "I shall, and gladly, but would you oblige me first? You call her 'mother'?"

"I call her 'Mamma'. It means the same, really, but when I say 'mother' I think of the woman who gave birth to me. I never knew her, but Papa has told me much about her, and I know he loved her very much. I never imagined he would marry again, until he met Railu."

"They first met at the Skilthorn Congress, I believe?"

"That's so, and I met her a few weeks later. I think I already knew Papa had thoughts of marriage, but he had to be sure I would like her."

"And did you? What were your first impressions? How old were you, by the way?"

"I was twelve, Master. Six years ago." Sumyra's mind went back to those first few days. "It was a little strange, just at first."

"Why so?"

She felt herself reddening "I'd never met any Dawnsingers, not then, so the only bald women I'd ever seen were enslaved." She faltered, almost feeling herself twelve years old again, but Master Berrivan's eyes were kind. "And I saw very quickly that she was... different. It's hard to say how. She was... who she was. I suppose she must have had some anxiety as to whether I would like her or not; I think my father would have drawn back from marrying her if I had really disliked her. But she didn't let that make her fulsome or condescending. She seemed perfectly natural.

"And very quickly I knew that I did like her, and then that I loved her. On the day they were married, I said to her, 'now I may call you Mamma'... and tears came to her eyes and she hugged me very hard."

"I'm very glad. And you have lived with her—and your father too, I presume, ever since?"

"I've been to all the summer-schools at Skilthorn, until this year, and I joined the school when it opened, five years ago. Since then I've spent less than half the time at home—but it still is my home."

"I dare say, then, you know their practice very well? They work together, do they not?"

"Not every minute of every day, but they do take major decisions together, consult each other on difficult cases, and so on."

"And they treat all manner of people?"

Sumyra hesitated a moment. "It's complicated. The clinic, the whole practice, has to pay its way. And not all owners are willing to pay for treatment for slaves, or only for major injuries and severe illness. I know it bothers Mamma that she can't do more for the enslaved. I don't mean that Papa is indifferent," she added hastily. "But Mamma's first practice was all in the care of enslaved; I believe the very first case she treated was the coachman at Duncal."

"And she was a slave herself for a time...?" There was something in Berrivan's voice, her look. It might almost be grief.

Sumyra did not know what to say, except for the plain facts. "Eleven years, all told, before the law finally acknowledged that her taking—and Jerya's—had been false."

"Eleven years..."

"Yes, Master Berrivan; but I'm sure she would tell you what she's told me, that she had more opportunity to practise, even as an enslaved, than she probably would have had as Dawnsinger in Delven."

Berrivan sat up in her chair; Sumyra half-thought she was about to spring up and stamp about the room. "I've often wondered what more I could—should—have done to stop that, that—" She broke off, shaking her head. Sumyra supposed she had been about to say something that reflected ill on Master Perriad, who had clearly been the architect of the decision to banish Railu to Delven.

Was 'banish' too strong a word? She didn't think so. She was about to say something about her own impressions of the place, when Master Berrivan spoke again. "I can't tell you how happy it makes me to hear you say that. Of course I've heard from people who've been in the Five Principalities how well she's doing now, but I still hate to think of her spending all that time as a slave."

"She did, but I think... I think she would say it is always a terrible thing to be enslaved, but that for her, and for Jerya, it turned out about as well as it possibly could have."

Berrivan looked somewhat relieved, but another emotion quickly overtook it. "All the same, none of it would have happened if Perriad hadn't..." She looked ready to grind her teeth. "I'm probably going to say things I shouldn't... you know about the Principle of Detachment?"

"I do, Master, and I wouldn't expect—"

"—You're Railu's daughter. Or—what is it you said? Stepdaughter?—saying this to you is probably as close as I'll get to saying it to her face. And by the Seven, I'm not going to hold back."

Sumyra could only nod, to show that she understood, or thought she understood, the strength of Master Berrivan's feelings. "What Perriad did...

We lost one of our best Healers... and I daresay Jerya was a great loss to the Guild, too."

In complete fairness to Master Perriad, thought Sumyra, you had to recognise that she didn't actually expel Railu and Jerya from the Guild; they had, in the end, made their own choice to leave. But she saw that Berrivan had been nursing this particular grievance for a long time. *Since before I was born...*

"Well," said Berrivan, glancing at a clock, "They'll be reconvening soon. Shall we walk together?"

# Chapter 32

# Sumyra

"Tutor Yanil? Is there anyone else you wish to call?"

"No one else, Master Prime."

"Dawnsinger Elidir, have you anything to add?"

"Nothing, Master Prime."

"Masters, has any of you anything further to add?" There was a brief silence; the gathered Masters looked at each other, but none spoke. "Very well, we shall now proceed to vote.

"Item One: that the sentence of confinement enacted against Jerya, former Novice of this Guild, in Conclave on 12th Wythamès 353, be immediately and unconditionally rescinded. My Masters, how say you?"

Apart from the Master Prime, withholding her vote unless required to break a tie, there was only one abstention, and no votes against.

"Very well," said Evisyn, beginning to tidy the papers before her. "That concludes the agenda for this Conclave... unless anyone has any other business to suggest?"

Master Berrivan raised a hand. "Masters, may I claim your indulgence for a minute or two?" On Evisyn's nod, she continued, "First, may I say that I was very happy to support the motion we have just passed. Of course, breaking one's Vow is a terrible thing, and we must be clear that we still regard it as such. Exoneration is only to be considered under the most exceptional of circumstances. But the very significant service Jerya has rendered to the Guild since must be weighed in the balance.

"With all this in mind, I request that the Conclave, while recognising that Railu also violated her Vow, make a clear commitment that no penalty shall be imposed on her, should she ever return to our lands. Simple equity demands it.

"Tutor Yanil argued that Jerya had also been penalised already, in her treatment on arrival in the Five Principalities. If that argument is valid for her, then it must apply with greater force for Railu. Jerya, as I think you know, endured the conditions of slavery for only a matter of months. Railu remained enslaved for more than ten years."

*And that's not all*, thought Sumyra.

"Very well," said Evisyn. "Item Two: for the avoidance of doubt, Conclave resolves that no censure or sanction, express or implicit, shall stand against Railu, former Ordained Singer of this Guild. My Masters, how say you?"

This time there were no abstentions, save Evisyn's formal one, and again no votes against. Again, Evisyn was ready to close the meeting, but again Berrivan requested a little more time. "There is another matter—a related matter—this Conclave may wish to consider, though as you will see, it warrants further investigation rather than immediate action.

"I am grateful to Conclave for removing any prospect of penalty against Railu. We cannot say she has rendered quite the same service to the Guild as Jerya, but let's recognise that her home in Drumlenn is frequently the first and last house to welcome Dawnsingers visiting the Five Principalities. And let's recognise that she has become a notable example for aspiring young women and girls in those lands. Her position as the only licensed female doctor in the Five Principalities complements the work that Jerya has done in furthering female education. All this strongly supports the feeling I have long had, that she would have been a great asset to this Guild.

"Which leads me to say a little about the circumstances just prior to her, and Jerya's, departure. As we have heard, after Ordination, Railu was posted to Delven. I imagine this dismayed her; I know that it dismayed me and every other Healer who knew her and her capabilities. I live with the regret that other demands on my time and attention meant that I did not protest as strongly as I should have.

"But how, my Masters, are we to understand this decision to send her there? It was said by the Tutorial Office that her marks in Finals fell short of expectations, but they were still more than adequate, and she was in my estimation and that of my colleagues one of the most gifted Healers we had seen. What sense in posting her to a remote village where she would have little opportunity to practise her craft?

"I have long been convinced that this posting was a punitive one. In fact I am inclined to call it vindictive. Railu had a habit of asking awkward questions. In particular she wanted to know why the benefits of our knowledge should not be extended to the wider populace. In the light of the emphasis on service which has been our guide since the accession of Master Evisyn to the Primacy, one might say Railu's only offence was to be ahead of her time."

A scowl compressed Berrivan's dark features. "Even if Railu had stumbled a bit in her Finals—and I'm not for one moment saying that she did—but even if she had, it would still have been wrong, quite wrong, to send her somewhere like Delven. The recorded marks were still easily good enough for her to proceed to probationary practice.

"My Masters, I shall take up little more of your time, but I have one more thing to say. I mentioned Railu's marks in Final Catechisms—respectable, but far from what was expected; enough so that I was shocked, but before I could do anything I was called away to an influenza outbreak at Kendrigg. No one else pursued the matter. I can't blame them, there's always so much to do between the announcement of results, Ordination, all the new assignments... But what happened? I came back from Kendrigg—after we'd quarantined everyone, myself included, for an extra week—and she'd been packed off to Delven. It seemed to be out of my hands, and I had the usual influx of new Novices to assess..."

Berrivan sighed. "And by then, of course, we'd all heard that Jerya and Railu had disappeared off the face of the Earth, as it seemed at the time.

The whole question seemed moot. I won't say I forgot about it—the loss of Railu nagged at me often over the years—but there seemed no point in pursuing the matter. Until...

"Just a few weeks ago I was in conversation with Dawnsinger Kerstyl, who had been assigned to the Adjunct House in Carevick for many years. I happened to mention Railu and Kerstyl reminded me she had been an examiner for a couple of her Catechism papers. So I said something about her disappointing marks and Kerstyl said, 'but her work was outstanding'.

"Now, Masters, what was I to think at that point? Was Kerstyl's memory at fault... or had there been some discrepancy? As you can imagine, I have been giving this matter some thought, and I lay it before you now as one which requires further investigation. If there is a discrepancy, where could it have arisen but within the Tutorial Office? And I need hardly remind you that responsibility for the conduct of the Tutorial Office rests with the Senior Tutor of the day."

There was a considerable stir, both among the Masters at the main tables and among the rest of the gathering. Sumyra did not understand the significance, but she had felt Jerya shift abruptly in her seat, saw that her face had a new expression; not just the alertness with which she had followed every moment of the discussions, but something... fierce. When her aunt caught Sumyra's inquiring gaze, she leaned closer, whispered, "The Senior Tutor of the day was Perriad."

As Master Berrivan sat down, Elidir rose. She looked more nervous than she had at any point in the proceedings, even when questioning Evisyn herself. "Your indulgence, Master Prime; would Conclave allow me to make a brief personal statement?"

"I trust the reason for this will become clear very quickly."

"It will, Master Prime."

"Then please proceed."

"Thank you, Master Prime. As Master Perriad was unable to be here in person, I felt honour-bound to present the case that she intended to make. I have endeavoured to do so to the best of my ability.

"However, now Conclave has ruled, and especially having heard what Master Berrivan has just said, I find my own conscience requires me to say that I no longer believe in the case I tried to present. Would you permit me a few moments to try and explain?"

Evisyn looked around the other Masters, then gave Elidir the nod.

"Until a week or two ago, I was convinced by Master Perriad's arguments. As the Master Prime said when I took my Vows, the Vow is what makes you a Dawnsinger. Jerya broke her Vow, and the Conclave decreed a penalty. I believed that penalty should be enacted in full."

Elidir's voice was soft, hesitant; the room was hushed as those in the farther corners strained to hear. "I believed in Master Perriad. She said some things that made sense to me, and I let that convince me that everything she said was true. But now...

"I've had several chances to observe Jerya now, and what I've seen doesn't fit with Master Perriad's account of her. Master Perriad said that Jerya hated the Guild, but it doesn't look that way to me.

"Most of all, though, I want to tell you about what happened in the Scorched Plains, what I saw there. Master Perriad had said we must... apprehend Jerya. We laid in wait at a deserted village—I think it was once called Sollom—and we... well, we attacked them."

She recounted the struggle in more detail than Sumyra thought really necessary. Before she reached the key moment, she broke off to pour herself a glass of water. Sumyra saw that her hand was shaking, and a few drops splashed on the table top; but when Elidir resumed her voice was firmer. "Master Perriad was fighting with Jerya when she suddenly... collapsed. And it was Jerya who called on the rest of us to stop, to take care of her. It was Jerya—as the most experienced rider—who took her on her own horse all the way to the Adjunct House at Aldgrave.

"Then the Singers at the House in Aldgrave received Jerya as an honoured guest. What was I supposed to think then? Either Master Perriad was mistaken, or she had deliberately misled us. And when I thought about it some more, I could only conclude that, if Jerya was an honoured guest, then what we had done was directly contrary to the wishes of the Conclave. And on further enquiry, on my return here, I found that Jerya had been received in the College too; received by the Master Prime herself. Jerya had already said the same, and said that Master Perriad had seen her here; but Master Perriad said nothing of this to us. I supposed, therefore, that Jerya had lied; but it was clear now that it was Master Perriad who'd deceived us.

"And then I had to ask myself how that was compatible with 'deference to duly constituted authority'. Which meant..." Her voice wobbled. "I had to ask myself: were *we* now Vow-breakers?"

Back in Aldgrave, Jerya had implied something similar, recalled Sumyra; and Elidir had reacted indignantly. Now she was singing a different tune. Well, she would have had plenty of time for reflection on her hard ride to the city.

Either Elidir had said all she wanted to say, or she wasn't able to continue. An older Singer stepped to her side, whispered a couple of questions, then helped Elidir to a seat.

"Thank you, Singer Elidir," said Master Evisyn. "We can all see how much it cost you to say what you've said. I applaud your courage. I'll say no more at this stage, except this: I cannot believe that inadvertent contravention of one's Vows is to be viewed in the same light as a wilful and flagrant breach."

"There was nothing 'inadvertent' about Jerya's contravention of her Vows twenty years ago," snapped a new voice.

"Singer Benz'yor," said Evisyn, "May I remind you, Conclave is still in session. You should know better than to interrupt. As to your point... I remember something my mother would say to me, before I was Chosen; 'two wrongs don't make a right'."

"But wrongdoing is not to be—"

"Singer Benz'yor! *What* did I just say about interrupting?" Benz'yor looked down, already rosy cheeks reddening further. "Conclave is still in session, but we have ruled on the matter you're alluding to. If you had anything pertinent to contribute, you should have done so earlier. Since you did not... this Conclave does not revisit its decisions unless new information comes to light. We shall not do so now. Is that clear?"

Benz'yor flicked a glance at her, under her brows, then looked away again.. She said nothing. "Is that clear?" repeated Evisyn, and this time received a grudging mumble, too low for Sumyra to catch, in reply.

Evisyn asked once more if there was any other business, and finally finding none, declared the Conclave at an end.

## Chapter 33

# Embrel

"Dawnsinger Elidir," he said, startled. For one mad moment the thought tumbled through his mind: *has she come to see me?*

Of course her words immediately dispelled it. "Is Jerya here? I would like to speak with her, if it's possible."

"She's here, but she can't come down just at present."

"May I ask why?"

He decided it couldn't hurt to tell her. "She's having a bath." For which Jerya herself, as well as he, Sumyra, and Sokkie, had carried heavy jars of hot water up two flights of uneven stairs. "You're welcome to wait, of course."

She nodded, but looked around as if uncertain. "Perhaps you'd like to sit in that booth?" he suggested, gesturing. "And would you... would you allow me to buy you a drink?"

Elidir's face (*beautiful eyes...*) first registered startlement. Then, he thought, she briefly contemplated refusing his offer. Finally she gave a slight shrug and said, "If you wish."

"It would give me great pleasure." In normal discourse at home, that would usually be no more than a polite formula, but right now it was no more than the exact truth; perhaps even less.

A minute later he conveyed the agreed half of pale ale to the booth. "I've asked Sumyra to let Jerya know you're here." And, suddenly bold, and almost breathless with it, "Would you object if I sat down with you for a minute? I would like very much to speak with you."

Again she hesitated before acquiescing. "Thank you," he said, sliding in on the opposite side, but not all the way in, so they sat on the diagonal, not directly facing. He thought she would find that easier, and he saw, or thought he saw, a slight nod as if to acknowledge the consideration.

But she said nothing, only giving him a fleeting glance and then gazing down into her mug. Clearly it was up to him—of course it was, he'd asked for the chance. But now he had it, now she was in front of him, all the things he had thought, dreamt, of saying seemed to have vanished from his head.

"I hope you've suffered no lasting ill effects from our... encounter," he fumbled out after an agonising pause.

"I'm quite well, thank you." Her tone was cool, but the 'thank you' seemed vaguely encouraging.

"I would have... I would have regretted it very much if I had caused you any harm. I had no wish for any kind of conflict with you."

"I suppose we did... initiate the situation. But at the time it seemed the right and necessary thing to do."

"At the time?"

She took a slow deep pull, the angle of the mug suggesting she had drained a good third of it, before she answered, "Perhaps you've heard what I said to the Conclave; how I'd lost faith in the case I presented." Her tone was bleak, tugging at his heartstrings.

"It was a complicated situation," he offered, hoping to give a little consolation. "Confusing."

Elidir sighed. "Yes... It seems I put too much trust in someone I sh—" She broke off. "But I surely shouldn't be telling you this."

"I suppose not. And I didn't ask..."

"No, I appreciate that." She drank again; there could hardly be more than an inch in the bottom of the mug now. "But I hardly know who I can..."

"Is that why you wanted to see Jerya?"

"I wanted to ask her something. I can hardly expect to load all my doubts and worries on her, though, can I?"

"You might find her more sympathetic than you think." He watched, but doubt lingered in her eyes. "But I'm sure there are people—Dawnsingers, I mean—who would be happy to offer help. Like Tutor Yanil; she seems very kind to me, and Jerya thinks very highly of her. Or... there's an old Singer called Sharess. She was Dawnsinger in Delven... I mean, she was the one who Chose Jerya. Jerya made a point of visiting her when we arrived." He thought a little more. "Maybe Master Analind would be best of all. She knows the Five Principalities as well as any Singer, and she's known Jerya a long time. But she's not here right now..."

"Thank you. I'll bear them in mind." She drained her mug.

"May I get you another?"

"I don't... are you quite sure?"

"It's still my pleasure." *I would expend my last penny for you.*

He fetched a fresh half for her, had his own topped up. As he carried the brimming vessels back to the booth, it came to him this would probably—surely—be his last chance to speak to her, certainly alone. It might—awful thought—be the last time he ever saw her.

Was it possible to say nothing? Was it even right to leave her in complete ignorance of the way she made him feel?

"Singer Elidir," he said, setting the mugs down. For all his care, a little beer spilled onto the table. Her was inexpressibly relieved he hadn't splashed any on her white garments; even the pale ale would show up.

He sat, wiped the base of her tankard on his sleeve, passed it across. "There is something I feel I must say, but I should say first that I know I can expect nothing from you. Perhaps I have no right even to say this."

A slight frown creased her perfect brow. She looked at him in silence, curious or perplexed.

"Elidir, ever since I first spoke to you, in the meadow below Delven... ever since that day I have... I have felt as if nothing mattered to me more than your good opinion."

There. He'd said it; said *something* anyway. He snatched up his mug, almost creating a fresh spillage.

"I'm not sure I understand," she said slowly.

He sighed. "I hardly know how else to say it without embarrassing you worse than I fear I have already."

Light seemed to be dawning, but she did not look as if the realisation pleased her. How could she be? She was a sworn Dawnsinger. And he... *maybe I'm just a fool.*

"I'm sorry," he said. "It was probably wrong of me, unfair, even to say it. But the feelings in my heart—"

From his perspective, there could hardly have been a worse moment for Jerya to appear, hair still black with damp and loose down her back. Or was it the perfect moment? Perhaps she had saved him from worse embarrassment—embarrassment for himself, or for Elidir..

Anyway. there they were, Sumyra close behind. His chance had surely gone... but really, chance of what? He made himself smile, and made way for Jerya to slip in and sit opposite Elidir, while Sumyra took the place facing him.

❄

"You wanted to ask me something?" said Jerya without preamble.

"I'm trying to understand what really happened between you and Master Perriad."

"Ten years ago, or twenty?"

"I suppose it goes back... I mean, it was twenty years ago you broke your Vow."

"It was, and I don't seek to minimise it. But the Vow I broke was to the Guild, not to Perriad. So why does she still feel so strongly when most of the Guild is happy to let bygones be bygones?"

"That's what I am wondering."

Jerya sat back, considering. "You know, in a way I owe everything to Perriad. I didn't really grasp until I got here, to the College, just how irregular my Choosing was. I was nineteen, hardly educated, Chosen by a village Singer rather than a troika of Peripatetics. As soon as I was brought before Perriad—Senior Tutor Perriad, she was then—I began to see. And it was pretty clear that she was thinking of sending me right back home again."

She smiled. "You may think it would have been better if she'd done just that. I don't know what difference it would have made to the Guild, but I know my life would have been utterly different. I'd probably have ended up back in Delven. I'd never have crossed the mountains, I'd never have met my husband, I wouldn't have my daughter." She blinked, evidently restraining emotion.

*And I wouldn't exist either...* It was obvious, really: if Jerya had been sent straight back—or if she and Railu and Rodal hadn't ventured the Crossing—if any of a dozen things, probably, had been even slightly different... *I wouldn't even exist.*

Sumyra would, he realised, and Sokkie, but he would never be there to call them sisters.

Jerya sipped her drink. "I wouldn't have had my time in the College, either. I know it was only four months, but it shaped me, and it gave me friends I still love."

"And yet you left," said Elidir.

Jerya nodded heavily. "Yes, and it was the hardest choice I ever had to make."

"And I'm still not sure I understand why..."

Jerya looked almost as if she were considering the question for the first time. "Certainly two reasons," she said at last. "Perhaps even three. First—in time, if not in order of importance... well, you've been to Delven. Did you ever go on up above the village, one of the crag-paths, up to the edge where you can see the mountains?"

Elidir admitted she had not. That was a shame, thought Sumyra. Jerya had made sure she and Embrel, and Sokkie, had done so. It was not that Delven's mountains, at least as seen from Wisket Moss, were higher or more savage in appearance than those they had passed on their Southern

Crossing—though they were. The real significance was that they were the mountains Jerya had gazed at and wondered about all her life—as she was now explaining.

"And then," said Jerya, "There was the moment I learned that the Dawnsong didn't have the power everyone in Delven had always believed it had. I didn't discover the truth till after I'd said my Novitial Vow. I felt like I'd been deceived, that I'd made the Vow under false pretences... but even that might not have been enough to drive me to do what I did."

"You said there might be three reasons?"

"Yes. And the third... well, you heard what Master Berrivan said about sending Railu to Delven. I'd grown up in Delven; I suppose I knew better than anyone just how wrong it was."

Elidir seemed satisfied, or at least to have run out of questions. After a few more minutes, she drained her glass, then gave him a glance; the first time, he thought, she'd really looked at him since Jerya had arrived. "Thank you for the drink."

He watched as she walked away.

# Chapter 34

# Sumyra

As the boys and their excited chatter moved away, Sokkie following, Sumyra abruptly found she could hear everything Embrel and Rodal were saying. She hadn't intended eavesdropping, any more than she had meant to overhear Mamma and Jerya, that day back at home, but she didn't want to disturb them by moving.

"You ought to be famous," Embrel was saying

"What, for our ale?"

Embrel laughed. "Yes, why not? But that's not what I meant. You were the first person to cross the mountains and return. The first to make a solo Crossing too. That should be better known, I think."

Sumyra kept her eyes on the steely blue water with its flashing white crests, but she couldn't so easily turn her ears away. "My proudest boast," said Rodal, "Was being the first to see both oceans. First in this Age of the world, anyroad." Finally his gaze came back to Embrel. "I sailed on the Eastern Sea, did you know that? Ship called the *Levore*."

"I think Jerya said something about the *Levore*. She's sailed on her too, I think."

"Did she, indeed?" Rodal chuckled. "Ha, I mighta guessed. Seems like there's not much Jerya ain't done. Not as crew, though, I don't reckon. Not for eight months." He sighed. "It was a good life, that. If I hadn't made promises, to Jerya and Railu as well as to Annyt, I don't know but what I'd probably have stayed with her."

A new urgency entered his voice "Did she say owt about her? About the Skipper? He were one o' the best men I ever knew, besure."

"Sorry, not that I remember. It was a while ago; when she was still my governess, I think. It was like a story she told. Climbing the mast and looking out at the horizon."

"Climbed the mast, did she? While she was at sea, too, I'll be bound; well, that's Jerya for you. Even in Delven, in long skirts and sandals, she was a climber. I mean, we all were, somewhat. Had to be, living there... but you've seen it. Did you see the bridge to the maidens' level?"

Sumyra had, and she'd crossed it with great care every time, always holding the single rope that was the only 'handrail'. More than once she'd shuddered to see girls younger than Sokkie scampering across it, just as Rodal said, in sandals and floor-skimming skirts.

Embrel must have nodded. "Well, then, you've an idea. But Jerya always went further than the rest. And when we made the Crossing..."

"The First Crossing," said Embrel. "How did... how did Railu go on the Crossing?"

"Tell you true, lad, she struggled. But then she hadn't been brought up wi' rock all around like me'n'Jerya. She'd been up on the hill, in the College, from a wee girl, and I don't reckon they teach 'em climbing there, nor even rough walking. It was strange to her, even just walking all day, carrying a load. It's no wonder she found it harder'n what we did. But she kept going and... you know, I don't recall her ever moaning. And now, you tell me, she's a doctor."

"She is. The only female doctor in the Five Principalities."

"Never mind saying I should be famous; what about her?"

"It's strange... I've known her all my life, or thought I did, but since we came here I've learned things about her I never knew, never even guessed at. Big things; huge things."

"Aye, lad," said Rodal, "It's a lot to take in, besure."

"But I still know even less about you. We're supposed to go back soon, but it's not been long enough. And... it just occurred to me. I met your parents in Delven, but Railu had parents too. Probably still has, they might not be more than sixty... Do you know anything about them?" he finished in a rush.

"Not really. Railu came from somewhere called... Kermey."

"Kermey? She called herself Railu Kermey, after she was free. And now it's Railu Kermey-Skelber... Where is it, do you know?"

"On the coast somewhere, I think, down in the Sou'west."

"Did she ever talk about it? Or them?"

Rodal sounded regretful, even apologetic. "Remember I mostly only knew her on our journey to Delven, and on the Crossing—and then we hardly had breath for talking, half the time. I don't recall she ever said much more than the name o'the place... You're better off asking Jerya."

"On the coast, you say. A place like this?"

"Nay, lad, I don't know no more about it. Jerya might, or there's books, ain't there? Descriptions of places, you know."

"Or maybe I could just go there."

"It's like to be a long journey. Farther'n Delven, I shouldn't wonder. And... ain't you got to be starting back next week?"

"Well, that's the plan." Jerya was anxious to get back to her daughter and her school. "But... they're my grandparents, you know?"

"And right now you don't even know if they're still in the same place." Embrel looked at him. "Well, people move, don't they? I'm proof o'that. So's Jerya... aye, and so's Railu."

Embrel said nothing. Beside him, Rodal shifted on the rock. "You'd think, growing up in Delven, I'd be used to sitting on stone. Happen my arse has got soft, living all these years in the city. But I've been a city fellow half my life now." He shook his head. "Where does the time go? And speaking o' time..."

He called out, "Sokkie! Lads! You ready for supper...? Don't rush, them weeds are slippery."

"I need more time here," said Embrel. "More time with you, and Sokkie, the whole family. And I'd like to find my grandparents."

"Don't you have to be back, though? You got your own College to go to, don't you?"

"It's the start of my final year. But I could try for a deferment." He didn't sound certain.

"Or you could come back next summer. Wouldn't that be better? Happen by then we could find out about Railu's folks..."

"She might have brothers and sisters, too," he said. "They'd be my cousins."

"And if she did, they could be anywhere. Anywhere in the Sung Lands, anyroad. Take time to find out, likely."

Sokkie came up, hair salt-tangled from the ceaseless breeze, her face gently flushed. There was a glow about her, perhaps just from being there in such a place, perhaps also pride at having safely shepherded her unruly brothers. Sumyra, freed to move now, felt a surge of affection, and she suspected Embrel would miss her sorely. His next words seemed to bear this out. "I don't know that I want to go back."

"Seems to me," said Rodal, getting to his feet, "There's one person in the Five Principalities you need to see, more than anyone."

Embrel only sighed. Sumyra could well imagine how mixed his feelings were about seeing Railu again.

Rodal said no more, but held Embrel's gaze a second before turning to his offspring. "Right, who's hungry? Fish'n'chips? No, I'm not giving anyone a back until we're off these rocks."

※

"I heard what you were saying, you and Rodal. Some of it, anyway."

They were out on the fore-deck of the canal boat, though a fretful breeze was keeping most of the passengers inside.

"I'm sorry," she added. "I didn't mean to—"

"—It's all right. Neither of us said anything I'd mind you hearing."

She gave a relieved smile. "I was going to try and quietly move away, but it'd be hard on those rocks. And then you started talking about grandparents, about Railu's parents. I can see why you'd want to meet them—but like you said, you have to be back before the start of term."

"I could get in a lot of trouble if I wasn't there. Specially as it's my final year."

"Well, that's what started me thinking. I don't have start of term to worry about. First time in years. And... well, who knows? Next year I might—just might—have it to think about again."

"In Velyadero."

"Exactly. But this year... I think I might stay a little longer. I could go down to Kermey. There'll be mail-coaches or something, I'm sure." She fixed her gaze on him. "I could go for both of us."

"She's my mother."

"But she's my Mamma."

He looked away, ahead; for a moment they both watched the patient, apparently tireless, horse, its gait so steady it seemed like it could go on for ever. But the canal curved to the right not far ahead, and then they would see Carwerid rising ahead of them.

He sighed. "I think there's also a part of me... going back's going to be strange. I feel like... Railu, my parents... I've known them all my life, but now..."

"You're going to feel awkward. Shy."

"That's it," he said. "Shy. You feel it too..."

"I know she's not my true mother, but she's my Mamma. For six years she's been the closest to a mother I've ever known. But now I know something about her I never knew before. And... just the fact that she kept that secret from me all that time... I really don't know how I feel about that." She squared her shoulders. "Maybe seeing where she came from, meeting her family; maybe that'll make things clearer. And I think—I hope—maybe hearing about them; maybe she'll be glad of that."

※

"I'm really not sure," said Jerya.

Sumyra had anticipated this. "Just remind me, aunt, how old were you when you set out on the First Crossing?"

Jerya's sigh had the air of I knew you'd say that. "I think you know that already."

"You were nineteen. And Mamma—Railu—hadn't even had her birthday. She was scarcely older than I am. And unless you're going to tell me eight months makes all the difference... Anyway, I'm not going to be doing anything like that. Not remotely like that."

"You might still be doing the return Crossing on your own."

"A Crossing with refuges, cairns, a good map." She almost laughed. "You mentioned good maps before, didn't you?"

"Did I? When?"

"When we were riding from Kerrsands Bay to Arklid. Don't you remember? It was just after you'd asked me if I'd like to teach geography."

"Ah..." said Jerya, soft as a sigh. Again Sumyra had the sense her aunt knew what was coming next.

She had no intention of disappointing her. "The more I see of the Sung Lands, the better I'll be able to teach about it."

Jerya pressed her lips together, pushed a breath out through her nose. "But what am I going to tell your Mamma?" It was the *am I going* that told Sumyra she'd prevailed.

And in that moment she didn't know whether to be elated or terrified.

# Chapter 35

# Embrel

"Well," said Jerya, "I'm still a little uneasy about leaving Sumyra behind, but the die's cast now. And I suppose this is the trip I originally promised you, just the two of us."

Embrel nodded, but made no immediate answer. The strath stretched before them; if anything it looked even browner than it had six weeks before.

"I'm not going to press you," she said after a spell. "You've had a lot to take in. And I may not be the person you most want to talk with anyway. But let me ask you one thing. Who do you want to see first when we get back to Drumlenn?"

He saw what she meant. The logical thing, on arrival, would be to go to Railu and Skelber's house first. If Sumyra had been with them it would have been unthinkable to bypass it.

He gave her a flickering glance, drew breath. "Whichever order I see them in, it's going to feel strange. I suppose seeing Railu first gets it done with sooner."

In the corner of his eye he saw her nod. "Makes sense. Anyway, you don't have to make any final decisions for a few days yet. Let me ask you something else. Are you any nearer knowing what you want to do after you finish your degree?"

He sighed. "What I want to do and what I *should* do may be two different things."

Jerya said nothing, just walked on beside him with that steady, seemingly tireless, stride. How old was she? he wondered suddenly. As far as he was concerned, Jerya had always been there. He could hardly say she'd never changed; she'd married Hedric, become a Countess, founded a school... and that was just the start. Still, something in her seemed to be always the same; even calling her 'aunt' really changed nothing, seemed rather to recognise what had always been true.

He could have asked, he supposed; he didn't think she would mind; but he left the question unspoken. The crunch of their boots and the faint whisper of breeze in dry grasses were all the sounds in the world.

Then a buzzard's mewing cry, somewhere high above, broke the train of his thought.

Jerya still didn't press him to say more, but her silence was as good as an invitation. "I know how much it's cost them to put me through University. Ever since Grevel..."

"I never liked him, you know," she said unexpectedly. "His wife, Nielle, she was kind to me. She spoke to me, the day of my manumission—"

"—It's hard to think of you being a slave."

"Not as hard as being one," she said, and her mild tone was almost harder to bear than wild rage. "Well, Nielle spoke to me when no one else did, none of the other guests, but then he—Grevel—called her away. I'd thought I might have found a friend, but he put a stop to that. I'd never warmed to him before, but I liked him a lot less after that."

"Of course."

"I blamed myself, you know. I kept the accounts—" She laughed, unexpected, almost shocking in the hushed valley. "D'you remember asking me once, 'what's accounts'? It was the day I first met Hedric."

"I remember that day. I don't remember asking you that question."

"Well, it was—what? Ten, eleven years ago? You were ten, I'm sure... I'd already been doing the accounts for some years by then, and I carried on until Hedric and I were married. I'd begun to suspect something was amiss, so we'd put a few precautions in place. Otherwise it could have been a good deal worse."

"Maybe that's why he didn't like you. He knew you were smart."

"Not smart enough to stop him completely. When I heard he'd absconded, and taken everything out of the trading account... I felt terrible.

"And I remembered what I owe them, your parents. If they hadn't been in the slave-market that day... I don't suppose I'd ever have met Hedric." Her voice was uncharacteristically tight. "If they hadn't bought me and Railu. I certainly wouldn't be a Countess... and I'd never have known you."

Embrel stopped walking. "If they hadn't bought Railu I wouldn't be who I am. I'd probably be a slave myself."

Jerya had gone on a couple of paces before realising; now she swung around, stepped back, reached for his hands. "That too... I know it's strange, all this, but... you just said it. 'Who I am.' You are who you are, and they are still your parents."

"Maybe I owe them even more than I thought..." She eyed him quizzically. "You see, I've been thinking, and it came back when you asked me about what I was going to do after my finals. I thought about all the sacrifices they've made to keep me in school, to put me through college... I thought the best thing I can do is go back home and help out however I can. Maybe I can be my father's estate manager. He's been trying to do it all himself since Grevel... It's wearing them down, I can see, and they're not getting any younger."

"They're fifty-five, not ninety-five."

"Even so."

She nodded slowly, released his hands, and by unspoken agreement they walked on. The cry of the buzzard came again, more distant now.

"Embrel..." said Jerya after a moment, but then she stopped.

"Yes, aunt?"

"Whatever else I might say about this, I admire you for it, for wanting to help; I admire that very much... But do you think that's what they made those sacrifices for? Do you think they put you through school and university just so you could come back and be estate manager?"

He hadn't thought of it like that, and after a moment he said so.

"They're proud people," said Jerya. "Proud in a good way, I mean. And they love you very much. That's two reasons why you might find... They'll think it just as admirable as I do, they'll be immensely proud of you, but still you might find quite a lot of resistance to your notion."

"But I can't just do nothing."

"I understand, but... you know I tried to help, too?"

"You bought the enslaved they had to sell."

"We did, but they wouldn't just let me make them an offer. They had to be sold at market price." She sighed. "I'd rather have paid three times market rate than go back to that slave-market... you know I hadn't been back since the day I was sold? It was bad enough going to other markets..."

"But you went. You didn't just get Hedric to do it."

"I did. I think I nearly crushed Hedric's hand, standing there. But I knew what I owed them. I'd have done more if I could... if they'd let me." She didn't spell out what else she might have offered, and Embrel didn't ask. He preferred not to know, because the most obvious thing he could think of was offering to pay for his education. Jerya would no doubt have said that Skilthorn could easily have afforded it, but even the wealth of that vast estate was finite. He knew they'd sold several sculptures and paintings to help finance the new enslaved-quarters and all the alterations in the main house.

They walked on in pensive silence for a while. The crags ahead were starting to look solid now, no longer mere hazy sketches of themselves.

"Just suppose..." said Jerya at last, "Just suppose your parents didn't have the problem. Suppose one of them inherited from a distant relative, or... well, it doesn't matter how. Just supposing you didn't have to worry about them; in that case, what would you be thinking of doing next?"

It wasn't a welcome question. He tried not to think about it too much, to dream. A distant relative... it sounded like a kids' story, not something that happened in real life. Real life was tough, and it only got harder to take if you let yourself harbour dreams that were never going to come to fruition.

But this was Jerya, the person who for most of his childhood had been almost closer to him than his real parents—

He almost stopped in his tracks at the thought of 'real parents'. That was real life, all right, getting even more complicated. But he supposed it showed that he still thought of them that way; and he'd discovered in the last few minutes that he was still resolved to do what was right by them, and for them.

But Jerya, whom he'd called 'aunt' before the revelation in Carwerid, and whom he still called 'aunt' now... Jerya had asked the question and he ought at least try to answer.

"You know what inspired me the most, last year?" he said. "We had a talk from Tavy Selton."

"You know I first met him not far from this very spot? But of course, I showed you on the way in."

"He talked about archaeology. A new subject, he said, but dealing with old things... You know, I suppose that abandoned village—where we had the fight with the Dawnsingers..." He stopped, because that brought back so many thoughts about Elidir. *Shebb! That spragging thing called Real Life again...*

He shook his head and made himself go on. "I suppose you could try and find out what was left there. That would be a sort of archaeology. Throw some light on why it was abandoned. Selton's done several trips into the South of Buscanya; there are abandoned settlements there too. Some possibly a lot older than the one on the way to Delven."

## Chapter 36

# Sumyra

There wasn't much at the crossroads except an inn, and that had a run-down, cheerless look. Sumyra hefted her pack and squared her shoulders and ventured in.

She saw only two other customers, hunched close together in a corner, talking low as if there were some actual risk of being overheard. Sumyra marched past them to the bar. There was no one in attendance, but she saw a small bell and after a few moments she lifted it and gave it a shake.

A woman appeared from somewhere behind, stocky, damp-eyed, with straggling grey hair. She didn't look overly pleased to see Sumyra, though the place looked like it could use all the custom it could get. Still, her greeting was civil enough. "What can I do for you, Miss?"

"Please, can you tell me how to get to Kermey?"

Perhaps the woman raised an eyebrow at her outlandish accent; perhaps she only imagined it. She appeared to give it careful consideration before answering. "Down th'road, facing when you step out."

"Thank you. How far is it?"

More cogitation. Were travellers to or from Kermey so rare? Was it further than the coachman had said ('just a few miles')? "Four—five miles, belike."

It was further than she'd hoped, but it had to be overall downhill. And she was a veteran of the Crossing—with a pack considerably heavier than the one she bore now. Still, "I could use a drink to set me on my way, then. And do you have anything to eat?"

"It's early for owt hot. I were just choppin' onions." That explained the leaking eyes. "I could do you a bit o' bread an' cheese, belike."

"That's perfect, thank you. And a small-beer, if you will."

※

There was indeed a gentle downhill trend, with switchbacks easing the gradient on a couple of sections of steeper ground. She could hardly be making less than three miles an hour, and she had been going, with only brief stops, once for water, once to relieve herself, for fully two hours. 'Four—five miles' had turned into at least six, and as yet she had seen only scattered houses, and clearly she was still some way above the sea.

The first person she saw—the first she'd seen since leaving the inn—was a woman stooping in a potato-patch. "Good afternoon," called Sumyra.

The woman straightened slowly, putting a hand to the small of her back. She was, Sumyra thought, probably in her fifties, stocky, and about as dark as herself. "How do."

"Can you tell me, please, is it far to Kermey?"

"Well," said the woman, screwing up her face as if the question required deep thought, "Belike you might say you're in Kermey a'ready, 'cos I don't know where else you'd call it." She smiled. "But most folks live about the cove. Past that bluff there and you'll see it."

"Thank you." It wasn't unalloyed good news, as the spot where the road disappeared around the bluff looked to be a good three-quarters of a mile away. She told herself it could have been worse. "Can you tell me... I'm looking for the family of a girl named Railu. She was taken—Chosen—for a Dawnsinger. Thirty years ago, near enough."

The woman shook her head. "I weren't here then. Only married-in twenty-four year since. But I daresay folks'll recall. Bain't that often a girl from here gets Chose. Only been one in my time."

"Well, thank you very much anyway."

She was about to move on, but her new friend now seemed inclined to chat. "Hot work walking this road in t'middle o't'afternoon."

"Not much choice. The coach dropped me at the crossroads after midday."

"Ah, that's be it. You got summat to drink?"

"I have water."

"Bain't doing you much good on your back, just weighing you down."

Sumyra thought the water would weigh the same on her back or inside, but it was good advice all the same. She unslung her pack and extricated the flask. Politeness impelled her to offer it to the woman, but she waved it away. "I'm a'reet, thanks. Got a flagon o'cider in t'shade just over there... belike you'd like a pull?"

"Thank you, but I won't deprive you. I probably should be getting along."

"Aye, belike. Well, good luck to you."

※

Sumyra did indeed find better luck at her next enquiry, though only in the form of directions to the village shop, with the explanation, "Karèmu knows everyone."

Though the directions had been simple, she almost walked past the shop, as it turned out to be no more than someone's front room with a few shelves of assorted merchandise; cooking pots and pans, a few knives, half a dozen bolts of cloth. Sitting in a chair, apparently dozing, was a girl, but she jumped up as Sumyra entered. She was about fifteen, Sumyra judged, slender and dark. Her hair was arranged in a curious fashion, the whole scalp sectioned off into squares, or approximate squares, the hair in each twisted into a tight knot. Sumyra had never seen anything quite like it, but it took only a moment to decide the effect was highly fetching.

She repeated her enquiry, but not with any great hopes, as this girl could not have been born until long after Railu's Choosing. Surely she could not be Karèmu, who 'knew everyone'. Indeed she showed no sign of recognising the name, but she went to an inner door, leaned through, hollered for 'Ma'.

Her mother, a shade or two lighter, had hair done in the same fashion. She looked to be at least Railu's age, forty or more, which gave Sumyra hope that she would recall something. And, as soon as the girl had relayed the question and Sumyra had corrected her pronunciation of Mamma's name, she was nodding. "Oh, aye, I remember Railu. She'd'a been a couple years younger'n me, I s'pose. Why, you seeking news of her? Or bringing news? Belike it's a reet long time since we heard owt."

Her curiosity was unmistakable, but Sumyra had a sense of her obligations. "I have news indeed, but I think I should tell her family first."

"Aye, reckon that's reet enough. Well, go on down t'street to t'harbour..."

She rattled off complicated directions, and Sumyra had to request a repeat. The woman obliged, but added with a smile, "You have any trouble, just ask anyone for Seyólu's house."

"Would she be Railu's mother?"

"Aye, she would that."

"Thank you very much. May I ask your name?"

"I'm Karèmu, and this is my daughter Avessu." Sumyra could hardly have missed that all the names she'd heard so far ended in —u, just as her Mamma's did.

She gave her own name in return, thanked them again, and exited, back into brightness and a strengthening breath of salt and ozone, seaweed and fish... and smoke. Yes, no doubt, in a place like this, so far from any significant market, any fish that wasn't for immediate local consumption would require preservation of some sort, salting or picking or smoking.

Hulking rough setts, walls of the same coarse granite, roofs of deep green slate. Then the harbour, a neat round pool sheltered by twin headlands, a dozen or more boats bobbing at anchor, one unloading at the quayside. Sumyra saw a basket full of mackerel, those lovely ripple-markings, a colour like the roof-slates against the silver.

She turned left, counted three streets, and turned left again into a street—or was it a mere alley?—steep enough to require intermittent steps. Doors were not numbered, nor mostly marked, but some were painted. *Second blue on't reet...*

She drew a deep breath and knocked.

# Chapter 37

# Sumyra

"Your name is Seyólu? You have a daughter called Railu?" Sumyra hardly needed to ask; the coppery skin and broad cheekbones were unmistakable. But she had to start somewhere.

"I had, once. They took her for a Dawnsinger." The tone was flat, but she could imagine there was sorrow or bitterness beneath.

"What was the last you heard of her?"

"Had a letter, she'd took her final Vows. Twenty year ago, must be."

"Yes, it would be."

Seyólu's look sharpened. "Beggin' your pardon, Miss, but who are you? You en't a Dawnsinger, so why're you askin' about my Railu?"

"I call her Mamma," she began. She got no further, as Seyólu almost barked a sharp, "No!" then, more quietly, "No, that can't be right. She's a Dawnsinger and that's all there is to it."

"It really isn't." Sumyra tried for a gentle, even an apologetic, note. "There's a lot more to her story."

Seyólu gave her a long considering look, finally said, "You'd better come in." It wasn't the warmest of welcomes, but it was a start.

Sumyra looked around as Seyólu waved her to a seat on a slightly sagging settle. "Is this the same house you lived in when she was young?"

"Aye. Changed a few things, but not too much... Now, Miss... what did you say your name was?"

"Sumyra."

"Sumyra. Ain't got much to offer you. It's tea or apple juice, that's all."

Sumyra opted for apple juice because she thought it would be quicker; for both their sakes, it would be best to get the gist of the story clear as soon as possible.

"Now, Miss Sumyra, what's all this about?"

She took a deep breath. "I'm sorry if this is a shock to you, but... You said they took her for a Dawnsinger. She isn't one any more."

Seyólu's countenance darkened. For a moment Sumyra wondered if she was about to be thrown out before she could get to the rest of the story. "Please... Saying that, it sounds bad, but believe me, it really isn't." She wondered how best to reassure the woman. "It might have been bad at the start, but six years ago, the Master Prime of the Guild of Dawnsingers was at her wedding."

Seyólu held up a broad brown hand. "I'm startin' to think this is goin' to be a long story. And I reckon my daughter ought be here to hear it."

Daughter... A quick question, and it turned out that there were two brothers and one sister. The men were both at sea, but the sister lived 'just round t'corner'. Seyólu was back within five minutes.

Péravu might have been five years younger than Mamma, but the resemblance was even stronger than in Seyólu's case. Péravu was a shade darker, and her cheekbones sharper, but she had the same arching eyebrows and the same umber eyes.

And she had a daughter with her: Railu's niece: Erassu, perhaps ten or eleven. Exactly the age Railu would have been at her own Choosing. Had Railu worn her hair like that, like Péravu's also, in a dozen or so tight braids, running front to back and close to the scalp, so the shape of her head was clear. Had Railu had the same solemn look, sat in the same kind of tongue-tied silence?

Meanwhile, Seyólu had clearly been thinking; Sumyra could almost see wheels spinning in her mind. "Six years... but you said you call her Mamma."

"She's my step-mother... do you have that expression here? She married my Papa."

"And the Master Prime..."

"Was at the wedding." *She even danced*. A grave and stately measure with Papa, though it had been obvious Master Evisyn was struggling not to laugh at her own ineptitude. Dancing did not seem to figure largely in the life of a Dawnsinger.

She looked at Seyólu, saw the bemusement. "I think I'd better start at the beginning." She drank down a good half of the apple juice to fortify herself.

※

She'd had plenty of time on the journey to think through how to tell the story, including the vital preamble. "I want to warn you, this might sound bad at first, but I promise you it gets better, so if you can bear with me till then end... And then you can ask me all the questions you like."

All three nodded, though their faces showed varying degrees of willingness. *If I were Mamma's true daughter*, she thought, *they'd be my aunt, great-aunt, and cousin*. Was there such a thing as a step-cousin, a step-aunt?

"First, though," she said, recalling those mental rehearsals, "Did you ever receive any word from her—or from the College? The Guild of Dawnsingers?"

"Aye," said Seyólu, "Two times." It was clear she didn't think that sufficient.

"When was that?"

"After t'first year, and then se'n year later."

"So when she took her Novitial Vows, and then when she was Ordained?"

"Aye, that's what they called him. T'headman came down and said t'Dawnsinger had told him."

Twice in eight years, and then at third hand. Sumyra could readily understand how a parent, a sister, might find that shabby, derisory. Back in Carwerid, she thought, she should find a chance to mention it to someone.

For now, though, she had a task to finish. "From early in her time as a Novice, Railu showed a particular talent as a Healer. It must have seemed certain that that's what she would be after Ordination.

"However... she made herself unpopular with some senior Dawnsingers. All she ever did was say what she thought, ask a few awkward questions. The Dawnsingers have the best Healers, the best medical knowledge, in the Known Lands, but... well, what does that mean to you, here? Railu would ask questions like that. Couldn't the Guild do more for the health of *all* the people?

"Now, the leaders of the Guild are asking the same questions, and they're starting to make changes. But then, over twenty years ago, by saying these things, Railu alienated some of them... including the ones who got to decide what happened to her after Ordination."

She paused, sipping at the juice. "And they decided—one person in particular—instead of keeping Railu in the College to finish Healer's training, to send her to a place called Delven.

"I've been there; it's far in the North, close to the mountains. Kermey's a fair way from any town, but Delven's two days' walk even from a coach service. And I don't know exactly how it is here, between you and your Dawnsinger, but in Delven, twenty years ago, the people left their Dawnsinger very much alone. She hardly ever spoke to anyone but the headman. If anyone saw her coming, they'd step aside, even turn away."

Her mind flashed back to Marit. She recalled the Singer's words; she'd been addressing Jerya, but Sumyra had been close enough. *When I started here, I was glad enough to be left to myself, to my misery. And by the time I was over it, loneliness had become a habit, so nothing changed until Master Evisyn became Master Prime.*

She pulled herself back to the story. "Railu had a friend called Jerya. I could tell you a lot about her, but this is Railu's story. But one thing to know about Jerya is that she'd come from Delven; she knew what it was like. And she thought it worst the worst place they could have chosen to send Railu. The cruellest place.

"Jerya had her own... disagreement... with some of the Guild too, but I won't go into that. Anyway, she managed to get permission to accompany Railu to Delven... but they didn't stop there. They left."

"Left?" said Péravu. All three had been quiet, honouring Sumyra's request, but now it seemed she couldn't help herself.

"I told you it would sound bad, but it really does get better.

"Yes, they left; left Delven, left the Guild. And yes, that does mean they broke their Vows. They set out into the mountains, and then for ten years no one in the Sung Lands had any idea what had become of them."

Her mouth was dry. Not a problem that had arisen in mental rehearsal. She sipped, swirling the liquid around her mouth before swallowing. It didn't improve the flavour, but it ought to help moisten her tissues.

# Part Four
## Homecomings

# Chapter 38

# Embrel

As they came into the outskirts of Drumlenn, Jerya looked over at him. "If you remember one thing... love isn't bound by the laws of physics. You can have more of it in one place without taking away from another."

"You're the scientist, aunt, not me... but is that good physics?"

She laughed. "It's central. Fourth-year physics; I teach it myself. Conservation of quantities. But more to the point, it's excellent *philosophy*."

He thought about that, looking around as they walked, seeing his home town as if for the first time, noticing how almost every doorway had a carved lintel bearing initials and a date; and most of those dates were from the old calendar. He thought how the creamy-gold stone stone was soft enough to carve but hard enough to last, to resist weathering. Harder, he thought, than the stone of which Delven was made.

But all the time, as they approached the final turning, he was also thinking about what Jerya had said.

※

Railu's first words were sharp with concern. "Where's Sumyra?"

For answer, Jerya merely reached into her pocket and handed Railu the letter. She pulled out her glasses, then tore open the envelope and began to read, but looked up after a moment. "Do you know what she says in this?"

Jerya shook her head. "Not a word. She might be saying I'm the worst aunt in the world."

"Not that..." Railu, obviously going back to the beginning, began to read aloud.

*"Dearest Mamma and Papa,*

*"You mustn't be angry with Jerya. She did her very best to dissuade me, but I was adamant."* Railu gave a soft snort. "Adamant, she says. What do you teach them in that school of yours? *I am travelling to Kermey to seek out your family. I know they are not related to me by blood, but I am keen to see the place, and the people, you came from.*

*"I thought too that you might like to be reminded of that, to know how your family went on after you were Chosen. I hope you will be glad to hear some news of them and will take it as my gift to you, my dearest Mamma. I could never have wished for a better mother."*

Railu lowered the letter, pulled off her glasses, wiped her eyes with her sleeve. "Stars, that girl. How can I be mad with her after that? Or with you?"

"Just don't, then," said Jerya. "Especially not with her."

Railu gave a shaky laugh, then resumed. *"If you are still inclined to rebuke me, Mamma, may I humbly remind you that you undertook a far more perilous journey when you were scarcely older than I am? I am not venturing into the unknown. I won't be crossing high places or descending slippery precipices. I have a map; I know exactly where the coaches stop each night on the way (four nights there and four back); I have enquired as to the best inns in each town. Peripatetics know most things, as you must know.*

*"In the same way, I have every reason to believe I'll be able to fall in with a party of Dawnsingers for the homeward Crossing. But even if not, the journey holds no terrors. Again, it pales into insignificance beside the journey you and Jerya made, when you were both nineteen.*

*"Expect to see me home within three weeks of receiving this. And believe me, I miss you and Papa very much and eagerly look forward to spending time with you; more time than I have had at home in years.*

*"So, dearest*—Well, you don't need to hear the last bit." She lifted her eyes, met Jerya's gaze. "I guess she really was adamant. She'd have to be, to get the better of you."

"You've raised her to know her own mind. And I only hope we can do as good a job with Torvyn."

Railu smiled. "Aye, and in ten years there'll be moments you'll wish you'd raised her to be a meek little Miss."

※

And then she turned to look at him, to fully take him in.

For a measureless interval they just looked at each other. He saw how her skin, though darker than his own, had the same warm hue; and her eyes... Shebb! he must have looked her in those eyes a thousand times—ten thousand, probably; how had he never seen how like they were to the ones he saw in the mirror every day when he shaved?

He was only remotely aware of Jerya moving about, hefting both packs, carrying them in by the kitchen passage. Voices within, hers and Skelber's, words lost. The only words that mattered now were between him and Railu.

"What do I even call you?" he asked.

"You've called me Railu since you learned to talk. Don't change now."

"But you're my mother."

"In a—in a medical sense, yes. And I'm a doctor, you'd think that was what matters most to me, but... Embrel, I'm not saying my opinion counts for more than yours, but I have had more time to think about it; twenty years more. And it's hardly been off my mind since you went off seven weeks ago."

"Mine too, ever since the first day in Carwerid." Perhaps that wasn't entirely true. For much of the time his thoughts had been taken up with Elidir. But maybe it was all connected anyway...

"I'm sure. But, Embrel, motherhood is so much more than pregnancy, than giving birth. Maybe, above all, motherhood, *parenthood*, is about responsibility. And that's what I couldn't—the part I wasn't ready for.

"I was nineteen; turned twenty before you were born. Younger than you are now. I know lots of women have babies at that age. But there's more to it."

She sighed. "I was—I'd been a Dawnsinger. Dawnsingers don't marry, don't have children; we never even talked about it. Since I was ten, I'd only lived in the College; a few trips to Kendrigg were the only times I even saw children, and then only a passing glimpse; babies were just bundles in the mother's arms. All I knew about pregnancy and birth was what I got from my classes. We didn't see healthy pregnant women or normal births in the Infirmary; that was all left to midwives. For eight years I never even saw a mother or a baby unless something had gone wrong. Was there ever a woman less ready to have a child than I was?"

She sighed. "If I didn't have to go back to surgery in an hour, I'd pour myself a stiff drink... Would you like something?"

It was tempting, but they'd have had to move, and he didn't want that. "Just tell me. I want to hear."

"Well," she said, sighing again, "When I realised I was pregnant, I was terrified. It's not too strong a word. If there'd been a way to... to end it, I think I'd have done it." Her gaze was almost unbearable, but then she grabbed his hands. "I'm glad now that I didn't. You have to know that."

He knew he should say something, but words wouldn't come. All he could do was turn their hands around so he could squeeze hers as she'd squeezed his.

"And when your... when they made the offer, Jerya was saying, 'they want to take your baby', like it was a terrible thing... but I was thinking, 'they want to take my baby', like it was the best possible thing. I wanted to say to her, 'you care so much, you have it'— you were still 'it' then, of course, before you were born. Jerya hadn't been in the College all those years, she had to know more about babies than I did. And Rhenya knew a lot more."

She tried to laugh. "I used to think either of them would have been a better mother for you... but of course I ended up caring for you anyway, wet-nurse and nursemaid and what-have-you. And... it's time to be honest, Embrel, isn't it? I did love you, I hope you know that, but it took me a while."

"I know that," he said. "Since I can remember... I loved you too. You and Rhenya and Jerya, all three of you. But you said it's time to be honest, and..."

"And it was Jerya you loved the best," she said when his courage failed him for a moment. Of course... she'd probably always known.

"I think I loved her better than anyone. When I was nine and she told me she was going back to the Sung Lands, it felt..." The memory was still uncomfortable. "I told her I hated her, but I only said that because I loved her so much. More than even..." He shrugged. "What do I even call them? What do I call you?"

"Call me what you did before. You know how Sumyra does it, as she has since she was twelve. The woman who bore her, Selence, is her mother. I'm her Mamma. Call your Mamma, Mamma.

"She's the one who... I said it was about responsibility. That's what I couldn't do. That's what they relieved me of, your Mamma and Papa."

She looked at him, those eyes so like his own. "I said I've been thinking a lot about this. I did know how I'd abdicated responsibility. And when Sumyra came along, all those years later, so obviously needing someone... then I told myself, *this time you have to take the responsibility.*"

"And you did."

There were tears in her eyes again. "I did my best. I only hope you don't feel bad because she got something from me that I couldn't give you."

He thought about it. "I think you did well enough. All of you."

## Chapter 39

# Sumyra

"Ma used to talk about Railu a lot," said Nóèttu. "I think it must ha' took her years to get over her being Chosen, going away. Are you sure she never mentioned her? Halveeru?"

They were sitting in what, in Kermey, passed for a tavern, though it looked like little more than someone's front room, a few extra chairs crammed in, cider or beer fetched in jugs from the back. It was Péravu who'd introduced her to Nóèttu, whose mother, she said, had been Railu's closest friend before the Choosing.

"Not to me," said Sumyra carefully. "Look, it's not just her, I think the Guild of Dawnsingers discourages girls from thinking about where they came from, about their families. At least, they did. I think things might be changing now." *And some people don't like it*. But she wouldn't waste thought or breath on Perriad now. "You know what I'm thinking? If you tell me some of her memories, things they did together, they might shake a few memories loose for her."

"They were best friends, did all kinds o'things together."

"Did they do each other's hair?" asked Sumyra in what felt like a moment of inspiration.

"I reckon so. 'Course, that age, you're just learning, so when it's important your Ma or someone'd do it for you..." A memory looked to come to mind. "Ma said Railu's Ma did her hair afore Choosing. Did the best job, like she *wanted* her girl to get Chose."

"It's funny. For me, Railu's always been bald, but of course she'd have had hair, before she was Chosen. Do you think it was like yours, like you have it now? I love the way it looks." Nóèttu's hair was partitioned and bound into a dozen or more... what would you call them? Stubby spikes, about three inches long, tightly bound in thread, each a different colour.

Nóèttu was looking at her. "I could do yours if you like. You've got the right kind of hair, looks like."

"Would you?" She laughed. "I can't ever keep it in order."

"I'm the same. Belike Railu was too. There ain't no better way. Lasts a good while too."

"Mamma says she doesn't remember ever having hair. Maybe if you do mine this way it'll be a reminder."

"Mebbe... so, you want to do this, then?"

"Yes, please."

"It takes a while, like.'

"I've got time. You can tell me a few more of your Ma's memories."

"And you can tell me about the Five Principalities."

※

Though her new hair made her less conspicuous in the streets of Kermey, Sumyra had no doubt everyone still knew who she was—including the Dawnsinger, who strode up to her without hesitation.

Light olive skin meant Kermey's Singer was paler than almost anyone in sight, including Sumyra herself. She was tall enough to stand out too; even without the white garments and bald head she would command notice.

"You are Sumyra," she said; it wasn't a question. "I am concerned about the stories you've been spreading."

"What stories?"

"Stories justifying Vow-breaking."

Sumyra quelled rising ire. "With respect, Dawnsinger, I don't believe I've attempted to justify anything. I merely wanted Railu's family to know what had become of her, and to carry some news back to her in return."

Green eyes fixed on hers. "You don't deny that Railu—and Jerya—are Vow-breakers?"

"I don't, and neither do they."

"That's not what I hear," said the Singer. "I have recently received a letter informing me that Jerya, having returned to the Sung Lands, has been spreading falsehood and slander... and worse, that she and her confederates *attacked* a party of true Dawnsingers who set out to stop them doing so."

"That's a lie!" The words burst forth, and she knew at once she could have chosen better, but there was no helping that now. "*They* attacked *us.*"

"A lie? Are you, then, calling me a liar?"

"No, Dawnsinger, of course not. I am saying that whoever wrote this letter is misinformed. Unless they were also there..." *In which case they're a liar.* But she doubted that. Perriad, when last she'd seen her, had been in no fit state to write letters to anyone; and she was sure Elidir's change of heart was genuine. That only left two other eyewitnesses, and it stretched credibility to think of either of them writing to a Dawnsinger who had been in Kermey since before they were Chosen. What Kermey's Singer had received was second-hand news at best, mere rumour at worst.

The Singer was silent, which strengthened Sumyra's intuition regarding her correspondent. "I was there, Dawnsinger. And I can assure you that Master Perriad and her party waylaid us with force. Even though one of our party was a girl still shy of her fourteenth birthday."

Sumyra had the sense that more onlookers were gathering, but she could not look around; all her attention was focused on the Dawnsinger.

"If Master Perriad ordered you waylaid, as you put it, I am sure she had good reason."

"Forgive me, Dawnsinger, but can you truly be sure? The last time I saw Master Perriad, she was being taken into the care of the Healers. It was clear she hadn't been well for some time. Even before that, at the confrontation in the Plains, she collapsed during the struggle. And do you know who took her up on her own horse to get her to the nearest Adjunct House as fast as possible?"

The Singer said nothing, but Sumyra thought she detected a tiny, probably involuntary, shake of the head. "It was Jerya," she said. "And let me tell you a few other things. Master Prime Evisyn has been a guest at Jerya's home in the Sung Lands. Other Masters, including Master Analind, have visited us at our home—Railu's home—in Drumlenn. Dawnsingers travelling to the Five Principalities almost always make their first call with us... And when we arrived in the Sung Lands this summer, about six weeks ago, Jerya was received personally by the Master Prime."

She took a somewhat shaky breath. It was impossible to tell if any of this was getting through to the stern woman in front of her. "And correct me if I'm wrong, Dawnsinger, but it's my understanding that Master Perriad is a Master in name only, a courtesy title. So I don't see that she had any authority to order Jerya and the rest of us to be arrested. I know that the Dawnsinger in Delven flatly refused to have anything to do with it."

"And why should I believe you? Why should any of these good people believe a word you say?"

This time Sumyra could not help but look around. Faces everywhere, watchful, intent; she could not tell where their sympathies lay.

"Everything I've said, I say as a direct witness, sometimes a participant. You only have hearsay and second-hand report. But if you, or anyone else, don't choose to believe me... everything I've said is readily verifiable." A thought struck here. "Dawnsinger, when do you next expect a visit from Peripatetics?"

"In a couple of months."

"It's a shame it's not sooner. There's a fair chance at least one of them will have been to the Five Principalities, and been welcomed in Drumlenn, perhaps at Skilthorn too. If not, they'll certainly know colleagues who have. And they'll have heard from Master Analind... I believe she was the first Dawnsinger to officially visit the Five Principalities."

"None of that tells us anything about the attack in the Plains."

Sumyra tried to think fast. Whoever the unknown correspondent was, she was hardly a good place to look for corroboration. "In two days I must begin my journey back to Carwerid, and then home to the Five Principalities. But while I'm in the city I'll find time to let them know, in the College, that you need... clarification... on a number of issues."

"That's hardly a speedy solution."

"I'm sorry, Dawnsinger, but it's the best I can think of."

## Chapter 40

# Embrel

A pumpkin sun hung close above the Western hills, and he realised how much earlier it was setting than when they had set off. The road wound ahead of him, empty of traffic.

He had an hour. A final hour all to himself.

It had gone well with Railu, he thought. What was obvious, though, was that her concern for Sumyra outweighed anything else. Perhaps it was simply that she could see he was safe, while her fate remained unknowable. But he thought it was more.

He was Railu's flesh and blood, but Sumyra was her daughter.

But what, he thought, if he had been her son in every sense? If his parents had never offered adoption, or she had for some reason refused?

He would—this she had said—he would have been the son of a slave.

He thought about that for a while, riding through bars of amber light and aquamarine shade. *Put yourself in someone else's shoes.* Yes, when Jerya was his governess, it had been one of her favoured ways of bringing a lesson to life: what would it be like to live there, or then? It had drawn him in to historical tales in particular, perhaps shaped the course of his life more than he had ever really seen before.

The son of a slave is a slave himself. That was the nub of it. He would have grown up in the same house, with the same people, but everything would have been different. Perhaps as a skinny bald boy he would still have been in and out of the same kitchen. Yes, even more than in reality—in *this* reality—his upbringing would have been shared by the same three women.

But the Master and Mistress would have been remote, even awe-inspiring figures. If one entered the kitchen when he was there, little slave-Embrel would have hidden behind his mother's skirts.

They might have taught him to read, he supposed, as they had taught Rhenya, but he would never have had those days, weeks, months and years, of Jerya's time, devoted solely to himself, to his education.

What would a twenty-year-old slave-Embrel be, then? A field-hand, most likely. There'd been no male slaves in the house since Whallin died. No coachman had replaced him; just one of the stringent economies forced by Grevel's embezzlement, the final act of thievery. The carriage had been little used, and on the rare occasions it was, the Squire (not my father, not in this tale) had driven it himself, or borrowed a man from a nearby estate.

But of course, he thought with the usual flicker of guilt, the need to economise had largely been driven by himself, the costs of school and now University. With no son to educate; well, the loss would still surely have been felt, but far less acutely. Perhaps they would have taken on a coachman after all. Though—he laughed silently at himself as he rode—they surely would not have given the responsibility to a lad of fifteen, his age when Whallin died.

No, he thought, realistically it would have been the fields. Or—if the need to raise funds still pressed—would he have been one of the ones to be sold? Might it have been him on whom Jerya bid? It would make sense. A healthy young male, not yet in his prime, intelligent, ready to be trained for anything, would fetch a good price. And to be at Skilthorn, under Jerya's eye... though he would not have been placed in the house, where male slaves—for the reassurance of nervous parents—were few and far between. Even the duties usually given to footmen were performed by females.

Perhaps he would have been close, though, he thought, anxious now for his other self to have that link with home, even if it were no more than an occasional glimpse of the woman who had been such a large part of his childhood.

He passed from the solid shade of a wood into an open stretch, and saw the slow fall of the Vale to his left. The sun was lost behind the hills now, the land sinking into a sombre haze, the sky above an odd sage-green.

Five more minutes to the turning, five more up the drive and then home; and he had not given a thought to what he would say to his parents. Well, let it happen as it might. He had not finished with this other self his imagination had conjured up.

He needed a name.

It would not be the Squire and Lady who named him, honouring some distant, years-dead, uncle; it would be Railu. What name would she have chosen for her slave-child? He had a lunatic urge to turn around, ride back, and ask her; but he did not. He kept on, on to the turning, past that little triangle of grass where this summer's adventure had really had its beginning—beginnings—in both the immediate and the more distant past. Six weeks, and ten years.

He chose to believe, because he wanted some connection with his present, this-reality, self, that she would keep—or stumble upon—the opening 'Em'. Or was there someone else, someone in her own past, she might have chosen to commemorate? Her own father, even; what had his name been? If Railu even remembered, she had never said. Sumyra would know, now, he thought suddenly, with a little pang that he had not thought more of her; was she still in Kermey, or back in Carwerid, or even already on her way toward the Crossing? He could not know; still less, at this moment, could he have any notion of who, if anyone, Railu might have thought of.

No, all he could do, in the two or three minutes remaining, was pluck a name from the air, the ether.

He glanced back at the last bend, as he always did, for the last view over the Vale, all indistinct now, lost to haze and twilight.

Ahead, the lights of the house were warm and inviting, and Embrel, with the name Emvrau suddenly in his head, steered the horse toward them

※

"And what sort o' time d'yow call this?" demanded Rhenya, hands on hips. "Five more minutes and I'd'a been platin' Squire an' Ladyship's dinner. Dinner for *two*," she added with an extra scowl.

He grinned and folded her in his arms. "If I could have warned you... but how could I? Would you rather I'd stayed in Drumlenn till the morning? Would they?"

"Don't be daft," she said, muffled against his chest.

He released her, holding on to her shoulders just long enough to bestow a kiss on her brow just below the growing Crest. "If you give me a slice of your good bread and the aged cheese, it'll be better than anything I've had this last week. But you might want to hold back Mamma and Papa's dinner a few minutes longer."

※

Mamma looked thinner. Rhenya had said something before their departure, but he hadn't seen it; he saw it now. Her hands in his felt frail, bird-boned. He didn't dare give her the kind of hug he'd given Rhenya.

"Mamma," he said, "Railu told me you'd been putting off the surgery. Please tell me you weren't doing it on my account."

Her silence was all the answer he needed. He sighed, but swallowed any rebuke; this was no time for harsh words. "Well, I'm here now. She's kept time free on Calansday, so let's make sure you're there. I'll drive the carriage myself if need be." *Emvrau would be proud of me*, he thought, and had to choke back a laugh.

"I think," said his father, "That I had better drive. You are sometimes, hm, a little inclined to, ah... recklessness. And with such a precious, hm, cargo..."

"Precious, yes. But hardly *cargo*."

"Well," said Mamma, "If you two have finished settling my fate, perhaps we can hear how you are, my son." She said the two words lightly, but there was no doubting the feeling behind them.

He gave her hands a squeeze, as from as he dared. "I am very well, and I have much to tell you. But I know what you most want to hear. And I can't tell you nothing has changed. I know things about myself I didn't know before. I know things about you, and Railu—and even Jerya—I didn't know. But it's as Jerya says; when is knowing more ever a bad thing?

"And Rodal… he's a good man, and I like him. But… well, he said himself, something like this: there are womenfolk watching, hoping we'll fall into each other's arms and declare undying love'. But we didn't, and we're not going to.

"Mamma, Papa, I haven't lost anything, I've only gained." He smiled. "I've gained a sister, and two brothers. And very soon I must tell you all about Sokkie. But I know it was time for your dinner, and I'm as hungry as a whole skulk of foxes. And something tells me in the ten minutes since I saw her Rhenya's worked some kind of miracle in the kitchen."

※

His mind was busy but his body felt the fatigue of his journey, the last long day—sunrise to sunset, near enough. He heard the sigh of the breeze in the cherry tree outside and then, more distantly, the acute sibilant call of a barn owl. Some called it eerie, sinister, but it was something he listened out for every time he came back, one of the sounds of home.

Some time before dawn he woke, a dimness outside his window. Before Dawnsong, he thought with a smile.

He sat upright. *The scenario didn't work.*

Oh, Emvrau would have been born a slave, still, and raised as one his first ten years; that was the same. But then… in his tenth year Jerya returned to the Sung Lands; and there was the Selton expedition. By the end of that summer the entire Five Principalities knew that there was another land to the West. The truth about Railu's and Jerya's origin emerged, and their enslavement was declared invalid. Jerya had already known Hedric more than a year by then; the following year they were married, and three years after that they became Earl and Countess.

But what of Emvrau? The son of a slave is a slave himself, but if his mother is set free, does he also benefit? He did not know the law well enough, but it seemed like it would be monstrously cruel if not. But monstrous cruelty was not always an obstacle.

It didn't matter, though. Railu had not been set free; the legal ruling clearly stated that she, like Jerya, had never been validly enslaved; and that meant that Emvrau's status as a slave was also invalid.

He felt an absurd sense of relief. Absurd, because... *Because what am I doing, getting worked up by the fate of someone who has no existence outside my own mind?*

But what was the difference between that and a character in a novel? Jerya and Railu had both read to him when he was small—Mamma too, though less often—and there'd been plenty of times he'd been upset, or breathless with excitement, over the fate of some character or other. How often had they had to remind him, 'it's only a story'.

*Perhaps I should be a novelist*, he thought.

He knew he would not go back to sleep, so he got up, threw on a dressing-gown, and headed for the kitchen. Rhenya would surely be up, and perhaps there would be hot water for a bath. If not, there would be coffee, and someone to talk to.

## Chapter 41

# Sumyra

The third night's room was small and stuffy, with a single skylight that refused to open, though Sumyra stood on the bed to give it a good shove. Those beds were niggardly-narrow, shoved in under the eaves so that at the bottom there was barely clearance for one's feet, and pushed together, leaving a space barely a foot wide on each side. A separate coverlet for each was a small concession to the claim of providing 'single beds'.

Some time in the night she woke. Vestiges of moonlight leaking in through the grimy skylight gave just enough light to see. They had both thrown off the covers, and Sumyra's hand was resting on Nóèttu's arm. The most innocent of touch, she thought, yet she felt all at once thoroughly awake.

Then Nóèttu's eyes opened.

Not a word was said, not a sound uttered, and in the dim light they could not even read the other's face with any clarity. Still, somehow, something was decided.

With fastidious slowness, Sumyra's hand glided up Nóèttu's arm, tracing the contours of her elbow, the slight flex of muscles in the upper arm, the firm roundness of the shoulder. With every centimetre, her eyes, the very tentativeness of her movements, asked 'is this all right?' and Nóèttu's gaze, the still-relaxed ease of her limbs, said yes.

She never knew who first moved, only that they were kissing. Then they slid apart, Nóèttu pulling off her nightdress, Sumyra her undergarments, languor gone, overtaken by urgency.

※

They woke in a tangle of limbs. Sumyra was briefly aware of a welcome sense of almost-coolness on bare skin, but it was rapidly overtaken by the realisation that someone was hammering at the door. "Coach due in half an hour."

They dressed in a rush, made an equally hasty breakfast, then spent twenty minutes trying to shelter from the rain waiting for the coach to appear. "It's always late," said someone, and Sumyra thought, *we could have had time to talk, like we need to.*

There was no chance for that on the coach. The woman in the facing seat left Sumyra in no doubt her ears would be as sharp as her eyes. It wasn't until the evening, seated in a secluded corner of a busy inn, that they could exchange anything more than casual remarks about the views from the coach window.

"I want to come with you," said Nóèttu.

"You are with me."

"No, to the Five Principalities, to see Denvirran and Sessapont and all them other places."

Sumyra laughed. "Is that the only reason?"

Nóèttu didn't seem to find it funny. "Course not. Not even t'main one." Her direct gaze filled in the rest, had Sumyra needed it.

She wasn't entirely surprised. She'd even had an inkling of what she might say in response, but most of those thoughts evaporated in the face of Nóèttu's palpable sincerity.

She sighed inwardly, hoping it really was only inward. "It's a lovely thought, but we have to think about this. If you come with me now, you'll probably have almost no time, a week or two at most, before you have to head back—if you can find someone to travel with. Leave it too long, and you're going to find the route closed by snow, and then you could be stuck in the Five Principalities for six months." Winter closures didn't usually last quite that long, but it was possible. "What would your family think about that?"

Nóèttu looked pensive. Even setting off for Carwerid had been a major step; it was clear that most people in Kermey—especially the women—had never been further than Milhara. If an absence of week or two was hard for Nóèttu's family to contemplate, six months would be terrifying. It was an awful lot to stake on the basis of a few days, and just three nights, however joyful they had been.

"Besides," added Sumyra, "You made a promise, to take word back to Kermey. And I'm sure—I know—you keep your promises." *Whereas there've been no promises between us.*

Nóèttu nodded, slow and obviously reluctant. Sumyra decided to soften the blow. "Come across next summer," she said with a bright smile. "It's a better time anyway, to see Sessapont and Troquharran and the Velya Lakes."

She thought the chances of Nóèttu undertaking that journey in six months time were probably slim indeed. Likely Nóèttu knew it too. Neither needed to say it.

"I wish we had more time," she added, and in this at least she was absolutely sincere.

❋

"Master Prime Evisyn is at Kendrigg just now," said the portress. "Master Analind is not yet back from the Five Principalities."

"Do you have any idea when they will be back?"

The woman looked at her. Sumyra wondered if this was information they would normally give out, but she'd seen the portress before, hoped that she'd remember that Jerya and Sumyra had been admitted to the Precincts, even received by the Master Prime in person. "The Master Prime will be back next week. Master Analind... I couldn't really say. It's not always possible for Peripatetics to keep us apprised of their movements."

This was a blow. Sumyra couldn't wait a week, unless she was prepared to attempt the Crossing alone, and at the tail-end of the season. She tried to recall the names of Jerya's other particular friends in the College. "Tutor Yanil?"

"I'm sure she's teaching right now, but I can take a message."

Another thought stirred. "Could I leave a message for Dawnsinger Elidir as well, please?"

※

Elidir's message had been brief and to the point: *I'll come soon as possible. Stay at the tavern if you can. E.*

She arrived soon after the five o'clock bells. "You're on your own?" she asked as soon as they had found a seat and given Sokkie their order for drinks.

"Yes, Jerya and Embrel went back almost three weeks ago." Elidir said nothing, but Sumyra was sure she could see relief in her eyes. Yes, dealing with a lovelorn Embrel had been awkward for her.

"But you stayed..."

"I'm starting back soon, but I've been down to Kermey..." She saw that the name meant nothing. "Beyond Milhara, in the South-West. And speaking of Kermey, there is someone I'd like you to meet." As Sokkie delivered their tankards, Sumyra asked her to fetch Nóèttu.

Nóèttu needed some persuasion to sit in the presence of a Dawnsinger, but Elidir's smile convinced her.

Sumyra explained the allegations that Kermey's Dawnsinger had repeated in front of of many of the village folk. No doubt everyone who wasn't at sea had heard them before the day was out. Elidir listened quietly, only breaking in once with, "She really said that?"

"She said that was what was in her letter. She didn't say who'd written it."

"And your part is to bear witness," said Elidir to Nóèttu.

"Yes, Dawnsinger."

"So you'll be heading back to Kermey soon?"

"Yes, Dawnsinger."

"Well, I can tell you what I know, but if your Singer's stubborn, she might say it's the word of someone she trusts against someone she's probably never heard of... do you know how long your Singer's been there?"

"Long as I can remember, Dawnsinger."

"Then before I was Chosen. Well, I can write something for her. There are words, phrases, that only a Dawnsinger would know. But I'm still unknown to her." Neither Sumyra nor Nóèttu knew the name of Kermey's Singer, but Elidir said she'd be able to find out.

"I had hoped to speak with Master Prime Evisyn or Master Analind," said Sumyra, "But they're not in Carwerid right now."

Elidir nodded. "I can speak to one or both of them when they get back. They won't want false rumours getting around, not within the Guild, still less being spread Outwith. But before then, Nóèttu, as you're here, you can tell your people...

"When Sumyra says Master Perriad's party attacked hers, she's telling the truth—and I know this as a certainty because I was one of them. With Master Perriad, I mean."

Nóèttu looked frankly bewildered and Elidir gave a soft laugh. "And now you're wondering, if that's true, why am I here?" Nóèttu nodded. "Well, I suppose I was already beginning to have doubts, and I saw things that day that made them stronger."

Nóèttu still looked bemused. Elidir laughed again. "Dawnsingers are just people, you know. We make mistakes, too, sometimes. I learned that too."

## Chapter 42

# Sumyra

Sumyra came home on a grey day, in intermittent drizzle. She kept her hood up most of the time, though she didn't like the way it pressed on the spikes of her hair. It was natural, coming from the mountain road, to slip in through the back gate, past the orchard, and in by the kitchen door. She stopped under the porch to slip out of her pack, remove her coat and shake off lingering moisture, then to unflatten her hair.

It was the porter, Cavlyn, who saw her first, and ran to stir the house, and in a minute there was a swirl of people around her, admiring her hair, asking this and that; her pack was carried up to her room, and she thought it would be a very long time before she had to carry such a weight again; her boots were taken away to be cleaned, there were slippers on her feet; there were questions about drinks, about food; but in all the flurry and hubbub, for all she was happy to be home and glad to see everyone, still there was one purpose in her mind and she was not ready to settle until she and Mamma were alone in the parlour.

The door closed, the bustle of the household receded into remoteness. The clock ticked quietly; for a moment there was no other sound. They faced each other, a pace apart. Mamma's eyes were full of questions.

Sumyra took a breath, gathered herself. "There's so much I have to tell you, Mamma; about Kermey, about your family, my journey. But there's something else I want—I need—to say first.

"I don't know if Embrel said anything, but... back in Carwerid, quite early on after he'd... after he'd found out; I saw how confused he was, but the strange thing was, I wasn't confused at all. I'd learned something about you that I never knew before, and that was an... adjustment. But somehow I felt like I saw things—saw *you*—more clearly, not less.

"I told him how I'd always reserved 'mother' for the woman who bore me, for Selence, and called you 'Mamma'; but I never knew her. She's a name, a pencil sketch, stories Papa tells, and Aunt Arlenys, but she's not a person I know. In all the ways that matter, you, Railu, *you* are my mother."

Railu's eyes were bright, fixed on her, but she did not move or speak. Sumyra took the single short step that closed the space between them, put hands on her mother's shoulders, and pressed brow to brow, as the Dawnsingers did.

How long they stayed like that she could hardly have said. The clock kept up its steady reserved tick, but she did not count, or care; but then it struck once, twice, and Mamma stirred and pulled back. "I have to get back..."

"Of course. But there's just one more thing, very quickly...?"

"Go on, then."

"You know I'd thought—we all had—that now I've finished school, and once this trip to the Sung Lands was done, that I'd be able to spend lots more time with you and Papa." She couldn't but recall her aunt's letter. "Ever since the school opened, I've been away more than I've been at home, and I do—you know I always miss you, don't you?

"But then before she and Embrel left Carwerid, Jerya said to me that I could—that she'd like me—"

Mamma saw that it was hard to say, and took pity. "She'd like you to be a teacher."

"She told you? No, stupid question, obviously she did."

"I dare say she wanted to forewarn me; and see what I thought about it."

There was only one thing she could say then. "And what do you think about it?"

"I was looking forward to you being at home for longer too. We both were, of course. But you're not a child any more. You have to find your own place in the world. And while we're on that, there's another thing..."

Mamma turned to pick something off the bureau; a letter. Sumyra took it from her hand. One line was written on the envelope:

*Trusting in your safe return, or your parents may never forgive me. I doubt I'd forgive myself.*

※

*My dear Sumyra*

*To make a long story as short as possible, when I reached Drumlenn, I found a letter from the Council of the University of Velyadero. It was sufficiently promising that, much as I longed to see Hedric and Torvyn again, I thought I should head South rather than North. Some tangled negotiations ensued (I shall tell you more when I see you) but ended with an agreement that the University Council will formally consider a proposal to admit females, potentially from the start of the Autumn Term next year.*

Sumyra looked up. "You know what she says here?"

Railu smiled. "Heard it from her own lips. I knew you'd be excited."

"I didn't dare think it would be so soon. Only a year after I finished school."

"Read the rest."

*However, many details remain to be finalised, so I am rushing home—literally Post-Haste—to collect husband and daughter, and return to Velya City. It occurred to me that it would be helpful to have the perspective of a potential student in a number of these decisions, and of course I immediately thought of you.*

*I don't suppose you will have been back long, if at all, before we reach Drumlenn, and it is hardly kind to prise you and your parents apart so soon, but they have not forbidden me from writing this. If, after discussion with them, you are willing to accompany us, please hold yourself in readiness.*

*In any case, I look forward to seeing you very soon and, in due course, hearing all about your solo adventures in the Sung Lands.*

*Your loving aunt,*

*Jerya*

※

A bath—deeply welcome—clean clothes, the rest of her unpacking; Sumyra had plenty to occupy herself until Papa came home a little after four of the clock. They had a pleasant half-hour catching up before Mamma returned from surgery. Soon after, Papa excused himself for the evening ward-round, and they were alone again.

"You know, my darling, when I first saw you, just for a moment… I do believe I had my hair like that when I was a little girl."

"I should think you almost certainly did."

"It's funny, if you'd just asked me, any other time, how I wore my hair before I was Chosen, I'd have said I didn't remember having hair at all. I always felt as if I've been bald all my life."

"Yes, you've said that."

Mamma looked at her more closely. "But when did you take it into your head to go all the way to Kermey? It must be as far to the South as Delven is to the North."

"Farther, I think, but there's a coach service all the way, except the last couple of hours. But to answer your question, I think I started to think about it when we were in Delven. Seeing how Jerya was still connected to the place, to people there."

Mamma nodded, swallowing. "I think seeing Delven might help you understand a few things about Jerya… but she was there till she was nineteen. I was only ten…"

"How much do you remember, Mamma? You've hardly ever talked about it."

"We were never encouraged to talk, or think, about it. In the College, I mean. I think the idea was it was better for us if we made a clean break."

"I wonder," said Sumyra, between sips of lemonade, "Whether anyone in the College considered whether it was better for the *families*…"

Railu laid down her knife and fork. "I'm guessing you don't think so."

"More that your family don't think so." She held Railu's gaze. "Mamma, how much do you really remember? Do you remember their names?"

Railu frowned. "I don't know if I even knew my parents' names. They were just Ma and Pa, you know?"

"I can see that. But your sister?"

"If you'd asked me any other time, I'm not sure I would even remember that I had a sister. But now, looking at you... I feel like I remember braiding someone's hair. Someone smaller."

She's three years younger. And her name?" Railu shook her head. "Péravu. And she has a daughter of her own now, Erassu."

"Péravu..." Railu seemed to be trying the feel of the name, almost tasting it. "Aye, it sounds like a name I knew."

"I asked if they wanted me to carry letters for you, but they both said they weren't much for writing. Péravu said, 'Not like Railu was'."

"Aye, it's one of the things they look for, in Choosing. At least for girls who like reading."

Sumyra smiled. "And do you know anyone who likes reading better than Vireddi?"

There was no time for more; at that moment they both heard the rattle of hooves on the cobbles, the rumble of carriage-wheels. They looked at each other, and Sumyra was sure Mamma's thought was the same as her own: *it's too soon.*

※

The coach, with the familiar Skilthorn crest blazoned on the doors, rolled to a halt, swaying gently. The horses stamped, breath steaming in the lamp-light that was beginning to outdo the fading sky.

On the driver's bench... she'd half-expected Mavrys, but the figure she saw was paler, and bald. *"Vireddi?"*

Vireddi, scrambling down, grinned over her shoulder. "S'prised yow, did I?"

"I didn't even know you could drive a carriage," she said, thinking, *this must have been the surprise Mavrys mentioned a while back.*

"Aye, I've been taking lessons this past year." She grinned again. "Don't tell Mav, but it's more comf'table than bouncing around on a horse's back."

"Besides," said Jerya, appearing beside them, "Who better to keep an eye on Torvyn when we're all occupied with University bureaucrats?"

Vireddi nodded. "Aye, nothin' we like better than readin' to each other. 'Cept when Tor's drawin'."

Sumyra looked around, saw Torvyn, in Hedric's arms, greeting Mamma and Papa.

"'Sides," added Vireddi, "I've never been further than this afore. Not even seen Drumlenn till today. Now I get to see places I only ever read about. And sitting up top drivin', I see a lot more than inside the carriage."

Of course it was normal for enslaved to ride in the rumble seats at the back, but Jerya's was not a normal household, and Vireddi was far from a normal enslaved—*whatever 'normal' means*, she added to herself. "I've never been to Velyadero either. I might join you up there sometimes... if that's all right?" she added hastily, not sure if it was Jerya's approval she was seeking or Vireddi's.

"Happy to have you," said Vireddi. "You ever driven a carriage?"

"Only a simple pony-trap."

"Well, if you fancy tryin' it..."

"When are we leaving?"

"No rush tomorrow," said Jerya. "We're just going as far as Denvirran. Sleep in familiar beds, catch up with Embrel."

"I can't wait."

It was true, she realised; but there was regret too. So much more she wanted to say to Mamma; Papa, too, but he would understand, better than anyone, why it was Mamma first and foremost just now.

All she had was a few minutes before dinner, as the household scurried to prepare rooms, and food, for four unexpected guests, and Mamma seemed to be the only one free to help her pack. At least this time, she thought, she would not have to carry everything on her own back.

"It's a little cruel," she said. "I thought we'd have a few days, at least."

"And we will." Railu gave her the merest side-glance, carefully folding russet satin. "More time than we've had in years. In a couple of weeks. Papa and I will plan it properly. Maybe we'll come down to the Velya Lakes."

"But then it'll be nearly the start of a new year at Skilthorn. And we haven't even talked about whether I want to teach, or *how*... And now there's the prospect of University too.."

"Hasn't it been your dream for years?"

"I'm not sure I ever dared let myself dream of it. It seemed too far-off, if it could ever happen at all."

"When you were Torvyn's age," said Mamma, "I dare say we'd all have said the same about a school for girls. Some dreams really do come true."

## Chapter 43

# Embrel

Embrel finished chewing, and washed the mouthful down with a swig of Elgol's excellent ale. Some things weren't so different, whichever side of the mountains you were; especially simple things. Better still, simple things done right. A sandwich made with decent sausages and decent bread, a pint of good beer, a snug corner of a favourite tavern, whether in Carwerid or here in Denvirran. When you were slogging over a mountain pass in driving snow, it wasn't fancy food and silverware that you dreamt of; it was this.

"Started without us, have you?" Verris's voice broke into his thoughts. His friend slipped into the facing seat, signalling to a server.

"Considering we arranged this meeting best part of three months ago, I didn't even know for sure you'd be coming."

"Drinking alone? Not a good habit to get into, my lad."

"Who said it's a habit?"

Verris grinned, brushing back his sandy hair. His languid elegance and general air of being at ease with the world gave the impression of a highly privileged background, but Embrel knew the truth was more complicated. Verris was of good family, but a great-uncle or grandfather had speculated unwisely and lost much of the family's wealth. The family seat, Thixenholme, was close to the scale of Skilthorn, but whereas the latter must have forty or fifty enslaved in the house alone, and probably twenty free staff, Thixenholme had a bare handful of enslaved. The family lived in half a dozen rooms in the most recent wing and the rest was gently decaying. The obvious solution was to sell the place, but Verris's father had set his face against it.

He wasn't even sure how his friend's parents had managed to fund his University career. He knew it had been tight for his own family, though it might have been a lot tighter had Jerya not begun to suspect Grevel's embezzlement before it was too late.

Jerya had reminded him he'd once asked her, 'What's accounts?' Now there was a flicker of memory: 'It sounds boring' had been his response at the time. Exactly what might have happened if she hadn't made the crucial discovery didn't bear thinking about, but 'boring' it surely wasn't.

"Never mind drinking alone," said Verris now, "You surely seem to be thinking alone."

"I'm sorry. Let me pay for your drink…" He fished a coin from his pocket and handed it to the girl. "How was your summer?"

"Not bad considering I had to forego the pleasure of your company. I still can't quite believe you gave me back-word for no better reason than a visit to the Sung Lands."

Another arrival saved Embrel from having to respond to this ludicrous charge. "Evening, gentlemen. Allow me to introduce myself. Claife Henty at your service."

"I knew that," said Verris. "Or had you forgotten us?"

"It's more that we thought you must have forgotten me, since I've not had so much as a line from either of you all summer." He turned to Embrel. "I know you've been in the Sung Lands, but you must have been back a few weeks."

"About three weeks, yes, but there's been a lot going on. My Mamma had to have surgery."

There was no banter now, just honest concern. They *were* good fellows. He was happy to assure them that all had gone well, but it reminded him again how strange it had been, waiting in the lounge of the clinic as… as his mother operated on his Mamma.

No matter how many times he'd told himself that Railu was the best surgeon in the Five Principalities, if not the known world, he felt like he hadn't taken a single breath since the doors closed behind them; and he felt like his heart would thrash its way out of his chest when Railu finally emerged. He didn't know who'd held the other's hand more tightly, himself or Papa.

Railu's smile, an instant later, had been, he thought, the sweetest thing he had ever seen.

Duly reassured, his friends were keen to revert to the subject of the Sung Lands, and he was also happy with the change of subject, though he still felt himself skirting around the question of his parentage. It wasn't the fact of meeting his natural father that most nagged at him; it was the powerful wish to tell them of his pleasure in discovering he had a half-sister. Two half-brothers too, but if he was honest with himself, they meant less to him. They were further apart in age, and he'd spent less time with them. But Sokkie… he felt great affection, and real pride in the way she'd conducted herself during the eventful days during and after the visit to Delven. Would she really be able to come to the Five Principalities next summer, as she'd declared was her intention? At fifteen? Would that make her the youngest to make a Crossing?

Verris's voice cut into his brief reverie. "And how is the lovely Sumyra?" He'd never actually met Sumyra, and though Embrel had talked about her a few times, he'd never dwelt on her looks. But Verris tended to preface almost any female's name that way, barring his own mother and his 'gaggle' (sometimes even a 'horde') of sisters.

"Sumyra's very well. At least, she was when we parted." He explained how she'd stayed behind when he and Jerya had left. But he had understood very well what Verris had really been asking. "We've decided, by the way, that our relationship is… well, we both call Jerya 'aunt', so we could be cousins of a kind, but it's more like brother and sister."

"No more than that?"

"And no less," he said with firm emphasis. He did not care for Sumyra any less; it was only that he was clearer about *how* he cared.

"I like how you so casually call the Countess of Skilthorn by her first name," said Henty, lowering a near-empty tankard.

"I've known her all my life, long before she became a Countess. I've always called her Jerya."

Henty took a final swig. "You're lagging, young Embrel." He signalled to the girl, holding up three fingers.

Embrel waited till the fresh drinks arrived, lifted his mug and took a sip. "Well," he said, trying not to grin. He'd been waiting for this moment. "Speaking of my aunt the Countess..."

Even as he said it, an idea suddenly began to blossom in his mind. But he'd say nothing of that till he'd spoken to Jerya. The fellows would be excited enough at the prospect of meeting the Countess. The fact that it would be tomorrow almost had them jumping up and down.

※

"The thing is, aunt... well, you remember how you discovered what Grevel had been up to, only just in time."

Jerya shook her head. "I should have got there sooner."

"Well, if he'd got away with it any longer, the consequences could have been a lot worse... well, Verris is in a similar situation. Not that their manager's been embezzling; they don't even have a manager. They haven't been able to afford one for years. I don't know how they've even managed to send him to University. I do know that, even in the cheapest place he can find that isn't actually infested, the rent is a stretch for him. He misses meals. He has to borrow textbooks. He can barely ever afford to buy us a drink. We don't mind that, of course, but he does. He has his pride, you know?"

"I know very well," said Jerya. "We all knew what it would have meant if Grevel had continued undetected a few more months. I don't know how your parents would have managed to support you here, if they could have even got you through school. Selling an enslaved, or more than one, was the only way I could think of, but who would they sell? And to whom? I wasn't at Skilthorn then, obviously, and finding any other buyer who supported the Movement's standards..." She paused, fixing him with intent brown eyes. "And I think I can guess what you're thinking. Rent is hurting him, and at the same time Hedric and I have a house right here in Denvirran. Pendeen House. It gets more use by Dawnsingers than we give it, and that's outside University terms anyway."

"You read my mind."

"Don't forget I've known you a long time, lad."

## Chapter 44

# Sumyra

Embrel's two friends had both been fittingly grateful for Jerya's offer, but while Embrel and Verris continued in earnest conversation with her, Sumyra soon found Claife Henty's attention turning to herself.

"Miss Sumyra, Embrel tells us you stayed on in the Sung Lands when he and the Countess started for home?"

"Yes, for another three weeks. I travelled down to the South-West."

"On your own?"

"On the outward journey, yes. Well, there were other people in the coaches, but strangers."

"And you felt safe?"

"The roads there are very safe," she said. *Unless there's a demented ex-Master of the Guild of Dawnsingers around...*

"I'm glad to hear it, Miss Sumyra, but I am impressed nonetheless. And more than a little envious. The Sung Lands..." His dark, finely-chiselled, features did suggest envy or yearning, and for a moment his freckled amber eyes went distant.

"It's not such a hard journey," she said, though thoughts of the blizzard did intrude. "Nothing like the First Crossing." She nodded towards her aunt.

"Aye, the true First Crossing, not Selton's."

"I'm glad you know that."

"Oh, Embrel made sure of that." He grinned. "Marched right up to the College Librarian and asked if he knew he had a misleadingly-titled book on his shelves."

"And how did the Librarian react?"

"Hid behind the full title. *The First Crossing of the Dividing Range by the Southerly Route*. Of course you only see *The First Crossing* on the spine, and the rest's in small print on the title page."

"It's not enough, is it?"

"We still meet people who believe Selton and his party did the First Crossing."

"I trust you set them straight."

"We do... although there was one fellow who wouldn't believe us, whatever we said. Embrel saying he knew the Countess just seemed to make it worse, as if we were biased. But then we heard that Selton's son was going to deliver a guest lecture, and we persuaded this fellow to take a wager. The lecture itself was about other things, his voyages to the East, but when he took questions at the end Embrel stood up and asked if he would confirm that his father's expedition was not the true First Crossing."

"And what did he say?"

"He said, 'I was on that expedition with my father, so I can tell you for a certainty that ours was only the first crossing *by the Southern route*.' And he told the story—which is in the book—of emerging from the mountains to be met by a party of women who were expecting them. Because among them was, well, that lady at the end of this table. But you must know the story. Better than I, I should think."

"Did your friend pay up?"

"Yes, the three of us had an excellent meal at the finest restaurant in Denvirran. But I don't know if I could call him a friend. He seemed to feel... I don't know, as if it was somehow our fault that he'd clung to his false belief against all the evidence."

"I've met someone else like that," said Sumyra, thinking of Master Perriad.

"Tell me, though." He leaned forward. "The Countess has obviously experienced both Crossing routes. Which does she think is harder?"

"Well, now, the Southern route has refuges and shelters all the way. You don't need to carry a tent... though I don't think she and her companions had one on the First Crossing either. So now it's clearly easier. But she says the Northern route is harder anyway, especially the crag climb, and there are two high passes to cross, not just one. You could ask her yourself, of course."

"Oh, I don't like to intrude." He gestured to the others, deep in their own conversation, and Sumyra saw: *he's shy*. Perhaps, specifically, he was in awe of the Countess; well, many people were. It was something Jerya herself hated, she knew. Many, probably most, of the nobility would be highly affronted if not addressed with full formality and deference, but she was always at pains to minimise it, to set people at their ease. In school, she insisted on everyone calling her 'Preceptor', not 'Countess', and servants and enslaved called her 'm'lady', not the more formal 'your ladyship'.

Well, she thought, at least he's not too shy with me. She gave him a brief smile. "Would you like to visit the Sung Lands, then?"

"Very much. You can't imagine how envious I was when I got Embrel's letter saying he was going."

"I think I can, actually. There was... there was some doubt at first about whether I'd be able to go with them. I'd have found it hard to bear, being left behind."

He was discreet enough not to ask why her participation had been in question. Instead he said, "And then you stayed on longer. Did you have some particular destination in mind? You said you travelled to the South-West."

"Yes. I was looking for my—" She broke off, took a quick sip of sweet, smoky porter to cover a moment's thought. "Do you know who my Mamma is?"

"Your step-mother? Yes, of course, Embrel's told us all about her."

*Not* all *about her*, she thought, certain Embrel had kept the secret about his own true parentage. Henty's next words seemed to bear this out. "The first lady doctor in the Five Principalities—and she was part of the First Crossing too."

"Yes, because she'd been a Dawnsinger with Jerya. And... you know about Choosing? How girls are taken from their homes, their families, at ten or eleven?" He nodded. "I went to find her family."

"And did you?"

"Yes, I met her mother, her sister, her niece." *Embrel's grandmother, aunt, cousin*. All the things she must not say... She tried to steer the conversation in a different direction. "What would you specially like to see in the Sung Lands?"

"I'm curious about Dawnsingers, of course."

"You don't have to go that far to see Dawnsingers. They pass through here every summer. And they start and finish every trip at our home."

"That sounds like one more good reason to visit Drumlenn," he said, glancing at her almost shyly—or was it slyly?

She decided to give him the benefit of the doubt. "We'd be glad to see you... and I'm sure any friend of Embrel's would be welcome at Duncal."

※

"Now," said Jerya, her glance taking in the whole table. "I think you all know Sumyra and I are on our way to Velyadero, and I hope we are going to come back with agreement that the University will open its doors to female students. What I'm wondering is how you, and your fellow students, might feel if the same thing happened in Denvirran."

A smile bloomed as she, unmistakably, thought of something. She looked at Embrel. "Do you remember, when you were nine, when Master Analind came to the Five Principalities for the first time? She was explaining how Dawnsingers were all female, and you said all the schools you knew about were for boys only, and you said a school where there were girls too might be nicer."

Embrel blushed. His colour only deepened as Henty, chuckling, said, "Sounds like you were smarter at nine than you are now."

"I think..." said Verris. "Well, you asked, Countess, how our fellow students might feel. And I cannot imagine such a move would be universally welcomed. I think many would regard the presence of females as a distraction. A very fine distraction, to be sure—a nice distraction—but definitely a distraction."

"All the better," said Sumyra with her sweetest smile. "While you're all distracted, we'll get on with winning all the prizes."

## Chapter 45

# Embrel

Their routes coincided as far as the steps of Pendeen House. As they said their farewells, Jerya said, "I'll speak to the staff tonight, and they'll send word when your rooms are ready for you. They won't be the grandest rooms in the house, you know."

"I'm sure they'll be a lot grander than what we have now," said Verris. "May I say again, Countess—"

Jerya waved off his thanks. "I never liked to think of a place like this sitting idle when there are people with barely a roof over their heads. If it weren't so useful to the Dawnsingers in the summer, I'd have been urging Hedric to sell it years ago, or find a better use for it."

As she spoke, Sumyra was trying to catch Embrel's eye. He raised inquiring brows and she gave a tilt of her head to draw him aside. "I haven't had a chance to speak to you properly all evening."

He nodded. Turning, he urged Henty and Verris to carry on without him. "I'll follow in a few minutes."

Verris only nodded, but Henty seemed to give him a dark look, and glanced back several times before they turned the corner.

"Oh dear," said Embrel. "Claife's smitten with you and he thinks I'm asserting a prior claim."

"I'm not here to be *claimed*," she said.

He raised both hands. "No, no, I never meant... I don't think he does either. But if he did, I would tell him; knowing you as I do, as close as a sister, exactly what you just said. You're not a prize—well, I think you are a prize—but not..."

Half-laughing, she laid a hand on his arm, a gentle pressure through coat and shirt. "Stop tying yourself in knots. I know you like a sister, remember."

"Step-half-sister," he said, summoning a grin. "But you *claimed* me for this conversation... was there something you particularly wanted to say?"

"Can I not just wish for a little time with my step-half-brother?" Her teasing tone gave way to something more seriousness. "I just want to know how you are. Especially after... well... Elidir."

He sighed. "I can't deny I still think about her; not all the time, but often. Ten, twenty, times a day; I don't keep count. But what's the use of yearning after the unattainable? Stupid to fall in—to become infatuated with someone like that."

"Not stupid," she said, pressing his arm again. Lanterns flanking the entrance, the light of a dozen candles streaming from the open door, painted one side of her face a rosy gold. He could quite see why Henty might be, as he'd said 'smitten'. Many things might have been simpler if he'd felt the same way himself. "Not exactly a rational thing to do, I grant you, but... I don't think words like 'stupid' apply."

"It feels pretty stupid to me. Pointless. Fruitless."

"The heart has its own ideas. It isn't a rational organ."

"We both know it's not really the heart. Your parents are doctors; I dare say you know better than me."

"Metaphorically. Metaphorically, I'm exactly right. None of us are completely rational creatures. But you said you're still thinking about her...?"

He sighed again. "Yes. And that *is* stupid."

"What's it been, Embrel? Three weeks? Four? Time... My parents are doctors and they both say time is the great healer. Their job is to give it the chance."

"And how do *I* give it a chance?"

She shrugged. He wondered suddenly if she was warm enough in her dress and short jacket; but she was speaking again. "Meet other people, I suppose."

He laughed. "Well, *that* would be easier if this University admitted females."

"You're saying you'd welcome the *distraction*?"

"That was Verris, not me."

"Embrel..." There was a new tone in her voice now. "I'm going to tell you something. I haven't told anyone else."

"Not even Railu?"

"Not even Mamma." She paused a second, and he supposed they were both thinking on exactly what it meant, now, to say 'Railu', to say 'Mamma', to think of her.

Sumyra gathered herself. "I met someone in the Sung Lands too. Someone in Kermey..."

"You... liked him?"

"Her."

*Oh*, he thought; but he thought, almost at once, of Mavrys and Vireddi. He did not know them as well as Sumyra did, of course, but well enough. He knew that they accounted themselves married, had held a ceremony which both Sumyra and his aunt had witnessed.

He thought of a school full of girls. And he thought of the College of the Dawnsingers...

Inevitably, he thought, again, of Elidir. But she was two hundred miles away, and in another world. His best friend—his *sister*—was right here, in front of him.

"You're not shocked?" she said.

"Surprised, perhaps, for a moment." He thought that was honest, more or less. "You liked her? What was her name?"

"Nóèttu." He remembered how she'd said that all female names in Kermey ended in —u. "Yes, I liked her. I liked her a lot. And maybe she liked me even more. I think she was more upset than I was when I had to leave."

"Whereas I don't suppose Elidir was upset at all—not that that's a great consolation. But why... are you telling me this because I said old Henty was smitten with you? Shall I be needing to let him down gently?"

"I don't know." Her face, usually so open, was harder to read in the flickering light. One of the lanterns needed its wick trimming, but he thought perhaps they'd be extinguished soon. "I liked him too, I think."

Sumyra considered for a moment. "Tell him... well, if he asks, just say I won't object to seeing him again. But say no more than that. I promise nothing, and, well, you can probably guess; I'm a little confused at the moment."

He took her hands. "Didn't you say time is the great healer?"

"I think, if I'm being picky, I said that Mamma and Papa say that."

"I'm sure it's too late in the evening to be picky. And I know Jerya's planning an early start. But was there any special reason for telling me about Nóèttu?"

She frowned. "I don't quite know. Just... yes, just to let you know, Embrel, if you're confused, you're not the only one."

He wondered if 'confused' was the word for his state of mind. He felt as though his feelings had been clear enough, unambiguous; just not reciprocated. Most emphatically not reciprocated. But he didn't need to say that. A little step-half-sibling solidarity wouldn't hurt.

He reached out and she stepped into the embrace. "Time," he said. "And speaking of time, I'll see you when you come back."

## Chapter 46

# Sumyra

As they were about to reboard after the midday break on the first day out of Denvirran, Sumyra looked up at Vireddi. "Would you mind some company up there?"

"Not at all, Miss. Plenty o'room."

She moved to the far side, clambered up, seated herself. She let Vireddi deal with the business of the moment, making sure the family were inside and settled, then easing the horses into a stately walk, working them around to bring the carriage in line with the arch of the inn-yard.

"There didn't seem much room getting out through there," she said when they were finally on the road and settling into their regular pace.

Vireddi grinned. "It's tighter at Skilthorn. First time I went through on this seat I couldn't believe we'd not scrape—and I wasn't even driving."

"How long have you been learning?"

"'Bout a year an' a half. Started after the worst frosts were done, last year. Aye, middle o'Tu'lander."

"Your idea, or Mavrys's?"

A broader grin. "All mine. I din't even let her know I was learnin', not at first. It's one thing—the only thing, likely—I can do better'n she can around horses. But, yow know, when I first started workin' at the stables, six—seven years ago, I was plain terrified of 'em."

"You've come a long way," said Sumyra, and she thought it was true in more ways than just this. Seven years ago Vireddi had been illiterate, like the vast majority of enslaved; now she was an avid reader. Sumyra had done volunteer shifts in Skilthorn's Library, and she'd seen Vireddi there numerous times; seen her name in the ledgers too, in a painstakingly neat hand quite unlike the hasty scrawls of most of the girls.

"It's nice to be up here," she said now. "Like you said, you see a lot more."

"D'yow know this road, Miss?"

"Please, Vireddi, call me Sumyra. We've known each other long enough... and I'm not even a Skilthorn student any longer."

"Thank yow very kindly. If yow'll forgive me when I forget—as I'm sure to. It's a habit; hard to break. Specially when time was I'd've been beaten for it."

Sumyra looked closer at her. Vireddi, she thought, was one of those people who would always look younger than her age, but she had looked much the same when they'd first met, during the first summer-school. She herself had been thirteen then; Vireddi had to be several years older. Which would mean... "You remember life under the old Earl, of course."

"I do, M—Sumyra, not that I care to dwell on those mem'ries."

"I'm sorry."

"It's all right. Though it's lucky I wasn't a few years older. Heard plenty o'stories. They used to say, when th' old Earl was still hale, no girl was safe... well, but I reckon Dortis could tell yow a lot more about him."

"That's true." Though Dortis, too, was always reticent about those times. Perhaps silence told its own story.

Anyway, the question that really occupied her was different. "You and Mavrys... you were quite young when you got married, weren't you?"

"Aye, we wed the day I turned eighteen... first time I ever knew it was my birthday, and the first present I got was the best I could've ever wished for."

"That's lovely," said Sumyra, and meant it; but then she thought a little more. "Of course, it's not lovely that you never even knew your date of birth before, never had a birthday."

"Ah, well, better late than never. That's what they say, ain't it?"

"You're not one to dwell on the past, I see."

Vireddi shrugged. "The past is done. Can't change a thing about it. And my life's so much better'n it was. For a lot o' reasons. Two of 'em sittin' in this carriage right now."

"And another one back at home. Vireddi, you and Mavrys being so young... you just eighteen..."

"She's not so much older. Just a few months."

"Just makes me wonder. I won't ask if you've ever lain with a man. But did you ever think about it? Did you ever feel... attracted?"

She watched Vireddi closely, hoping first that her question wouldn't offend or upset her. There seemed no sign of that, but Vireddi said nothing for some time. Her eyes were on the horses and the road ahead.

She'd slowed to manage the narrow gap left by an overladen hay-wain lumbering up the shallow gradient they were descending. Only once she'd brought the team back to pace did she speak.

"Funny thing. There's lots o'books about love. Stories, I mean, novels. But I ain't ever read about love like Mav and me. Love between two women." She spared a quick sidelong glance. "You know what I reckon? Ever since someone told me what pen-names were... I reckon a lot o' those books are really written by men."

Sumyra laughed, but then she thought about it. "I'm not a great novel-reader... but I think you might be right."

"I read a lot at first... yow have to, don't yow, afore yow can figure out what yow really like?"

*Especially*, thought Sumyra, *if you didn't even get started till you were... maybe my age.* But then another thought surfaced. "If no one's written your kind of story, maybe you should do it."

Vireddi jerked the reins in her surprise, had to settle the horses before she could reply. "Me? Write a book? I'm only a—"

"—You're a reader. You read a lot; that means you know what makes a good book. But most important of all, you've got stories to tell. Important stories."

Vireddi considered this. "But if I did tell *our* story... I mean, it's not 'xactly a secret, but we don't shout it around. There's not that many people know; outside o'Skilthorn, hardly any. 'Bout us bein' married and all that."

"How many, do you think?"

"Well... there was about twenty at the wedding. Yow and yowr Mamma, th'Earl and Countess, all of the hands. Torvyn was there but she'd be too young to remember. A few others. People we trusted. A few more since... But there's many more as don't know." She sighed. "Even Mav's mother doesn't know."

"Really?"

"Mav reckons it's better that way. But it makes it awkward when she comes visitin' or Mav goes to see her. She's always askin' is Mav seein' anyone, and what can Mav say?"

Sumyra smiled. "My aunt's like that with me."

"If she's bad now, see what it's like when yow're twenty-four. If yow're not wed by then, I mean."

"Well, that's what I was trying to ask you about, when I asked if you'd ever been attracted to a man."

Vireddi gave her another sideways look, and Sumyra was reminded again just how shrewd she could be. She thought Vireddi probably had a very good idea of the situation she was facing; but she turned her gaze back to the team and the road, and answered the specific question. "Depends what yow mean by 'attracted', I s'pose. I can look at a man and think he's beautiful—Mav does too—but it don't mean I'm wantin' to cuddle up to him."

Sumyra took a slow breath, thinking. The road turned a bend and she saw a narrow bridge ahead. Another carriage was starting to cross, so Vireddi drew their team to a halt. She said nothing more until the wait was over, the bridge safely crossed, the carriage rumbling up the slope beyond. "You know what it's like at Skilthorn. A school full of girls. Where else can you look for... for intimacy, for affection? And when you're like me and you've spent every summer there too... Well, it's one of the things my aunt worries about, I guess."

"It's much the same as slave-quarters, I s'pose," said Vireddi. "Yow know the household slaves are nearly all female. Separate quarters for the men, and for the married ones, o'course."

"Well, anyway" said Sumyra, "It's not like I'd never... well, you said 'cuddle'. Never cuddled with another girl. Cuddled and... well, you know."

"I reckon I do." It was hard to read Vireddi's face now; in profile, dappled light flickering across it as they rolled down an avenue lined with poplars.

"But it always seemed like something that was just for school. I suppose I thought that when I left and got out into the world I'd... that things would be different. Only..."

"Only they're not so diff'rent after all?"

"I'm just confused. This summer... well, I've been out in the world all right. Seen a good deal of the Sung Lands, North and South. But the first thing that happened was back home in Drumlenn." She took another deep breath, hardening her resolve. "I kissed—well, she kissed me first, really. Someone I'd only just met." She trusted Vireddi, no question, but there was no need to mention names. "She kissed me first, but two seconds later I was kissing her back...

"And then, in the Sung Lands, when I was travelling on my own, there was someone else."

"Another girl?"

"Girl, woman, whatever you want to say. Similar age to me, anyway. We travelled together for a while, shared a bed for a few nights. And I'm sure if I'd been able to stay longer we'd have continued, but I really had to come home, and..." She stopped, still feeling a little guilty about the way things had ended with Nóèttu. If they have ended... "But then when we were in Denvirran..."

"Yow liked that friend o' Master Embrel's."

She didn't know whether to be glad or sorry; she shouldn't have been surprised. Vireddi really was no-one's fool. "Yes, I did, and I told him I'd be happy to see him again... but am I just trying to be the way Aunt Arlenys thinks I should be? And should I? I mean, she's right about one thing. Somebody has to have children, or there'll be no one left in a hundred years. But then again, why shouldn't I be like you and Mavrys? I've always thought you're as well-suited as any other couple I know. Maybe better than most."

"Well, thank yow for that, Mi—Sumyra." Vireddi chewed her lip, pondering. "Seems to me, a lot o' problems happen because people care too much about 'should' and 'shouldn't'. Girls shouldn't be too educated. Slaves shouldn't marry frees. Women shouldn't wed women... Ask me, a lot o' people make themselves mis'rable 'cause their heart's tellin' 'em one thing and 'should's' tellin' 'em another."

"I believe you... but I think my problem is I don't know what my heart is telling me."

"Time," said Vireddi. "Don't 'xpect to know right off, whate'er they say in those novels about love at first sight. And I ain't sayin' it never happens, but it wasn't like that for Mav'n'me. Not right off."

"But did you know, before, that the love of your life would be another woman?"

Vireddi pondered, as if she'd never considered that particular question before. "I don't know that I did. I think maybe Mav'd always thought she'd wind up wi' a man, 'cause that's what everyone expected. All she knew when I first knew her was she didn't want to marry the man they'd lined her up for. Twice her age and practic'ly a stranger. But her'n'me... it wasn't love at first sight, but it wasn't too long either. Weeks rather than months. We knew soon enough."

She'd kept her eyes ahead through this; now she flicked one swift glance at Sumyra. "Way I see it, love's love, and yow'll know when it... when it finds yow."

They drove on in contemplative silence for a mile or more, side by side, close but not touching. Then Vireddi gave her another glance. "There's a good straight stretch comin' up. Maybe yow'd like to take the reins for a bit?"

## Chapter 47
# Sumyra

Almost as soon as they'd crossed the border, Sumyra had felt she was going to like Velyadero. Jerya remarked that the forested slopes that rose on both sides of the road reminded her of some of the country around Delven, and Sumyra had seen immediately what she meant.

It didn't hurt that it was a sweet summer day; in lower lands the riding might be hot and dusty, but here the temperature was perfect, and the air had that freshness that seemed to be endemic in mountains, or at least their foothills. Within the first hour she'd seen a black woodpecker and several hoopoes, and every time she looked up there seemed to be an eagle above, though too distant to identify precisely.

She didn't believe in omens or auspices, but she saw no harm in taking encouragement from what she saw around her. People in the three Northern Principalities were often disparaging about their Southern neighbours, often lumping Velyadero and Buscanya together. But the scattered farms and cottages she'd seen thus far had all looked clean and well-kept. It wasn't proof that the inhabitants were comfortable and well-nourished, but it seemed unlikely that people who struggled to feed and clothe their children would have excess energy for the maintenance of turf-roofs or the regular lime-washing of walls.

Her first view of Velya itself brought further cheer. They came over a rise and within a few of the horses' strides found the whole of the town spread out below, lining a river and climbing the slopes of flanking hills. It wasn't a city on the scale of Denvirran, let alone Sessapont, but the first impression immediately gave the lie to the suggestion that it was little more than a cluster of hovels. She began to suspect that those who pronounced so definitively had never even been here.

She'd noticed that most of the people she saw working in the fields or elsewhere were frees, not enslaved. It was no surprise, as she'd heard that enslaved were a lower proportion of the population in Velyadero. In fact this was one of the reasons the Principality was often regarded as 'impoverished'. Since the number of slaves owned was commonly taken as an indicator of the wealth of an individual or family, there was a twisted logic in using it as a measure of the wealth of a whole province too.

※

"Stop," said Jerya in a low, urgent tone. She turned aside for a moment, lowering the veil attached to her formal hat. That done, she walked briskly on. It wasn't far from their lodging to their first destination; Sumyra wasn't surprised she'd elected to walk. Carriages rolled by over square setts, overlooked by tall narrow houses with distinctive stepped gables.

"I want to be sure that woman is who I think she is," Jerya explained now. "Let's pass her and then stop to look in a shop window."

When they stopped, and knowing what she was about, Sumyra was able to see how Jerya angled her view to watch her quarry's reflection, time her turn so it looked natural yet allowed her a good view of the woman's face.

Jerya waited a moment, then turned to Vireddi. "Would you do me a favour and follow that woman? Stay back, don't let her see you're following, but if you can see where she goes, that would be very helpful. The street name, and the house number? Meet us back at the hotel, and if you need refreshment just ask them to put it on my account."

Vireddi nodded, "Yes, m'lady," and moved off.

"Who was that?" asked Sumyra as they started again.

"A woman called Nielle. I'm sure now. She looks older, and she's gained some weight; well, she must be past forty, and she's had at least three children that I know of. Well, I'm older too... I don't know if she'd have recognised me even without the veil. Last time she saw me, I was still a governess." She'd pushed back the veil again, and there was a wry smile on her face now.

"That must be ten years ago."

"Eleven, I should think. But she'll have good reason to remember me... or bad reason, she's likely to think it."

"Pardon me, aunt, but who is she?"

"It's not so much who she is but who she's married to. You might have heard the name of Grevel?"

"Oh, yes... wasn't he the estate manager who'd been embezzling?"

"The very same. They did a flit with a fair chunk of Duncal's money, but fortunately I'd started to suspect. We'd blocked his access to the main account—just in time, as it proved—but we hadn't got enough proof to take to the authorities. Grevel presumably realised the game was almost up. He tried to get in to that account but when the bank declined, he seems to have jumped into a carriage that was already waiting, along with wife, children, and a significant amount of loot. The bank sent a messenger to Duncal, but by the time we could organise a pursuit they'd been gone for half a day." She blew out a long breath. "I'd hardly thought of Grevel, or Nielle, for years, but now, suddenly, here she is."

"She looks prosperous."

"Aye, seems they've invested the money well. Only it wasn't theirs to invest in the first place." Another out-breath, almost a snort. "It's a complication I could do without. I'll send a bird for Duncal later; can't think about it now. We'll be there in five minutes."

※

Riber was either prematurely greying or unusually smooth-faced for a mature man. He greeted Sumyra courteously, but there was an almost boyish enthusiasm in his greeting for Jerya. "Countess Jerya! I am truly honoured and delighted to see you again!"

"It's only been a couple of weeks..."

"Indeed, and I must express my gratitude that you have returned so soon. And... well, the truth is, I dreamed of meeting you... well, most of my life. I was still but a lad when I first read... it was a report of your wedding, I recall, and there was an account of your previous exploits. First and Second Crossings of the Dividing Range! May I say I am always at pains to correct those—far too many, I am afraid—who still credit the Duke of Selton with that achievement."

"I can't entirely blame Selton. Anyone who reads his book closely must know the truth."

"Quite so—and very gracious of you, Countess, if I may say so. You hit the nail on the head when you say they must read closely! Yes, he did give you the credit, but in a niggardly manner."

Jerya shrugged. "It was a long time ago." *Before I was born,* thought Sumyra. "In any case, Doctor Riber, I don't believe you invited me here to discuss the merits, or otherwise, of Selton's book."

"No, very true... I can but hope that later in your visit there may be more chance to hear some first-hand accounts of your adventures. Well, let me approach the business of the day by bemoaning another injustice; the fact that degrees awarded by our University—be they Bachelor's, Master's, or Doctoral—are not always recognised by our counterparts in other Principalities."

"I've noticed too that they often refer to you as a College rather than a University. Though if you take a moment to consider the College of the Dawnsingers, you might see why I wouldn't take that as an insult."

He smiled, showing white but rather uneven teeth. "A nice point, Countess, but you must know as well as I do that it is intended as a slight."

Jerya inclined her head. "Well, I shall continue to call you Doctor, and to refer to the institution as a University. Now, what do you have in mind for today?"

"Well, I had hoped—with your consent, of course!—to offer you a guided tour this morning. Then some refreshment, and then I will bring you to the Council of Senate this afternoon."

"That all sounds admirable. Please, lead on.

## Chapter 48

## Sumyra

"With your permission, Countess, I shall first invite Doctor Riber to make his case in support of the proposal." The Chancellor smiled. "We are all familiar with at least the gist of his argument, but this will see it entered into the minutes. Then Professor Birchen can make the case against the change; and then, having seen both sides of our discussions, we will be glad to hear your response."

"I'm your guest," said Jerya. "I'm happy to proceed however you think best."

"A guest, my lady, and an honoured one. I thank you for your acquiescence. Doctor Riber..."

Riber almost bounded to his feet. "Chancellor, Councillors of Council, fellow scholars... and of course, Countess... As the Chancellor says, my case has already been aired and widely discussed; and I can hardly believe that you, Countess, will need any convincing. I shall, therefore, be as breviloquent as possible."

Sumyra saw Jerya restraining a smile. How much time did men spend telling their listeners how concise they intended to be? And would anyone who really prized concision use a word like 'breviloquent'?

"As I informed our gracious guest this morning, our University is unfortunately and, as I'm sure we all here agree, unfairly, disparaged by many beyond our own Principality. It is undeniable that our institution is somewhat smaller in scale, and that we teach a slightly narrower range of subjects, but our guiding principle has always been the pursuit of quality rather than quantity. To further our development, to broaden the scope of our teaching and research, to maintain and enhance our standards... these aims are, I am sure, shared by every member of this Council."

He looked around as if seeking confirmation, and was rewarded with a few nods; but Sumyra saw impatience in other faces too. Breviloquent, she thought.

"The question," continued Riber, "And one to which we have devoted many hours of debate, is how best to further these aims. I know this is all too familiar to all but one of my listeners, but permit me to summarise for the benefit of the noble lady. Very broadly, there are two competing schools of thought. One might be encapsulated in the mariner's phrase, 'steady as she goes'. We have reached our present position almost entirely without benefit of investment from outwith the Principality, or the presence of non-native scholars. Why should we not continue on the same upward path while continuing to draw on our own resources?

"To this, as my fellow Councillors know, I, and those of similar mind, respond as follows: we recognise, of course, that our present condition represents a very notable achievement, one in which we can all justifiably take pride. However, we must recognise that none of the other institutions against which we are measured—against which, indeed, we do and must measure ourselves—none of them consider 'steady as she goes' an adequate or acceptable guiding principle. None of them have, to switch metaphors, reached a plateau on which they rest while we complete our own ascent. If we continue as we are, I fear that we... well, the metaphor begins to look stretched, but it is somewhat like continuing to toil over the foothills while others scale ever higher summits.

"With this in mind, I and my allies argue that we must embrace more radical, more daring, strategies. We must be bolder. We must seek new ideas, new investors... new blood. Also in metaphorical terms, of course." No one laughed. With a faintly crestfallen air, Riber continued. "And this, Council, is why the proposal that we consider the admission of young ladies is so timely."

He looked at Jerya. "Countess. It is, I believe, seven years since the first great Congress hosted by you and your noble husband at Skilthorn?"

"That's correct."

"A Congress at which our University was, alas, unrepresented. I was but a junior lecturer at the time, or I should have leapt at the chance. Be that as it may, it remains a landmark in the history of the Five Principalities. From that time it became impossible for any rational man to maintain the notion that females are incapable of advanced thought or intellectual endeavour. The other Universities were happy enough to send delegates to your great Congress, and in other ways too have been eager to take advantage of the scholarship of the Guild of Dawnsingers, but have so far shown no obvious inclination to extend any new opportunities to females of our own lands.

"Were the University of Velyadero to do so, it would, at a stroke, place itself at the forefront. It would be, I submit, a move both bold and visionary. Never again could we be dismissed as a place of no consequence, an intellectual backwater. From being a place of which people in Sessapont or Troquharran might say, 'oh, is there a University there?', we would be the academy of which everyone is talking. Gentlemen, I put it to you that this is an opportunity whose like we shall not see again."

He nodded to the Chancellor and resumed his seat.

"The Council thanks you, Doctor Riber," said the Chancellor. "I now invite Professor Birchen to respond."

Sumyra had been expecting the opposing speaker to be one of the elder statesmen of the gathering, men whose minds had been shaped long before Jerya's second Crossing, and all that had unfolded that turbulent summer. It was eleven years ago; Riber might still have been an undergraduate, but some of the fustier-looking dons she saw would already have been in their fifties, one or two perhaps even older.

However, Professor Birchen appeared only a few years older than Riber, not past his mid-thirties. Old enough to recall the first news of the existence of the Sung Lands; young enough for his ideas to have been shaped by it.

She felt a little discouraged, but his first words were emollient. "Council will indulge me if I address a few opening remarks to our esteemed guest. My friend the Chancellor was eloquent in his welcome, Countess, but I fear he was remiss in one particular, omitting to mention what I believe to be the case, namely that you are the first lady ever to be invited to attend a meeting of this Council, let alone to speak."

"Thank you. May I just say no other University has extended me this honour?... Yet."

Birchen smiled. "The honour is ours. So I pray you not to imagine that my questioning of this proposal in any way indicates a disrespect for you or for your achievements. I too count myself among your admirers, and I heartily applaud all that you have done to further the education of young ladies." He gestured broadly. "A few of my colleagues may still question the basic principle of women's education, but I am not among them. I made a note of Doctor Riber's exact words at one point, and I should like to quote them now. *'From that time it became impossible for any reasonable man to maintain the notion that females are incapable of advanced thought or intellectual endeavour.'*

"The question as I see it, therefore, is not whether ladies should be educated, or at least have the *opportunity* to be educated; the question now is whether they should be educated alongside gentlemen, or separately.

"Might I ask you, Countess, if I am correct in understanding that the College of the Dawnsingers is entirely composed of females? Students, academic staff, ancillary staff?"

The question was surely rhetorical, but still required an answer. "That's correct."

"In fact, I believe, the Precincts of the College are exclusive to the female sex? As far as I know, no man has been admitted, beyond an annexe reserved for the purpose, for decades if not centuries?"

"Not to my knowledge. But I am not an expert in the history of the Guild."

"And it is also true that your own establishment, which has achieved so much in a short time, is exclusively female?"

"The student body is, yes. The teaching staff, and the household, no. In fact—but perhaps I should save any further response for my own turn."

"Thank you, Countess. I look forward to it. Well, lady and gentlemen, no doubt you can already see the direction of my argument. We have two significant pieces of evidence to prove the capacity of the female mind to benefit from higher education. The very great accomplishments of the Guild of Dawnsingers, which in some fields exceed the achievements of the finest minds of the Five Principalities, are the first. And then we have the Skilthorn Academy, whose students have, as Doctor Riber reminded us, been assessed to the same standards as their male counterparts in the Principality of Denvirran, and have consistently performed at levels equal to the best of the boys' schools. Two noteworthy and compelling pieces of evidence… and both from institutions where the student body, at least, is entirely female.

"We can, on this basis, say a good deal about the real and potential achievements of female students in an all-female student body. However, we have no comparable evidence on how females—or indeed males—might fare in an environment where the two sexes are taught together. That would most certainly be an interesting experiment." He smiled. "Interesting, and perhaps enlightening, but surely not without risk. Risk for the students, perhaps of both sexes, certainly for the females, but a risk too for the University itself.

"My good friend Doctor Riber said much that I agree with. I most assuredly agree with him that the admission of young ladies would be a bold move, and that it would draw attention throughout the Five Principalities and perhaps beyond. The corollary is that any untoward outcomes would also receive a great deal of attention.

"I do not think I need to spell out for you the kind of risks attendant upon bringing together groups of young ladies and young gentlemen on a daily basis. We are not bumpkins in Velyadero, whatever some unenlightened people may think; we are men of the world. Still, our gracious guest has seen more of the world than any of us. I am bound to ask how many parents would be happy to see their daughters in such a situation."

He glanced at Jerya as if half-expecting her to leap up with a rebuttal. Sumyra was sure she had an answer, but presumably she thought it best to save it for her own turn.

"Well," he said, looking slightly disconcerted, "Like Doctor Riber, I have no wish to trespass on the valuable time of this august assembly any more than I have to. I will therefore draw my argument together. I trust we can all agree that the education of young ladies is a worthy cause, and I certainly wish to further it, not to impede it. Indeed, one of my greatest concerns is that anything but a wholly triumphant outcome might set back the cause rather than advancing it.

"Perhaps a day will come when we can view this in a different light, but sadly I fear that day is not yet here, nor is it anywhere on the near horizon. Until then, I am very much afraid that Doctor Riber's proposal, though wholly admirable in intent, is premature. Believe me, my friend, learned colleagues, noble guest, it gives me no pleasure to say this, but I am obliged to conclude that at the present it presents too great a risk both for our putative future students and for this institution we all hold so dear."

※

Even after seven years, Sumyra knew, Jerya still saw something absurd in holding the rank of Countess. She had confessed, one day in the carriage, that being addressed as such still sometimes filled her with a wild urge to laugh—usually on the most inappropriate occasions. No one, she added, ever paid any particular heed to what Miss Jerya Delven had to say; few paid more than polite attention to Jerya, Mistress of Kirwaugh. But the moment she became Jerya, Countess of Skilthorn, people sat up and took notice. Embrel had told her how the headmaster of his school, who had barely deigned to notice the governess, turned almost cringingly obsequious when presented, barely two years later, to the Countess.

It was absurd, and Sumyra well understood why Jerya felt it was wrong; but there were times when it was useful, when she would overcome her misgivings, and her aversion to elaborate finery. Today, naturally, was one such, and Sumyra had taken every care to present herself as a worthy companion.

With a rustle of tiered skirts, Jerya stood and stepped forward. "Thank you, Chancellor, Councillors. I am deeply appreciative of the opportunity you have given me today. Simply by inviting me to address you, you have placed your University in the forefront of progress, ahead of every other in the Five Principalities. And to add to this, both the previous speakers have clearly endorsed the principle of education for females."

Jerya smiled. "I'm almost disappointed. I had prepared a pretty speech, elaborating on your estimable motto, *Knowledge is the first step to Wisdom*. I was ready, too, to dazzle you with the excellence of the results our students have achieved in the Matriculation papers of the University of Denvirran—including my niece here." Sumyra wished she was darker, the better to mask a blush. "Now I find I don't need to.

"Well, never mind. Let me proceed directly to the arguments raised by Professor Birchen. I hope no one imagines I am insensible of the concerns he raised. I am a mother myself, though my own daughter is still more than a decade away from the age of University admission.

"I have also been responsible for the care of the daughters of others, from the age of eleven or so, for five years now. And as an aside, our first graduands, who achieved such excellent results, had been in school only for those five years, though some had attended summer-schools with Dawnsingers before then.

"Which brings me to a key point of Professor Birchen's argument; that we at Skilthorn have chosen to educate girls apart from boys. One answer to this is that, as I just mentioned, our girls are younger than university students, but there is another.

"In fact, we did consider the possibility of admitting both sexes. I used to be governess to one lad who had said to me that he thought such a school would be 'nicer'. And he may very well have been right. Of course we were aware that we were already asking parents to commit to something unprecedented, and that the additional presence of boys might have been a step too far for some, but that was not the main reason we chose not to pursue that option. The real reason was a very simple one. There were already many schools for boys. There were none for girls. We could not justify halving the number of places available to them."

She paused a moment, looked around. She seemed to have everyone's attention. "I must admit that the challenges of establishing and developing a school for girls were pretty much all-consuming. To my lasting shame, when one of the girls from our first graduating class asked me 'what next?', I had no ready answer. We have done what we could, and we have enabled a couple of girls to pursue further study in the subjects in which my husband and I have advanced knowledge, principally mathematics and astronomy. Another has taken part in fieldwork on the movement of glaciers, and helped in the preparation of papers on the subject. We have done what we can, but we are nowhere near possessing the resources that would be needed to establish a fully-fledged University. I am sure you know better than I just what a great undertaking this is. There is a need, and I am very glad that both previous speakers have acknowledged it, and we cannot meet it unaided.

"Since Professors Riber and Birchen have both endorsed the *principle* of education for females, including University education, I conclude that it is the *practical* questions which remain to be addressed. I turn, therefore, to the specific concerns raised by Professor Birchen."

At this moment, Riber raised a hand. When Jerya yielded, he said, "Forgive my interruption, Countess, but I hope you will agree that I have good reason. I should like to request the Chancellor to put the matter of the admission of females to the vote."

"In principle?" asked the Chancellor.

"As a first step, yes, Chancellor. Might I suggest the following form of words? *Council supports equal education for females as a binding principle. Council further stipulates that the admission of females be brought forward at the earliest date at which practical considerations can be satisfactorily resolved.*"

There was a good deal of discussion, some of which struck Sumyra as extraordinarily pernickety. The word 'binding' was removed, reinstated, and finally replaced with 'fundamental', which either satisfied everyone or, perhaps, satisfied no one. There was equally convoluted debate as to whether specific criteria should be set to determine what 'satisfactorily resolved' might mean, or whether—as any reasonable person would surely think—you would know when a matter was *satisfactorily resolved* because, well, you were satisfied.

It took a full twenty minutes by the clock over the side door, before the final wording was agreed. After that the actual vote was almost an anti-climax, over in a blink; a simple show of hands.

By seventeen votes to seven, with three abstentions, the Council of Senate of the University of Velyadero committed the institution to *equal education for females* as a fundamental principle, and further agreed that the admission of females was to be brought forward *at the earliest date at which practical considerations can be satisfactorily resolved.*

Looking at Jerya, Sumyra thought her aunt's eyes seemed suspiciously bright.

※

"Now that we are addressing *practical considerations*," said Jerya. "I'd like to make an observation that some of you may find reassuring.

"We only graduated our first class a few months ago." Half-turning, she indicated Sumyra. "My niece here was one of them. Five years ago we admitted our first thirteen girls; a slightly motley group in terms of age, and in the extent of their previous education. Two of them were, sadly, withdrawn after two or three years; two more will graduate next year. We took nine girls through the examinations of the Denvirran Matriculation Board, and they all comfortably achieved the marks required for admission to the University of Denvirran. In five years, with only the tuition of governesses before then..." She broke off with a laugh. "But I mustn't disparage governesses; I've been one myself.

"Well, I don't need to reiterate my arguments about the quality of these girls. My point here is quantity. As I said, there are nine of them. Next Meadander, at most, sixteen. If every one of them wished to take up a place at the University... well, I'm pretty sure most of them would, but their parents may be another story. I hear one of our nine is likely to be married in the spring...

"Anyway, even in theory, we could not be talking about more than twenty-five girls. In practice, I should be pleasantly surprised if more than half are both willing and able to take the opportunity." Sumyra could think of two, at least, who might be disappointed, perhaps bitterly, but not all would be able to rely on parental approval—and the essential financial support. She only needed to consider how it might be if Aunt Arlenys had the ordering of her affairs, rather than Papa and Mamma.

Jerya continued. "At the absolute outside, Doctor Birchen, fifteen girls. It's hardly a horde, is it? Not what some of your more alarmist undergraduates are shouting about. Not a regiment."

"You heard about that?"

"I saw a pamphlet. 'Sacrificing opportunities for men, who will have to be the support of their future families, on the altar of female vanity...' Do they think the Guild of Dawnsingers is all vanity?"

"Some of the hotheads say some... unpleasant things about Dawnsingers," he said with visible reluctance.

"Perhaps they need to see a few Dawnsingers for themselves. A few guest lectures, maybe?"

"Perhaps. And perhaps you yourself...?"

"I spend too much of my time on my hind legs, spouting, already, but in a good cause... I'll consider it. But let's get back to the point. We're not talking about dozens, let alone hundreds, of women; no regiments. I'm not sure women are particularly good at marching in step anyway. There's no immediate need for a whole College to accommodate twelve or fifteen. An ordinary largish house would do very well. Nor should there be any immediate need for many extra teaching staff."

## Chapter 49

# Embrel

"Now," said Tahstib, the Crested cook at Pendeen House, "M'lord and m'lady were clear, I'm not to cook for yow reg'lar, 'cept breakfast. And..." She grinned. "That's to be at proper time, not middle o'th' mornin'. But I reckoned yow's all got enough to do movin' yowrselves in, so I'm fettlin' up a simple supper for yow. Would seven o'th'clock be to yowr likin'?"

"Any time that suits you, Tahstib," said Embrel, smiling at her. She was a good ten years older than Rhenya, taller, thinner, and very much paler, but there was still something about her that reminded him inescapably of Duncal's much-loved cook-housekeeper. The world might call her a slave, but in her own domain, she was in charge.

❈

A few hours later it had become abundantly clear that Tahstib's idea of 'a simple supper' would be reckoned closer to a feast in many households. Verris had complimented her extravagantly. "It's probably a good thing the College requires us to dine in Hall at least three nights a week or I'd be badgering you to cook for us every night."

"It's right kind o' yow to say so, Master Verris, but yow heard what her ladyship said. I'm not to do dinner for yow more'n once a week."

Verris carried on, exercising all his considerable charm. Embrel had long thought he did the whole 'charming rascal' act just because he could, to keep in practice, not because he automatically thought there'd be some benefit for him at the end of it.

Henty, meanwhile, had said little throughout the meal. After Tahstib and the maid had brought their dessert, he tasked him about it. "You're not usually this quiet."

Henty still said nothing at first, but then he burst out. "Do you think Miss Sumyra might want to see me again?"

Embrel grinned. "Why not? Next to Verris you look quite human. Nothing to object to at all. "

This was a monstrous slur on Verris, and they all knew it, but Verris only smiled, running a finger round the bowl and licking off the last of the ice-cream as if he were five years old. Henty seemed almost not to have noticed; he was after a more serious answer.

"Look, old man," said Embrel, "I don't in the least blame you for being very taken with Sumyra. I've known her for years, and I've seen her in some… unusual circumstances. I can honestly say she's one in a million."

"It's a wonder you haven't snapped her up for yourself, then," said Verris.

"It would seem logical, wouldn't it? But I suppose… love isn't logical." If only they knew, he thought. But he wasn't ready to tell them about Elidir, perhaps never would be.

Anyway, none of that for now. "We finally decided during our time in the Sung Lands, once and for all, that what we are to each other is more like brother and sister.

"But," he added, giving Henty the full force of his gaze, "Since she's a sister to me, I shall be very displeased if you do anything to cause her distress."

Henty looked indignant. "Believe me, Embers, if I did cause her distress, it would be entirely inadvertent… and I would like it even less than you."

"I'm glad to hear it."

"Well, what can you tell me about her? Whatever I should know."

*Well, I can't tell you everything you might* want *to know, and I won't.* "I'll tell you this. She said she wouldn't object to seeing you again."

"She did?" Henty's face had brightened, but then he frowned. "When was this?"

"When she was here. Right outside this house, in fact."

"That was nearly a week ago. You didn't think to tell me sooner?"

"You never asked." Henty still looked put out, so he added, "Look, lad, I could see you enjoyed talking to her, but I didn't know if that was all there was to it. I reckoned if it was nothing more than casual conversation, there'd be no reason to say anything. If it was, then sooner or later you'd be bound to ask."

"All right, all right, I forgive you. You've known her a long time...?"

"Six and a half years, near enough."

"And her mother's the lady doctor?"

"I can see you've only got part of the story... This could take a while." He looked around, found Tahstib. "I'm sure you'd like to be clearing up and get to your bed. Could you just fetch us a bottle—or a jug of beer?"

The cook shook her head, the tail of her silvery Crest brushing her shoulders. "Beggin' pardon, sir, but her ladyship said yow weren't to have th'run o'th cellar. And we dun't got no cask beer in right now. It dun't keep, yow knows, so unless there's a good number in..."

He sighed a little, but really Jerya had made it very clear that there would be limits. "Perhaps we'll find a watering hole for an hour. Then we'll be out of your hair." Too late, he saw the absurdity of the expression; well, as she was Crested, it made partial sense.

"Very good, sir. There'll be some'un about to let yow in till midnight. After that, I couldn't be answerable for the consequences."

"We all have lectures tomorrow; we'll need to be back in good time."

※

"Right," he said, once they'd all taken a first draught of ale. "First thing, Railu's Sumyra's *step*-mother."

*And my real mother, but that's another thing I won't be sharing with you any time soon...* "Sumyra's real mother died when she was very young; she doesn't remember her at all, as far as I know. Her father was away a fair amount and so she spent a lot of time with her aunt; her mother's sister. She's good deal older and it sounds like she's rather straight-laced.

"Anyway, her father met Railu at the the first Two Lands Congress. You're a historian, Verris, you'll recall the date."

"'96," was the prompt answer. "Gleander, I believe."

"Very good, give that fellow a Distinction. They got married a few months later. That's when I first met Sumyra."

"So you were—what? Fourteen? How old was she?" Henty was avid for every detail.

"Twelve, I think. But we were talking about Railu. Were you aware she used to be a Dawnsinger?"

Henty's eyes widened, at which Verris shook his head. "How'd you manage to miss that minor detail, lad? She was on the First Crossing with the Countess too, wasn't she?"

"You've an unfair advantage, you history fellows."

"Of course Jerya wasn't the Countess then," said Embrel. "They'd both been Dawnsingers, but Jerya only for a few months. That's why she's not still bald." He explained, as far as he understood, how Dawnsingers eventually became permanently bald. "But what it meant when they first arrived on our side is that they were taken for runaway slaves."

"And it was your parents who acquired them," said Verris, keen to show he knew the story—if only to score a few points off Henty.

Embrel explained how Railu had been his nursemaid when he was small, before graduating to the role of housekeeper, while Jerya became his governess. This was still too close to the part that must remain secret—the part he was still coming to terms with himself—so he moved briskly along to the aftermath of Jerya's return to the Sung Lands in '92, the first visit by a Dawnsinger to the Five Principalities.

"I know all that," said Henty, anxious to redeem his reputation.

"I should think everyone from Glimhaven to Withenstake knows that," riposted Verris. Embrel gave him an admonitory frown.

He related how Railu had already been quietly practising her healer's art on the Duncal estate, and once she was freed she spread her wings further, though always with great discretion. It was only after the Skilthorn Congress that she was able to practise openly. "But there's still no way for any woman native to the Five Principalities to become a doctor. I know Sumyra felt that keenly at one time."

Henty, of course, was soon keen to revert from Railu to her daughter; but as they walked back to Pendeen House, comfortably the right side of midnight, he was thinking that he'd reminded himself just how remarkable Railu was.

The world at large tended to take more notice of Jerya, and that was understandable. She was remarkable too, and for various reasons had attracted more attention, while Railu remained largely in the smaller world of Drumlenn.

But, yes, Railu was extraordinary; a woman anyone would be proud to own as a mother.

That, however, took him back to the same question that kept gnawing at him; where, exactly, did he stand in relation to his parents, or the people he'd always thought of as his parents?

# Chapter 50

# Sumyra

"Is Mistress Nielle at home?"

"I'll see, ma'm. May I ask who's calling?"

Jerya handed her a visiting card. The girl accepted it without looking at the text and disappeared down a short passage and through a door. A moment later there was the distant sound of voices, a woman's and then a man's.

But when the girl returned it was with apologies that the Master and Mistress had gone out.

"I'm sorry, to hear that," said Jerya, but instead of leaving she stepped round the girl, walked briskly to the door, and entered without knocking. Sumyra close on her heels. Two startled faces turned as one.

"Your enslaved gave me the message," she said. "Not her fault; you ordered her to lie. But it's really not a good welcome for someone you haven't seen for ten years."

"No, I..." said Nielle. "Countess, I... it's good to see you." Grevel drew in a sharp breath at that but said nothing.

"I'm glad you think so. Your husband doesn't seem to agree." She turned to face him. "But then you never did like me, did you? I often wondered why. Did it begin when I started doing the accounts? You must have been worried I'd find evidence of your peculation."

Nielle turned a sharp look on her husband. "Did you not know?" asked Jerya. "If not before, you must have suspected something when he uprooted you all at a moment's notice."

"He said he'd got word of a better position..." Nielle tailed off under her husband's fierce glare.

"Aye, and it does look like you've done pretty well for yourself." The room was at least as large as the parlour at Duncal, but a deal more fashionable. They'd already seen that the house had four storeys; it was a common pattern for town-houses. A basement for the main offices, kitchen, scullery, laundry, store-rooms, and so on; ground floor for reception rooms; first floor for family bedrooms, a bathroom, perhaps a study or library; and an attic where enslaved and servants slept. Pendeen House in Denvirran followed the same scheme, albeit on a slightly grander scale.

"There's no shame in that," said Nielle.

Grevel spoke for the first time. "If anyone's done well for themselves it's surely you, my lady." There was a distinct edge to the honorific.

"No doubt about it," agreed Jerya, "But my good fortune never rested on the proceeds of theft."

"Theft?" Nielle's tone was shrill.

"There are other words for it. Larceny, misappropriation, embezzlement, pilferage. I dare say all apply. But clearing out the deposit account, as you intended, is theft, pure and simple."

"Jerya," said Nielle. "I'm sorry, I mean Countess... you must be mistaken, surely."

"One thousand, three hundred and forty-four Denvirran thalers and eighty-six pence. That's how much we know you took from the trading account. Confirmed by the manager of the Drumlenn branch of the Denvirran Rural and Commercial Bank—who resigned immediately afterward on the grounds he'd authorised the withdrawal without checking with Squire Duncal, and attempted to pay back what he could from his own pocket."

"The Bank didn't compensate Duncal?" asked Grevel.

"Is that how you salved your conscience? If you had any... Supposing they had repaid in full, that would only mean you stole from them, rather than from your own employer. You know, if they had, the Bank would probably have put a lot more into tracking you down than the Duncals were able to do."

Grevel said nothing. Nielle looked as if she couldn't; her brown skin had taken on a grey tinge.

"I blamed myself, too," said Jerya. "I'd done the accounts for years, couldn't help feeling I should have spotted something sooner. When it came out fully, after you absconded, I went back to Duncal, went through everything again. You'd been clever, all those years, never lifting too much cash at once—at least as far as I could see. It was all about a bag of seed or a calf that you took for yourself, wasn't it, to sell privately? A sheep or two that ended up with someone else's mark... We never could put a final number on it, the total. I wonder... do you even have any idea, yourself?"

"Why don't you just cut to the chase?" said Grevel sourly. "What is it you want?"

"What I want is not the issue. It's not me you stole from."

"But you're the one who's here... who forced her way into my house."

"I hear the Velyadero Constabulary are quite efficient," said Jerya. "Perhaps you want to summon them?"

Nielle swayed, eyes rolling upward. Sumyra sprang to her side and guided her two steps backward to a chair. Spotting a decanter and glasses on a side-table, she poured a small measure and pressed it into the woman's hands.

Grevel had scarcely looked at his wife. "If you're so keen to involve the Constabulary, I wonder you didn't bring an officer or two with you."

"Involving the Constabulary would mean enquiries, legal hearings, summoning witnesses. The Duncals would have to relive it all... and that poor bank manager. It may have been even worse for him and his family... The Duncals have left it to my discretion and I think it would be better for everyone if we can avoid all that."

"Then what do you want?"

"One thousand, three hundred and forty-four Denvirran thalers and eighty-six pence."

Nielle gave a soft moan, clutched the glass to her chest. Again Grevel appeared oblivious. His gaze remained fixed on Jerya. "I can't raise that much."

"I'm sure you can. This house must be worth a lot more than that."

"The house is rented."

Nielle stirred. "That's not what you told me…"

"Be quiet, you little fool!"

"It seems to me," said Jerya, "The two of you may have a few things to talk about. And I have other business here in Velyadero. I'll be here for two days more, at the Filyorn Hotel. I'd like to hear from you by the morning of the day after tomorrow how you plan to repay the stated sum. Shall we say nine of the clock? If I don't hear anything, then perhaps I will have to, reluctantly, bring in the Constabulary.

"You might want to reflect that if it comes to that, there will be further sums to be taken into consideration. We can at least make an estimate of your embezzlements, and there's nine years interest on that thirteen hundred. And I'm sure you know how legal expenses can mount up…"

She looked at them; the glowering man, the slumped, ashen-faced woman. "I saw myself in. I can see myself out."

Something shifty in the young enslaved's look made Sumyra wonder if she'd been listening at the keyhole. She wondered, too, if selling an enslaved or two might be one option—if Grevel had spoken truly when he said he couldn't readily raise the money. It would be a kind of justice, since that was exactly how the Duncals had been obliged to act.

## Chapter 51

# Sumyra

"My daughter, Meirzem," said Riber.

The girl pulled up a lever just below the arm of her chair; a brake, Sumyra realised, in principle like the brakes on the carriage-wheels. She gripped firmly on both arms and pushed herself upright. She took one step forward, right foot dragging a little, then dipped from the knees.

Sumyra knew Jerya hated being curtseyed to, and discouraged any such display whenever she could; but here, today, she was struck dumb.

The girl plumped back down into her seat with evident relief, but also a smile of satisfaction.

Jerya, clearly deciding there was only one way to respond, made the very best and deepest courtesy she could.

For a moment there was absolute silence in the hallway. Then Riber puffed out an audible breath. It was enough to dispel the solemnity.

The girl smiled, once again looking more child than woman. "I'm honoured to meet you, Countess."

"I think the honour is mine." On the face of it, a conventional response, but Sumyra was sure Jerya meant it from the bottom of her heart.

Meirzem smiled. "I have been wishing to meet you for a long time, m'lady. I don't think you have been wishing to meet me quite so much?"

"Meirzem!" Riber sounded scandalised.

Jerya gave him a reassuring smile. "I'm sure I would have, if I had known about you. Unfortunately, I can't do what the Guild of Dawnsingers does, sending out their Peripatetics to seek out bright girls all over the Sung Lands. But I expect you know all about that."

"I'm sure I don't know all about it," said Meirzem. "I'm sure you know much more than I do. You were a Dawnsinger once, were you not? You were Chosen, as they call it."

"I was, though not in the usual way. I... how old are you, Meirzem?"

"I am ten, your ladyship. I shall be eleven in Brumander."

"Just the sort of age at which girls are—normally—Chosen."

"Yes, m'lady, but I don't suppose they would take a girl like me..."

"I think they look for girls very much like you," said Jerya firmly. "Bright girls, girls who want to learn, to understand, as much as they can. I know I've only known you for about three minutes, but I have a feeling those words describe you very well. In fact I'd say the only mark against you, for the Guild, would be that you don't live in the Sung Lands."

"But that makes all the difference..." said Meirzem. The wistful note quickly gave way to eagerness as she added, "But do you really think they would Choose a girl in a chair? A girl who can't walk more than a few steps?"

"I know they would. The first time I ever saw a chair like yours was in the College. And one of my tutors used one occasionally. Mostly she walked with a stick, but with great difficulty." She meant Tutor Brinbeth, Sumyra realised.

Jerya smiled again. "Will you excuse us now, Meirzem? Your father and I have things to discuss. But I hope very much I'll see you again before we leave Velyadero."

※

"I think we understand each other," said Jerya. "And I think we can present a reasonably unified message to the Council tomorrow. Now, shall we talk about Meirzem?"

"Of course, Countess. It's very good of you to pay such attention to her."

"Not at all. There are few things in life I like more than talking with bright girls. And she *is* bright, I feel sure."

He smiled, and there was no mistaking the fatherly pride and love. *Now, she thought, I think I know why Riber stands for the education of females.*

"My conversation with Meirzem showed me something," Jerya continued. "Something I'm rather ashamed I haven't considered before. As I said, there were Dawnsingers who used a wheelchair, who walked only with aid of a stick. One of the Tutors in Harmony was very nearly blind, I gather, but she could play almost any instrument, though how she learned new pieces I never quite knew...

"I knew all this, but I never thought of applying it to Skilthorn. I can excuse myself to a degree; as I told Meirzem, we don't have Peripatetics to range across the Five Principalities seeking out the brightest girls. We're almost entirely reliant on parents bringing their girls to us... tell me, Doctor Riber, had you ever thought of approaching us on Meirzem's behalf?"

He reddened a little, which seemed answer enough in itself. After a moment, he said, "Would it be possible, Countess?"

"She's ten, isn't she, going on eleven? At the start of next school year she'll be at an ideal age—and that gives us twelve months to make sure Skilthorn is fully ready to accommodate, not just wheelchairs, but a range of different needs. But I thought I had better say no more in front of her until I knew what you—and her mother, of course—would feel about it. I wouldn't want to raise hopes..."

"Thank you." His voice was full of feeling. "Of course I've thought of her, and what having a College for women right here in Velya would mean for her... but Skilthorn's a long way away..."

"And I dare say there are complications to travel..."

"Yes, but also... You understand, Countess, parents of daughters already tend to keep them closer than they do their sons, but I think with Meirzem we have always been more protective, kept her closer still."

Jerya nodded. "I have a daughter myself. And however fiercely I advocate for freedom and independence, I too feel that urge to keep her away from any possible hazard. I often wonder how far I should resist that urge; I feel sure I'd do her no favours by wrapping her in cotton wool."

"But I'm sure you would miss her very much if you were so far apart. And she would miss you."

"I was in the Sung Lands for six weeks; the first time I've been away from Torvyn for more than a week. It was harder for me than for her, I think."

He nodded slowly, several times. "I must have a good talk with my wife, I think. And perhaps we should see Skilthorn for ourselves... but my duties will hardly permit me to travel before the winter break. It must be six days' journey, I think?"

"It's possible in five, by the fast coaches, and supposing there are no delays."

"And if Meirzem did become a student with you, that would prolong her absences even more... Indeed, Countess, there is much for us to think about. May I make one request? As you said, you wouldn't want to raise hopes that might come to naught, so would you, please, say nothing more to her about Skilthorn until my wife and I have had the chance to consider?"

"Of course. But you can't be sure she won't work it out for herself, if she is the bright girl I take her for."

## Chapter 52

# Sumyra

Facing a table of men—*University* men, Sumyra was very glad to have Vireddi with her, though in the assumed role of 'attendant' she would be expected to remain silent. She could not even see Vireddi without turning, but at least she knew she was there.

Her first interlocutor had been introduced as Professor Swanscoe. "Tell me, Miss Kermey-Skelber, what motivates a young woman like you to devote another three years to study? Surely most ladies of your age are thinking of dresses and dancing?"

There were so many ways she could answer that she hardly knew which one to pick. To gain a moment, she said, "I was under the impression that the decision to admit women had already been taken. I thought we were here to discuss details, practical issues."

"You are quite correct, madam, but I am curious. For me, and I should imagine for most of my colleagues here, this is our first opportunity to meet one of our prospective new lady undergraduates. Or shall we say undegraduatesses?"

"I would be happy just to call myself a student."

He nodded. "Consider my question, if you will, as a way for us to better understand what we are dealing with. To establish context, you might say."

Sumyra had her doubts as to his motives, but she kept them to herself. "Very well. The first thing I would say is that I very much doubt most of my contemporaries are thinking of dresses and dancing. You seem to be forgetting that more than half of the population of the Five Principalities are enslaved. I know the proportion is lower here, but it's still significant. And of the rest, the vast majority are either married, perhaps already mothers, or working. Often both. It is only young women of the privileged class who have the choice between a life of study and a life of leisure."

"Do you, then, consider yourself to be of the privileged class?" asked another.

"I've had a good education. That's a very great privilege."

"But you are not satisfied...?"

"The more I learn, the more I realise how much there still is that I don't know."

"Very well," said the first interlocutor. "This may seem like a personal question, but I hope you will see that it is pertinent... How do you intend to reconcile three further years of study with the prospects of courtship, marriage, and motherhood?"

He was right on both counts, she thought. It was a personal question... but it was pertinent too. As she was considering her answer, another added, "If I might put in another way—or perhaps you will regard this as a supplementary question—do you envisage remaining unattached until after your undergraduate course is over?"

'Unattached'... that was too loose a term. She might have expected greater precision from a professor, but it would hardly be diplomatic to rebuke him. Instead, she began, "I don't know exactly how it is here, but I have a... close family friend, currently studying in Denvirran.." Again she wondered what was the best term for Embrel: cousin? honorary brother? "As far as I know neither he nor any of his friends are currently attached." *Though perhaps there's one who'd like to be...*

"I'm sure the same is true of our young gentlemen here. No doubt there are a good few who have some family understanding, but it's usually short of a formal betrothal. Of course, what they do in vacations is no concern of ours, unless they transgress spectacularly." Sumyra decided it was better not to think about what might count as a 'spectacular' transgression. "However, you can hardly be unaware that gentlemen... and men of the lower orders too, I believe... generally marry women younger than themselves. Thus, girls of your age, or in the next few years, are frequently engaged and it's by no means uncommon for them to be already married, even to have had their first child."

Sumyra was well aware of this. The Sung Lands trip had clashed with the wedding of her good friend Oyenda. Her letter of regret had been heartfelt and painstakingly wrought, but had not yet brought a reply. She could only hope Oyenda had been fully occupied otherwise, rather than mortally offended.

"I'm aware that it's common," she said. "Even customary. But it's hardly mandatory. The Countess, I think, didn't marry until she was around thirty, and she is older than her husband; and my step-mother didn't marry my father until she was thirty-two. And it may be just coincidence, or it may not, that they, of all the women I have ever met, are the two I most admire... and who have managed to combine marriage and motherhood with other notable achievements."

"You mentioned the privileged class," said Professor Mottran. "It is true, is it not, that women of the privileged class are not expected to undertake all the work of child-rearing themselves?"

Sumyra took a moment to dampen her ire and frame a careful response. "That is true, but I would not have you think that my Mamma left all of my care to governesses or enslaved. From the age of fourteen I have, *by my own choice*, spent the greater part of the year at Skilthorn, but in the years before that she gave me a great deal of her time, even though she and Papa were very busy establishing their practice and rejuvenating the clinic in Drumlenn."

"You call your step-mother Mamma?"

"I do."

"And is that also by your own choice?"

"It is, sir, but... I begin to feel that is too personal a question."

"I think," said Riber, looking impatient, or perhaps embarrassed, "We have mined this particular seam long enough. Our brief here today is to consider the *practical* aspects of the admission of females. And in that light,

Miss Kermey-Skelber, perhaps you could tell us which subjects you and the other young ladies might wish to study?"

She gave him a small smile, hoping he would see her gratitude. "I can answer that for myself, sir; and I can make a reasonable surmise as to the preferences of my classmates. I can't be so sure about the preferences of any future classes."

"I understand. Very well, then... why not begin with your own choice?"

"Of course. Though I'm not sure I can give you a final answer, not yet."

"I'm sure whatever thoughts you have will be most illuminating."

Sumyra wished she could be as sure of that as he sounded, but all she could do was begin. "For most of my life, growing up as I did, I dreamed of medicine."

"Your father is a doctor, I believe."

"*Both* my parents are doctors, sir." She could not entirely keep a reproving note from her voice, but thought she had kept it mild.

"Ah, yes, of course... A remarkable woman, your step-mother."

"I believe so, but I think she would say only that she's had opportunities denied to most women." She looked around. "And that's what we're here to address, isn't it?"

Riber nodded vigorously, and several of the others smiled.

"But as I grew I had to accept that being a doctor would, for me, remain a dream. Even now, as we're talking about a University admitting women... I am right, am I not, in thinking Velyadero does not have a school of medicine?"

"Alas, no. Though there are foundational courses in Anatomy and Physiology, and some of our students then proceed to a shortened version of the medical degree in Denvirran."

"But that would only be of use to me if the University of Denvirran could also be persuaded to admit females, and I'm afraid there's no sign of that at the moment."

Riber was saying something about hoping Velya's example would encourage Denvirran to faster progress, but Sumyra was thinking *and if it didn't I'd be left high and dry...*

"In any case," she went on, "I have had a close acquaintance with the medical world all my life, and I have helped in whatever ways I can as my parents have established the clinic in Drumlenn." *Dortis said I'd make an excellent nurse...* "And though I admire them both deeply, I am not now sure I share their vocation. Five years at Skilthorn, five summer-schools learning from Dawnsingers, have opened my eyes to many other possibilities. And this summer, travelling in the Sung Lands..." She thought again of Jerya's offer, to return to Skilthorn as a teacher. "I was reminded that many of the lessons which most fascinated me were given by Earl Hedric, on subjects like his investigations into glaciers. Crossing the Dividing Range, though we only had distant glimpses of the actual ice, we saw many things which aligned with his theories about the land being shaped by it. And then, in the Sung Lands themselves... I'm not sure which fascinates me more, how the landscape itself is formed, or how people live in it."

She could have said more. The places which had left the deepest impression on her, she realised, had been Delven, and then Kermey; two places on the edges of civilisation. In Delven, homes themselves were literally carved out of the land; but in both, life and livelihood were forged at an elemental level.

It was a moment of clarity. She knew, in that moment, what she wanted to study. Perhaps for the rest of her life... But she could not sink into those thoughts now.

"From what you say, Miss Kermey-Skelber," said Professor Yarnslaw ,"I surmise that your inclinations would be toward either History or Geography."

"I think so, sir."

"Well, History is a well-established discipline, though still we know regrettably little about the history of the Sung Lands. Geography and Geology are encompassed within the School of Natural Philosophy."

"I would need to look closely into both before committing myself."

"Of course, quite understandable. And you will have, at least, the better part of a year to do so."

*At least*. Aye, there it was; and whether the Council did commit to that timetable might depend, in part, on what she said, how she comported herself, today.

"Miss Kermey-Skelber," said Mottran now, "What can you tell us about the inclinations of your classmates?"

She thought of them. Oyenda, now married, could be ruled out. Of the others, some were easy. Olusin, surely, would plump for Mathematics; Jazelyn would throw herself into Literature, especially poetry. The rest she could not be quite so sure about, but with a few moments' thought, recollections of conversations under the canopies in Skilthorn's inner court or late at night in someone's room, she managed to suggest a probable spread.

"And you yourself may be destined for Natural Philosophy. I confess I'm a little surprised that your company appear to have a greater predilection for the sciences than the arts."

Sumyra gave him a look as guileless and amiable as she could make it. "And I'm a little surprised that you're surprised, sir. We've already noted that my Mamma is a doctor. And of course our Preceptor, the Countess, is a fine mathematician and has done original work in Astronomy. And that's without even mentioning the Dawnsingers..."

He *hmmphed* and muttered something that might have been 'quite so'.

"I'd like to add something," she said. "I think I alluded to it already, in fact. If I can't even be sure what most of my own classmates might choose, I'm even further from knowing what next year's students might do. But I'm sure their choices will be just as various as among my own class."

Another, who had barely spoken thus far, stirred. "But therein lies a problem, does it not? To arrange separate teaching for one or two subjects is one thing; but if there has to be provision across the—"

Sumyra was staring at him, and she was very glad when Riber broke in. "Pardon my interruption, Professor Quarnford, but did you say *separate teaching*?"

"Why, yes, of course."

"I don't believe I ever even considered that was what we were discussing," said Sumyra. "And I must say I think it would take away much of the value of a University education. I have a... close friend who's a student in Denvirran. Several of my classmates have brothers. And it's clear... how should I put this? A University is a community. Just as Skilthorn is; just as, in my limited experience, the College of the Dawnsingers is. Equal education for female students surely means being full members of that community."

Riber and a couple of others were nodding, but Quarnford seemed unconvinced or uncomprehending. "You would wish to attend the same lectures as the male students? The same tutorials? In science subjects, the same laboratory sessions?"

"I would, sir, absolutely."

"I entirely take your point, Miss Kermey-Skelber," said Mottran, "But would your parents be quite happy with such arrangements? Would they not at least expect there to be some sort of... chaperonage?"

*I travelled the Sung Lands on my own for three weeks*, she thought. *Alone—unchaperoned—or with Nòèttu.*

She thought about saying it, asking whether the lecture theatres and laboratories of the University of Velyadero were to be considered less safe than the roads and inns of the Sung Lands. But before she could decide, the moment had passed, and she had to endure ten minutes of discussion about the most acceptable form of chaperonage; whether, for instance, having a slave-attendant would sufficient.

The temptation to turn and look at Vireddi was stronger than ever. Sumyra could well imagine how she might feel about spending her days attending lectures, passing hours in libraries...

It would appeal greatly, no doubt of that, but not for one moment did she suppose that it would appeal enough for Vireddi to contemplate a prolonged separation from Mavrys.

※

As the clock indicated they were nigh the end of their allotted time, a younger man, silent so far, whose name eluded her, spoke up. "Miss Kermey-Skelber... I wonder if you have any thoughts as to a suitable name for this nascent Ladies' College?"

Sumyra smiled. She had indeed thought about this. "In my opinion, there could be no more appropriate name than Countess of Skilthorn College, but I rather think her ladyship herself might veto it. She's a remarkably modest woman."

"And we could hardly use her name without her consent..." mused the young man. "Have you, then, any other thoughts?"

Sumyra glanced at her 'maid', who had been observing intently throughout. Wickedly, she had the impulse to suggest 'Vireddi College'. *That would set the cat amongst the pigeons, she thought.* However fitting a tribute she might think it, it was surely not to be. And just like Jerya, she was sure Vireddi would veto any such idea. Oh well... "I'm afraid I've no other suggestions at this moment."

※

"I'd like to call it Mavrys College," said Vireddi as they walked back to the hotel.

Sumyra chuckled. "I'm sure you would. But what do you think she would think of that?"

"Same as yow said for th'Countess; she'd veto it. She's always sayin' she ain't academic. Sayin' the senior girls know far more'n she does. Girls like yow, Miss." Vireddi's turn to chuckle. "Sayin' I know more than she does, on account of readin' so much."

"You may laugh, but I'm sure you do know more than her—more than most of us—about all manner of things. Remember, I've seen the Library records."

Vireddi shrugged. It was, thought Sumyra, her usual reaction to almost any compliment.

"It's hard, isn't it? There are so few women even named in histories of the Five Principalities."

"Not in the ones already written," agreed Vireddi. "But if someone's writin' a history of our times, there'll be a few. Why, yowr Mamma'll have to be one of 'em."

"That's true." Sumyra almost hugged Vireddi in her delight; but even in liberal Velyadero, hugging an enslaved on a public street in broad delight would not be accounted respectable behaviour. "Oh, what about Railu Kermey College? That sounds well enough, doesn't it?"

"Sounds proper fine to me, Miss... but do yow s'pose she'd allow it?"

Sumyra didn't need to think for more than a second. "No, she'd be just the same as... the Countess, Mavrys, Mamma... you too, Vireddi. Why do all the most remarkable women have to be so modest?"

## Chapter 53
# Embrel

"Here's the official statement," said Jerya. "*The Council of Senate of the University of Velyadero, being committed to equal education for females as a fundamental principle, has determined that the admission of females shall commence from the Autumn Term of the year 104 of the Unified Calendar, subject only to the acquisition of suitable premises to serve as the initial base of a Ladies' College.*

"*The name of said College is yet to be determined, but will be announced in due course, at or before its official inauguration. Pending such decision, it will be referred to herein as the Ladies' College.*

"*Council affirms that female students are to be admitted as full members of the University, with all the rights, privileges, and obligations attendant on such status.*

"*Council reaffirms that all students, male or female, are required to satisfy the Admissions Office, and the Master and Fellows of their chosen College, of their academic qualifications and their personal good character. Council notes that females are not at present officially permitted to sit the examinations of the Matriculation Boards of Denvirran, Sessapont, or Troquharran, and strongly urges all said Boards to rectify this omission. In the interim, Council recognises that other arrangements will have to be made for the assessment of female candidates, and advises all interested parties that this is being addressed as a matter of urgency. Council firmly rebuts any suggestion that the standards required of female candidates will be in any way less rigorous than those applied to their male counterparts. Council also notes that internal examinations of the University, for progression and for final degrees, are marked anonymously and that close attention has always been, and will continue to be, devoted to ensuring that all students' work is assessed fairly, objectively, and without bias.*

*"Council names Jerya, Countess of Skilthorn as the first Master of the Ladies' College and gratefully acknowledges her ladyship's willingness to serve in this capacity, especially in the light of her extensive pre-existing commitments. Recognising that her ladyship may not be able to attend all meetings of the Governing Body, Council names Doctor Dunmall Riber as Deputy Master.*

*"Council acknowledges the potential difficulty in identifying qualified females to serve, at present, as Fellows of the Ladies' College, but invites nominations. Council, however, recognises that interim Fellows will almost certainly need to be named from among the Fellowships of the existing Colleges. The first tasks of this new Governing Body will be to identify suitable premises for the College, and to make such arrangements as are necessary to ensure the comfort and security of its members.*

*"Council concludes by expressing eager anticipation for the historic innovations which will be observed in Fructander and Veremander of next year and look forward to welcoming the first undergraduate members of the Ladies' College."*

"Oh, bravo," said Embrel.

※

They'd dined at the long table in Pendeen House's servants' hall; as Jerya said, it was more comfortable than the formal dining room, easier for the staff because it was closer to the kitchen. It was clear that this was their normal routine when visiting as a couple or family, but he suspected that he and his friends were also being gently reminded not to expect any pampering. The grander rooms would remain unused, dust-sheets left on the furniture.

Jerya and Hedric retired relatively early, and Sumyra and Verris moved into their places to make conversation easier. This put Sumyra opposite Henty, and Embrel could see how his eyes kept settling on her.

Before long the talk turned to novels, and then specifically to Lamorne's *An Honourable Estate*, which had been the sensation of the previous winter. "Have you read it, Miss Kermey-Skelber?" asked Henty at the first momentary lull.

"Please, that's too much of a mouthful. Call me Sumyra—you too, Mr Verris," she added quickly. In seconds they were all agreed on first names. She resumed, "I must confess I haven't—and I wager I'm the only one here who hasn't." She turned toward Vireddi. "Am I right?"

Vireddi blushed gently. There'd been raised eyebrows from Verris and Henty when Hedric brought her to the table, but as it was his house they hadn't questioned the move. Embrel thought it primarily a practical one; she had probably been helping with Torvyn's bath and bedtime when the other slaves were eating.

The colour slipped from her cheeks as she answered, "I did, Miss."

"And what did you think of it?"

"Well, Miss, it's well-written, I'm sure, but I kept thinkin', like I do with half the novels I read, 'where're all the slaves?' It's three hundred pages or whatever and I don't s'pose there's more'n three mentions of slaves." Since no one spoke immediately, she went on, "There's this one scene where Galdeen's givin' Maddren dinner, and there's about a whole page o' description o' the food—how the skin on the chicken's perfectly golden and crispy and so on—and Maddren says at the end, 'thank you for a wonderful meal' and Galdeen's just saying 'I like things to be done well'... but does he say who actually cooked it all? There's not even a mention of anyone bringin' the food in."

"At least I can promise you we know the name of our cook here," said Henty, which would have carried off better if he'd not sneaked a glance at Sumyra while he was saying it.

"Aye, Tahstib's a marvel," said Verris, smiling at Vireddi. "Tell me, Vireddi, are you a great reader?"

"I like to read, Sir. I wouldn't claim more'n that."

"She's too modest," said Sumyra. "I've assisted in the library at Skilthorn, and I'm sure I see Vireddi's name on borrower slips as often as any and more than most."

Henty was regarding Vireddi with more respect now; whether because of Sumyra's testimonial or the reply she herself had given, he could hardly tell. She certainly seemed to have better recall of the book, and of characters' names, than he himself did, though he could excuse himself that neither Maddren nor Galdeen were the ill-fated lovers at the centre of the tale. Perhaps, like Embrel, he had struggled to finish those three hundred pages—and wondered, after, whether it had been worth it.

"Well," said Henty now, "Galdeen's hardly the most likeable character."

"'Tis true, sir, but like I said, it's the same in half the novels I've read."

"And the other half?"

"Well, sir, I ain't sure but what they're worse, 'cause when you do see slaves they're lazy, or stupid, or both. D'yow know that one, *A Summer in the Archipelago*?"

"I have read it, but I can't say I remember it well."

"But I dessay yow remember there's this fellow and his 'tendant goin' through th'Archipelago on a boat, and the 'tendant—can't quite call his name to mind—"

"Vairth, isn't it?" said Verris helpfully.

"Thankin' yow, sir, I believe yow're right. So Vairth—every time he's goin' about the deck, seems like, he trips over a rope or somethin', and then 'ventually he goes overboard an they have a right to-do fishin' him out, and when they do he just stands there on th'deck sayin' 'thank yow, Sir, waitin' yowr orders', an' we're all s'posed to think he's too stupid to think o' gettin' dry, changin' his clothes."

"Well," said Verris, "He's there for comic relief, as his master's rather a tormented soul, isn't he? I'm sure you're not saying there are no slaves like that?"

"In real life there's a few, sir. In novels they're all over th'place."

"That's a very interesting observation," said Henty. This time it was Sumyra who turned toward him, and her look was approving. Yes, compliments to the slave—whom she knew well, and clearly respected—would be a better way to her heart than compliments to herself. The question, he thought, was whether Henty had divined that this was a good tactic, or whether he was merely caught up in the discussion.

"I said you should write a book," said Sumyra.

Embrel saw that his friends were as surprised as he was; but Vireddi wasn't. "Yow did, Miss. And I won't say I ain't been thinkin' about it. Only, like I said, I don't know if I could write my own story."

"I think a lot of people would be very interested," said Henty, "To know how a slave—I beg your pardon, I should say an enslaved, shouldn't I?—comes to be so well-read. Ha! I should think you're better-read than half the young ladies I know."

"Only half?" said Verris with his customary sardonic smile.

"I wouldn't know 'bout that, sir," said Vireddi, though she conspicuously did not deny the suggestion. "I'd like to—what do they say—set the record straight 'bout a few things. But tellin' my own story—there's reasons, sir; Miss Sumyra knows why."

Embrel also had a good idea what underlay her reticence. Living with Mavrys, calling it marriage, was not anything that would bring legal sanction upon them; it was merely inadmissible, unrecognised, on two counts. However, though they made no public show, did not even wear rings, he had a clear impression that their bond was as real and enduring as any he knew. *When will I find that kind of love?* There was a painful suspicion that he might already have found it, and lost it.

Vireddi was continuing. "But I was wond'rin' if there'd be some other way... tell the story of a slave—like a novel, but tellin' it true—the real life of a slave, e'en if it's not exactly my life. I 'xpect yow know, sirs, how diff'rent Skilthorn is under this Earl'n' Countess to how 'twas under his uncle."

"I dare say you have some tales to tell," said Verris.

"Truth, sir, I was too young for th'worst of it. By th'time I was..." She blushed again. "By th'time I was old enough for him to turn his eyes on me, he were ailin'. Mostly bedridden." She glanced at Embrel. "Yow know Dortis, sir, what's at Drumlenn now? She were his nurse, those last years, weren't she?"

"I believe she was."

"I dessay she could tell yow a few tales—if she had a mind to. There's many as don't like to talk about it. B'sides... what he did, pers'nally, that's only the half of it. Beatin's, whippin's... Th'Countess herself, she's got a 'tendant who'd been tongued. Most times they never learn to speak again, but she took it on herself—her ladyship, I mean—and Elleret talks pretty good now.

"All o'that, the cruelty, that stopped the day they arrived; day after th'old Earl died. More'n ten years ago now, I reckon...?"

She looked to Sumyra for confirmation. Sumyra would remember it very well; it was the same year her father had met Railu, the year of the Congress.

The year he'd danced with her at Railu's wedding...

Her father, and, had he but known it then, his true mother.

❄

Soon after that two of the enslaved appeared, hovering at the kitchen door, and immediately Vireddi jumped up, offering to help clear the table. "Nay," said Tahstib, behind the others. "Not yowr work."

"It's what I do most o'th time at home."

"That's as may be, but yow've other work while yow're trav'lin. Mindin' Miss Torvyn and drivin' th'carriage seems like enough for anyone."

Embrel and Sumyra had set the example by rising just moments after Vireddi and moving toward the door, but Henty and Verris had been quick to follow suit. But they had gone no further, so they all heard the exchange, heard Tahstib say, "Get to yowr bed, lass. Yow've got th'grand bed, so I hear."

Vireddi shrugged. "Soon as Miss Torvyn saw th'low bed, it were the one she had to have."

"Don't s'pose yow've slept in a four-poster afore."

"Nay, but I do well enough." They all said their goodnights and filed out. Because Vireddi was in Torvyn's room, she was accompanying them as far as the first landing, where they parted; Sumyra, Vireddi, and himself to the left and the state-rooms, the boys to the right, and somewhat humbler quarters.

"Well, thank you, Miss Vireddi," said Henty. "A most enlightening half-hour."

Vireddi blushed once more, no doubt at being addressed—probably for the first time in her life—as 'Miss'. Although, reflected Embrel, her marriage—her honourable estate—would make 'Mistress' more accurate.

Vireddi and Verris took their leave, but Henty lingered, clearly anxious for a moment with Sumyra. Seeing this, Embrel paused a little further along the passage, in the relative gloom between lamps. Not that he suspected Henty—still less Sumyra—of entertaining any thoughts of illicit trysts, but... well, pesk, he could call himself her brother, and he was Henty's friend. And he'd never been deficient in curiosity.

"Thank you for what you said to Vireddi," she was saying now.

"I meant every word," he assured her. "And if she ever does write that book, I shall be one of the first to read it. But, you know, if she requires a little... assistance, or merely moral support, I should think you would be well-placed to provide it."

"Well," she said, her tone becoming thoughtful, "I shall be at Skilthorn most of next year."

"You are returning there, then?"

"Yes. I've agreed to teach the geography of the Sung Lands. For one year."

"And then you go to Velyadero."

"Yes," she said, adding with a modesty he felt sure was genuine, "Provided they accept my qualifications."

"Well, Skilthorn is a good deal closer than Velyadero; and I suppose you will be coming home to Drumlenn from time to time?"

"As often as I can." She said it with a fervour that Embrel thought he understood; she might not regret a moment of the time she'd spent at Skilthorn, but she would still wish for more time with her parents.

"Perhaps, then, I may hope to see you a time or two?"

"Perhaps," was all she said, but her tone could be read as more encouraging than not.

## Chapter 54

# Embrel

Embrel sat, tapping his pen against his teeth. What was the point—what would the fellows think—of writing a letter that no one would ever read? Least of all its supposed recipient.

Well, no one else need ever know. If Henty or Verris should happen to pass his door and see the faint gleam of candlelight beneath it—itself unlikely—they would no doubt think he had an essay to finish.

As indeed he did, and it would become urgent soon enough; but it was not the reason he was sitting up now. There was too much in his mind; he knew he would not sleep. He could only hope that getting the thoughts on to paper might stop them circling in his head. And he hoped that the best way to get them down was to address himself to the person who was at the centre of it all.

He dipped his pen.

*My dear Elidir*

*I write from Denvirran, so between us lies a week's hard travelling, and all the savage grandeur of the mountains. And yet, having done the Crossing twice, I know mere geography is not the insurmountable obstacle. What truly divides us is not terrain or distance, but the fact that I am a young man of the Five Principalities, and you are a Dawnsinger.*

*I know something of Dawnsingers—more than most men here, and perhaps more than most in the Sung Lands. The first time I met a Dawnsinger—apart from Jerya and Railu, whom you might not count—I was, I suppose, about nine or ten. For some years, our house at Duncal was the first port of call for Dawnsingers arriving from the Crossing, and the last before they departed.*

*I have heard of the Principle of Detachment, and I know that you are bound to eschew all attachments beyond ordinary, friendly acquaintance. I would never wish to place you in an awkward position, and sincerely hope that I never did any such thing this summer.*

*And yet…*

*How can I express this? Though I don't envisage that you'll ever read this, I feel I am addressing you, and sincerely wish to cause you no embarrassment. But my feelings demand expression.*

*Elidir… did you notice anything, that first time we spoke, in the meadow below Delven? Anything in my demeanour? Because, believe me, I noticed many things.*

*I noticed you.*

He paused, chewing the end of his pen. It was strange… He had decided—almost certainly decided—that the letter would never be sent. And yet he still felt concerned about embarrassing her…

However, if the point of the thing was really to explain himself to himself, then he needed to be candid.

*Elidir, I noticed you. The first thing I noticed—my first thought was 'you have beautiful eyes'. But I noticed the grace of your movements, the play of light and shade on your scalp, the timbre of your voice. I think of them still, though memory can never recall them with the absolute clarity of the moment. How I wish I could be back there again, to walk with you on that path.*

*That night I hardly slept. Rationally, I knew—as I've already explained—that whatever I was feeling could never be expressed, let alone reciprocated. But what the head knows and what the heart wants can be entirely different.*

*Our second meeting in the meadow was the same exquisite torture. And, I must now confess, a torture I brought on myself, having chosen to follow you there.*

*But if I call that 'torture', how to describe our third encounter, at Sollom? To be so close, to be touching you; I had scarcely dared dream of it. But to be in a situation that almost demanded that I hurt you was the stuff of nightmares. All I can say is that I trust you know it was none of my choosing, and I would have gone a very long way to avoid it. I hope you know that.*

*And the final time, when you came to the tavern... for one impossible moment I imagined you had come to see me. I tried, then, to say something of what was in my heart—treading a delicate line between saying too little and saying too much. Perhaps... did you gain an inkling, then, of how I felt? Perhaps you were glad that Jerya and Sumyra appeared when they did. Perhaps I was, or should be.*

*And have I, even now, in the isolate security of this letter, really said how I feel? How can I describe the torrent of feeling... yes, torrent is a fair word for it. Writers of romances are apt to speak of being 'swept away'. Call it infatuation, call it being besotted... no, there is only one true way to say it. I fell in love.*

*Elidir, I loved you then and believe I love you still.*

*There is one more thing that might help you to understand... When I first encountered you, that day in the meadow, I was already in an unsettled frame of mind. I need not burden you with all the details, but on our arrival in Carwerid I made a discovery. All I need say is that I learned that the people who raised me, whom I had always called Mamma and Papa, were not my true parents—not, that is, in the bluntly physical sense. My true mother I had known all my life, but in another guise, while I only met my father for the first time in Carwerid.*

*Can you imagine how this made me feel? The sense of dislocation; the sense, almost, of no longer knowing who I was. Did this, somehow, set me on the path to falling for you? I don't know; I can't know. I feel as if, in saying this, I do you an injustice. Because what I realise I have not said is that I do not only find you beautiful beyond compare: I* admire *you. Your dignity throughout; your determination in riding on to Carwerid after what had already been a hard day; your commitment (as reported to me by Sumyra) in standing up for Master Perriad at the Conclave, even though you had begun to lose faith in her message; and that very willingness to admit you had been misled... All these, Elidir, mark you as worthy of the highest respect.*

*I should be honoured to know you better... but I suppose that is unlikely. I suppose it's possible, even probable, that I'll never see you again. And probably that's for the best, though it's hard for me to feel it is.*

*I should draw this to a close, or I fear I shall simply go round again. I am loath to do so, as it feels too much like a final farewell, another almost-bereavement. I must hope that time, as they say, is the healer.*

*Still, I cannot quite rid myself of the hope that we might meet again. I have other reasons to return to the Sung Lands, or perhaps one day you may make the Crossing yourself. If this should come to pass... may I hope that we can meet as friends? However much I might wish it in my heart, my head knows well that I can ask for no more.*

*And now it is well past one, and the candle flickers ever more fitfully. I must either light another, or get to my bed, and surely that is the wiser course. I think now I can hope for at least a few hours of restful sleep. And, though I still don't think I have properly expressed what I feel, that is due to you.*

*With all my heart,*
*Embrel.*

## CHAPTER 55
# SUMYRA

Sumyra drew a rather shaky breath. She had prepared assiduously for this moment; she had thought, if anything, that she was overdoing it; but now she felt woefully unready. Forty faces gazed expectantly at her; students of all ages. Since her topic was a late addition to the curriculum, and since she would almost certainly be unavailable to teach it again for the following three years, it had been decided to present it as a series of lectures on Jovesday evenings, in the hiatus before dinner. Attendance was optional, but open to all who were interested.

Forty faces, perhaps nearer fifty. Fifty students would be almost half the school.

And, sitting quietly near the back, Vireddi; and beside her, pencil and paper before her, Torvyn.

Jerya rested a hand lightly on her shoulder. "You might ask, since I was born and raised in the Sung Lands, lived there until I was nineteen, why I am not delivering these talks. I have two answers. First, I have my own classes to deliver, the administration of the school, a daughter to raise, and now I have commitments in Velyadero too. Second; yes, I grew up there, but for the first nineteen years all I knew was one remote village; for four months I was in the College in Carwerid, and of the rest I had seen nothing but the road between Delven and the city. Plainly put, Sumyra has seen more of the Sung Lands than I have. I may occasionally have additional insights to contribute, particularly concerning the Guild of Dawnsingers, but really I am as eager as any of you to hear what Sumyra has to tell us."

She released Sumyra's shoulder, smiled, stepped back.

"Thank you…" *Don't say aunt, don't say Countess, don't say Jerya.* "Thank you, Preceptor. I think, as always, you are too modest, but I thank you for your gracious commendation, and I only hope I can live up to it."

She glanced at the papers before her on the lectern, and knew in that moment that it was fine to have them there to refer to for facts, figures, details, but it would be better by far not to simply read them out. She looked up. "My subject is the geography of the Sung Lands, so naturally I am going to begin by considering the Five Principalities."

That made a few sit up, a few smile, one or two to put hand to mouth as if stifling a laugh; that was all right. She'd snagged their attention.

"How many of you have visited all five of the Principalities? Raise your hands…?"

Not a single hand was raised. She glanced at Jerya, now seated a few yards to her right. "Have you, Preceptor?"

Jerya shook her head. "I only visited Velyadero for the first time this summer, and I've never been to Buscanya."

"Thank you.." She faced forward again. "We have already established that our Preceptor was born and raised in the Sung Lands, but unless I'm very much mistaken, everyone else in this room is a native of the Five Principalities…?" Inflection and inquiring gaze made it a question; no one gave any answer but a nod.

"We are all natives of the Five Principalities, yet none of us has seen all five. How far, then, can any of us say that we *know* the Five Principalities?" She let that simmer a moment before adding. "Or does it maybe not matter? Do we think that if we know one or two, or even just one—if we know Denvirran city, say, and Skilthorn, and the road between—do we know what the rest is like? Do we suppose that Denvirran, Troquharran, Sessapont, Velyadero, Buscanya, are all essentially alike?"

There was a stronger reaction then, almost universal shaking of heads.

Just for a moment, she glanced down, and Jerya gave her a smile. *It's working*, she thought. *Maybe I can actually do this.*

At the end, after various teachers and students had congratulated her, she realised Vireddi had been waiting patiently and unobtrusively nearby. "That was fascinatin', Miss."

"Thank you, Vireddi. D'you think, though, you could call me by my name, as you did in Velyadero?"

"Happy and honoured, Miss..." She glanced around. "When we're alone."

"Whatever you're comfortable with. And I'm glad you liked what I said."

"I'll try to get along every week. But I was thinkin' just now... yow know how yow was sayin' I should write a book?" Sumyra nodded. "Yow should too. Tain't just girls here that'll want to know 'bout the Sung Lands."

"Well..." It sounded like a lot of work. But then she thought, *I'm preparing for these talks anyway. Those notes would be a start...* And then she saw something else. "Vireddi, you've given me an idea."

"What'd that be, Miss?"

"Why don't we help each other? I show you what I've written, and you tell me what you think. And I'll do the same for you. If you think what you write is a bit rough, I can help you polish it."

Vireddi's response was slow, full of doubt. "I don't know... Sumyra. I mean, I'd be happy to read anythin' yow wants to show me, if yow think I can say anythin' of use... but I still don't know how to write a book. Shebb!—pardon th'expression—I ain't ever written more'n a few lines together."

Vireddi calling her by her name made Sumyra realise everyone else had left. By unspoken agreement, they too started to move.

"I don't know how to write a book either. I don't think anyone does until they start. But don't think about that: think about one story, one moment. Write that story, as if you were telling it to me or to Mavrys." They left the room, and the sunset glow through the windows, for the relative gloom of the passage. A new thought came to her. "Maybe you'd rather have Mavrys's help than mine?"

"I don't know, Mav's heard a lot o' these stories already. Don't seem quite fair, makin' her sit through 'em all again. Specially when we don't get so much time together anyway."

"Well, think about it; talk to her if you want. But I mean it when I say I'm willing—eager—to help. You saw how Embrel's friends thought about it. It might sell really well."

"Are yow sayin' I wouldn't just write Miss? That we'd actually publish it?"

The return to 'Miss' alerted Sumyra that they had company. She saw Shevra approaching.

The housekeeper gave a small curtsey; Jerya and Hedric had discouraged anything more elaborate. Her ornate silver Crest added to her imposing presence. Sumyra knew that many of the younger girls were intimidated by her, but most learned soon enough that there was a kind heart behind the grave facade. "Beggin' yowr pardon, Miss Sumyra, but there's a letter for yow. Come by late post, and by th'time I found someone to tell me where yow'd be, yow'd'a been startin' yowr lecture."

"Not to worry. Thank you, Shevra."

She'd assumed it would be a missive from home, but as soon as she looked at the envelope she realised it was something far less routine.

✤

*Sumyra ??*
*℅ Countess Jerya*
*Skilthorn*
*Denvirran Principality*

*The College*
*Carwerid*
*19th Degfamès, 365 GR*

*My dear Sumyra*

*I had thought of writing to you sooner, but never managed it before (as we all thought) the Crossing route was closed by the first snows. However, an unusually warm and settled spell has allowed a re-opening, and I learned that the Couriers, as we are now calling them, were anxious to test out the feasibility of a swift traverse, as a trial for a more regular mail service next year. I shall say more about this shortly, but let me finish this tale first. Having done the Crossing yourself, in both directions, you'll know better than I what it entails. It is well-known that the normal schedule, from Blawith to Drumlenn, is six days. Their intention is to do it in three. When asked, they point out that a faster Crossing requires them to carry less food—as one said, "the faster you go, the lighter you can go, and the lighter you go, the faster you can go". Also, there are other would-be Couriers already on the move ahead of them, to leave caches of food and fuel in the high refuges*

*I have seen a little of their preparation, and know that they have gone from here to Kendrigg and back in a day, relying on a boat only to cross the river. Still, it is a bold undertaking, and there is an ever-present risk, if the weather turns, that they will not be able to return before spring. At least there are now several places in the Five Principalities where they can be assured of good hospitality—including, I believe, your own home, as well as at Skilthorn.*

*Now, as promised, I must explain how I know so much about all this. In truth, I think every Singer in the College is aware of what is afoot, but I have had a closer view than most, as I am now in training to become a Peripatetic myself. Having distanced myself from Master Perriad, I was anxious also to move on from the Faculty of Records. Master Brinbeth is not—as you yourself saw—an ally of Master Perriad, but there are others in that office who are, and who may now regard me as a turncoat. Well, perhaps I am, but that die is cast.*

*And our ill-advised journey was not wholly without beneficial consequences. I learned that I could ride substantial distances, on consecutive days—and I gained an appetite to see more of the land. With this in mind, I applied to Master Analind and was accepted into the company of Peri-*

*patetics. Perhaps, in a few years, this may even allow me to travel to the Five Principalities—if so, be assured that I would hope that this would afford an opportunity to see you again.*

*There is other news which will surely interest you.*

*Master Perriad returned to the College just a few days after I saw you last. She had travelled by coach from Aldgrave, and by short stages—I think the Healers there released her only on that condition. She came from the stableyard on her own feet, but leaning heavily on Chamion's arm. She looked gaunt and is clearly still weak, but the force of her glare is undiminished. I had never really been on the receiving end before, but she had clearly heard about my closing words to the Conclave. To my relief, she said nothing, but it was a sticky moment nonetheless.*

*I know that Master Analind is writing to Countess Jerya, so I presume she will convey this news, but you may wish to mention it anyway. It was she who suggested I write to you at Skilthorn, on the presumption that the Countess, or someone there, would be able to forward this if you were elsewhere.*

*I have little time, and I have another missive to write (as you will see), so I will just close by saying what I think I failed to say face to face. I am grateful to all of you for helping me see some important things in a new light—but I think nothing made me reshape my ideas more than seeing the care both you and Countess Jerya took to ensure Master Perriad was conveyed safely and comfortably, but with all due haste, to the Healers at Aldgrave. It was this, quite as much as the evidence of Master Perriad's cavalier attitude to matters of fact (all the more shameful in one whose métier is as a historian, and who was once Master of Records), that truly sapped my faith in her.*

*I must thank you even more for bearing no grudge toward me afterward. It is more than a little chastening to see such generosity of spirit in people against whom we had conspired, and whom we had so fiercely ambushed. Would that all my Sisters showed equal grace.*

*Well, Master Perriad's influence is undoubtedly on the wane, and Master Prime Evisyn seems emboldened, renewing her stress on 'service not superstition'. Which, when I think about it, is not too far from what Jerya took as grounds to leave the Guild. The Master Prime is clear that, even if we wanted to, we can no longer rely on people believing that we have some mystical power over the sun and the seasons. Now, more than ever, we must recognise that we are utterly dependent on the goodwill of the populace—they give us their tithes and, even more important, they give us their daughters. If the people do not feel that both sacrifices are worth making, the Guild will crumble, and it will deserve to. That is her message. Master Perriad and a few other diehards may still oppose it, but they have had their day.*

*This is a new world, a world twice the size of the one we knew until eleven years ago. We must accept that and strive in every way we can to make the best of it.*

*And on that subject, I close with the thought that I should very much like one day to see the other half of the world for myself, and my earnest hope that in doing so I shall also see you again. And if before then you find yourself once more West of the mountains, I hope you will count me among those you will seek out.*

*With warmest wishes*

*Elidir of the Guild of Dawnsingers.*

*PS. I should be most grateful if you would forward the enclosed. I am sure you will understand why I did not send it separately.*

# Chapter 56

# Embrel

The moment he realised what he was holding, he wanted nothing more than to rip open the envelope, but he made himself read Sumyra's note first.

Embrel Duncal
Pendeen House
Denvirran

*Skilthorn*
*27th Fructander, UC 103*

Dear Embrel

Forgive brevity, I am in some haste to get this in the mailbag, to ensure it reaches at least as far as Drumlenn today. I shall write more fully soon.

The enclosed... do you recognise the sigil of the Dawnsingers embossed on the envelope? You would have seen it over the doors of the Adjunct Houses in Kerrsands Bay and Aldgrave. If you are wondering why anyone from the Guild should be writing to you... or perhaps you have guessed, and I should put an end to your suspense. It is from Elidir. I do not know why she writes, or what she has to say; perhaps in due course you will be able to settle my curiosity. I can more easily surmise why she has sent it under cover of writing to me, but I am sure she will explain herself.

Just a few lines more; I have little time, and I am sure you are impatient to see what she has to say. I have given my first lecture, and I can at least say I did not make a complete fool of myself. People have been kind enough to say nice things about it; the Countess was complimentary, and so was Vireddi, and *if they were both satisfied, I must be too. But it seems to take so many hours to prepare that I cannot imagine how Jerya, or any of the others, manage to teach five or six hours a day, five days a week. It seems to me they would need about five hundred hours a week for preparation.*

*So, I know I can do this, eight lectures this term and probably the same in spring term. Otherwise, I shall help out wherever I am able. And in whatever time remains I shall seek to prepare myself for next year; for University. Did you feel this sense of anticipation? I feel a little like I did standing in the high places of the Crossing; a vast exhilaration at the prospect, an intense eagerness to explore it, but also an edge of awareness of the consequences of a misstep. Yes, that is how I feel, overwhelming exhilaration tinged with dread.*

*I really must go. I am attempting to create a map of the Sung Lands that I can display when I speak, and Earl Hedric is going to help me, both in preparing a board and in the techniques of transferring from a small map to a larger one. Then, this evening, I have the pleasant anticipation of a ride with Mavrys, followed by dinner with Vireddi and all of the stable-hands. Did you know there are more females than males there now?*

*Really, there are times when Skilthorn seems very close to perfect. If Mamma and Papa, and you, were a little closer, it would be even more so. Yet I often find myself thinking of the Sung Lands, of our travels, and of my own further wanderings. And receiving a note from Dawnsinger Elidir has awakened such thoughts once more. I begin to think I have not made my last Crossing.*

*With much love,*
*Your affectionate sister,*
*Sumyra*

❋

*Embrel*
*% Sumyra*
*Skilthorn*
*Denvirran Principality*

*The College*
*Carwerid*
*19th Degfamès, 365 GR*

*Dear Embrel*

*I am sure you had no expectations of receiving any missive from me. To be candid, I had no thought of writing to you until two days ago. As I have explained to Sumyra, it only then became known that the fine spell had re-opened the Crossing and that a 'mail run' was being speedily arranged—and as the possibility appeared, I came to the realisation that there were a few things I should say to you—that I needed, above all, to express my gratitude.*

*You are no doubt no wondering why I should be grateful to you. I think if I am to explain it clearly I must begin at the beginning.*

*I am sure you know that we are Chosen as Dawnsingers at the age of ten or eleven—in my case I was about two months past my eleventh birthday. Peripatetics came to my home village, a place a few miles outwith Kilnwick—they Chose me—in short order took my First Vow, shaved me, dressed me in white. The next morning I was whisked away—I was a Postulant of the Guild of Dawnsingers.*

*The custom in the College is—or was—to encourage Postulants and Novices to look forward, not back—I will not say we are bidden to forget, but we are not encouraged to remember. People often say, "The Guild is your only family"—or words to that effect. I suppose I took this to heart as much as most. I know I had a father—everyone does—but I couldn't tell you much about him. If I wanted to know his occupation, I could consult the records of my Choosing, but I have never been sufficiently curious. As a Novice I would have needed to request access, and I think I always knew—not that it would have been refused—but that it would have been noted, and perhaps not with approval. More recently, having served in that office myself, I had the possibility of doing so without drawing attention—but any curiosity had dwindled to vanishing point.*

*You will know that men never enter the College—save those received, occasionally, in the Annexe. As a Postulant, I never left the Precincts, so I never even saw men, or boys. In my first years as a Novice there were annual trips to Kendrigg—we peered curiously from the carriage windows—we stole many a sidelong glance at the men who worked the river-boats—but we never spoke to any of them. Then, as my direction became clearer (as I then thought), even those trips ceased—once again my entire life was compassed within the bounding walls. The grounds are extensive, with gardens—both ornamental and productive—orchards—pastures—and paths and rides aplenty. I had friends who rode regularly—one who is now a Peripatetic—and they encouraged me to join them sometimes, so for two or three years—every week or two—I have spent an hour on horseback. All of us whom Master Perriad chose for her company this summer had some experience—though clearly we knew much less than we should about the care of the animals. But I'll return to this.*

*I think you have the picture. I had barely seen a man since I was eleven—near enough ten years—and in all that time never spoken to or been addressed by any member of the male sex.*

*Inexperience is one thing—ignorance another. All I knew of men is what I was told, and I was under the influence of Master Perriad and others who thought much as she did. Men shattered the One Moon—poisoned those plains we saw in the North, the blighted tracts in the South—men in the Five Principalities enslave half of their people, and free women fare little better—if you can call them free at all. Jerya herself told us that even as a Countess—whatever that means— the law says she cannot own a house, or a horse, or anything of significance.*

*So some of this, at least, is true. Perhaps we cannot know—not with the utter certainty that some would claim—that men alone were wholly responsible for the calamities that ended the Age Before—but we know that it is men who benefit from, and enforce, the injustices endemic in the Five Principalities.*

*I believed it all—I believed, too, what Master Perriad told us, that Jerya was responsible for the first appearance of men from the Five Principalities in our lands. I believed also that she had gone unpunished for her Vow-breaking, and should be brought to book. I learned to reconsider that—to question my views on many matters—but before all that I had reason to reassess my opinion—which I thought was fact—about men.*

*And that process began that day when you encountered me in the meadow below Delven—when I as good as accused you of stealing our horses and you responded—first with forbearance and then with kindness—a kindness I surely did not deserve. I suppose I had not considered before that men even were capable of kindness. Now I look at that sentence on the page and it seems foolish—imbecilic.*

*That day, I suppose, planted a seed—a kernel of doubt—but it did not bear fruit all at once. Indeed I think that at first that challenge to what I had believed—and to the mission we had undertaken—made me cling even more fiercely to my prior tenets. Instead of thanking you for your kindness, for your help with the horses—just a couple of days later I threw a rock at you and tried to choke you. May I now sincerely say, I am glad the rock missed.*

*Many things impelled me to revise my thinking. Jerya's kindness, that day at Sollom—her taking up Master Perriad on her own horse to get her to Aldgrave as quickly and safely as possible. The growing sense that other things Master Perriad had told us as fact were nothing of the kind. A few precious minutes with the Master Prime when I returned to the College. And further converse with you—I had visited the tavern because I needed to speak to Jerya—but when I got there I found I needed to speak with you again too.*

*Yes, many things caused me to reconsider, but you began the process—and you were an important part of its resolution. I feel I owe you thanks for that.*

*And I am grateful for more reasons than one. As I told Sumyra, I have been accepted for training as a Peripatetic. I learned that I could travel—and that I had a relish for it—but also I wished to make a break with my former position. There are still some in that office who feel some allegiance to Master Perriad. Such feelings—if they exist at all—are much rarer among the Peripatetics. The fact that travel—the life of a Peripatetic—brings one into contact with men in a way most Dawnsingers will never experience—this would formerly have been a deterrent to me. Now it is very much less so—and for that I must thank you.*

*And as a Peripatetic—there is no certainty at this stage of my training—but the fact is that Peripatetics have a greater chance than other Singers of making the Crossing to the Five Principalities. If that should transpire—in a few years—and if it should further transpire that our paths might cross again—I wish you to know that I should not be sorry. May I express the hope that—if that should happen—we could meet on friendly terms? It would give me very considerable pleasure.*

*I have conveyed my regards to Sumyra directly—and through her to Countess Jerya also—but if or when you see either of them, please feel free to reiterate my respect and thanks to them both.*

*With kind regards*
*Elidir of the Guild of Dawnsingers.*

❃

It was a kind of agony. If he didn't respond immediately, the chance might be gone, and then it would be six months or more before anything could get through. But he could not just drop everything in the middle of the week, not without consequences.

He thought harder. Denvirran to Drumlenn by coach was the better part of a day. If he rode hard, changing horses at every opportunity, he could do it in four hours. Potentially, there and back in a day. It would be hard, but mail riders did it. It would also be expensive, but he'd manage that somehow. It was his final year, after all, and there ought to be fewer nights drinking. And maybe he could persuade Tahstib to feed them just a bit more often.

If he went tomorrow, first thing, he would only be away the inside of a day. He would miss a few lectures, but nothing worse. Verris would let him read his notes. As for the essay due on Venerday; he'd have to burn some midnight oil, that was all.

He didn't even want to think about the possibility that the Dawnsingers—the Couriers—had already departed.

Decision made, he reached for fresh paper and dipped his pen.

❈

*Pendeen House*
*Denvirran*
*29th Fructander, UC 103*
   *My dear Elidir*

*It was a wholly unexpected delight to receive your letter, forwarded by Sumyra, this afternoon. I can hardly thank you enough for taking the trouble. I can only hope that the irregularity of doing this (at least I think it must be quite irregular for a Dawnsinger to write to a man of the Five Principalities) does not lead to any trouble for you.*

*I imagine you had some inkling of the feelings you stirred in me. Feelings, I'm sure, which were not welcome to you, were an embarrassment and an imposition. I fully understand—as I did from the start—that the best there could ever be between a Dawnsinger like you and one such as me would be a cool and remote kind of friendship. I would wonder if even 'friendship' is too strong a word, but I have seen Dawnsingers, including Master Analind and the Master Prime herself, relaxed and genial in the company of men such as Jerya's husband, Earl Hedric, and Railu's, Doctor Skelber.*

*I am highly gratified, and even more surprised, that you felt able—felt it necessary—to express thanks to me. I do not think that my behaviour, in the meadow or on any subsequent occasion, showed anything more than the consideration and courtesy that any true gentleman would show toward a lady. You may have guessed—intuited—that I was sorely tempted to stray beyond those limits, but I hope very much that I was successful in restraining myself.*

*And now I think I must explain the second letter enclosed herewith. Or perhaps I should say, 'first letter', as it was written two days ago. You will see—IF you choose to open it—that at the time, for all that it's addressed to you, I had no thought of ever actually sending it. You may wonder, then, why I took the trouble of writing 'to you' at all? I find it hard, myself, to answer clearly. Why do some people keep diaries that are never shown to anyone? Why do some, even, write these in a private code? It seems that the act of writing sometimes has value in itself, even if there is no other reader.*

*And as, again, you will see if you open the letter, I have addressed myself to... well, am I addressing you, or some imaginary version of you? This may confuse you; I think it has confused me. I left unexplained some things that, in a real-life conversation, would need to be explained. And I poured forth much of my inmost feelings and emotions in a way that I surely would never have done were we face to face.*

*But, then, if I would not impose myself on you in that way in real life, why am I now sending this to you?*

*I can only say that in the act of writing I find that I have reached a clearer understanding of my own feelings, both in regard to yourself and in relation to the ambiguous nature of my own parentage. If you felt impelled to thank me for (in whatever small way) helping you to clarify your own position, I feel doubly, trebly, vastly more grateful to you. Somehow I feel much clearer now. The question 'who am I?' had been plaguing me ever since first arrival in Carwerid.*

*And so I think, if you can feel grateful toward me, it might conceivably interest you to know why I feel grateful toward you. But I warn you that my letter is a lengthy and no doubt chaotic effusion, and that it might very well occasion embarrassment or discomfort. Please know, therefore, that I would fully understand if you chose not to read it all, even to destroy it out of hand; or, if you did open it, if you should choose to stop after the first page, even the first paragraph. I have no right to ask anything more of you than to know of my gratitude. It is only on this understanding that I have decided to offer this to you.*

*With all my heart,*
*Embrel.*

※

"Well, this is an unexpec—" Railu got no further.

"I'm sorry, really... explain later. Are they still here?"

"Who?"

"The Couriers."

"They left..." His heart dropped toward his boots, but Railu was looking at her watch. "About half an hour ago."

He seized her by both shoulders and kissed her fervently. "I'll see you in an hour, then." Seconds later he was back on his horse.

※

"Just you wait a minute," said Railu with a firmness that reminded him of when he was much younger. "You can relay horses, but you can't relay yourself."

"I need to get back tonight." Now his mission was accomplished, his focus had shifted to that.

"How long did it take you to get here?"

"Four hours, near enough."

"And there's a good six hours of daylight left. Sit down, have something to drink, something to eat, give yourself a rest. And I want an explanation. You come racing in, then dash off again with hardly a word... what was so important that you had to go chasing after the Couriers like that?"

He sighed. He knew she was right. And he knew, if he took just one moment to think, that it would be good to sit down with her for a little while; and not just to rest and refresh himself.

She was his mother, after all. Not his Mamma, but his mother.

More than that, even. She was *Railu*.

# About the author

Jon Sparks has been writing fiction as long as he can remember, but for many years made his living as an (award-winning) outdoor writer and photographer, specialising in landscape, travel and outdoor pursuits, particularly walking, climbing and cycling. His name is on 60 books all told, plus four self-published novels (and counting). He lives in Garstang, Lancashire, with his partner Bernie and several bikes.

**If you enjoyed this book…**

To be receive updates about future books, and to get other news and insights, please consider following one of my social media accounts:

Substack: https://theshatteredmoon.substack.com

Bluesky: https://bsky.app/profile/jonsparksauthor.bsky.social

Mastodon: https://writing.exchange/@JonSparks

I have a Facebook Page at https://www.facebook.com/profile.php?id=100089266940531

The Shattered Moon website is at https://www.jonsparksauthor.com.

My mailing list is no longer active (personal essays etc. are now on Substack), but the sign-up page still gives you a free short story from the world of The Shattered Moon: tinyurl.com/4dvf7pt.

Finally, a small plea. Reviews and ratings are really valuable to indie authors like me. If you can find a moment to leave a few thoughts, or just to add a star rating, it all helps. You can do this on whatever platform you got the book from, and there are also general review platforms, notably

Goodreads, where my profile is at https://tinyurl.com/2p9znuhh. Thank you very much.

# Acknowledgements

Terry Pratchett once said, "Writing a novel is as if you are going off on a journey across a valley. The valley is full of mist, but you can see the top of a tree here and the top of another tree over there. And with any luck you can see the other side of the valley. But you cannot see down into the mist. Nevertheless, you head for the first tree."

This perfectly encapsulates what writing a novel feels like for me. But what Terry didn't say, at least on this occasion, is that few, if any, writers undertake the journey entirely alone.

As with *The Sundering Wall* and *Vows and Watersheds*, parts of this story deal with a mountain journey. Once again, I'd like to mention some of the people with whom I've shared great mountain days over many years. For sharing the first tentative forays on rock, thanks to Robin Taylor and Mike Thompson. For later climbing partnerships, Judith Brown, Jonathan Westaway, Dave Smith, Alan Sealy, and of course Bernie Carter. For Alpine and Karakoram days, Judith again, along with other members of Clwyd Mountaineering Club especially, Ian Nettleton, and Pat Cossey. Thanks too to several generations of Lancaster University MC, notably Colin Wells and the late Matthew Walsh.

I reiterate my thanks to all who've read and commented on my work, notably Marion Smith and Jago Westaway. For the only formal writing tuition I've ever had, thank you Steve Ashton. Thanks to the many excellent editors I've worked with in my non-fiction career, particularly Ronald Turnbull, Sue Viccars, John Manning, and Seb Rogers. Many other members of the Outdoor Writers and Photographers Guild have also helped me in manifold ways.

First, last, and always, I cannot overstate what I owe to my partner Bernie, who's been an essential part of unforgettable experiences from Morocco to New Zealand, as well as a host of hikes, climbs and treks in the Lakes, Scotland, and the rest of the UK. As I said in Book One, she's also my principal beta-reader, and so much more besides. Our conversations on walks and in pubs and cafés have helped refine my ideas and I'm sure this book, and this series, are much the better for them.

Of all the places we've had such conversations, none means more to us than Cobblers Bar and Bistro in Garstang. Passages from all the books have been written or edited here too. It's a particularly welcoming and nurturing place.

It's very likely I wouldn't have been around to bring this book, and this series, to fruition without the amazing work of many dedicated health professionals. Deepest thanks to all of them, notably Dr David Howarth and Dr Scott Gall.